THE PIRATE

HAROLD ROBBINS

The daring tale of the richest sheikh in Islam. In his private jet, he flashed from financial capitals to the world's luxury playgrounds, always seeking to conquer new worlds—and new women. But none could hold him: neither Maryam, his lovely Arab wife, nor Jordana, the golden girl from California who bore him sons to inherit a prince's throne.

Books by Harold Robbins

Published by POCKET BOOKS

HAROLD ROBBINS

THE PIRATE

PUBLISHED BY POCKET BOOKS NEW YORK

POCKET BOOKS, a Simon & Schuster division of
GULF & WESTERN CORPORATION
1230 Avenue of the Americas, New York, N.Y. 10020

Published by arrangement with Simon and Schuster
Library of Congress Catalog Card Number: 74-13407

ISBN: 0-671-41715-0

First Pocket Books printing June, 1975

20   19   18   17

POCKET and colophon are trademarks of Simon & Schuster.

Printed in the U.S.A.

To my daughters, Caryn and Adréana . . .
May their world be filled with
understanding, love and peace.

In the name of Allah, the Beneficent, the Merciful.
Abundance diverts you,
Until you come to the graves.
Nay, you will soon know,
Nay, again, you will soon know.
Nay, would that you knew with a certain knowledge!
You will certainly see hell.

—THE HOLY KORAN
From Chapter 102,
The Abundance of Wealth

... who were his ... when he unfastened her seat belt and
... settled ... in ... Harriet and Theresa ...
... then he ... the corner, leant it ... down on ...

THE PIRATE

PROLOGUE : 1933

IT was the eighth day of the storm. There had never been a storm like this one before. Not even in the memory of old Mustapha, the camel keeper, who was himself an old man when all the others in the caravan were boys.

Holding his ghutra close to his face, he made his way laboriously toward the tent of Fouad, the caravan master, pausing every few moments to peer through the narrow cloth slits, to make sure he did not lose his bearings and wander away from the tiny shelter of the oasis out into the ripping, swirling sand of the open desert. Each time he stopped, the grains of sand tore into his face like so many shotgun pellets. He hawked and summoned up his spit to clear his throat before he entered the small tent. But there was no moisture, only the grainy dryness of the sand.

Fouad looked up at the camel keeper from his chair next to the small table on which the oil lamp flickered, lending only shadows in the darkness. He did not speak. A giant of a man, he was not much given to words.

Mustapha drew himself up to his full height of almost five feet as he always did when talking to the caravan master. "There is sand in the eyes of God," he said. "He is blind and has lost sight of us."

Fouad grunted. For once he found words. "Ass," he said. "Now that we've made the journey to Mecca, do you think He would lose sight of us on our way home?"

"There is death in the air," Mustapha said stubbornly. "Even the camels can smell it. For the first time they are nervous."

1

"Put blankets over their heads," Fouad said. "If they cannot see, they will dream their camel dreams."

"I have already done that," Mustapha said. "But they toss the blankets away. I have lost two blankets in the sand."

"Give them some hashish to chew on then," Fouad said. "Not enough to make them crazy. Just enough to make them quiet."

"They will sleep for two days."

The caravan master looked at him. "It does not matter. We are not going anywhere."

The little man stood his ground. "It is still a bad omen. How goes it with the master?"

"He is a good man," Fouad answered. "He does not complain. He spends his time tending to his wife, and his prayer rug is always turned toward Mecca."

The camel keeper smacked his lips. "Do you think their prayers will be answered now that they have made the pilgrimage?"

Fouad looked up expressively. "All is in the hands of Allah. But her time is growing very near. Soon we will know."

"A son," Mustapha said. "I pray Allah to give them a son. Three daughters are enough of a burden. Even for such a good man as he."

"A son," Fouad repeated. "Allah be merciful." He rose from his chair, towering over the little man. "Now, donkey," he suddenly roared. "Go back and tend to your camels or I will bury your old bones in their dung."

THE large tent pitched in the center of the oasis between the four giant palm trees was aglow with light from the electric lamps placed strategically in the corners of the main room. From behind one of the curtains came the faint sound of the small gasoline-powered generator that supplied the electricity. From behind another curtain came the sweet smell of meat roasting on tiny charcoal braziers.

For the twentieth time that day Dr. Samir Al Fay

lifted the curtain and went to the outside wall of the tent and peered out into the storm.

The sand tore at his eyes through the tiny crack and he could not even see to the tops of the trees fifteen feet above the tent nor to the edge of the oasis, where the swirling sand seemed to form a wall that climbed up into the sky. He closed the opening and rubbed the sand from his eyes with his hand as he walked back into the main chamber of the tent. His slippered feet moved soundlessly as they sank into the soft woven rugs that completely covered the sand floor.

Nabila, his wife, looked up at him. "No better?" she asked in her soft voice.

He shook his head. "No better."

"When do you think it will stop?" she asked.

"I don't know," he answered. "At any rate there are no signs of it letting up."

"Are you sorry?" Her voice was gentle.

He crossed to her chair and looked down at her. "No."

"You would not have made this pilgrimage if I had not insisted."

"It was not because of you that I made this pilgrimage. It was because of our love."

"But you did not believe that the pilgrimage to Mecca would change anything," she said. "You told me that the sex of a child is determined at its conception."

"That is because I am a doctor," he said. "But I am also a believer."

"And if the child is a girl?"

He did not answer.

"Would you then divorce me or take a second wife as your uncle, the Prince, wishes?"

He took her hand. "You are being a fool, Nabila."

She looked up into his face, shadows darkening her eyes. "It is almost time. And I am growing afraid."

"There is nothing to be afraid of," he said reassuringly. "Besides, you will have a son. Did I not tell you the child's heartbeats are those of a boy?"

"Samir, Samir," she whispered. "You would tell me anything to keep me from worrying."

He raised her hand to his lips. "I love you, Nabila. I do not want another wife, another woman. If we do not have a son this time, it will be the next."

"There will be no next time for me," she said somberly. "Your father has already given his word to the Prince."

"We will leave the country. We can go to England to live. I went to school there, I have friends."

"No, Samir. Your place is at home. Our people need you. Already the things you have learned are helping them. Who could ever have dreamed that the generator you brought from England to light your operating room would lead to a company that is bringing light to our land?"

"And more wealth to our family," he added. "Wealth that we do not need, since we already have everything."

"But it is only you who can see to it that the wealth is used for the good of all rather than just the few. No, Samir, you cannot leave. Our people need you."

He was silent.

"You must make a promise to me." She looked up into his eyes. "If it is a girl, you will let me die. I cannot bear the thought of life without you."

"The storm," he said. "It has to be the storm. There is no other explanation for the crazy thoughts you have in your head."

Her eyes fell before his gaze. "It is not the storm," she whispered. "The pains are already beginning."

"You're sure?" he asked. According to his calculations, it was about three weeks early.

"I have had three children," she said calmly. "And I know. The first one was about two hours ago, the last one just now while you were looking out into the storm."

*   *   *

MUSTAPHA was sleeping, sheltered from the storm by the three blankets over his head and warmed by the heat of the camels on either side. He dreamed of paradise filled with golden sunshine and lovely houris of the same golden color, with fat breasts and bellies and buttocks. They were beautiful hashish dreams, for he would not have been selfish enough to refuse to share the hashish he gave his camels and let them wander alone into paradise without his guidance. Without him the poor creatures would be lost.

Above him the storm raged and the sand blew on his blankets, then blew off as the wind changed. On the edge of paradise a camel shifted and a sudden cold crept through to his old bones. Instinctively, he moved toward the heat of the animal but it moved farther away from him. Pulling the blankets around him, he moved toward another camel. But that one, too, had shifted and now the cold was attacking him from all sides. Slowly he began to awaken.

The camels struggled to their feet. As usual, when they were nervous, they began to defecate, then urinate. The spatter from one of them on his blankets brought him wide awake. Swearing angrily at having been torn from his dream, he scrambled away from the hot acidy stream.

Raising himself on hands and knees, he peered out from beneath the blankets. And suddenly the breath froze in his throat. Out of the wall of sand came a man riding toward him on a donkey. Behind that man was another donkey whose saddle was empty. The rider turned to look at him.

It was then that Mustapha screamed. The man had two heads. Two white faces on one body fixed him with their baleful glare.

Mustapha leaped to his feet. Forgetting the sand that bit at his face, he ran toward the caravan master's tent. "Ai-yee! Ai-yee! It is the angel of death coming for us!"

Fouad came out of his tent like a thunderbolt, caught Mustapha in his giant arms and held him in the air,

shaking him as he would a child. "Shut up!" the caravan master roared. "Has not our master enough on his
mind with his wife in labor to listen to your dope-
ridden dreams?"

"The angel of death! I saw him!" Mustapha's teeth
were chattering. He pointed. "Look. By the camels!"

By now several of the other men had run up to
them. They all turned to look in the direction of Mustapha's pointing finger. A collective sigh of fear was
released as the two donkeys came out of the darkness
and blinding sand. And on the first donkey was the
man with two heads.

Almost as quickly as they had come, the other men
disappeared, each vanishing into his own private shelter, leaving only Mustapha still struggling in Fouad's
arms. Involuntarily, Fouad loosened his grip on the
camel keeper, and the little man slid from his grasp
and dove into the tent, leaving him alone to face the
angel of death.

Almost paralyzed, Fouad watched the donkeys
come to a stop before him. A man's voice came from
the rider. "As-salaam alaykum."

Automatically, Fouad answered. "Alaykum as-salaam."

"I beg your help," the rider said. "We have been
lost in the storm for days and my wife is ill and near
her time."

Slowly, carefully, the rider began to dismount. It
was then that Fouad saw that the rider's blanket had
been covering two people. He moved forward quickly.
"Here," he said softly. "Let me help you."

In the darkness, Samir appeared, clothed in a heavy
beige mishlah. "What is happening?" he asked.

Fouad turned, the woman lying like a feather in his
arms. "Travelers who have been lost in the storm,
master."

The man stood leaning weakly against his donkey.
"I don't know how many days we have been out
there." He began to slip toward the ground.

Samir caught him and slipped an arm under the man's shoulders. "Lean on me," he said.

The man slumped against him gratefully. "My wife," he whispered. "She is ill. Without water."

"She will be all right," Samir said reassuringly. He looked at the caravan master. "Bring her to my tent."

"The donkeys," the man said.

"They will be taken care of too," Samir said. "You are welcome in my house."

THE man's face was scraped and bleeding from the windblown sand and his lips swollen and blistered. The scarred hands completely hid the small teacup he clutched in them. He was tall, taller than Samir, almost six feet with a large nose and piercing blue eyes that were hidden behind puffed lids. He watched Samir as the doctor straightened up from the pallet on which the man's wife lay.

Samir turned to him. He did not know what to say. The woman was dying. She was almost completely dehydrated, with a faint, erratic pulse and an alarmingly low blood pressure. "How many days were you in that storm?" he asked.

The man stared at him. He shook his head. "I don't know. It seemed forever."

"She is very low," Samir said.

The man was silent for a moment. He stared into his teacup. His lips moved but Samir could hear no sound. Then he looked at Samir. "You're a doctor?"

Samir nodded.

"Will she live?"

"I do not know," Samir said.

"My wife wanted our child to be born in the holy land," the man said. "But the British would not give us visas. So we thought if we could cross the desert, we could enter from the rear and slip into the country."

The shock showed in Samir's voice. "With just two donkeys? You have still almost six hundred miles of desert to cross."

"The storm came and we lost our supplies," the man said. "It was a nightmare."

Samir turned back to the woman. He clapped his hands and Aida, his wife's serving woman, came into the room. "Prepare some sugared water," he told her. As she left the room, he turned back to the man. "You must try to get her to swallow some," he said.

The man nodded. For a moment he was silent, then he spoke. "You know, of course, that we're Jews."

"Yes."

"And still you are willing to help us?"

"We are all travelers on the same sea," Samir said. "Would you refuse me if our positions were reversed?"

The man shook his head. "No. How in the name of humanity could I?"

"Then it is so." Samir smiled and held out his hand. "I am Samir Al Fay."

The man took his hand. "Isaiah Ben Ezra."

Aida came back into the room with a small dish and spoon. Samir took it from her. "Bring a small clean cloth," he said.

He sat down beside the pallet with the cloth she gave him. He soaked the cloth in the warm sugar water and pressed it against the woman's mouth. "Here, watch what I am doing," he said to the man. "You must gently force her lips apart and let the drops trickle into her throat. It is the only substitute I can think of for glucose intravenous feeding. But very slowly, for she must not gag."

"I understand," Ben Ezra said.

Samir rose to his feet. "Now I must tend to my own wife."

Ben Ezra looked up at him questioningly.

"We are on our way home from a pilgrimage to Mecca and the storm caught us here. Like you, we wanted our child to be born at home but now it is not likely to be. She has begun labor three weeks early." Samir made an expressive gesture. "The ways of Allah are mysterious. Had we not gone to Mecca to ask Him for a son, had you not wanted to have your child born in the holy land, neither of us would have ever met."

"I thank the Lord you are here," Ben Ezra said. "May He grant you the son you pray for."

"Thank you," Samir replied. "And may Allah stand guard over your wife and child."

He left the curtained chamber that separated the rooms, as Ben Ezra turned back to his wife and began pressing the moistened cloth to her lips.

IT was in the hour just before dawn that the storm reached its zenith. Outside the tent the wind roared like the echo of distant cannon and the sand beat against the tent like hailstones flung from an angry sky. It was at that moment that Nabila screamed in pain and fear, "The child within me is dead. I can no longer feel its life and movement."

"Hush," Samir said gently. "All is well."

Nabila reached for his arm. There was a note of desperation in her voice. "Samir, please. Remember your promise. Let me die."

He looked at her, the tears beginning to blur his vision. "I love you, Nabila. You will live to give me a son." He was swift, so swift that she never felt the hypodermic needle find her vein, only the sweet surcease of the pain as the morphine took her.

He straightened up wearily. For more than two hours now he had not been able to find the child's heartbeat with his stethoscope. All the while, Nabila's pains had been increasing but there had been little dilation.

"Aida," he said to the old serving woman. "Call the caravan master. I will need his help to take the child. But have him wash thoroughly before he enters the tent."

She nodded and fearfully ran from the chamber. Quickly, Samir began to lay out the instruments on the clean white cloth next to the bed.

Suddenly Nabila shuddered and blood began pouring from her. Something was seriously wrong—Nabila was hemorrhaging. Her heaving body seemed to be trying to push the child out. But Samir could not feel the baby's head. He knew now what the trouble was. The afterbirth was blocking the outlet of the womb.

The stain on the sheets was growing rapidly and Samir worked madly against a quickening fear. With his hand he went into Nabila and dilated her cervix so that he could pull out the afterbirth. When he'd removed the bloody tissue, he broke the waterbag and guided the baby down and out of her body. Swiftly he cut the umbilical cord and turned back to Nabila. He held his breath for a moment, then let go a sigh of relief as the bleeding stopped. Now, for the first time, he looked at the child.

The baby was a girl and she was dead. He knew that even without touching her. The tears rushed to his eyes as he turned and looked down at Nabila. Now she could never bear him a son. Nor any child. He would see to it that she would never become pregnant —the threat to her life would be too great. He felt a flood of despair. Perhaps she had been right. Death might have been preferable.

"Doctor!" Ben Ezra stood at the curtained door.

He stared at the Jew; his eyes blurred. He couldn't speak.

"My wife, doctor." Ben Ezra's voice was frightened. "She stopped breathing!"

By reflex, Samir picked up his medical bag. He looked again at Nabila. The morphine had done its work well. She was sleeping comfortably. He went quickly into the other chamber.

He knelt over the silent woman, searching for her heartbeat with his stethoscope. There was no sound. Quickly, he prepared an injection of adrenaline and shot it directly into the woman's heart. He forced open her mouth and tried to breathe some air into her lungs but it was of no use. Finally, he turned to the man. "I'm sorry," he said.

Ben Ezra stared at him. "She can't be dead," he said. "I see her stomach moving."

Samir looked down at the woman. Ben Ezra was right. The woman's stomach seemed to be heaving. "The child!" Samir exclaimed. He reached into his bag and took out a scalpel.

"What are you doing?" Ben Ezra demanded.

"The child," Samir explained. "It's not too late to save the child."

Samir had no time to open the woman's clothing. He cut it away swiftly. Now the woman's belly was exposed, blue-tinged and swollen. "Now, close your eyes—do not look," Samir said.

Ben Ezra did as he was told. Swiftly, Samir made an incision. The thin skin cracked with an almost popping sound. Samir opened the abdomen and a moment later he had the child in his hands. Quickly, he cut the cord and tied it off. Two sharp slaps on the child's bottom and the healthy wail of the baby filled the tent.

He looked at the father. "You have a son," he said.

Ben Ezra stared back at him with a strange expression. He didn't speak.

"You have a son," Samir repeated.

Ben Ezra's eyes filled with tears. "What will I do with a son?" he asked. "With no woman and six hundred miles of desert still to cross. The child will die."

"We will give you supplies," Samir said.

The Jew shook his head. "It won't work. I am already hiding from the police. There is nothing I have to offer the child."

Samir was silent, still holding the child in his arms.

Ben Ezra looked at him. "Your child?" he asked.

"Dead," Samir answered simply. "I guess Allah in His wisdom saw fit not to answer our prayers."

"Was it a son?" the Jew asked.

Samir shook his head. "A girl."

Ben Ezra looked at him. "Maybe Allah is wiser than both of us and that is why He brought us together in the desert."

"I don't understand," Samir said.

"If it were not for you, the child would have died with the mother. You are more his father than I."

"You're mad," Samir said.

"No." Ben Ezra's voice seemed to gain strength. "With me, he will die. And the burden of taking him could lead to my death also. But Allah has answered your prayer for a son. With you, he will grow safe and strong."

Samir looked into the Jew's eyes. "But he will be Muslim, not a Jew."

Ben Ezra stared back at him. "Does it really matter?" he asked. "Did you not tell me that we are all travelers on the same sea?"

Samir looked down at the tiny boy-child in his arms. Suddenly he was filled with a love such as he had never felt before. Truly Allah had in His own way answered their prayers. "We must be quick," he said. "Follow me. Take the other child."

Ben Ezra picked up the stillborn baby and went back through the curtain. Samir placed his son on the the table and wrapped him in a clean white sheet. He had just finished when Aida and Fouad came in.

He looked at the woman. "Clean and wash my son," he commanded.

The woman stared into his eyes for a moment, then her lips moved. "Allah be praised."

"There will be time for that at morning prayers," he snapped. He looked up at the caravan master. "You come with me," he said, leading the way through the curtain.

As suddenly as it had come upon them, the storm had gone. The day dawned bright and clear. The two men stood at the side of the new graves at the edge of the oasis. Beside Ben Ezra were his two donkeys, one loaded down with water and supplies, the other with the old worn leather saddle. Ben Ezra and Samir looked at each other awkwardly. Neither knew what to say.

Isaiah Ben Ezra held out his hand.

Silently, Samir took it. There was a warmth and

bond between them. After a moment they let go and the Jew swung up into the saddle. "Khatrak," he said.

Samir looked up at him. With his right hand, he made the traditional gesture. He touched his forehead, his lips and finally his heart. "As-salaam alaykum. Go with peace."

Ben Ezra was silent for a moment. He looked at the graves. then at Samir. The eyes of both men were filled with tears. "Aleichem sholem," he said and turned the donkey away.

For a moment, Samir stood looking after him, then slowly walked back into his tent. Aida was waiting at the entrance for him, an excitement in her voice. "The mistress is awakening!"

"Did you tell her?" he asked.

The serving woman shook her head.

He went through the curtain and picked up the child. He was standing next to his wife when she opened her eyes. Smiling, he looked down at her.

"Samir," she whispered. "I'm sorry."

"There's nothing to be sorry about," he said softly, placing the child in her arms. "Allah has answered our prayers. We have a son."

For a long moment she looked down at the baby, then she turned her face up to him. Her eyes began to fill with tears. "I had the most terrible dream," she half-whispered. "I dreamed that the baby had died."

"It was a dream, Nabila," he said. "Just a dream."

Nabila looked down at the child, her fingers moving the white sheet away from the infant's face. "He's beautiful," she said. Then a startled expression came into her face. She looked up at him. "Samir," she exclaimed. "Our son has blue eyes!"

He laughed aloud. "Woman, woman," he said. "Will you never learn? All newborn children have blue eyes."

But Allah had really performed a miracle. For Baydr Samir Al Fay grew up with dark, almost violet, blue eyes, the color of the sky over the desert at night.

BOOK ONE

The End of Spring

1973

CHAPTER 1.

THE needlepoint spray of the shower on his scalp drowned out the sound of the four big jet engines. Steam began to fog the walls of the narrow shower stall. Quickly, he rubbed the rich soap into a perfumed lather over his body, then rinsed and cut the water from hot to ice cold. Instantly, fatigue left him and he was wide awake. He turned off the water and stepped from the shower stall.

As usual, Jabir was waiting, the heavy terry-cloth robe and thick towels over his arm. He draped the towels over his master's body. "Good evening, master," he said softly in Arabic.

"Good evening, friend," Baydr said, rubbing himself vigorously. "What time is it?"

Jabir glanced at the heavy stainless steel Seiko chronograph that his master had given him. "It is nineteen hours, fifteen minutes, French time," he said proudly. "Did the master spend a restful time?"

"Yes, thank you," Baydr said, dropping the towels and slipping into the robe being held for him. "Where are we?"

"Over the English Channel," Jabir answered. "The captain has asked me to inform you that we will be in Nice at twenty hours and forty minutes."

"Good," Baydr said.

Jabir held the door of the small bathroom open as Baydr went through into his cabin. Though the master cabin was large, taking up almost one-third of the interior of the Boeing 707, the air was heavy and over-laden with the pungent scents of hashish and amyl nitrite.

17

Baydr paused for a moment. He didn't mind the odors while he was using them but afterward they were distasteful to him. "It stinks in here," he said. "Too bad we can't open a window and air the room out. But at thirty thousand feet that might prove embarrassing."

Jabir didn't smile. "Yes, sir." He went through the cabin quickly, opening all the air jets, then picked up a perfumed aerosol spray and sprayed the room. He came back to Baydr. "Has the master decided on his costume?"

"Not yet," Baydr answered. He looked down at the giant king-sized bed that took up almost half the cabin.

The two girls lay in each other's arms, their naked bodies gleaming in the soft golden light of the cabin. They were dead to the world. Baydr's memory of what had happened hours before was as vivid as if it were happening now.

He had been standing at the side of the bed, looking down at them making love. Their heads were between one another's legs, their mouths and tongues viciously devouring each other when suddenly they rolled over one on top of the other and the twin half-moons of a pair of white buttocks was shining up at him. He felt the excitement race through him and glancing down saw his erection, hard and pulsing. Moving quickly, he scooped up the amies from the table and, kneeling over the girl, placed his penis at the opening of her anus. He slipped one strong arm under the girl's belly and held her tightly against him. He reached down with his hand until he felt her mound. The other girl's tongue, licking her clitoris, touched the edge of his fingertips. Savagely, he pulled her back against him and with a powerful thrust pushed himself deep into her anus.

The girl froze for a moment at the unexpected assault, then opened her mouth to scream. As she sucked in her breath for air, he broke two capsules under her face. Instead of screaming she climaxed in a frenzied spastic orgasm. A second later, he cracked an amie for himself and exploded in an orgasm he thought would never end. The room began to reel around him and he slipped into the dark. His next conscious act was awakening and going into the shower.

Now he stood at the side of the bed looking down at them once again. But this time he felt nothing. It was over. They had been used, and served their function. They had eased the boredom of the long flight from Los Angeles. Now he could not even remember their names. He turned away and went to the cabin door. He turned to Jabir from the doorway. "Wake them and tell them to dress," he said, and closed the door behind him.

He walked through the narrow corridor past the two guest cabins into the main salon. Dick Carriage, his executive assistant, was in the office at the forward end of the salon, seated at the desk, next to the telephones and telex. As usual, the young attorney was formally dressed: white shirt, tie, dark suit. Baydr could never remember having seen him in his shirtsleeves.

Carriage got to his feet. "Good evening, chief," he said formally. "Have a good rest?"

"Thank you, yes," Baydr said. "And you?"

The young attorney gave a brief grimace, the most expression he would allow himself. "I've never learned to sleep on planes."

"You will," Baydr smiled. "Just give yourself time."

Carriage didn't smile. "If I haven't learned in two years, I'm afraid I never will."

Baydr pressed the service call button. "Anything happening?"

"Everything's quiet," Carriage answered. "Weekend, you know."

Baydr nodded. It was Saturday. He hadn't expected any action. By the time they'd left Los Angeles it had been one o'clock in the morning.

Raoul, the chief steward, came from the galley. "Yes, sir?"

"Coffee," Baydr said. "American coffee." His

stomach wasn't quite up to the harsh filter coffee the steward preferred to serve. He turned back to Carriage. "Have you been in touch with the yacht?"

Carriage nodded. "I spoke with Captain Petersen. He has everything set for the party tonight. The Rolls and the San Marco will be at the airport. If the seas are good, he says the San Marco can get you to Cannes in twenty minutes. The car will take over an hour because of the film festival traffic."

The steward came back with the coffee. While he filled a cup, Baydr lit a cigarette. He took a sip of the coffee. "Would you care for something to eat?" the steward asked.

"Not just yet, thank you," Baydr said. He turned to Dick. "Is my wife aboard the yacht?"

"The captain told me she was at the villa. But Youssef came down from Paris and is already aboard. He asked me to inform you that he has some sensational talent lined up for tonight."

Baydr nodded. Youssef Ziad was chief of his Paris office. He had one in every country. Bright, charming, educated young men who loved money and being next to the seat of power. Their main function was finding pretty girls to decorate the parties that Baydr gave in the course of business. "Get Mrs. Al Fay on the phone for me," he said.

He walked back to the dining area and sat down at the round mahogany table. Raoul refilled his cup. Baydr was silent as he sipped his coffee. A moment later the phone buzzed. He picked it up.

Carriage's voice came through. "Mrs. Al Fay is not at home. I just spoke with her secretary, who informed me that she went to a film and said she would proceed directly to the yacht from there."

"Thank you," Baydr said, putting down the phone. He was not surprised. He hadn't expected Jordana to be at home—not when the film festival was on or there was a party going. She had to be where the action was. For a moment he was annoyed, then it passed. After all, it was that which had attracted him to her in the first place. She was American, not Arab. American girls did not stay at home. He had once tried to explain it to his mother but she never really understood. She was still disappointed that he hadn't married another Arab girl after he had divorced his first wife.

The phone buzzed again. He picked it up. It was the pilot, Captain Andrew Hyatt. "With your permission, sir," the pilot said. "I'd like to have Air France service the plane if we'll be in Nice long enough."

Baydr smiled to himself. It was the captain's polite way of finding out how much ground time he could give the crew. "I think we can plan on remaining here until Wednesday. Will that be time enough, Andy?"

"Yes, sir."

"It's been a good flight, Andy. Thank you."

"Thank you, sir." The pilot's voice was pleased as he rang off.

Baydr punched the button for Carriage. "Book the crew into the Negresco until Tuesday."

"Yes, chief." Carriage hesitated. "About the girls, shall we invite them to the party?"

"No." Baydr's voice was flat. Youssef had already taken care of that item.

"What shall we do with them?"

"Check them into the Negresco with the crew," he said. "Give them each five hundred dollars and a return ticket to Los Angeles."

He put down the telephone and stared out the window. It was almost dark and far below him lights were beginning to twinkle on the French countryside. He wondered what Jordana was doing. It had been almost a month since he had seen her in Beirut with the children. They had arranged to meet in the south of France on her birthday. He thought of the diamond Van Cleef necklace and wondered whether she would like it. He just didn't know. Everything was tie-dyed jeans and fake jewelry now. Nothing was real anymore, even the way they felt about one another.

* * *

JORDANA got out of the bed and started for the bathroom, picking up her clothing as she went.

"What's the hurry, darling?" the man's voice came from the bed.

She paused in the bathroom doorway and looked back at him. "My husband's coming in," she said. "And I have to be on the boat in time to change for the party."

"Maybe his plane will be late," the man said.

"Baydr's plane is never late," she said flatly. She went into the bathroom, closing the door behind her. She bent over the bidet and turned the taps, balancing the flow of hot and cold water until it was just the temperature she liked. Opening her purse she took out a plastic container of her own soap and straddling the bidet began to wash. "Someday I just won't wash," she thought. "I wonder if he would know when he ate me."

She rejected the idea, laughing to herself. Men were so obsessed with the idea of the irresistible power of their invincible cocks they could not imagine that any woman they penetrated would do anything but have orgasm after orgasm. She could almost count the number of times she had truly climaxed on the fingers of both hands. But of one thing she was sure. If they ever got around to handing out Academy Awards for acting out orgasms, she would win one every year.

She pressed the plug and stood up, drying herself as the water gurgled down the drain. French hotel bidets always sounded the same whether in Paris, Cannes or the provinces. Glug, glug, pause, glug, glug, glug. Dry now, she put some perfume on her fingertips and brushed it lightly across the silky soft pubic mound. Then quickly, she dressed and came out of the bathroom.

The man was sitting up, naked in the bed, playing with his penis, which was erect again. "Look what happened, darling."

"Goody for you," she said.

"Suces moi," he said. "Pas partir comme ça."

She shook her head. "Sorry, darling. I'm running late."

"Perhaps later at the party," he said. "We can find a quiet corner, away from the crowd."

She met his eyes. "You're not coming to the party."

"But, darling," he protested. "Why not? I have been on the boat with you all week."

"That's why," she said. "Baydr is no fool."

"Then when will I see you?" he asked, his penis already beginning to droop.

She shrugged her shoulders. "I don't know." She opened her purse and came out with a small envelope filled with hundred-franc notes. She dropped it on the bed beside him. "This should cover your hotel bill and expenses," she said. "With something left to tide you over until you can make another connection."

The man's voice was hurt. "But, darling, do you think it was only for the money?"

She laughed. "I hope not. I would hate to think I was that bad."

"I will never find another woman like you," he said sadly.

"You just look," she said. "There are a lot of us around. And if you need any references, you just tell them that I said you were the best."

She was out of the room before he could answer. As she stood in the hallway waiting for the elevator, she looked at her watch. It was a quarter to eight. She would just have time to get to the boat and take a hot tub before dressing for the party.

CHAPTER 2.

YOUSSEF noticed Jordana's white Corniche convertible parked in front of the Carlton Hotel when he got out of his taxi. He looked for her as he paid the driver but all he saw was her chauffeur, Guy, talking with some other drivers. He turned and went into the lobby.

It was the day before the official opening of the film festival and already most of the signs were in place on the posts and the stands of the smaller film vendors. He paused for a moment to look at them.

The most prominent display was the giant banner overhanging the entire lobby. ALEXANDER SALKIND PRESENTS THE THREE MUSKETEERS. Slowly he read the list of credits: Michael York, Oliver Reed, Richard Chamberlain, Raquel Welch, Charlton Heston, Faye Dunaway. It was truly an all-star cast. Even he, a film fan from the time he had been a child, was impressed. He turned toward the concierge's desk.

Elie, the chief concierge, smiled and bowed. "Monsieur Ziad, so good to see you again."

Youssef returned his smile. "It is always good to be here, Elie."

"And what can I do for you, Monsieur Ziad?" the little man asked.

"I am to meet Mr. Vincent here," Youssef said. "Has he arrived?"

"He awaits you in the little bar," Elie said.

"Thank you," Youssef said. He turned away and then back as if with an afterthought. "By the way, have you seen Madame Al Fay?"

Without hesitation, Elie shook his head. "I have not. Would you like to have her paged?"

24

"It's not important," Youssef said. He turned and walked toward the little bar near the elevators.

Elie picked up a telephone from behind the counter and whispered a number into it. The operator in the descending elevator answered. A moment later he put down the telephone and turned to Jordana.

"Monsieur Elie suggests that madame might like to descend by the elevator at the Rue de Canada side of the hotel. He has sent a man there to pick you up on the mezzanine floor."

Jordana looked at the operator. The man's face was blank; the elevator was already stopping at the mezzanine. She nodded. "Thank you."

She stepped out and walked down the corridor to the far corner of the hotel. True to his word, Elie had a man waiting there in the small old-fashioned cage elevator that still served that end of the building on special occasions.

She left the hotel through the Carlton Bar and walked out onto the terrace and then up the driveway to the hotel entrance. Guy, her chauffeur, saw her and sprang to the door of the Rolls. She turned and looked into the lobby before she went down the steps. Through the crowd of people in front of the conciergerie, she caught Elie's eyes. She nodded her thanks. Without changing expression, he bent his head forward in a small bow.

Guy held the car door as she got into it. She didn't know why Elie had flagged her down but it was enough that he had. The concierge was probably the wisest man on the Riviera. And probably the most discreet.

THE little bar was crowded but Michael Vincent had a table away from all the others between the bar and entrance. He got to his feet as Youssef entered and held out his hand.

Youssef took it. "Sorry to be late. The traffic on the Croisette is just awful."

"No problem," Michael answered. It was amazing to hear the gentle voice emerging from a six-foot-four giant of a man. He gestured to the young women seated at the table with him. "As you can see, I have been most pleasantly occupied."

Youssef smiled. He knew them. They were part of the group he had brought down from Paris. "Suzanne, Monique," he murmured as he sat down.

They rose almost immediately. They knew the signals. This was a business meeting. They had to go to their rooms and prepare for the party that evening.

The waiter hurried over with a bottle of Dom Pérignon and held it out for Youssef's approval. Youssef nodded. The waiter quickly opened the bottle and offered the glass for him to taste. Again Youssef nodded and the waiter looked at Michael Vincent.

"I'll stick with the Scotch," the producer-director said.

The waiter finished filling Youssef's glass and left. Youssef raised the wine. "I trust your accommodations are to your liking."

The big man smiled. "The best suite in the place and you ask if I like it? What I want to know is how you did it. Two weeks ago when I called there wasn't a room available anywhere in town during the film festival. And you call one day in advance and, like magic, there is room."

Youssef smiled mysteriously. "Let us say that we are not without influence."

"I'll drink to that," the American said. He finished his whiskey and signaled for another.

"Mr. Al Fay asked me to express his appreciation for your trouble in arranging to be here. He is very much looking forward to your meeting."

"So am I," Vincent said. He hesitated a moment, then spoke again. "I find it almost too much to believe."

"What is that?" Youssef asked.

"The whole thing," Vincent said. "It took me more than five years to raise the money to make *Gandhi* and here you come to me with ten million dollars and ask if I am interested in doing the life of Muhammad as a film."

"It is not surprising to me," Youssef said. "And it won't be to you when you meet Mr. Al Fay. He is a man of great instincts. And after seeing your films of the great philosophers—Moses, Jesus Christ and Gandhi—what could be more natural than his turning to you, the one man who could possibly bring this great story to life?"

The director nodded. "There will be problems."

"Of course," Youssef said. "There always are."

Vincent frowned. "It will not be easy to get a release. There are many Jews in the film business."

Youssef smiled. "We will worry about that when we get to it," he said smoothly. "Perhaps Mr. Al Fay will buy one of the major companies and distribute the film himself."

Vincent took another sip of his Scotch. "He must be quite a man, this Mr. Al Fay of yours."

"We think so," Youssef said quietly. He studied the film maker and wondered if the man would feel the same way if he knew how carefully he had been investigated before Baydr chose him. Everything Vincent had done since he had been a child was in a dossier on Baydr's desk. No element of the man's private life was unknown. The girls, the women, the drinking, even his membership in the secretive John Birch Society and certain other subtly anti-Semitic groups. It was all there. Down to an analysis of why he was persona non grata in the film industry. Anti-Semitism was hard to hide in an industry as sensitive as the film business. It had been five years since *Gandhi* had been made and it had not yet been released in the Western world. And not a single new project had materialized for the man since then. He had been living on friends and promises for the last few years. And the whiskey bottle.

Youssef didn't tell him that Baydr had approached many others before coming to him. But they had all turned down the offer. Not because they did not agree that the Prophet was a good subject for a film, but because they thought its purpose at this time would be more propagandistic than philosophical. All of them knew better. It was the Jews they feared; the Jews had a stranglehold on the business and they were afraid to antagonize them.

He glanced at his watch and rose to his feet. "I'm sorry but I must be off. There are some important matters that I must attend to."

Vincent looked up at him. "Of course, I understand. Thank you for looking in on me."

"It was my pleasure." Youssef looked down at him. "The yacht will be in the bay in front of the hotel. From ten-thirty on there will be a fleet of speedboats at the end of the Carlton pier to ferry you out to the boat. You're welcome anytime after that."

The waiter came up with the check. Youssef signed it as Vincent rose. The two men shook hands and Youssef left the bar as Vincent ordered another Scotch.

He noticed that Jordana's car was gone when he came out of the hotel. He glanced at the Piaget on his wrist. It was a few minutes after eight o'clock. He went down the steps and turned toward the Martinez. Already the curious were gathering. There would be a mad scene every evening during the next few weeks as people came from all over to gawk at the celebrities and movie stars. He walked rapidly through the crowd, looking neither left nor right. He had at least another hour to spare before he had to return to the boat and meet Baydr.

The Martinez lobby was not as crowded as the Carlton had been. He went directly to the elevator and rode to the top floor. From the elevator, he walked down the corridor to the corner penthouse suite. He pressed the button. Inside a chime rang softly. He waited a moment, then impatiently pressed the button again.

The husky resonant voice came through the closed door. "Qui est là?"

"C'est moi. Ouvrez la porte."

There was the sound of the chain being removed,

then the door swung open, revealing a tall blond young man. He looked at Youssef truculently. "You're late," he accused. "You said you'd be here an hour ago."

"I told you I had some business," Youssef explained, walking past him into the suite. "I have to work for a living, you know."

"You're lying!" The young man's voice was angry as he shut the door. "You were with Patrick."

"I told you Patrick's in Paris," Youssef said. "I didn't want him down here."

"He's here," the blond young man said flatly. "I saw him on the plane this afternoon. He was with that Englishman who owns the department stores."

Youssef was silent, controlling the anger that seethed inside him. He had given Patrick express orders to stay in the hotel and not come out until tomorrow. "The bitch!" he swore. "I'll take care of him when I see him."

He crossed the room to the table, where a bar had been set up. There was an open bottle of Dom Pérignon in an ice bucket. He poured a glass for himself and turned to the younger man. "Would you like some wine, darling?"

"No." The young man was sullen.

"Come on, Jacques," Youssef said placatingly. "Don't be like that. You know the plans I have for you."

For the first time since he had entered, Jacques looked at him. "When am I going to meet her?" he asked.

"This evening. On the yacht," Youssef said. "I have it all arranged."

"I am going with you?" Jacques asked.

Youssef shook his head. "No. You do not even know me. If she suspects that we are friends, you will have no chance. I have arranged that you will escort the Princess Mara to the party. She will present you to the hostess."

"Why Mara?" Jacques protested. "You know I can't stand her."

"Because she will do what I say," Youssef answered flatly. "She will take Jordana aside sometime during the evening and tell her how great you are in bed and what a magnificent cock you have."

Jacques looked at him. "And that will make the lady fall in love with me?"

"No," Youssef answered. "That is up to you. But Jordana is still enough of an American to be impressed when a woman as experienced as Mara recommends you. Besides, Jordana is cock crazy."

The younger man was silent as he crossed to the bar and poured himself a glass of champagne. "I hope you're right," he said as he took a sip. "But what if there's someone else she is interested in?"

"There was," Youssef said. "I picked that up from the crew on the boat. But if I know Jordana, she has gotten rid of him because she will have no complications while her husband is around."

"What if she doesn't like me?" Jacques asked.

Youssef smiled and put down his glass. He walked over to the young man and pulled the sash that held his bathrobe. The robe fell open. Youssef took Jacques' penis in his hand and stroked it gently. "Ten beautiful inches," he murmured. "How can she not help liking it?"

CHAPTER 3.

THE teletype began to clatter as soon as the plane came to a stop at the west end of the field near the warehouse. Dick Carriage unfastened his seat belt and walked over to the machine. He waited until the sound ceased, then he tore the message from it, sat down at

the desk and opened the code book he always carried
with him.

Baydr glanced at him, then turned back to the two
girls. They were already unbuckled and getting to their
feet. He rose with them and smiled. "I hope you enjoy your stay on the Riviera."

The blond girl returned his smile. "We're very ex-
cited. It's our first trip here. The only thing we're sorry
about is that we won't see you."

He gestured vaguely. "Business. Always business."
His mind was on the message. It had to be important
if the teletype worked on the weekend. "But if there's
anything you need, just call Carriage; he will take care
of things."

"We will," the dark girl said. She held out her hand
formally. "Thank you very much for a lovely trip."

The blond girl laughed. "It was a real trip."

Baydr laughed with her. "Thank you for coming
along."

Raoul approached them. "The ladies' car is waiting
at the gate."

Baydr watched the women follow the steward to
the exit and turned back to Carriage. A moment later
the young man finished decoding the message. He tore
it from the pad and handed it to Baydr.

TEN MILLION £ STERLING DEPOSITED YOUR AC-
COUNT BANQUE DE SYRIE GENEVE ACCORDING TO
AGREEMENT. CONTACT ALI YASFIR MIRAMAR
HOTEL CANNES FOR FURTHER DETAILS.
                              [signed] ABU SAAD.

Baydr looked at the message impassively, then carefully tore it into shreds. Carriage did the same with
the teletype and put the pieces in an envelope. He
walked back to the desk and, from under it, pulled out
what looked like an ordinary wastepaper basket with
a slotted cover. He opened the basket and threw the
papers into it, closed it and pressed a small button on
its side. The button glowed bright red for a moment,

then faded to dark. He opened the container and looked in. All that was left of the papers was crinkly gray ashes. He nodded and went back to Baydr.

"When would you like to see Mr. Yasfir?" he asked.

"Tonight. Invite him to the party."

Carriage nodded and went back to the desk. Baydr leaned back in his chair, thinking. It was always like this. No matter how carefully he planned his holidays, something always came up that interfered. But this was important and had to be attended to. Abu Saad was the financial agent for Al-Ikhwah, one of the most powerful of the Fedayeen splinter groups, and the sums of money that passed through his hands were astronomical. Contributions came from the rulers of oil-rich sheikdoms and monarchies like Kuwait, Dubay and Saudi Arabia that were anxious to keep their images in the Muslim world intact. And with typical Middle Eastern caution, part of the money was set aside for investment and safekeeping in case the movement should fail. Perhaps no more than fifty percent of the total amounts received were funneled back into the struggle for liberation.

Baydr sighed gently. The ways of Allah were strange. Freedom had always been an elusive dream for the Arab world. Perhaps it was written that it would always remain so. Certainly there were those like himself upon whom He smiled, but for the others there was only bleak existence and struggle. But the gates of paradise were open to all who believed. Someday they would reach those gates. Maybe.

He rose to his feet and walked over to the desk. "Get the necklace from the safe," he told Carriage. He slipped the velvet-covered box into his jacket pocket and walked to the door of the aircraft. He looked back at Carriage. "I will see you on the boat at eleven o'clock."

Carriage nodded. "Yes, sir."

Jabir was waiting for him at the foot of the ramp. "The car is waiting to take you to the speedboat, master."

The big black Rolls limousine was on the field beside the plane. Standing next to the car was Raoul and a man in the uniform of the French customs service. The man touched his cap in a semisalute. "Vous avez quelque chose pour déclarer, monsieur?"

Baydr shook his head. "No."

The douanier smiled. "Merci, monsieur."

Baydr got into the car. Jabir closed the door behind him and got into the car beside the driver. The motor started and the car swung around and headed for the western tip of the airfield.

The San Marco was there, tied to a rickety old pier. Two sailors and the first officer of the yacht were waiting for him. The first officer saluted as he got out of the car. "Welcome back, Mr. Al Fay."

Baydr smiled. "Thank you, John."

A sailor held out his hand and Baydr took it as he stepped down into the speedboat. Jabir followed, then the sailors. Baydr moved forward and stood behind the controls.

The first officer held up a yellow slicker and cap. "I have some wet gear here, sir. There's a bit of wind and this baby kicks up quite a spray."

Silently, Baydr held out his arms as the sailor helped him into the slicker. Jabir picked up a slicker and got into it, as did the sailors. Baydr turned back to the controls and touched the starter button. The engine sprang into life with a roar that shattered the night. Baydr looked back over his shoulder. "Cast off."

The sailor nodded and snapped the tie line. The rope jumped up from the post like a rippling snake and the sailor pushed the boat away from the pier. "All clear, sir," he said, straightening up and coiling the rope at his feet.

Baydr threw in the clutch and the big speedboat began to move slowly forward. Gently Baydr advanced the throttle and headed the boat out to sea. Effortlessly, it slipped through the water. Baydr sat down and fastened the seat belt across his lap. "Tie yourselves in," he said. "I'm going to open her up."

There was the sound of movement behind him, then the first officer's voice shouted over the roar of the engine. "All ready, sir."

Baydr moved the throttle all the way up. The boat seemed to climb out of the water in a sudden forward surge and the spray from the bow made an incandescent arch over their heads. The wind whipped his face and he bared his teeth in a grimace as he caught his breath. A glance at the speedometer told him they were already doing forty knots. He almost laughed aloud as he turned the wheel gently to head the boat for Cannes. The strength of three hundred and twenty horses at his fingertips, the wind and water tearing at his face. In some ways it was better than sex.

THE telephone began to ring in Ali Yasfir's apartment. The pudgy Lebanese waddled to the telephone and picked it up. "Yasfir."

The American voice crackled in his ear. He listened for a moment, then nodded. "Yes, of course. It will be my pleasure. I am looking forward to meeting with his excellency." He put down the telephone and waddled back to his friends.

"It is done," he announced with satisfaction. "We are to meet on his boat tonight."

"That is good for you," the slim, dark Frenchman on the couch said. "But it still does not solve our problem."

"Pierre is right," the American in the brightly colored sport shirt said. "My contacts in America have a greater problem."

Ali Yasfir turned to him. "We understand and we're doing all we can to resolve it."

"You're not doing it fast enough," the American said. "We're going to have to do business with other sources."

"Damn!" Pierre said. "Just when we had the processing plants operating smoothly."

"And there has been no shortage of the raw material," Ali said. "The farmers have come through. The harvest has been good. And deliveries to the plants here have been without interference. It seems to me, Tony, that we're bearing the brunt of a breakdown in your own delivery system. The last two major shipments from France have been intercepted in the United States."

The American's face hardened. "The leaks came from here. Otherwise the Feds never would have got on to them. We're going to have to find another route into the country."

"From South America," the Frenchman said.

"It won't help," Tony said flatly. "We did that the last time and it was picked up. If it starts here, we're in trouble."

Ali looked at the Frenchman. "The leak has to be in your organization."

"Impossible," the Frenchman said. "Every man working for us has been checked and rechecked."

"We may have no choice," Ali said. "We cannot keep financing your operation if the merchandise can't get to the market."

The Frenchman was silent for a moment while he thought. "Let's not be hasty," he said finally. "We have a shipment leaving this week. Let's see what happens."

Ali Yasfir looked at the American. The American nodded. Ali turned back to the Frenchman. "D'accord, Pierre. We will wait and see."

After the Frenchman had gone, Tony looked at Ali. "What do you think?"

Ali shrugged. "Who knows what to think?"

"He could be selling us out," Tony said. "The stuff's still getting into the West Coast. We're paying premiums to the mobs out there just to get enough to keep us in business."

"Their merchandise comes from Indochina?" Ali asked.

Tony nodded. "And it's cheaper than ours."

Ali shook his head. "With good reason. Our costs would be lower too if we were financed by the CIA."

"That's only one part of the problem," Tony said. "The hot item in the States now is coke. And that's where we're weak."

"We've been looking into that," Ali said. "I have some contacts in Bogotá and will be going there myself next week."

"The boys will be glad to hear that. We'd rather stay in business with you than go looking for new partners."

Ali rose to his feet. The meeting was over. "We're going to be in business together for a long time."

He walked to the door with the American. They shook hands. "We will meet in New York at the beginning of next month."

"I hope things will improve by then."

"I'm sure they will," Ali replied. He shut the door behind the man, bolted it and placed the chain across the latch. He went from the door directly to the bathroom, where he fastidiously washed his hands and dried them. He then went to the bedroom door and knocked softly.

The door opened and a young girl stood there. Her olive skin, dark eyes and long black hair belied her modern St. Tropez studded jeans and shirt. "Is the meeting over?" she asked.

He nodded. "Would you like a cold drink?"

"Do you have a Coke?"

"I'm sure," he answered. He went into the kitchen and brought a Coca-Cola from the refrigerator. He poured it into a glass and handed it to her.

She drank thirstily. "When will we be leaving?" she asked.

"We're booked on tomorrow's plane for Beirut," he answered. "But there might be a delay."

She looked at him questioningly.

His eyes met her gaze directly. "I have a meeting with your father tonight."

A startled expression came into her eyes. "You're not going to give me away?" She put the drink down.

"They promised me he would not know. I would not have left the school in Switzerland otherwise."

"It has nothing to do with you," he reassured her. "Your father suspects nothing. We have some business with him."

"What kind of business?" Her tone was suspicious.

"Your father handles many investments for us. He has entrée into areas that we could not penetrate otherwise. He can also purchase supplies and matériel that we cannot."

"Does he know that it is for the cause?"

"Yes."

A strange expression crossed her face.

"He is a sympathizer," Ali said quickly.

"I don't trust him!" She was vehement. "My father sympathizes with nothing but money and power. The suffering of people and justice mean nothing to him."

"Your father is an Arab," he said stiffly.

She stared at him. "He is not! He is more Western than Arab. Otherwise he would not have divorced my mother to marry that woman. It is the same with his business. How much time does he spend with his own people, in his own land? Two weeks out of the year? It would not surprise me to discover that he even trades with the Israelis. He has many Western friends who are Jewish."

"In his own way your father has done much for the cause." Ali found himself defending a man he had never met. "Our battle cannot be won by soldiers alone."

"Our battle will be won by those who are willing to spill their blood and give their lives, not by men like my father whose only interest lies in the profits he can make." Angrily she stamped back into the bedroom and slammed the door behind her.

He knocked on the door. "Leila," he said gently. "Leila, would you like me to order some dinner?"

Her voice came faintly from the room. "Go away. Leave me alone. I'm not hungry!" A faint sound of sobbing came through the wooden panels of the door.

He stood there indecisively for a moment, then went to his bedroom to dress for dinner. The young were filled with ideals. To them everything was black or white. There were no shadings in between. It was good and it was bad.

But he was not in the business of passing judgment. Causes were not run on ideals alone. The young never knew that it took money to make things happen. Money to buy their uniforms, to feed them, to give them guns and weapons and training. Modern warfare, even guerrilla warfare, was expensive. And that was the real reason so much time had been spent indoctrinating her. They had used her resentments against her father until she had reached the point where she was ready to commit herself physically to the Fedayeen. It was not just for what she herself could do. There were many other girls who could have performed as well.

But none of the others had a father who was among the richest men in the world. He felt a sigh escape his lips. By the day after tomorrow she would be in a training camp in the mountains of Lebanon. Once she was there and under their control perhaps Baydr Al Fay would be more amenable to some of the plans he had already rejected. She would be better than a gun pointed at his head.

CHAPTER 4.

"YOUR call to the United States is ready, Mr. Carriage," the hotel operator said in English.

"Thank you," Dick said. There was a whine and series of clicks, then a voice came on. "Hello," Dick said.

There were more clicks then a buzzing sound. "Hello, hello," he shouted. Suddenly the line cleared and he heard his wife's voice.

"Hello, Margery?" he shouted.

"Richard?" she sounded doubtful.

"Of course, it's Richard," he snapped, strangely annoyed. "Who did you think it was?"

"You sound so far away," she said.

"I am far away," he said. "I'm in Cannes."

"What are you doing there?" she asked. "I thought you were working."

"Jesus, Margery, I am working. I told you the chief was planning to spend the weekend here for his wife's birthday."

"Whose birthday?"

"His wife's," he shouted. "Oh, forget it, Margery. How are the kids?"

"They're fine," she said. "Only Timmy has a cold. I kept him out of school. When are you coming home?"

"I don't know," he said. "The chief's got a lot of things going."

"But you said it would only be for three weeks this time."

"Things piled up. It's not my fault."

"We were better off when you worked for Aramco. At least then you came home every night."

"I also made a lot less money," he said. "Twelve thousand a year instead of forty."

"But I miss you," she said; there was the faint edge of tears in her voice.

He softened. "I miss you too, darling. And the kids."

"Richard," she said.

"Yes, dear?"

"Are you all right?"

"I'm just fine," he said.

"I worry all the time. It seems to me that you're always flying, that you're never in one place long enough to get proper rest."

"I've learned to sleep on the plane," he lied. "I'm just fine." He reached for a cigarette with his free hand

and lit it. "At any rate we'll be here until Wednesday. I'll be able to catch up by then."

"I'm glad," she said. "Will you come home soon?"

"As soon as I can," he said.

"I love you, Richard."

"I love you," he said. "And give the kids a big kiss for me."

"I will," she said. "Goodbye."

"Goodbye, darling." He put down the phone and took a long drag at his cigarette. He looked around the hotel room. It seemed strangely empty and sterile. Hotel rooms everywhere in the world were alike. They were designed so that you could not feel you belonged.

He wished he were more like Baydr. Baydr seemed to belong anywhere he put himself down. Strange rooms and strange places seemed to have no effect on him. Of course, he had his own homes or apartments in most of the major cities. New York, Los Angeles, San Francisco, Paris, London, Geneva, Beirut, Teheran. But even when he did stay in a hotel he had a way of changing the room to fit his own style.

Perhaps it was because he had spent all of his life in foreign lands. When he was a boy his father had sent him to school in England, then to college in the States, first Harvard Business School, then Stanford. In a curious manner, his life had been planned for him even before his birth. A first cousin to the reigning Emir and the only male descendant of his family, it was only natural that they would entrust him with their business affairs. With the development of the oil leases, the money had begun to flow into their coffers. And the family's investments were turned over to Baydr because they could not bring themselves to trust the Westerners. In addition to the basic differences in philosophy and religion, there had been too long a history of colonial oppression. Rich to begin with, Baydr became even richer. Just on commissions alone his income began to run in excess of five million dollars a year and he controlled an international investment fund of over five hundred million dollars. And perhaps the most curious part of it all was that he conducted his business without a centralized organization. In each country there was a small group of employees reporting directly to him. In the end he made all the decisions. He was the only one who knew where it was all going. Now after two years, Dick was beginning to get a feel of the scope of the operation but still he found each day would bring some new development that would take him by surprise.

The first time that he realized that Baydr might be involved in Al-Ikhwah was when he had seen the cable signed by Abu Saad, the group's financial representative. He had always thought that Baydr, with his basic conservatism, frowned upon the Fedayeen's course of action, that he had thought it more harmful than helpful to the Arab cause. Yet, he appeared to be doing business with them. Carriage was bright enough to know that there had to be a reason. Something was happening of which only Baydr was aware. He wondered what it could be. But there was no way he could guess. In time, he would find out. When Baydr was ready to disclose it.

Carriage looked down at his wristwatch. It was almost ten o'clock. Time to get dressed and go to the yacht. Baydr liked him to be around when there was business being done.

BAYDR stopped at the connecting door between their staterooms. He stood for a moment in thought, then walked back to his dressing table and picked up the velvet-covered jewel case. His slippers were noiseless in the deep pile of the rug. The only sound was the rustle of his polished cotton jellaba as he crossed into her room.

The room was in total darkness except for the light spilling through the open doorway. He saw her huddled form hidden beneath the sheets. Softly, he closed the door and went to the bed and sat down. She didn't move.

After a moment, he spoke. "Jordana."

There was no sign that she had heard him.

"Are you awake?" he whispered.

There was no answer. He leaned forward and placed the jewel case on the pillow beside her head, then got to his feet and started back to the door. As he reached for the knob, the lights suddenly came on. He blinked and looked back.

She was sitting up in the bed, her long blond hair spilling down over her white shoulders and full rose-tipped breasts. She didn't speak.

"I thought you were asleep," he said.

"I was," she answered. "Did you have a good flight?"

He nodded. "Yes."

"The boys will be glad to see you," she said. "Will you be able to spend some time with them this trip?"

"I plan to be here until Wednesday," he said. "Perhaps tomorrow we can take them down to Capri and spend a few days there."

"They would like that," she said. She threw off the sheets and stepped out of the bed. Her robe lay over a chair and she picked it up. In the mirror at the far end of the stateroom, she saw him watching her. "I have to dress for the party," she said, turning toward him as she slipped into her robe.

He didn't answer.

"You'd better dress too."

"I will," he answered.

He watched her walk into the bedroom and close the door behind her, then he turned back to the bed. The black velvet case still lay there on the pillow. She hadn't even noticed it.

He walked back to the bed and picked it·up, then quietly went back into his own stateroom. He pressed the button for Jabir.

Jabir appeared as if by magic. "Yes, master?"

Baydr held out the jewel case. "Have the captain place this in the safe. We will return it in the morning."

"Yes, master," he replied, putting the jewel case in his pocket.

"I have prepared the blue shantung dinner jacket for this evening. Will that be satisfactory?"

Baydr nodded. "It will be fine."

"Thank you," Jabir said. He bowed and left the stateroom.

Baydr stared at the door the servant had closed behind him. It was impossible. She could not have failed to see the jewel case on the pillow beside her. She had chosen to ignore it.

Abruptly, he turned and went back into her room. She was seated at her dressing table, looking into the mirror. She saw his reflection and turned toward him.

His open palm caught her across the face. She crashed from the chair to the floor, her arm sweeping the perfume and assorted bottles of cosmetics off the dressing table. She stared up at him, her eyes wide, more in surprise than fear. She touched her cheek and could almost feel the imprint of his hand. She made no move to get up. "That was stupid of you," she said, almost impersonally. "Now I won't be able to come to my own birthday party."

"You'll come to the party," he said grimly. "Even if you have to wear a veil like all good Muslim women."

Her eyes followed him as he walked back to the door. He paused and looked down at her. "Happy birthday," he said, and closed the door behind him.

DICK stood near the bar looking across the deck at his employer. Baydr was standing with Youssef and several other people, listening in his quietly attentive manner as Youssef told one of his interminable stories. Dick glanced at his watch. It was almost one o'clock. If Baydr was disturbed that Jordana had not yet appeared, he did not show it.

The music came through the loudspeakers that had been placed above the canopy over the sundeck. Several couples were dancing, their bodies fluid in the lights that had been strung across the ship for the party. Other couples were seated on the banquettes along the railings and at small cocktail tables around the dance floor. The buffet had been set up on the main deck below, but Baydr had not yet given the signal for dinner.

Ali Yasfir came toward him. The pudgy Lebanese's face was shining with perspiration despite the coolness of the evening. "This is a beautiful ship," he said. "How big is it?"

"A hundred and eighty feet," Dick said.

Yasfir nodded. "It seems larger." He glanced across the deck at Baydr. "Our host seems to be enjoying himself."

Carriage smiled. "He always does. I know no other man who can combine business and pleasure in the same way that he does."

"Apparently pleasure comes first." Yasfir's voice was faintly disapproving.

Carriage's voice was polite but cold. "This is madame's birthday after all and he did not expect to do business this trip."

Yasfir accepted the implied rebuke without comment. "I haven't met the lady yet."

Carriage allowed himself a smile. "It's her birthday and you know how women are. Perhaps she's planning a grand entrance."

Yasfir nodded solemnly. "Western women are very different from Arab. They take liberties our women would never dream of. My wife—" His voice trailed off as he stared at the stairway from the lower deck.

Carriage followed his gaze. Jordana had just made her appearance. All sounds of conversation faded away. Only the music blared from overhead, and abruptly it changed to the wild strains of "Misirlou."

A light seemed to envelop Jordana as she moved to the center of the dance floor. She was dressed as an Oriental dancer. A hammered gold brassiere covered her breasts, below which she was bare to the jeweled band from which hung the multicolored panels of sheer chiffon that made up her skirt. On her head, she wore a coronet and her long golden hair flowed down over her shoulders. A silken veil covered her face so that only her seductive eyes were visible. She raised her hands over her head and stood poised for a moment.

Carriage heard the Lebanese catch his breath. Jordana had never looked so beautiful. Every line of her magnificent body was revealed. Slowly, Jordana began to sway with the music.

First the finger cymbals on her hands picked up the rhythm, and as the beat became more pronounced, she moved into the dance. Carriage had seen many belly dancers in his time. He came from a Middle Eastern family and had known the dance since he was a child. But he had never seen it performed like this.

This was the height of sexuality. Her every movement brought back memories of the many women he had known, all concentrated in the eroticism of her dance. Deliberately, he tore his eyes away from her and looked around the deck.

Everyone there felt it, man and woman alike. Their passions and hunger were revealed in the way they looked at her as the dance thrust wildly toward its peak. All except Baydr.

He stood there silently watching her every move. But his face was impassive, his eyes withdrawn. And his expression did not change even as she moved in front of him and kneeling made him the classic offering movements. The music crashed to its climax and she sank to her knees before him, her forehead touching his feet.

For a moment there was silence, then applause. There were cries of brava mixed with the Arabic ahsanti. Still Jordana did not move.

After a moment, Baydr bent over and, taking her hand in his, raised her to her feet. They were still applauding as he turned toward them. He raised a hand to still them. The applause died away.

"On behalf of my wife and myself we thank you for being with us on this joyous occasion."

There was more applause and cries of happy birthday. He waited until they were silent again. "Now, there is nothing more we can say, except that . . . dinner is served."

Still holding her hand, he led her to the staircase and they began to descend. Once again the sounds of conversation began to fill the night as the others moved to follow them.

CHAPTER 5.

UNIFORMED stewards were standing at the buffet table to help the guests. The table was laden with food —roast beef, baked hams, turkeys and a giant loup caught fresh that day in the Mediterranean. The centerpiece was a huge fish carved of ice on the top of which was set a crystal bowl holding five kilos of Malossol grosgrain beluga caviar.

Many of the tables and banquettes were already occupied by hungry guests when Carriage saw Baydr excuse himself and cross to the salon doors. He turned and looked back at Carriage, then nodded in the direction of Yasfir, who was still waiting in line for the buffet. Baydr turned and entered the salon without looking back.

Carriage crossed to the Lebanese. "Mr. Al Fay waits at your convenience."

Yasfir looked at the buffet table, then at Carriage. The little man's stomach had begun to rumble at the sight of food. Reluctantly, he began to put down the empty plate he had been holding.

Dick took the plate from his hand. "I will arrange for a steward to bring you dinner."

"Thank you," Ali said.

Dick gave the plate to a steward and instructed him to bring it to Mr. Yasfir in the study, then turned back. "If you will follow me."

Yasfir followed him through the salon into the corridor which led to the staterooms. Midship, he paused at a closed mahogany door and knocked.

Baydr's voice came from inside. "Enter."

Carriage opened the door and stepped aside to allow Yasfir to precede him into the study. He did not enter. "Will there be anything further, sir?" he asked.

"Turn your beeper on," Baydr said. "I may want you later."

"Yes, sir," Carriage answered. A steward arrived with Yasfir's dinner plate. "Place it inside," he directed. When the steward came out he closed the door. He heard it lock as he went back down the corridor.

"I apologize for the inconvenience," Baydr said.

The Lebanese was already seated and eating. "It is no problem," he said, between mouthfuls of caviar. A black driblet escaped from the corner of his mouth and he patted it deliberately with his napkin.

Baydr walked over to the small desk and took out a folder from the center drawer. He placed it on the table next to Yasfir's plate. "In accordance with my discussions with your principals," he said, "I have prepared a portfolio of investments, comprising blue chip stocks and real estate, which we conservatively estimate should throw off a return of twelve percent annually over a ten-year period. This includes a growth rate of six percent and cash dividends in the same amount. It means that at the end of the ten-year period we will have received a cash return of better than forty percent, or ten million pounds sterling, while our principal will double in value."

"That's very good," Yasfir said, his mouth working on a piece of chicken.

"All I need to put the plan in operation is approval from your principals," Baydr said.

Yasfir made no move to look at the folder. He put the chicken bone back on the plate and smacked his lips politely to show how much he had enjoyed the food. "May I wash my hands?" he asked.

Baydr nodded. He took the Lebanese to the small lavatory just off the study. When the little man returned, Baydr was sitting behind his desk. The Lebanese left the folder on the table next to his empty plate and took a chair opposite the desk. Baydr waited politely for him to speak.

"Man proposes, God disposes," Yasfir said.

Baydr was silent.

"Circumstances necessitate a change in our plans," Yasfir said. "I am afraid we will not be able to go forward with the investment plan."

Baydr's face was impassive. He did not speak.

"Other commitments had to be made for the funds," the Lebanese said.

"I understand," Baydr said quietly. "I will arrange to have the ten million pounds returned to you immediately."

"That will not be necessary," Yasfir said quickly. "We see no reason why you cannot handle this affair for us. At your usual rates of commission, of course."

Baydr nodded silently.

"As you know, Israel is growing more powerful every day. And more oppressive. The suffering of our people under their domination continues to increase. They cry out to their brothers for help. Time is growing short. Soon we must move or all will be lost forever." The Lebanese paused for breath. "We have entered into certain arrangements with the Société Anonyme Matériel Militaire for supplies in the amount of six million pounds. Because of the trust we have in you, we have agreed that you would be an approved purchasing agent. For this we are prepared to pay you your usual ten-percent commission above the expenditure."

Baydr was still silent.

"For the balance of three million four hundred thousand pounds left after that purchase, we have earmarked a million pounds for investment in Colombian farmlands, coffee plantations, of course."

"Of course," Baydr said. But both realized that he knew better. "That leaves two million three hundred."

Yasfir smiled. The little man was pleased. He knew that once the money had been placed in Baydr's account, there would be no problem in securing his assistance. No matter how rich he was, he always wanted more. "We have made no plans for the balance," he said. "We thought perhaps that you might prepare a portfolio for that amount and we would give you a list of certain numbered accounts in Switzerland and the Bahamas to which it would be credited."

"I see," Baydr nodded.

"You would, of course, receive your ten-percent commission on that balance also," Yasfir said quickly. "That means you would receive almost a million pounds just to clear the money through your account."

Baydr looked at him. This was the weakness of the Arab world. Corruption and graft had almost become an integral part of their commerce. Out of ten million pounds, only six million pounds was going to be used for the benefit of the people. And that benefit was highly questionable. What the people needed was food and education, not guns. And certainly they did not need to enrich their leaders at their own expense.

The Lebanese took his silence for assent. He rose to his feet. "Then I can inform my principals that you will attend to the matter for them," he said with satisfaction.

Baydr looked at him. "No."

Yasfir's mouth fell in surprise. "No?" he echoed.

Baydr got out of his chair. He looked down at the little man. "The money will be returned when the banks open Monday morning," he said. "You will express to your people my regrets at not being able to be of service to them. But I am not equipped to function in that capacity. I am sure they can find others more qualified in those matters than I."

"It is written that a decision made in haste is often regretted," the little man said.

"It is also written," Baydr quoted pointedly, "that an honest man lives his life without regret." He pressed a button on the signaling device built into the digital clock on his desk. He started for the door.

"Mr. Al Fay," Yasfir said.

Baydr turned to him. "Yes?"

"There will be war before the winter comes." The Lebanese spoke in Arabic for the first time. "When it is over we will be in control of the Middle East. Israel will no longer exist because we will force the world to its knees. The old order is changing—a new force is coming from the people. If you join us now, you will be with the victors."

Baydr didn't answer.

"The sands of the desert will turn red with the blood of our enemies," Yasfir added.

"And our own," Baydr answered. "And when it is over, nothing will be changed. A few hundred yards here, a few hundred there. We are merely pawns in the hands of greater powers. Russia and America cannot afford to let either side win."

"They will have to listen to us," Yasfir said. "We control their oil supply. If we turn it off they will come to their knees."

"Only to a point," Baydr said. "Then they will force us to our own knees."

There was a knock at the door. Baydr unlocked and opened it. "Please escort Mr. Yasfir back to the party," Baydr said to Carriage. He turned back to the Lebanese. "If there is anything you should require to make your visit more pleasurable, we are at your disposal."

Yasfir stared at him. The bitterness of his disappointment rose like gall in his throat. But he forced himself to smile. Things would change quickly once Baydr discovered they had his daughter with them. "Khatrak," he said. "With your permission?"

"Go with peace," Baydr said formally in Arabic.

He closed the door behind them and crossed to the table and picked up the portfolio. He looked at it for a moment, then dropped it into a wastebasket.

It had merely been a ploy to involve him. They had never intended to go through with the portfolio. He knew that now. He also knew that they would not give up. They would not rest until they dragged the world down to their own level. Or, failing that, destroyed it.

Suddenly weary, he went back to his desk, sat down and closed his eyes. He saw the gentle, earnest eyes of his father looking into him, almost to his very soul. The scene was one from childhood. He had been ten years old at the most.

The children had been playing at war and he had been beating his playmate with a wooden scimitar, shouting at the top of his lungs, "Die, infidel, die! In the name of the Prophet, die!"

He felt the scimitar snatched from his hands and turned in surprise to see his father. His playmate was sniffling and crying. "Why did you stop me?" he asked angrily. "Ahmad was pretending to be a Jew."

His father knelt so that their faces were on the same level. "You were blaspheming," he said gently. "You were taking the name of the Prophet to justify your own actions."

"I was not," he retorted. "I was defending the Prophet."

His father shook his head. "You forget, my son, that the Prophet you try to defend by an expression of violence is also known as the Messenger of Peace."

That had been thirty years ago and now other yesterdays crowded and fought their way into his memory.

CHAPTER 6.

THE airstrip shimmered in the heat of the noonday sun as the twin-engine DC-3 circled the field at the edge of the desert in preparation for its landing. Baydr looked down from the window at the field as he heard the landing gear lock into place. At the far end of the airstrip, there were several large black Cadillac limousines waiting; beyond them, resting in the shade of a cluster of palm trees, were some camels and their drivers. The grinding sound of the flaps signaled that the plane was on its final approach.

Baydr turned back to the cabin. The stewardess was already in her seat, with her seat belt fastened. Opposite him, Jabir, too, was strapped in. He fastened his own belt as the plane dropped smoothly toward the desert.

The sand was rushing below his window and it seemed as if the pilot were about to land on the desert floor. Then the concrete landing strip raced beneath him and a shudder ran through the plane as the wheels touched down. A moment later, the pilot hit the brakes and Baydr felt himself thrust against the seat belt. Abruptly, the pressure ceased and the plane rolled gently toward the end of the airstrip. The noise of the motors lessened in the cabin and the stewardess rose from her seat and came down the cabin toward him.

A blond American, she had the same impersonal, professional smile that stewardesses seemed to cultivate no matter what airline they worked for. The fact that this was his father's private plane seemed to make no difference in her attitude. "I trust you enjoyed the flight, Mr. Al Fay."

He nodded. "It was fine, thank you."

"We made good time," she said. "Only eighty-seven minutes from Beirut."

"Very good time," he said.

The plane came to a stop. Through the windows he could see the limousines begin to move in closer. A number of men dressed in semi-uniforms emerged from the first car. Each carried a submachine gun, and they ran to take up their assigned places around the plane. The doors of the second limousine remained shut. Baydr could not see into it because of the heavily shaded brown sunglass. The landing ladder rolled toward the plane, pushed across the airstrip by four workmen.

Baydr pulled the buckle and got to his feet. He started toward the door. Jabir held out a restraining arm. "If the master would be kind enough to wait for a moment."

Baydr nodded and let the servant advance toward the door in front of him. The copilot had come from the flight cabin and was standing with the stewardess at the exit. They made no move to open it. Jabir opened his jacket and from under his sleeve withdrew a heavy Luger automatic. He pulled back on the safety and held the gun at the ready.

A knock came at the door. One, two, three. The copilot raised his hand. He looked at Jabir.

"One, two," the servant said. "They should answer with one, two, three, four. Anything else and we leave."

The pilot nodded. His fist rapped on the door. One, two.

The reply was instant and correct. The pilot pulled the latch on the door and it swung open. Two guards with guns were already at the top of the landing ramp and two more were at the foot of the stairs.

Baydr started for the door but again Jabir held out his hand. "With your permission, master."

He stepped out onto the ramp and exchanged a quick word in Arabic with one of the guards, then turned back to Baydr and nodded.

The intense heat of the desert hit the young man even before he reached the doorway. Baydr stepped out into the sun, blinking his eyes in the white light. He started down the ramp just as the door of the second limousine opened and his father emerged.

His father stepped out in front of his guards and slowly walked to meet Baydr. He wore the soft traditional robes of the desert sheik, and his head and neck were protected from the hot rays of the sun by his ghutra. Baydr moved quickly to his father and took the outstretched hand and pressed it to his lips in the traditional gesture of respect.

Samir reached out and raised his son's head. For a long moment, his eyes searched the young man's face, then he leaned forward, to embrace him and kiss him on each cheek. "Marhab. Welcome home, my son."

"Ya halabik. I am happy to be home, my father." Baydr straightened up. He was a head taller than his father.

Samir looked up at him. "You have grown, my son," he said proudly. "You have become a man."

Baydr smiled. "It is nineteen fifty-one, Father. One does not remain a boy forever."

Samir nodded. "We are proud of you, my son. We are proud of your achievements in the American schools, proud of the honors you have brought to us, proud that you have been accepted in the great University of Harvard in Boston, Cambridge, Massachusetts."

"I only seek to bring honor and pleasure to my parents," Baydr said. He looked toward the car. "How are my mother and sisters?"

Samir smiled. "They are well. You will see them soon enough. Your mother awaits you eagerly at home and tonight your sisters and their husbands will come and join us for dinner."

If Baydr felt disappointment at their not being at the airfield to greet him, he knew better than to show it. This was not the United States, where he had been living the past five years. Arab women did not appear in public, at least not the respectable women. "I look forward to seeing them," he said.

His father took his arm. "Come, get into the car. We will be cool in there. It is the latest model and air-conditioned against this unbearable heat."

"Thank you, Father." Baydr waited politely until his father got into the car before he entered.

A guard with a submachine gun ran quickly to the car and closed the door behind them, then got into the front seat beside the driver. Other guards piled into the limousine in front of them. As the cars began to move away, Baydr saw the drivers beating the pack camels toward the plane to collect the luggage and supplies. The car left the airfield and turned onto a concrete road that led to the mountains a few miles distant. An armored Land Rover with a mounted machine gun fell into the lane behind them.

Baydr looked at his father. "The war has been over this many years—I thought guards would no longer be necessary."

"There are still many bandits in the mountains," his father said.

"Bandits?"

"Yes," his father said. "Those who slip across our borders to steal, rape and kill. There are some who think they are Israeli guerrillas."

"But Israel has no borders near here," Baydr said.

"True," the older man replied. "But they could be agents in their employ. We cannot afford to relax our vigilance."

"Have you ever been bothered by these bandits?" Baydr asked.

"No. We have been fortunate. But we have heard of others who have." Samir smiled. "But let us talk of other more pleasant matters. Have you heard that your eldest sister is expecting a child in a matter of weeks?"

The automobiles began to climb into the mountains. After a few minutes Baydr saw the first hint of green on the sides of the road. Cacti gave way to scrub pine, then to flowers, bougainvillea and green grass. His father reached over and pressed the button to let down the windows. The fresh scented air flowed into the car, replacing the stale, cooled air of the machine.

His father took a deep breath. "There are many inventions of man but they cannot duplicate the scent of mountain air."

Baydr nodded. They were climbing rapidly to the crest of the mountain. Their home was on the far side overlooking the sea. He wondered if it was as he remembered it.

The house came into view as they turned at the top of the hill and started down. Baydr, looking from his window, saw the white roofs of the house below him. It was larger than he remembered. More buildings had been added. A large swimming pool had been built at the far end of the property, looking out toward the sea. There was something else he had never seen before. A high wall had been erected all around the complex, and stationed on top of the wall at approximately fifty-yard intervals were small booths, each manned by a guard with a machine gun.

The house itself was hidden by trees. Baydr turned back to his father. "Are all the homes like this?"

His father nodded. "Some have even more guards. The Prince has more than one hundred men at his summer estate."

Baydr didn't comment. Something had to be wrong if men had to make prisoners of themselves in order to feel safe. The car turned off the road onto the driveway leading to the house. A moment later, they passed the trees that concealed it from the road and came to the giant iron gates in the wall. Slowly the gates, powered by silent electrical motors, began to swing open. Without stopping, the automobiles rolled through. A quarter-mile farther, they stopped in front of the huge white house. A servant ran to the doors of the car. His father got out first. Baydr followed.

His eyes looked up the giant marble steps that led to the door. It was open. A woman, unveiled but wearing a headcloth and a long, white tob appeared in the doorway.

"Mother!" he cried, running up the steps and taking her in his arms.

Nabila looked up at her son, tears in the corners of her eyes. "Forgive me, my son," she whispered. "But I could no longer wait to see you."

SINCE it was not a formal occasion and only members of the family were present, they all ate together. On formal occasions the men dined alone, and the women ate afterward or not at all.

Baydr looked down the table at his sisters. Fatima, three years older than he, her face round and body heavy with child, was beaming as she sat proudly next to her husband. "It will be a boy," she said. "There have been nothing but boys in Salah's family and they all say that I look just like his mother did when she was carrying him."

Her father laughed. "Old wives' tales. Not very scientific but until we do find a way that is more exact, I'm willing to go along with it."

"I will give you your first grandson," Fatima said pointedly, looking at her sister Nawal, whose first child had been a girl.

Nawal said nothing. Her husband, Omar, a doctor who worked in his father-in-law's hospital, was also silent.

"Boy or girl," Baydr said, "it will be the will of Allah."

To that they could all agree. Samir rose to his feet. "The Westerners have a custom," he said. "The men retire to another room to enjoy a cigar. I find that very pleasant."

His father led the way to his study. Baydr and his brothers-in-law followed. A servant opened and closed the door behind them. Samir opened a box of cigars on his desk. He took a cigar and sniffed it with satisfaction. "Cuban cigars. They were sent to me from London."

He held out the box. Salah and Omar each took one

but Baydr shook his head. He took a package of American cigarettes from his pocket. "I'll stick to these."

Samir smiled. "Even your language is more American than Arabic."

"Not to the Americans," Baydr said. He lit his cigarette and waited while the others lit their cigars.

"What do you think of them?" Samir asked curiously.

"In what way?" Baydr asked.

"They are mostly Jews," Salah said.

Baydr turned to him. "That is not true. In proportion to the whole population there are very few Jews."

"I have been to New York," Salah said. "The city is crawling with Jews. They control everything. The government, the banks."

Baydr looked at his brother-in-law. Salah was a heavy-set, pedantic young man whose father had made a fortune as a money lender and now owned one of the major banks in Beirut. "Then you deal with Jewish banks?" he asked.

An expression of horror crossed Salah's face. "Of course not," he said stiffly. "We deal only with the biggest banks, the Bank of America, First National and Chase."

"They're not Jewish?" Baydr asked. Out of the corner of his eye he caught his father's smile. Samir had already gotten the point.

"No," Salah answered.

"Then the Jews do not control everything in America," Baydr said. "Do they?"

"Fortunately," Salah said. "Not that they wouldn't if they had the opportunity."

"But America is pro-Israel," Samir said.

Baydr nodded. "Yes."

"Why?"

"You have to try to understand the American mentality. They have sympathy for the underdog. And Israel has very successfully played upon that in their propaganda. First against the British, now against us."

"How can we change that?"

"Very simply," Baydr said. "Leave Israel alone. It is only a tiny strip of land in our midst, no bigger than a flea on an elephant's back. What harm can they do us?"

"They will not remain a flea," Salah said. "Refugees from all over Europe are coming in by the thousands. The scum of Europe. They will not be content with what they have. The Jew always wants it all."

"We do not know that yet," Baydr said. "Perhaps if we welcomed them as brothers and worked with them to develop our lands, rather than opposing them, we would find out differently. A long time ago it was said that a mighty sword can fell an oak tree with one blow but cannot cut a silken scarf floating in the air."

"I'm afraid it is too late for that," Salah said. "The cries of our brothers living under their domination are ringing in our ears."

Baydr shrugged. "America does not know that. All they know is that a tiny nation of a million people is living in the midst of an enemy world which surrounds and outnumbers them one hundred to one."

His father nodded solemnly. "There is much thinking to be done. It is a very complex problem."

"It is not complex," Salah said heavily. "Mark my words, in time you will all see what I tell you is true. Then, we will unite to destroy them."

Samir looked at his other son-in-law. "What is your opinion, Omar?"

The young doctor cleared his throat with embarrassment. He was inordinately shy. "I am not political," he said. "So I really do not think of these matters. In the foreign universities of England and France where I studied, there were many professors who were Jews. They were good doctors and good teachers."

"I also," Samir said. He looked at Baydr. "I trust you have made no plans for tomorrow."

"I am home," Baydr said. "What plans do I need to make?"

"Good," Samir said. "Because tomorrow we are to

have dinner with his excellency, the Prince Feiyad. He wishes to celebrate your eighteenth birthday."

Baydr was puzzled. His birthday had passed some months before. "Is his excellency here?"

"No," Samir said. "He is in Alayh, enjoying a holiday from his family and duties. We are invited to join him tomorrow."

Baydr knew better than to ask the reason. His father would tell him in his own good time. "It will be my pleasure, Father," he said.

"Good," his father smiled. "Now shall we rejoin your mother and sisters? I know they are waiting eagerly to hear more of your stories about America."

CHAPTER 7.

ALAYH was a tiny village in the mountains thirty miles from Beirut. There was no industry, no trade, no farming. It had only one reason to justify its existence. Pleasure. Both sides of the main street that ran through the center of the village were lined with restaurants and cafes which featured Oriental dancers and singers from all over the Middle East. Western tourists were discouraged and seldom if ever seen here. The clientele were the rich sheiks, the princes and businessmen, who came here to escape the rigid moralities and boredom of their own world.

Here they could indulge in all the things that were not acceptable at home. They could drink the liquor and taste the foods and delights that strict Muslim law forbade them. And perhaps most important was the fact that here they were anonymous. No matter how well one man knew the other, he did not recognize him or speak to him unless invited to do so.

It was after ten o'clock the next evening that Samir's limousine rolled to a stop in front of the largest cafe on the street. In keeping with his importance, Prince Feiyad had taken over the entire establishment for the night. It would not be proper for him to mix with the casual visitor. He was absolute monarch of a thousand-square-mile piece of land bordering on four countries, Iraq, Saudi Arabia, Syria and Jordan. That his land infringed somewhat into each of these countries did not matter because it served a useful purpose. It was to his country that each could come with impunity and in safety to work out disagreements and problems between them. Baydr's grandmother was the sister of Prince Feiyad's father and as cousins to the royal family the Al Fays were the second most important family.

It was to Baydr's father that the Prince had given the rights to all public utilities. The electric and telephone companies were owned by Samir and in return the family had built schools and hospitals where free care was provided for all who sought it. They had been rich to begin with, but with the grants they had grown even richer almost without effort.

It was a great disappointment to the whole family that the Prince had no male heirs to whom he could pass the throne. He had married a number of times and always performed his duties. And as each wife failed to produce the required heir, he had divorced her. Now, sixty years old, he had long ago decided that if it was the will of Allah that he should have no direct heir, he would see to it that his cousin would provide one for him.

It was for this reason that eighteen years earlier, Samir had made his pilgrimage to Mecca. His prayers had been answered with the birth of Baydr. But, despite his promise, Feiyad had still not designated the boy as his heir. Instead, he had insisted that Baydr be educated in Western ways and live and learn about the Western world. In many ways, Samir had been pleased. His son would become a doctor as he had been and together they would work, side by side.

But the Prince had other ideas. There were others who could become doctors. Baydr had to be educated in more important matters—trade, investment. It was only through increased sophistication in commerce that the country, meaning himself and his family, would continue to grow in wealth and stature. He had the basic Arab distrust of the Western people he did business with: he felt they regarded him as somehow inferior, almost childlike in his lack of knowledge. And so it was that he decided that Baydr would not go to England to follow in his father's footsteps, but to America, where business was the admired and respected profession.

Samir looked proudly at his son as he stepped from the limousine. Dressed in traditional Arab clothing, the ghutra falling down his neck, the robes clinging to his tall lean frame, he was a handsome figure. The strong chin, prominent nose and blue-black eyes set deeply into high-boned, olive cheeks gave promise of the strength and character of the young man. The Prince would be pleased. Perhaps, now, he would designate Baydr as his heir.

Mentally, he begged Allah's forgiveness for his earthly hopes and vanities. It was enough of a miracle that he had brought a son to him in the desert. With that he should be content. Allah's will be done.

He gestured to Baydr, who followed him up the steps into the cafe. The Prince's major-domo was at the door with two armed guards. He recognized Samir. He bowed in the traditional greeting. "As-salaam alaykum."

"Alaykum as-salaam," Samir replied.

"His excellency has been awaiting the arrival of his favorite cousin with great anticipation," the major-domo said. "He has requested that I bring you to him as soon as you arrive. He is in his apartment upstairs."

They followed the major-domo through the empty

cafe to the staircase at the rear of the great room. The cafe itself was quiet. The usually busy waiters stood around in clusters gossiping with one another, and near the stage, the orchestra sat smoking and talking. None of the singers or dancers was visible. Nothing would begin until the Prince gave the signal.

The apartments over the cafe were reserved for very special clients and their guests who, after a night of amusement in the cafe, might be too tired to make the journey home or who wished to stay and partake of further pleasures that could be provided by the management. The major-domo paused in front of a door and knocked.

"Who ith it?" a young boy's voice answered.

"The Doctor Al Fay and his son are here to see his excellency," the major-domo replied.

The door was opened by a young boy clothed in silken shirt and trousers. His eyes were heavily made up and his cheeks rouged and his fingernails long and painted. "Pleathe come in," he lisped in English.

Baydr and his father entered the room. The faintly sweet odor of hashish hung in the air. The room was empty. "Pleathe be theated," the boy said, indicating the sofas and chairs. He left them and went into another room.

Baydr and his father looked at each other without speaking.

The boy came back into the room. "Hith exthellenthy will be with you in a moment. Ith there anything I can do for you? A thweet? A refrethment perhapth? We have Englith whithkey if you prefer."

Samir shook his head. "No, thank you."

The door opened again and Prince Feiyad entered. He was fully dressed in his royal robes, his head covered in white muslin. He crossed the room to his cousin.

Samir and Baydr rose and made the traditional obeisance to their monarch. Feiyad brushed Samir's arms aside with a smile. "Is that a way for cousins to meet after they had not seen each other for a long time?" He put his arms on Samir's shoulders and kissed him on each cheek, then turned, still smiling, to Baydr. "And this is the little boy who cried when he went away to school?"

Baydr felt himself flushing. "That was a long time ago, your excellency."

"Not too long," the Prince said and laughed. "I think you were six then."

"He's eighteen now," Samir said. "And a grown man, praise be to Allah."

"Al-hamdu li-llah," the Prince echoed. He looked up at Badyr, who stood a head taller than either of them. "He is tall, your son. Taller than anyone I remember in our family."

"It is the diet, your excellency," Samir said. "The food in America is enriched with many vitamins and minerals. The entire younger generation is growing taller than their parents."

"What miracles you scientists perform," the Prince said.

"The miracles are Allah's," Samir said. "We are nothing but His instruments."

The Prince nodded. "We have much to talk about, my cousin," he said. "But we can do that in the morning. Tonight we must enjoy the pleasure of our reunion and each other's company." He clapped his hands. "I have had a suite made ready for you so that you may freshen yourselves after your journey. At midnight we will gather in the cafe below, where a feast has been prepared for us."

Samir bowed. "We are most grateful for the kindness of your hospitality."

The young boy appeared again. "Show my cousins to their apartments," the Prince commanded.

The boy bowed. "It will be my pleathure, your exthellenthy."

Baydr's room was separated from his father's by a large living room. He left his father and went into his bedroom, which was luxuriously furnished in rich silks and satins. The couches were covered with velour cushions. No sooner than he had entered, a soft knock came at the door. "Come in," he called.

A young maidservant came into the room. She bowed her head respectfully. "May I be of service to the master?" she asked in a soft voice, her eyes properly averted.

"There is nothing I can think of."

"Perhaps I can draw the master a hot bath so that he may wash away the fatigue of his journey?" she suggested.

"That would be nice," he said.

"Thank you, master," she said and crossed the room to the bathroom.

Baydr looked after her thoughtfully. Now he knew he was home. Service was not like this in America.

THE noise of the kanoon and the drums flooded the cafe. On the small stage a dancer whirled, her multicolored scarves floating around her, the silver metal of her brassiere reflecting the sparkling lights. At a horseshoe-shaped table at the front of the stage, the Prince's party watched intently.

The Prince was seated at the center of the table, Samir in the place of honor on his right, Baydr on his left. Behind the Prince, on small stools, were several young boys, all wearing the same elaborate makeup as the young boy who had greeted them in the Prince's suite. Standing behind them was the major-domo, who supervised the service of the waiters and other members of the staff. There were bottles of champagne in buckets near each guest and their glasses were constantly filled. The table was covered with more than fifty varieties of hors d'oeuvres and delicacies of the region. The guests ate with their fingers, and a servant delicately wiped their hands after each mouthful with a fresh warm damp cloth. At the door and against the wall stood a dozen of Feiyad's personal guards, who never took their eyes from the Prince.

The music reached a crescendo and the dancer sank to her knees in finale. The Prince led the applause.

At a gesture from him, the waiters snatched bottles of champagne from their buckets and kneeling before the stage popped the corks from bottle after bottle, shooting them high over the kneeling dancer's head. Idly, the Prince picked up a bank note from a pile in front of him and, crumpling it in his hand, threw it onto the stage in front of the dancer.

With a fluid graceful motion, the dancer picked up the money and placed it in her belt just below her navel. She bowed again and smiling seductively backed off the stage.

The Prince signaled the major-domo and whispered in his ear. The major-domo nodded. He turned and made a gesture to the boys sitting behind the Prince, then signaled the orchestra to begin again.

At the first sound of the music, four girls came on the stage and began their dance. Gradually, the lights went down until the room was in almost total darkness, with the exception of tiny blue spots on the dancers. As the music grew wilder, the spotlight would lose a dancer, then find her moving more excitingly than ever before. The dance lasted more than fifteen minutes, and when it was finished, the girls seemed to be in a frenzy, finally falling to the floor as the stage went completely dark.

For a moment there was silence, then for the first time the Prince began to applaud enthusiastically. Slowly the lights came up. The dancers, still prostrate on the floor, began to rise to their feet. Baydr stared unbelievingly. The dancers on the stage were not the girls who had begun the dance. Instead, their places had been taken by the boys who had been seated behind the Prince.

This time the Prince didn't bother to crumple the bank notes. He threw the money on the stage in handfuls while the champagne corks popped wildly.

Baydr glanced at his father. Samir's face was impassive. He wondered what his father thought of the evening. Those were one-hundred-pound notes that the Prince was so carelessly throwing at the dancers

—more money than the average workman earned in a year.

The Prince looked at Baydr and spoke in French. "C'est beau, c'est magnifique, non?" Baydr met his eyes. They were watchful and appraising. "Oui." He hesitated for a moment. "C'est tout pédéraste?"

The Prince nodded. "Vous aimez? Choisissez quelqu'un pour votre plaisir."

Badyr still looked into the older man's eyes. He shook his head. "Merci, non. Pas pour moi. Je préfère les femmes."

The Prince laughed aloud and turned to Samir. "Your son is lovely and he has sound taste," he said. "He is also very American."

Samir looked at his son and smiled proudly. Somehow Baydr knew that he had passed the Prince's first test.

It was five o'clock in the morning and dawn was breaking in the mountains when Badyr bid his father good night and went into the bedroom. The drapes were drawn and the room was dark. He reached for the light switch.

A hand stopped his arm. The woman's voice was soft and held the faintest Egyptian accent. "We will have candles, your excellency."

The faint scent of musk came to his nostrils as she moved away from him. He stood very still in the darkness, his eyes trying to make her out, but he could see nothing until the match scratched and glowed. Then the dark, heavy-lashed eyes smiled at him and she turned to the candle.

The soft yellow light spilled into the room. He recognized the woman as one of the dancers who had performed earlier that evening. The only portion of her costume that had been changed was her brassiere. Her breasts were no longer contained by the silver metal plate. Instead, they were covered by a diaphanous silken scarf through which the dark areola of her nipples could clearly be seen. She smiled again at him. "I have had a warm bath prepared in case his excellency should be weary."

He didn't answer.

She clapped her hands. Two more women came from the corners of the room, where they had been standing in the shadows. They wore even less costume than the first. Only the thinnest of veils covered their breasts and fell from their hips around their legs. As they moved toward Baydr, they crossed in front of the light, and he could clearly see the shape of their nude bodies and their carefully depilated hair-free mounds. Only their lower faces were hidden by the traditional Muslim veil.

The first woman clapped her hands again and still another woman came from a far corner. She turned on a record player and the soft sound of music began to come into the room. She began to sway gently to the rhythm.

The two women took his hands and led him toward the bed. Their touch was light and swift as they undressed him. He still hadn't spoken.

The first woman lit a cigarette and gave it to him. He took a drag. The faintly sweet pungent odor of hashish floated into his nostrils, and he felt a gentle rush of warmth. He took another deep puff and gave back the cigarette.

He looked at her. "What is your name?"

"Nadia, your excellency," she said, making the gesture of obeisance.

He smiled at her, feeling the surge of sex rising within him. He stretched out on the bed. "Must we bathe?" he asked.

She laughed. "Whatever your excellency desires."

He looked around at them. He could feel the hashish in his loins. He looked down at his phallus, long and lean and hard against his belly, then back at the first woman. "I desire all of you," he said.

CHAPTER 8.

HE awoke with the sunlight spilling into the room and Jabir standing next to his bed, with a cup of hot steaming Turkish coffee. He took a sip. It scalded his mouth. "What time is it?" he asked.

"It is noon, master," the servant said.

He looked around the room. He could not remember when the women had gone. His last memory of them was a wild tangle of bodies and warmth. He had been lying on his side. One of them had anointed his entire body with oil and then they were all licking at him with their tongues, at his anus, his scrotum, his nipples, his phallus, his belly until the sensation had become so exquisite that the juice burst from him in a final exhausting geyser. Then he had fallen asleep.

He took another sip of the scalding coffee and shook his head. "Is my father awake?"

"Yes, master. He is with the Prince and they await you for breakfast."

He took another gulp of the coffee and got out of bed. "Tell them I'll grab a shower and be right there."

He let the water run cold, then hot, then cold again. In a moment he was wide awake. He ran his fingers quickly over his chin and decided that he could shave later. When he came out of the bathroom, Jabir had laid out shirt and slacks for him.

The Prince and his father were still seated at the breakfast table when he came into their room. The major-domo was just clearing away the breakfast dishes.

Baydr kissed his father, then the Prince's hand. At

the Emir's gesture he sat down. "Would you like something to eat?" the Prince asked politely.

"No, thank you," Baydr said. It would have been impolite for him to eat after they had finished.

"Some coffee then," the Prince said.

"Thank you." Badr nodded.

The major-domo hurried to fill his cup. Baydr tasted it. It was thick and sweet. He waited quietly, respectfully. Though the shades were drawn so that the sunlight could not enter the room, the Prince still wore dark sunglasses, behind which his eyes could not be seen. He waited until Baydr put down his cup. "Your father and I have been discussing your future."

Baydr bowed his head. "I am your servant."

The Prince smiled. "First, you are my cousin, my blood."

Baydr didn't speak. He was not expected to say anything.

"The world is changing rapidly," the Prince said. "Many things have happened since your birth. Our plans must change accordingly." He clapped his hands sharply.

The major-domo withdrew from the room, silently closing the door behind him. They were alone in the room.

The Prince waited for a moment. His voice dropped almost to a whisper. "You know that I have always looked upon you as my heir and believed that someday you would take my place as ruler of our country."

Baydr glanced at his father. Samir's face was expressionless. He turned back to the Prince.

"But times have changed," the Emir said. "There are other, more important matters that confront us. All through the Middle East the tide of the future flows from beneath the sands of the desert, promising riches such as we have never envisioned. The source of this wealth is oil. The lifeblood of the modern industrialized Western world. And our little country sits upon some of the greatest pools of oil ever known to man."

He paused for breath, raising his coffee cup to his lips to taste the hot sweet mixture. "I have this past month concluded an agreement with several American, British and European companies to develop this resource. For exploration rights, they have agreed to pay us ten million dollars. If oil is discovered, they will pay us additional sums for each operating well and a royalty on the oil that is exported. They have also committed themselves to build refineries and help develop the country. All of this has great promise but I am still not at ease."

"I don't understand," Badyr said. But he did. It was for this reason that he had been sent to learn the ways of the Western world."

"I think you do," the Emir said shrewdly. "But let me continue in my own way. Though the world has renounced imperialism and colonization as a way of life, there are other ways to enslave a country and its people. By making them economically dependent. I do not intend to let the West do that to us, but it suits my plan to let them pay for our progress."

Baydr nodded. He began to feel a new respect for the Prince. Behind all the strange peculiar ways lurked a man of thought. "How can I be of help?" he asked. "I am yours to command."

The Prince looked at Samir and nodded approvingly. Samir smiled. The Prince turned back to Baydr. "I have a more important task for you than to succeed me. I want a man who can walk in the Western world and take these riches they grudgingly give to us and use them in the Western way to acquire even more riches. And if you will undertake this task for which you have been trained and will be trained even further, I promise you that your first-born son will become my heir and the next prince."

"I need no promise from my sovereign prince," Baydr said. "I will take my joy in carrying out his wishes."

The Emir rose to his feet and embraced Baydr. "My own son could not do more for me."

"I thank your excellency for your trust. My only prayer is that Allah sees fit in His wisdom to make me worthy of it."

"It will be as Allah wills," the Prince said. He returned to his seat. "You will return to America to school. Only now your education will be in the hands of certain men recommended to me by the American oil companies. You will not take the ordinary schooling. Your education will be specialized and completed within a three-year period."

Baydr nodded. "I understand."

"And now there is just one further matter to be arranged," the Prince said. "Your marriage."

Baydr stared at him in surprise. This was something he had not expected. "My marriage?" he echoed.

The Prince smiled. "You need not be surprised. From the reports I have had about last night, you should provide me with many sons."

Baydr was silent.

"Your father and I have been discussing the matter very carefully and after a great deal of thought have selected a bride for you of whom you can be very proud. She is young and beautiful and comes of one of the best families in Lebanon. Her name is Maryam Riad, daughter of Mohammed Riad, the famous banker."

"I know the girl," his father said hastily. "She is indeed very beautiful. And very devout."

Baydr looked at his father. "How old is she?"

"Sixteen," Samir answered. "Though she has never been abroad, she is very well educated. At the present time she is attending the American Girls College in Beirut."

"Sixteen is young for marriage," Baydr said.

The Emir began to laugh. "I have chosen wisely. Perhaps in America a maiden of sixteen is young. In our lands, she is just ripe."

* * *

BAYDR was silent in the car on the drive back to Beirut. It wasn't until they were at the outskirts of the city that Samir spoke to him. "What is it, my son?"

"Nothing, Father."

"Are you disappointed that you are not to be the Prince's heir?"

"No."

"Then is it the thought of your impending marriage?"

Baydr hesitated. "I don't even know the girl. I never heard of her before this afternoon."

Samir looked at him. "I think I understand. You wonder why we go to all the trouble to educate you in the Western ways and then revert to our own in arranging your marriage. Is that it?"

"I guess that's it. In America, at least, you get to meet the girl first and find out if you like each other."

"That happens here too, son," Samir said quietly. "But we are not ordinary folk. We have responsibilities that go beyond our own personal feelings."

"But you and Mother knew each other before you were married. You practically grew up together."

Samir smiled. "That's true. But our marriage had been arranged while we were still children. Somehow we knew that and it brought us closer together."

"Would you have married someone else if it had been arranged? Knowing how you felt about Mother?"

Samir thought for a moment, then he nodded. "Yes. I might not have liked it but I would have had no choice. One must do what one must do. It is the will of Allah."

Baydr looked at his father, and sighed. The will of Allah. That covered it all. Man himself had very few options. "I would like to meet the girl," he said.

"It is already arranged," Samir replied. "Her family has been invited to spend the weekend with us in the mountains. They will arrive the day after tomorrow."

A sudden thought crossed Baydr's mind. "You have known about this for a long time?"

"Not long," his father answered. "The Prince just told me of his decision last week."

"Does Mother know?"

"Yes."

"Did she approve?"

"Of the marriage? Yes."

"You seem to hesitate," Baydr said.

"Your mother had grand dreams of you becoming the Prince." Samir laughed. "Women aren't always very practical."

"And you, Father, were you disappointed too?"

Samir looked into his son's eyes. "No." He thought back to the night his son was born. "You always were and always will be my prince."

CHAPTER 9.

MARYAM Riad, like most Lebanese girls, was small, no more than five feet tall, with large dark eyes. Her black hair was worn high on her head in the latest Paris fashion to give an illusion of greater height. Her skin was pale olive and she had a tendency toward plumpness, which she continually fought by dieting, much to the despair of her parents, who preferred the roundness of the Arab woman. She spoke French fluently and English uncomfortably, hated going to the American Girls College and made a point of continually letting her parents know that she felt she should have gone to Swiss or French schools like the children of other well-to-do families.

To this complaint her father had one answer. Girls had no need of education because after they were married they had only to run a house and bear children. Bitterly, Maryam had watched her brothers go away to school while she herself remained at home without even being allowed the freedom that many of her friends who attended the school enjoyed. She had to be home immediately after classes, was never allowed dates and could not go out unless chaperoned under circumstances approved by her father.

In the limousine with her parents on the way to Baydr's home, her father looked at her with satisfaction. "Now, my daughter," he said in his heavy manner, "perhaps you understand why your parents looked after you the way we did. Perhaps now you will appreciate us more."

She turned from the window. "Yes, Father," she said obediently.

"Do you think you would have been chosen for this marriage by the Prince himself if you had been away in foreign schools?" he asked. "No," he said, answering his own question. "What he wanted was a true Arab woman, not one who had been tainted by foreign influences."

She glanced at her mother, who was silent. Her mother never spoke when her father was near. "Yes, Father," she said again.

"Now I want you to remember your manners," her father said. "Above all, be respectful and decorous. I want none of the frivolous ways that you learned from friends at the college."

"Yes, Father," she said wearily for the third time.

"This marriage will be the most important in the country," her father said. "Everyone knows that your first son will become heir to the Prince."

She glanced at her father out of the corner of her eyes. "But what if I have nothing but girls?"

Her father was shocked. "You will have sons!" he shouted, as if saying it would make it so. "Do you hear me? You will have sons!"

"If it pleases Allah," she said with a secret smile.

"His will be done," her mother said automatically.

"It is the will of Allah," her father said with conviction. "Why else would He have arranged this marriage?"

MARYAM was very impressed by what she saw as the car drove through the gates of the vast estate. She had known wealth, but nothing like this. Compared with Samir, her father, who was one of the richest men in Beirut, was just comfortable. Here there were endless servants and guards. It was like another world.

In honor of the occasion, the family wore traditional clothing but in their suitcases were the latest Paris clothes, into which they would change for the grand dinner that evening.

"Adjust your veil," her mother said as the car came to a stop and a servant advanced to open the door.

Quickly, Maryam covered her face so that only her eyes were visible. Looking up the steps, she saw Dr. Al Fay descending toward them. A half-step behind him was Baydr. Her breath caught in her throat. They, too, wore traditional clothing and there was something in her fiancé's bearing that bespoke a desert heritage. Only a true sheik could look like that.

Her father got out of the car. Samir advanced toward him, arms outstretched. "Ahlan, Ahlan."

"Ahlan fikum." The two men embraced, kissing the other on each cheek.

Samir turned and introduced his son. Baydr made the gesture of obeisance and respect, bidding his future father-in-law welcome. Then he held out his hand, Western fashion.

They shook hands and turned back to the car. Mrs. Riad got out of the car and was greeted by Samir. A moment later Maryam descended. Her father held out his hand toward her and led her to the doctor. "You remember Dr. Al Fay?"

She glanced up for a moment, then averted her eyes as was proper. She nodded and made the gesture of obeisance.

Samir took her hand. "My child," he said. "Welcome. May our home forever be your home."

"Thank you," she whispered. "May it be the will of Allah."

Samir gestured and Baydr came forward. Decorously, she kept her eyes down so that all she saw were the tips of his shoes under the flowing jellaba. "Maryam," he said, "may I present my son, Baydr, your future husband?"

She made the gesture of obeisance before looking up, then she raised her head. For a moment, she was startled. No one had ever told her that his eyes were blue. Then her heart began to beat and she could feel the blush creeping up under her veil. There were so many things that no one had ever told her about him. He was so tall. And so handsome. Her eyes fell and she could hardly hear his words of welcome, the sound of her heart was pounding so strongly in her ears. For the first time in her life she was truly grateful that her parents had not sent her abroad to school. She was hopelessly in love.

DINNER was a formal affair. Samir had ordered the French chef to come from their house in Beirut to prepare it. Instead of the usual Lebanese mezzeh, the hors d'oeuvres were pâté de foie gras and grosgrain Iranian caviar. Rather than the customary moulou-khieh, rabbit and rice, the entrées were coq au vin and gigot, but the dessert was typical—baklava in more than twenty of its honey-sweet variations.

Champagne was served throughout the meal—the single exception to Muslim law. The women in their long Paris gowns and the men in dinner jackets carried on casual, polite conversation as the two families became acquainted.

As the meal drew to its close, Mr. Riad rose to his feet. "If I may be permitted," he said in his most important manner, "I would like to propose a toast to our most gracious host, the good doctor Al Fay. May Allah shower His blessings upon him and his family."

He raised his glass and took a sip of the champagne. "And another toast," he said quickly, still holding his glass. He smiled down the table at Baydr. "To my future son-in-law, whom I already think of as my son, and to my daughter. May Allah bless their union with many sons."

Maryam felt herself blushing at the sound of the warm laughter. She did not dare look across the table at Baydr. Her father was speaking again.

"And though the question of dowry never arose between our families, I would not like to lose sight of this ancient and honored custom. For in what other manner can a man show his affection for his daughter and appreciation of her husband?"

Samir rose protestingly. "No, Mohammed, the gift of your daughter is riches enough."

"My dear doctor." The banker smiled, overriding him. "Would you deny me this simple pleasure?"

"Of course not." Samir returned to his chair.

"My son," Riad said, turning to Baydr. "On the day of your wedding, an account will be opened in your name at my bank in Beirut in the amount of one million pounds Lebanese. It will be yours to do with what you wish."

Baydr glanced across the table at Maryam before he rose to thank his father-in-law. Her face was flushed and she did not look up from the table. He turned to the banker. "My honored father," he said slowly, "may Allah be witness to your generosity and kindness. There is only one thing more that I ask and that is that you give me your guidance so that I may make wise use of your great gift."

"You shall have it," Mohammed said quickly. He was pleased. It was working as he had planned. He was sure that this account was only the beginning of the business his bank would be doing with the Al Fay family.

Samir rose to his feet. Dinner was over. He looked at Baydr. "It would be nice if you showed your fiancée the gardens," he said, "while we go into the library to relax."

Baydr nodded, went around the table and held

Maryam's chair as she rose. He smiled at her. "They seem to want to get rid of us."

She nodded. He took her arm and they started for the garden doors.

As they went through the doors, Mrs. Riad turned to Nabila. "Don't they make a beautiful couple?" she asked.

THEY had reached the pool at the far end of the garden before either of them said a word. Then they both began speaking almost at the same time.

Maryam stopped. "I'm sorry."

"It's my fault," Baydr said quickly. "What was it you wanted to say?"

"Nothing important," she said. "What was it you wanted to say?"

They laughed, each a little embarrassed for the other. He looked down at her. "I was wondering how you felt. I mean, about our getting married?"

Her eyes fell. She didn't answer.

"You don't have to answer that," he said quickly. "It wasn't fair of me. You don't have much choice, do you?"

Her eyes came up. "Do you?"

It was his turn not to answer. He fished in his jacket pocket and came out with a package of cigarettes. He held them toward her. "Do you smoke?"

She shook her head.

He lit one and drew a deep breath. He let the smoke out slowly. "It's kind of old-fashioned, isn't it?"

"Yes."

"In America I almost forgot how we do things."

"I always wanted to go abroad," she said. "But my father wouldn't let me. Did you like it?"

"Yes," he answered. "People are simpler there. Most of the time you know exactly what they are thinking."

She hesitated. "Did you have a girl there?"

"Not one special girl. But we had lots of dates. And you?"

"My father is very strict. I wasn't allowed out much.

There was even a fight when I wanted to go to the college."

They fell silent again. He looked at the glowing tip of his cigarette. This time it was she who spoke first. "You have blue eyes."

"Yes," he said. "My father says it goes all the way back to the holy wars. Ever since then blue eyes show up in the family now and then."

She turned away and looked out to the sea. Her voice was very low. "I must be a great disappointment to you after all the Western girls you have known."

"That's not true," he said quickly. "I could never take them seriously. They're too empty-headed. Not like us."

"Still, they're very beautiful. They're tall."

"Maryam," he said.

She turned toward him.

"You're very beautiful too."

"I am?" she asked. "Do you really think so?"

"I think so." He reached for her hand. "Would you still like to go abroad?"

"Yes."

He smiled. "Then we'll go to Europe on our honeymoon."

And that is what they did. Married at the end of July, they spent the month of August traveling the Continent. When in September Baydr brought Maryam back to Beirut and left her to return to school in America, she was already pregnant.

CHAPTER 10.

DANCING had resumed on the upper deck when the guests wandered back after dinner. As usual, Baydr had disappeared as soon as the food was served. It was his habit to hold his meetings while everyone was eating so that by the time they were finished he would come out again and join the party. In that fashion he would not be missed.

Jordana joined one of the tables and seated herself so that she could watch for Baydr's reappearance in the salon. He was still strange to her, even after nine years of marriage. There was something about him she would never understand. At times it seemed as if he were completely unaware of her and then, suddenly, out of nowhere, he would bring her up short and she would realize that there was very little about her that he was not aware of.

Like tonight. She had seen the Van Cleef box on the pillow but for some perverse reason which even she did not fully understand, she had decided not to acknowledge it. Perhaps it was just that she could not excuse his comings and goings with another gift. Unlike American men she had known, she could not manipulate him with guilt. He was the way he was and there was nothing anyone could do about it. His reaction was direct and simple. The savage roared out of the darkness within him.

It was her own reaction that surprised her. There was something comforting in his violence. It was as if she had been a child provoking a parent into punishment so that she could be reassured of his love. Her

own guilts were clarified and she began to think of
ways to win back his pleasure.

No sooner had the door slammed behind him than
she rose and looked in the mirror. His handprint was
turning bright on her cheek. She pressed the button
for her secretary and asked for an ice pack, then sat
in her room for over an hour holding the cold pack
to her face until the swelling was gone.

It was then that she decided on her costume. She
would be a Muslim wife if that was what he wanted. A
wife, a houri, a slave. Wasn't that what Allah promised when they entered the gates of paradise?

She raised a glass of champagne to her lips as she
watched the salon doors. Baydr had not yet come out.

"Jordana, darling," a voice gushed in her ear. "Your
dance was so beautiful."

She turned to the speaker, recognizing the voice.
"Mara," she said, holding up her cheek for the customary kiss. "You're more than kind."

"No, darling," the Princess said quickly. "It's true.
It was the most erotique thing I have ever seen. Had
I been a man I would have raped you then and there."
She laughed and added, "As a matter of fact I still
might."

Jordana laughed with her. "That's the greatest com-
pliment of all, Mara."

The Princess bent her head closer to Jordana's ear.
"What you did was unbelievable. Did you notice the
young man I brought with me? He went out of his
mind. I thought he would burst his trousers."

Jordana looked at her. It was not like Mara to be
so effusive. "Really, darling?"

"Really," Mara answered. "And he's dying to meet
you. Do you have a moment?"

Over the Princess' shoulder, Jordana saw Carriage
coming out of the salon with Mr. Yasfir. "Not just
now," she answered. "Baydr should be coming out
soon."

Yasfir made his way directly to her. "Madame Al
Fay." He bowed.

"Mr. Yasfir," she said formally.

"I wish to express my thanks for a gracious evening and present my apologies for leaving so soon but I have pressing affairs ashore."

She held out her hand. "I'm sorry too."

He kissed her hand.

"Perhaps next time we will have the opportunity to become better acquainted," she said.

"I will look forward to that," he said. "Bon soir, madame."

As Yasfir made his way down the deck to the ladder that led to the speedboat which would take him back to shore, she saw Carriage go over to Youssef. Youssef and the American film director Michael Vincent followed Carriage into the salon and down the corridor leading to Baydr's study.

"Another meeting?" Mara asked.

Jordana shrugged silently and raised her champagne. The Princess slipped into the chair beside her.

"One of my husbands was like that. I forgot which one. Always meetings. It was so boring, I divorced him."

Jordana smiled at her. "Baydr may be many things but he is not boring."

"I did not say he was. But some husbands do not realize there are other things in life besides business."

Jordana did not answer. She sipped at her champagne. Suddenly she was down. Nothing seemed to work for them anymore.

"Come, darling," the Princess urged. "Meet my young man. It will make him happy and may amuse you for a few minutes."

"Where is he?"

"Over there. The tall blond one standing near the steps."

Jordana glanced at him. "He seems young."

The Princess laughed. "He is young, darling. Twenty-five and with the staying powers of an ox. I have not known a man like him since Rubi was in his prime."

"Gigolo?" Jordana asked.

"Of course, darling," Mara said. "Aren't all the beautiful young men? But that makes life simpler when you get tired of them. Give them a few francs and they go away. No complications."

"Tired of him already? Is that why you're giving him away?"

Mara laughed. "No, darling. It's just that he exhausts me. I can't keep up with him. He keeps sticking his big beautiful cock at me and I'm not as young as I used to be. I'm exhausted."

"At least you're honest."

Mara's voice was hurt. "I'm always honest. Now will you meet him?"

Jordana glanced toward the salon. Carriage was coming back alone. Youssef and Vincent had remained with Baydr. She shrugged her shoulders. "All right," she said. "Bring him over."

BAYDR handed the Scotch and water to Vincent and gestured him to a seat. Youssef retired discreetly to a corner of the room as Baydr sat down opposite the American.

"I have been an admirer of your work for a long time, Mr. Vincent," Baydr said.

"Thank you, Mr. Al Fay. I'm truly flattered."

"I'm sure I'm not alone," Baydr said, and decided to come right to the point. After all, the man was American and he didn't have to beat around the bush. "That is why I decided to ask if you would be interested in doing a film based on the life of the Prophet. Have you ever thought about it?"

The director pulled at his drink. "Honestly, Mr. Al Fay, I never have."

"Any particular reason, Mr. Vincent?"

Vincent shook his head. "It just never occurred to me. Maybe it's because we Americans know very little about Muhammad."

"But there are more than four hundred million people who do," Baydr said.

Vincent nodded. "I know that now. Mr. Ziad very carefully explained that to me. He also gave me several biographies of the Prophet and I must admit that I was fascinated with the idea."

"Do you think there is a film there?"

"I do, a very good film."

"One that could be successful in the Western world? One that could help them understand that we have a civilization founded on morality much like their own?"

"Successful? I don't know. There will be problems in exhibition," the director answered. "In terms of understanding, I would say, yes. Conditional, of course, on the film being shown."

Baydr nodded. "I understand that. But suppose that were possible. What is the first step we would have to take to get the film made?"

"All films begin with a script."

"You've written the scripts for your other films. Would you consider writing this one?"

"I would if I knew enough, but I'm afraid I lack knowledge."

"If you could obtain the help you need, would you then consider it?"

"If I were sure that when I was finished with the script a picture would be made."

"And if I guarantee that the picture will be made?"

Vincent looked at Baydr and took a deep breath. If he said yes and the picture were abandoned, he would be finished in the industry. The Jews would see to that. But if it were made, and it was good, they would even play it in their theaters. They didn't care what the film was if it brought money into the box office. "I'm expensive," he said. "I don't come cheap."

"I already know that, Mr. Vincent. Would a fee of one million dollars plus a share of the profits of the picture be too little?"

THE music that came through the loudspeakers was slow and romantic and the floor was crowded as Jacques took the glass of champagne from her hand, put it down and led her onto the floor. He smiled down at her. "I have waited a long time for the right music so that I could ask you to dance."

Jordana felt the champagne buzzing in her head. She smiled back at him. "How nice."

He pulled her close to him. "You Americans. Is that all you can say? 'How nice.'"

She looked up into his face. "American? I'm not American. Can't you tell from my dress?"

"Don't talk," he said. "Just dance." He moved her head against his shoulder and with his other hand in the small of her back pressed her hips tightly against him. He moved very slowly in time with the music, allowing her to feel his growing erection.

After a moment, he looked down at her. Her eyes were closed. He let the hand that held her drop to his side, then moving toward the railing where no one could see what they were doing, he began to rub her hand against his rocklike shaft. "I have buttons on my trousers," he whispered. "Not zips. Open them."

She stared up at him, her eyes wide. "You're crazy!" she whispered. "There are people watching!"

"No one can see!" he whispered fiercely. "We have our backs to them. I have already masturbated twice since your dance. This time I must have you touch me!"

Still looking into his eyes, her fingers found the buttons and opened them. He wore no undershorts and his phallus leaped out into her hand. He pressed her head against his chest so that she would have to look down at him. "Pull it!" he commanded.

The palm of her hand covered no more than one-third of its length. In the dim lights she could see the glistening red glans bursting from his foreskin. She felt the moisture fill her palms.

"Harder!" he said.

She no longer heard the music. The only rhythm was that of her hand moving back and forth, back and forth over the length of him.

"Now!" he whispered. "Through the railing into the sea!" He let it come.

Staring down, she could see the spurts of semen as they shot from his shuddering penis. Then it was over. She looked up into his face.

"Thank you," he said, smiling. He took the handkerchief from his breast pocket. "Dry your hands."

She took the handkerchief and rubbed it against her palm, then gave it back to him.

He shook his head. "Dry me too."

She wiped him and he slipped himself back into his trousers. "You can throw the handkerchief away," he said.

The handkerchief fell toward the sea and they moved from the railing back onto the crowded dance floor. "I must see you again," he whispered. "Where can I call you?"

"You can't call me. I will call you."

"I'm at the Martinez. You will call? You promise?"

She nodded. The music stopped just as she saw Baydr followed by Youssef and the American director come to the top of the stairs. "My husband," she whispered. She began to leave him but he held onto her hand.

"Tomorrow?" he whispered.

"Yes!" She pulled her hand free and made her way across the floor toward Baydr. Her face was flushed and she felt as high as if she had just finished a joint of hash.

"Darling!" she exclaimed. "What a lovely birthday party. How can I ever thank you enough?"

CHAPTER 11.

IT was past midnight and Leila was getting bored with sitting in her room. She stood at the window looking out at the Croisette. The crowds were still milling back and forth in the warm night. The lights on the billboards on the center islands were still advertising the films that were to be shown during the coming festival and there was a bright, gay feeling in the air.

She turned from the window. She had had enough. She had to get out for a walk or she would go crazy. She picked up her denim jacket and her key and went out into the hall. She put on her jacket while waiting for the elevator. When she emerged from the building, she looked much like the other young women wandering the night in their jeans and shirts.

She started down toward the Carlton, stopped and bought an ice cream on the corner of the Rue du Canada, then crossed the street to the beach side, where the crowds were less. Opposite the Carlton, she sat down on the slanting concrete railing along the esplanade and watched the people entering and leaving the hotel.

She finished the ice cream, ate the sugar sweet cone down to the last tiny fragment and then licked her fingers clean. She heard the noise of a speedboat motor and turned around to look.

A big Riva was pulling up to the Carlton dock. It was empty except for two uniformed sailors in white T-shirts and duck trousers. One leaped up on the dock and tied the line to a small stanchion. A moment later the other sailor climbed up beside him, then both stood idly smoking and talking.

She looked past the speedboat. Her father's yacht was anchored several hundred yards out in the bay; the party lights across the upper deck twinkled in the night. The faint sound of music drifted toward the shore. She took out a cigarette and lit it.

She glanced back at the hotel. Nothing was happening there. She dragged on the cigarette. A small car going by on the Croisette slowed down, then stopped opposite her. The driver leaned across the seat, rolled the window down and yelled something at her.

She didn't hear what he said but she knew what he wanted. Contemptuously, she shook her head and, getting to her feet, turned her back on him. The driver hooted his horn in reply and drove off with a clashing of gears.

Impulsively she started down the steps to the beach and walked out on the jetty. Automatically, the sailors began to come to attention, but when they saw her, they relaxed and continued smoking. Their eyes watched her as she approached.

She halted on the upper portion of the pier and looked down at them. She didn't speak.

"Bon soir," the taller sailor called to her.

"Bon soir," she replied. She studied the Riva. It was the big one, elaborately furnished with radio telephone and stereo tape deck. There was no doubt in her mind that it belonged to her father. He was into all the American toys.

"No business tonight?" the shorter sailor asked slyly in French.

She ignored him.

The taller one laughed. "Come down here," he said. "We'll pay you ten francs each for a quickie."

She stared at him. "What's the matter?" she asked tauntingly, gesturing toward the yacht. "The girls out there too expensive for you?"

The taller sailor was undaunted. "Twenty francs each. That's our top offer."

She smiled at him. "I'll give it to you for free, if you take me out there."

The two sailors looked at each other, then at her. "We can't do that," the taller one said.

"Afraid you'll lose your jobs?" she taunted. "What's going on out there that's so important?"

"It's the birthday of the wife of our patron, the Sheik Al Fay," the smaller one said.

Teasingly, she undid the buttons of her denim jacket and let it fall open. She put her hands under her full breasts and held them out so that they could see them. "Regardez ces tétons," she said. "How would you each like one of these beauties in your mouth?"

They shook their heads almost sadly. "Twenty-five francs," the taller one said finally.

"Sorry," she said. Quickly she did up the buttons. She began to turn away. "You had your chance."

"Tomorrow," the tall one called after her. "Come to the old port. We'll take you out then."

"Tomorrow I won't be here."

"Wait!" the shorter one called. He said something quickly to the other that she could not hear, then turned back to her. "Okay. Out there and once around the yacht, then back. Agreed?"

"Agreed." She climbed down to the boarding jetty while the taller sailor jumped into the speedboat. The roar of the engine filled the night. The shorter sailor held out his hand to help her down into the boat. She stepped in without his assistance, went to the back and sat down.

The shorter sailor cast off the line and stepped down into the moving speedboat. He turned to her. "Better come forward. You'll get soaked with spray back there."

She smiled up at him. "I don't care," she said. "I love the water."

As the Riva picked up speed, he came and sat beside her. He reached over and undid the two buttons on her blouse. A calloused hand cupped her breast roughly. "Magnifique," he said. "Epatant."

"What's your hurry?" she asked. "There's plenty of time."

He bent forward and placed a greedy mouth on her nipple. His teeth were rough against her skin. She pushed him away. "Wait," she said angrily. "When the ride is finished."

He stared at her, his face flushed.

She smiled sweetly at him. "I won't cheat you, don't worry." She took off her jacket and handed it to him. "You can hold that as collateral."

He stood there stupidly holding the jacket and looking at her. "What kind of a game are you playing?"

The radio telephone buzzed before she could answer. The taller sailor picked it up. A voice crackled angrily. He put it down and looked back at them as he turned the boat in a wide arc. "We have to go back to the dock," he said. "The captain is pissed at us. There are people waiting there to come aboard."

"Damn!" the shorter sailor said. He gave the jacket back to her. "Put it on."

"I told you we shouldn't have done it," the taller sailor said.

"Merde!" the shorter sailor snapped.

Silently, Leila buttoned the jacket. She looked at the dock where some people were standing, dressed in elaborate evening clothes. The sailor cut the engine and the boat drifted in toward the dock.

Smartly, the little sailor, holding the line in his hand, leaped to the dock and fastened it. The taller sailor remained in the boat.

There were two men and two women. They stared curiously at her as she got out of the speedboat but didn't speak. She climbed to the upper portion of the pier before she turned around. The smaller sailor was helping the ladies down into the Riva with exaggerated solicitude. Suddenly he looked up at her.

"C'est la vie," she called down to him with a smile.

The men were already in the speedboat and it began to move away slowly. The smaller sailor leaped into the boat and turned back to her. Then he laughed and held up his hands in a typically Gallic gesture of help-lessness.

Leila started down the pier to the beach when he suddenly appeared out of the shadows under the ca-banas. "What's the matter with you?" he shouted. "Have you lost your mind? You could have given ev-erything away!"

She was startled. "I didn't see you come from the boat."

"When I got to the apartment and saw you weren't there," Ali Yasfir said, "I almost went crazy. You know you weren't supposed to leave the rooms."

"I was bored," she said.

"So you were bored," he repeated sarcastically. "So you had to come out and take a ride on a boat?"

She stared at him. "Why shouldn't I?" she asked. "Who has a better right? After all, it belongs to my father."

It was after four o'clock in the morning when the last of the guests boarded one of the speedboats to go ashore. Jordana was bidding good night to the Princess Mara and Jacques when Youssef crossed the deck to Baydr, who was standing alone. "Shall I leave the girls?" he asked, gesturing to the two actresses who were standing with Vincent.

Baydr shook his head.

"Do you want me to stay aboard?"

"No. I'll reach you at the hotel in the morning."

"Okay." Youssef smiled. "Good night."

"Good night."

Baydr was gone when Jordana turned back from the ship's ladder. Slowly she went into the salon.

A steward came up to her. "Anything I can get madame?"

"Nothing, thank you," she said. "By the way, have you seen Mr. Al Fay?"

"I believe he's gone to his stateroom, madame," the steward said and left the salon.

She went down the corridor to her stateroom. Only the lamp at the side of the bed was on; her nightgown and robe were already laid out. Slowly she undressed. Suddenly she felt drained and exhausted. Her face where he had slapped her began to ache again.

She went into the bathroom, opened the medicine cabinet and took out a bottle of Percodan. She tossed two of the yellow tablets back into her throat and washed them down with a swallow of water. She looked into the mirror. She thought about taking off her make-up but it was too much effort.

She went back into the bedroom and slipped into her nightgown. Wearily she got into the bed and, turning off the night lamp, sank back against the pillows.

The light spilled into her room from the crack under his door. He was still awake. She closed her eyes as the pain began to subside. She was almost asleep when his door opened suddenly. Her eyes flew open.

He stood in the doorway, still fully dressed. For a long moment he didn't speak. "I want the children on board by nine o'clock in the morning," he said finally.

"Yes, Baydr," she said. "I'll see to it. It will be nice. It's been a long time since we've been together with the children."

His voice was cold and expressionless. "I asked for my sons. Not you."

She was silent.

"I'll return them on Sunday."

"You can't make it to Capri and back by then."

"We're not going to Capri. I have to be in Geneva early Monday morning. We'll just go up to St. Tropez and the Porquerolles."

The door closed behind him and again the room was dark. She looked at the illuminated dial of the digital clock on the table next to her. It was after five.

She reached for a cigarette and lit it. Too late to go to sleep here if she had to have the children at the boat by nine o'clock. Wearily, she turned the light on and pressed the signal button for her maid.

She might as well dress and go back to the villa now. By seven o'clock the children would be awake. She could catch up on her sleep after they had gone.

CHAPTER 12.

MICHAEL Vincent came into the dining room of the hotel. His eyes were puffed from lack of sleep, his face lined and whiskey worn. He peered through the morning sunlight looking for Youssef. He found him at a table near the window.

Youssef was freshly shaven. His eyes were clear. On the table next to his coffee was a pair of binoculars. "Good morning," he smiled.

"Morning," Vincent grumbled as he sat down. He blinked his eyes. "How do you do it? It had to be six o'clock before you got to bed. Yet here it is only nine-thirty and you call for a meeting."

"When the chief's around, nobody sleeps," Youssef said. He picked up the binoculars and gave them to the director. "See for yourself. He's out there water-skiing already."

Vincent peered through the binoculars adjusting the glasses until the view of the yacht was clear and sharp. He picked up the Riva as it raced across the bay. Behind it, holding on to the tow lines with one hand, was Baydr; the other hand held a small boy sitting on his shoulders. "Who is the boy?" Vincent asked.

"The chief's younger son, Samir," Youssef answered. "He's four and named after his grandfather. The older son, Prince Muhammad, is skiing off the Riva just behind his father. He's ten."

Vincent, who had been following Baydr, hadn't noticed the second speedboat. He swung his glasses and picked up the boy. The ten-year-old was a miniature of his father; slim and strong, he too held the tow with one hand. "Prince Muhammad?" he questioned. "Is Baydr a—"

"No," Youssef said quickly. "Baydr is first cousin to Prince Feiyad, the reigning prince. Since he has no male heirs, he has indicated that Baydr's son will be the successor to the throne."

"Fascinating," Vincent said. He put the glasses down as the waiter came to the table. "Is it too early to get a Bloody Mary?"

"Not here," Youssef smiled. "Bloody Mary."

The waiter nodded and disappeared. Youssef leaned toward the director. "I apologize for disturbing you so early but the chief called me this morning and I must leave with him for a few days so I thought it important that we conclude our business."

"I thought everything was agreed on last night," Vincent said.

The waiter returned with the drink. Youssef waited until the man left and Vincent had taken his first sip. "Almost everything," he said smoothly. "Except the agent's commissions."

"I have no agent," Vincent said quickly. "I always conduct my own negotiations."

"You have this time," Youssef said. "You see, it's a matter of custom. And we are great people for custom."

Vincent was beginning to understand but he wanted to hear Youssef say it. "And who is my agent?"

"Your greatest fan," Youssef said urbanely. "The man who recommended you for the job. Me."

Vincent was silent for a moment, then he took another sip of the Bloody Mary. He felt his head beginning to clear. "The customary ten percent?" he asked.

Youssef shook his head, still smiling. "That's the Western custom. Our custom is thirty percent."

"Thirty percent?" Vincent's voice expressed his shock. "That's an unheard-of amount."

"It's not unfair in view of your fee for this film. A million dollars is an unheard-of amount. I happen to know it's five times what you received for your last film. And you would not have been offered that if I hadn't known that this picture had been a dream of Baydr's for a long time and that he should make you an offer that would ensure your cooperation."

Vincent studied Youssef's face. The Arab was still smiling but his eyes were deadly serious. "Fifteen percent," he offered.

"I have many expenses," Youssef said. He spread his hands in a deprecating gesture. "But you are my friend. I will not bargain with you. Twenty-five percent."

"What expenses?" Vincent was curious. "I thought you worked for Baydr. Does he not pay you well?"

"Well enough for a good existence. But a man must think of the future. I have a large family to support and must put a few dollars aside."

Vincent fished in his pocket for cigarettes. Youssef anticipated him. He clicked open a gold cigarette case and held it toward the director. "That's a beautiful case," Vincent said, taking a cigarette.

Youssef smiled. He placed it on the table in front of the director. "It's yours."

Vincent stared at him in surprise. He just didn't understand this man at all. "That's solid gold. You just can't give it to me like that."

"Why not? You admired it."

"Still that's not enough reason," Vincent protested.

"You have your customs, we have ours. We consider it a blessing to give gifts."

Vincent shook his head in resignation. "Okay. Twenty percent."

Youssef smiled and held out his hand. "Agreed."

They shook hands. Vincent put the cigarette in his

mouth and Youssef lit it with a gold Dupont lighter. Vincent dragged on the cigarette, then laughed. "I don't dare admire your lighter or you'll give that to me too."

Youssef smiled. "You learn our customs quickly."

"I'll have to," Vincent said, "if I'm going to make this picture."

"Very true," Youssef said seriously. "We will work very closely together on this film and when the time comes I think I can show you how we both can make a great deal of money."

Vincent picked up his Bloody Mary and sipped it. "In what way?" he asked.

"The money they would ask you to pay for services and material is much more than they would ask from me," Youssef said. "Together we might be able to save the chief a great deal and at the same time find some reasonable benefit for our diligence."

"I'll remember that," Vincent said. "I'll probably call on you a great deal."

"I am at your disposal."

Vincent looked across the table. "When do you think the contracts will be ready for signature?"

"Within the week. They're being drawn in Los Angeles and will be telexed here when completed."

"Why Los Angeles? Aren't there good lawyers in Paris?"

"Of course there are, but you have to understand the chief. He demands the best in everything. And the best film attorneys are in Hollywood." He glanced at his watch. "I must go," he said. "I'm late. The chief wants me to gather up the girls and bring them on board with me."

Vincent rose with him. He was puzzled. "The girls? But won't Mrs. Al Fay object?"

"Mrs. Al Fay has decided to remain in the villa in order to give the chief more time to spend alone with his sons."

They shook hands and Youssef walked out into the lobby. Vincent sank back into his chair. There was so much about these people he would have to learn. They were not quite as simple as they had first seemed. The waiter came up and he ordered another Bloody Mary. Might as well start the day right.

The actresses and Patrick were waiting in the lobby with their luggage when he came out of the restaurant. He asked Elie to have the bagagiste carry the bags to the pier and place them on board the Riva.

"You go ahead," he told them. "I'll be with you in a minute. I have one more call to make."

He made his way up the small landing to the telephones and placed a call to Jacques at the Martinez. The telephone rang ten times before the sleepy voice answered.

"C'est moi, Youssef," he said. "Did I wake you?"

"Yes," Jacques' voice was surly.

"The chief has asked me to go on the boat with him for a few days and I am leaving now. I wanted to know how you left it with her."

"She is supposed to call me."

"Do you think she will?"

"I don't know. I didn't have much trouble getting her to whack me off."

"She will call then," Youssef said with satisfaction. "The first step in getting it between her legs is getting it in her hands."

"When will you be back?" Jacques asked.

"Sunday evening. The chief is leaving for Geneva that night. And if you haven't heard from her by then, I will give a dinner party for the American director and you will meet her then."

"I don't have to come with that Princess Mara again, do I?" Jacques asked. "I can't stand that woman."

"No. This time you will come alone." Youssef came out of the booth and gave the telephoniste a few francs tip. He fished in his pocket for the cigarette case, then remembered he had given it away. He swore to himself, then smiled as he went down the steps toward the street. It wasn't a bad deal. The three-hundred-dollar cigarette case got him the last five percent. And fifty thousand dollars was not to be laughed at.

SHE was standing at the window looking out at the sea when he came into her room. "Are you packed?" he asked.

"Yes," she said without turning back to him. "My father's boat is leaving."

He came to the window and looked out. The yacht was turning and moving out to sea toward the Estérel. The sky and the water were a matching blue and the sun was bright. "It will be warm today," he said.

She still didn't look at him. "He was water-skiing with his sons."

"Your brothers?"

Her voice was bitter. "They are not my brothers! They are his sons." She turned back into the room. "Someday he will find that out."

Ali Yasfir was silent as he watched her cross the room and sink into a chair near the bed. She lit a cigarette. She didn't realize how much her father's daughter she really was. That slim strong body was not her mother's lineage. Her mother, like most Arab women, ran to weight.

"I remember when I was little he would take my sister and me water-skiing with him. He was very good and it was such fun. Then after he divorced my mother, nothing. He never even came to see us. He threw us away like old shoes."

Despite himself Ali found himself defending Baydr. "Your father needed sons. And your mother could bear no more children."

Leila's voice was contemptuous. "You men are all alike. Maybe someday you will learn that we are not just creatures of your convenience. Even now, women are giving more to the cause than most men."

He didn't want to argue the point with her. That wasn't his job. His job was to get her to Beirut and then into the mountains to the training camp. After that she could argue all she wanted to. He pressed the button for the porter.

"What plane are we making?" she asked.

"Rome via Air France, then MEA to Beirut."

"What a drag," she said. She got out of the chair and walked back to the window and looked out. "I wonder what my father would think if he knew I was here?" she asked.

CHAPTER 13.

BAYDR looked at his wristwatch. "We have five hours before the market opens in New York," he said.

"That doesn't leave us much time to refinance ten million pounds sterling, Monsieur Al Fay," M. Brun, the swiss banker, said. "And it's too late to recall the buy orders."

John Sterling-Jones, his British associate, nodded in agreement. "It will be impossible. I suggest you reconsider your position, Mr. Al Fay."

Dick Carriage watched his employer from the far side of the room. No expression crossed Baydr's face though he knew what the British banker was suggesting. It would be simple enough to pick up the telephone and let Abu Saad know that he would go along with their new proposition. But once he did that they would own him. And he was not about to let that happen. Not after all the years he'd spent building his independence. No one could own him now. Not even his sovereign prince.

"My position remains the same, Mr. Sterling-Jones," Baydr said quietly. "I do not intend to go into the armaments business. If I had, I would have done so years ago."

The Englishman didn't answer.

Baydr turned to the Swiss. "How much can I cover from here?" he asked.

The Swiss looked down at his desk. "You have a free cash credit balance of five million pounds, Monsieur Al Fay."

"And a borrowing credit?"

"Under the present circumstances?" the Swiss asked.

Baydr nodded.

"None," the Swiss said. "Unless you alter your position. Then, of course, you can have any amount you want."

Baydr smiled. Bankers were always the same. "If I did that, I wouldn't need your money. Monsieur Brun" —he reached into his pocket and took out a checkbook—"may I borrow a pen?"

"Of course, Monsieur Al Fay." The Swiss handed over his pen with a flourish.

Baydr placed the book on the corner of the desk and quickly wrote a check. He tore the check from the book and pushed it together with the pen back to the banker.

The banker picked up the cheek. "Monsieur Al Fay," he said in a surprised voice, "if we pay this check for five million pounds it would empty your account."

Baydr rose to his feet. "That's right, Monsieur Brun. And close it. I'll expect a copy of your transfer advice to my bank in New York at my hotel within the hour." He walked to the door. "You will also receive instructions on the disposition of the funds in the other trustee accounts under my jurisdiction before the morning is over. I trust that you will give the same attention to the closing of those accounts as you did to their opening."

"Monsieur Al Fay," the banker's voice rose to a squeak. "No one has ever withdrawn forty million pounds from a bank in one day."

"Someone has now." Baydr smiled, then gestured to Carriage, who followed him out the door. They started through the bank toward the street.

They were almost at the street entrance when Sterling-Jones caught up with him. "Mr. Al Fay!"

Baydr turned to look at him. "Yes, Mr. Sterling-Jones?"

The Englishman almost stammered in his haste to get the words out. "Monsieur Brun and I have reconsidered your position. What kind of bankers would we be if we did not grant a loan to an old valued client? You shall have the loan of five million pounds."

"Ten million pounds. I see no reason why I should have to use any of my own money."

The Englishman stared at him for a moment, then nodded. "Ten million pounds."

"Very good, Mr. Sterling-Jones." He turned to Dick. "You go back with Mr. Sterling-Jones and collect the check I just gave them. I'll go on to the Aramco meeting and you catch up with me there."

"Yes, sir."

Baydr nodded pleasantly to the banker and without saying goodbye went out through the doors to the curb, where the limousine was waiting. The chauffeur leaped out of the car to open the door for him.

Baydr sank into the comfortable seat with a sigh of relief. What the bankers did not know was that it all had been a bluff. There was no way he could close the trustee accounts without the consent of the principals. But that check for five million pounds had made them forget that.

He lit a cigarette. By tomorrow it wouldn't matter. Chase Manhattan in New York would give him seventy percent of the market value on the stock as collateral. He would return that to the Swiss bank because the New York bank's interest rates were much lower. That would leave his exposure here at only three million pounds, which he could cover from his own account if necessary.

Meanwhile it wasn't all bad. Perhaps he really owed

Ali Yasfir a note of thanks. Because of the withdrawal of their support, he had wound up as the controlling stockholder of a small bank in La Jolla, California, a mail-order insurance company based in Richmond, Virginia, and a home-loan and finance company with forty branches in Florida. The three companies alone had assets of over sixty million dollars, of which at least twenty million was in cash with an annual profit of ten million dollars after taxes.

Abruptly, he decided not to go to the Aramco meeting. There was really nothing to be accomplished. Production and sales quotas for the year were being met. Instead, he directed the chauffeur to take him back to the President Wilson Hotel, where he maintained a suite.

He picked up the phone and called Aramco, apologized for canceling the meeting at the last moment and asked that Carriage be sent to the hotel when he got there. Then he called his pilot at the airport and asked him to prepare to depart for the States immediately.

He went into the bedroom, took off his jacket and stretched out on the bed. Jabir appeared, almost immediately, from his little room behind Baydr's.

"Would the master like me to draw him a bath?"

"No, thanks. I just want to lie here and think."

"Yes, master." Jabir turned to leave.

Baydr called him back. "Where is the girl?" He had almost forgotten that he had brought Suzanne, the little red-headed French actress that Youssef introduced to him in Cannes.

"She went out shopping, master," Jabir answered. "She said she would return shortly."

"Good. See to it that I am not disturbed for at least an hour."

"Yes, master. Shall I draw the drapes?"

"Good idea." When the servant left, Baydr closed his eyes. There was so much to do and so much to think of and so little time. It was hard for him to believe that just yesterday afternoon he had been water-skiing with his sons.

He had spent every hour of daylight with the boys. They had gone to beaches, looking for shells which they never found, rented paddle boats at St. Tropez, snorkeled off the Porquerolles, picnicked on the Isle of Levant. In the evening after their dinner, they watched the Disney films he kept for them in the film library on the boat. He also had other films but they were not for children.

But it hadn't been until they were on their way back to Cannes on Sunday evening that he realized something had been troubling him.

They were in the salon watching *Snow White and the Seven Dwarfs* when it came to him. He looked down at their rapt faces watching the screen. He held up his hand, signaling the steward who was performing as projectionist. The film stopped and the salon lights came up.

The boys looked at him. "It's not bedtime yet, Daddy," Muhammad said.

"No, it's not," he answered in Arabic. "It's just that I realized we've been so busy having a good time we haven't had time to talk."

"Okay, Daddy," the boy said agreeably. "What shall we talk about?"

Baydr looked at him. Muhammad had answered him in English. "Supposing we talk in Arabic," he said with a gentle smile.

An uncomfortable look crossed the boy's face but he nodded his head. "Yes, Baba," he answered in Arabic.

Baydr turned to his youngest son. "Is that all right with you, Samir?"

The little one nodded without speaking.

"Have you both been studying your Koran?" he asked.

They both nodded.

"Have you come to the Prophecies yet?"

Again they nodded without speaking.

"What have you learned?" he asked.

"I have learned that there is but one God," the older boy said haltingly. "And that Muhammad is His prophet." From the child's answer, Baydr knew that he had forgotten his lessons.

Indulgently, he turned to Samir. "And what have you learned?"

"The same thing," the little one replied quickly in English.

"I thought we were going to speak Arabic," he said softly.

The little one met his eyes. "It's hard to say, Daddy."

Baydr was silent.

A look of concern came over Samir's face. "You're not angry with me, are you, Daddy?" he said. "I know the words in French—la même chose."

"I'm not angry with you, Samir," he said gently. "That's very good."

The little one smiled. "Then can we go back to watching the movie?"

He nodded and signaled the steward. The salon lights went down and the picture came back on the screen. A few moments later they were again lost in Snow White's adventures. But there was a hint of tears in Muhammad's eyes.

He reached over and drew the boy to him. "What is the trouble, my son?" he asked in Arabic.

The boy looked up into his face for a moment, then the tears began to roll down his cheeks. He tried to stifle his sobs.

Baydr felt helpless. "Tell me, my son."

"I speak so badly, Father," the boy said in Arabic with a heavy English accent. "I feel you are ashamed of me."

"I'll never be ashamed of you, my son," he said, holding the child close to him. "I'm very proud of you."

A smile burst through the boy's tears. "Really, Father?"

"Really, my son. Now watch the movie."

After the children had gone to bed, he sat in the

darkened salon for a long while. Youssef and the two French women came into the room and Youssef turned the lights on before he realized that Baydr was there.

"I'm sorry, chief," he apologized. "I didn't know you were here."

"That's all right," Baydr said, rising. "I was just going to my room to change." A thought flashed through his mind. "You were here when Jordana and the children arrived from Beirut?" he asked in Arabic.

"I saw them through customs."

"Was their Arabic tutor with them?"

Youssef reflected for a moment. "I don't think so. Only the nanny."

"I wonder why Jordana didn't bring him."

"I don't know, chief. She never said anything to me."

Baydr's face was impassive.

"But then, Jordana and I don't have much chance to talk. She's always busy. There are so many parties here."

"I guess so. Remind me to cable Beirut in the morning. I want my father to send a tutor on the next plane."

"Yes, chief."

Baydr started for his room.

"Mouscardins okay for dinner at ten o'clock in St. Tro?" Youssef asked.

"Les Mouscardins will be fine." Baydr went down the corridor to his room. Leave it to Youssef. Les Mouscardins was the finest restaurant in St. Tropez and Youssef wanted nothing but the best.

Baydr called Jordana from the airport the next morning before the plane took off for Geneva. "What happened to the Arabic tutor?" he asked. "I thought he was coming with you."

"He was ill, and there was no time to get another."

"No time?" he said sarcastically. "You could have called my father. He would have found one and sent him right out."

"I didn't think it was important. After all, it is their summer vacation. They shouldn't have to study."

His voice was cold with anger. "Not important? What gives you the right to decide what is important and what is not? Do you realize that Muhammad is going to be the ruler of four million Arabs and he cannot even speak his own language?"

She was silent.

"I see I've left too much in your hands," he said. "I've cabled my father to send a tutor and when they return this fall, I'm sending them to my parents' home to live. Maybe there they'll be brought up properly."

She was silent for a moment. When she spoke there was hurt in her voice. "And me?" she asked. "What plans have you made for me?"

"None at all," he snapped. "You can do anything you goddamn well please. I will let you know when I need you."

CHAPTER 14.

JORDANA was drunk, drunker than she had ever been in her life. It was the kind of peculiar drunken high that comes only after a deep depression, a high that let her watch herself as if she were outside her own body. She was being gay, charming, witty and brilliant all at the same time.

She had been down all day after Baydr's call that morning. The two things she truly loved in all the world were her sons. Once she thought she had loved Baydr like that. But now she did not know how she felt about him. Maybe it was because she did not know how he felt about her.

For the first time, she had been pleased to receive Youssef's invitation. She didn't like Youssef, but then she never had liked any of Baydr's full-time flunkies and part-time pimps. She never understood Baydr's need to surround himself with those kind of men when he could get any woman he wanted with just a snap of his fingers. He was still the most exciting and attractive man she had ever met.

When Youssef had explained that he was giving a small dinner party for Michael Vincent, the man who was to direct Baydr's film, *The Messenger,* she had agreed that it would be a nice gesture if she were to act as hostess. Especially when Youssef had hinted that Baydr would be very pleased by her action.

Youssef's small dinner party was for twenty people at La Bonne Auberge, a restaurant halfway between Cannes and Nice. As hostess, she was seated at the head of the table with Vincent, the guest of honor, on her right. Youssef sat on her left. Since Baydr was not there, the foot of the table was left significantly vacant. Halfway down the table, between two pretty women, sat Jacques, the blond gigolo whom Princess Mara had introduced to her the night of her birthday party. Idly, she wondered who he was with.

The dinner, ordered by Youssef, was superb. And the Dom Pérignon came in a never-ending flow. She knew from the very first sip that she was going to feel the wine. But tonight she didn't care. Michael Vincent was a bright man even though he drank nothing but Scotch, and also he was an American with whom she could share jokes that no one else at the table really understood.

Halfway through dinner, she became aware that Jacques had been watching her continually. Each time she would look down the table, his eyes would try to fix her gaze. But they were too far away from one another to engage in conversation.

After dinner, Youssef suggested that they all go to a discotheque to continue the party. By that time, she was high enough to think it was a wonderful idea. She

loved to dance. It was not until they had been at
Whisky for almost an hour that she looked up and
saw Jacques standing in front of her.

He bowed almost formally. "May I have this dance?"

She listened to the music, responding to the hard
driving beat of the Rolling Stones. She looked at Vincent. "Excuse me," she said.

He nodded and turned to talk to Youssef, who was
sitting on his other side. She was dancing even before
she was on the floor.

Jacques turned to face her and began to dance. For
a moment she looked at him critically. Rock really
wasn't a Frenchman's style. He danced with the uptight
stingy movements that to a Frenchman passed for cool.
He would be better off if he stayed with ballroom num-
bers. But she soon forgot about him as she lost herself in her own dancing.

His voice rose over the sound of the music. "You
said you would call me."

She looked at him. "I did?"

"Yes."

"I don't remember," she said. She honestly didn't.

"You're lying," he said accusingly.

Without a word, she turned and started off the floor.
His hand caught her arm, pulling her back.

"I apologize," he said earnestly. "Please dance with
me."

She stared at him for a moment, then let him lead
her back to the floor. The record changed from rock
to ballad. He took her into his arms and held her
tightly against him.

"For the past three days I have not been able to eat
or sleep," he said.

She was still cool. "I don't need a gigolo."

"I, better than anyone else should know that," he
said. "Someone as beautiful as you. I want you for
myself."

She looked up at him skeptically. His hardness
pressed into her. "Feel how much I want you," he
said.

Her eyes closed and she rested her head against his shoulder. She allowed herself to enjoy the pressure. The high inside her head seemed to take on a rosy hue. Maybe he was telling the truth after all.

What she didn't see was the smile that passed between him and Youssef.

THE coarse cotton khaki of her shapeless shirt and trousers scratched at her skin as she followed the five other new women into the barracks of the commanding officer. The stiff leather boots clumped heavily on the wooden floor. The yellow light of the oil lamps cast an unsteady glow in the room.

The commanding officer sat at a table at the far end of the room, a uniformed soldier seated on each side. She was studying a paper on the table and did not look up until they came to a halt in front of her.

"Attention!" their sergeant barked.

"An-nasr. Victory," they shouted as they had been trained to do on the very first night they arrived in camp a few days before.

Leila felt her brassiere pull tight against her breasts as she snapped her shoulders back. The brassiere too was made of coarse cotton. She looked straight ahead.

Slowly the commanding officer rose to her feet. Leila saw that she wore the equivalent of a colonel's pips on the shoulders of her blouse. She stared at them silently for a moment, then abruptly in a surprisingly strong voice she shouted, "Idbah al-adu!"

"Slaughter the enemy!" they yelled back.

She nodded, a faint smile of approval coming to her lips. "At ease," she said in a more normal voice.

There was a rustle of the coarse cloth as the women settled into a more relaxed position. The CO came around the front of the desk.

"In the name of the Brotherhood of Palestinian Freedom Fighters, I welcome you to our holy struggle. The struggle to free our peoples from the bondage of Israel and the enslavement of imperialism. I know that each of you has made many sacrifices to come here, estrangement from loved ones, perhaps ostracism from your own neighbors, but I can promise you one thing. At the end of our struggle lies a freedom greater than has ever been known.

"And because of this, your struggle is only beginning. You will be called upon to make many more sacrifices. Your honor, your body, even your life may have to be given to win the freedom we seek. For we will have victory.

"Here, you will be taught many things. Weaponry. Guns, rifles, knives. How to make bombs. Small and large. How to kill with your bare hands. How to fight. All so that we, together with our men, can drive the Zionist usurpers back into the sea and restore the land to its rightful owners, our people.

"You have already, each of you, taken the sacred oath of allegiance to our cause. And from this moment on your real names will be forgotten and never used in this camp. You will answer only to the name assigned to you and in this manner, in the case of unforeseen capture, you will never give away the names of your comrades. From this moment on your only loyalty is to your cause and your brethren in arms."

The commanding officer paused for a moment. The women were silent in rapt attention. "The next three months will be the most difficult any of you have ever known. But at the end you will be able to go forth to take your place beside Fatmah Bernaoui, Miriam Shakhashir, Aida Issa and Leila Khaled, others of our sex who have proven themselves the equals of their brothers in the struggle."

She walked back around the table and took up her position between the two men. "I wish you luck."

"Attention!" the sergeant barked.

"An-nasr," they yelled, straightening up.

"Idbah al-adu!" the CO cried.

"Idbah al-adu!" they shouted back.

The commanding officer saluted. "Dismissed."

They broke ranks and followed the sergeant back out into the night. "Get to your barracks, girls," the sergeant said dryly. "Your day begins at five tomorrow morning."

He turned and went off to the men's section of the camp as they started for their own small building. Leila fell into step with the tall young woman who occupied the bed next to hers.

"Wasn't the CO wonderful?" Leila asked. "For the first time I feel my life has a meaning."

The woman looked at her as if she were a creature from another planet. "I'm glad you feel that way," she said in a common-sounding voice. "The only reason I came up here is to be near my boyfriend. But I haven't even been able to get anywhere near him and I'm getting so horny that I wouldn't be surprised to find myself in your bed eating your pussy tonight."

THIRTY-FIVE thousand feet over the Atlantic Ocean in a dark blue star-filled sky, Baydr slept as his plane raced time on its way to New York. Suddenly he awoke with a start. He sat up in the bed, his eyes wet with tears.

He brushed them away with his fingers and reached for a cigarette. It must have been a bad dream. But there was a presentiment of dread within him, a curious foreboding that lay heavily on his heart.

The girl beside him stirred. "Q'est-ce que c'est, chéri?" she asked in a sleepy voice.

"Rien," he said. "Dors."

She was silent and after a while the drone of the engines made him drowsy. He put out the cigarette and went back to sleep.

ANOTHER PLACE: JUNE 1973

THE black Cadillac limousine bearing diplomatic plates rolled to a stop in front of the administration building and three men got out—two men dressed in civilian clothing and an American Army colonel. They started up the steps toward the building. The Israeli soldiers standing guard at the entrance presented arms. The colonel saluted and the three men went into the building.

The senior staff sergeant at the reception desk rose from his chair, saluting. The colonel returned the salute. The sergeant smiled. "You know where to go, colonel?" It was more a statement than a question.

The colonel returned his smile, nodding. "I've been here before, sergeant." He turned to the other two men. "If you'll follow me—"

He led them down a corridor to an elevator and pressed the call button. The doors opened silently and they boarded the car. He pressed a button on the panel and the elevator began its descent. Six levels underground it stopped and the doors opened again.

The colonel led them out into another reception area, where another senior staff sergeant sat. This time the sergeant did not get up. He looked at them, then sat down at the list on his desk. "Please identify yourselves, gentlemen?"

The colonel spoke first. "Alfred R. Weygrin, Colonel, United States Army."

The civilian in the three-button suit: "Robert L. Harris, United States Department of State."

The man in the rumpled sports jacket: "Sam Smith, American Plumbing Supply Company."

The sergeant didn't crack a smile at the absurd cover name for the CIA agent. He ticked the names off the list and gave each of the men yellow plastic identification cards, which they affixed to their lapels. He pressed a signal button on his desk and a corporal appeared from a door on his right. "Please escort these gentlemen to Conference Room A."

Conference Room A was at the end of a long narrow gray corridor, guarded by two soldiers and still another sergeant at a desk. The corporal halted in front of the desk while the sergeant checked their plastic ID cards, then pressed a signal button which opened the electronically controlled doors. The visitors went into the room and the doors shut automatically behind them.

There were approximately nine men already in the room, only two of whom were in the uniform of the Israeli Army, one a brigadier general, the other a colonel. The brigadier came forward, his hand outstretched. "Alfred, it's good to see you again."

The American smiled as he shook his hand. "Good to see you, Lev. I'd like you to meet Bob Harris of State and Sam Smith. Gentlemen, General Eshnev."

They exchanged handshakes. The general introduced them to the others and then gestured to a large round table set at the far end of the large conference room. "Supposing we find our seats, gentlemen."

Printed nameplates indicated their places, and when they had all been seated there was only one vacant chair remaining at the table. It was positioned just to the left of the Israeli general, and inasmuch as he was the highest-ranking officer it meant that the vacant place belonged to his superior. The Americans glanced at the nameplate curiously but without comment.

General Eshnev caught the glance. "I'm sorry for the delay, gentlemen, but I am informed that General Ben Ezra is on his way. He has been tied up in traffic and should be here at any moment."

"Ben Ezra?" Harris whispered to the colonel. "I never heard of him."

The soldier smiled. "I'm afraid he was a little before your time, Bob. The Lion of the Desert is almost a legendary figure. Honestly, I thought he was long since gone."

General Eshnev caught the tail end of the remark. "Was it your MacArthur who said, 'Old soldiers never die, they just fade away'? Ben Ezra proves how wrong that statement is. He refuses to die or to fade away."

"He must be in his seventies by now," the CIA man said. "The last we heard he'd gone back to his kibbutz after the sixty-seven war."

"He's seventy-four," the Israeli said. "And as far as the kibbutz is concerned, there's no way we have of knowing just how much time he actually spends there. He's got the whole kibbutz under his spell. Not even the children will tell us about him. We never know whether he is in or out."

"It would seem to me if you wanted to know what he's up to you'd keep him in Tel Aviv," Harris said.

"It could become embarrassing," Eshnev said, smiling. "The Lion of the Desert was never known for his tact. It seems your President still remembers his comments when Eisenhower stopped the British and French takeover of the Suez Canal in fifty-six. You know he planned that operation for the British."

"I didn't know that," Harris said. "But why should the President be angry? He wasn't President then."

"He was Vice-President and Ben Ezra was very out-spoken on the subject of his support of certain Arab elements which he held responsible for Eisenhower's decision. Ben Ezra even went so far as to advise the British to tell Eisenhower to mind his own affairs, and I'm afraid his language was not very diplomatic. After that embarrassment, Ben Gurion had no choice but to accept his retirement. That's when he went to the Sinai to live in a kibbutz."

"You mentioned that he came out in sixty-seven?" Harris asked.

"Yes. But not officially. And that proved to be an-other embarrassment. He didn't want us to stop until we reached Cairo and got a total surrender. He said his own intelligence could prove that if we didn't we would have to do it all over again within seven years."

"What makes him feel that his sources are superior to our own?" the CIA man asked.

"His mother was Arab, and there are still some who maintain he's more Arab than Jew. At any rate, he lives out there among thousands of them and in a strange manner they seem to trust him and come to him for justice. The Arabs call him 'Imam'—holy man, reader, a man who lives by the honored principles. He crosses borders with impunity and alone."

"Was he married?" Harris asked.

"Twice," General Eshnev replied. "Once when he was a young man. His first wife died in the desert giving birth to a child, who also died while they were trying to slip through the British lines into Palestine. The second time was after he had retired. He married an Arab girl and as far as I know she is still alive and living with him in the kibbutz. They have no children."

"Does his coming here mean that you expect trouble then?" Colonel Weygrin asked.

The Israeli shrugged. "We Jews always expect trouble. Especially when there are things happening we don't understand."

"Such as?" Harris asked.

"That's why we're meeting," Eshnev said. "Let's wait for Ben Ezra. He just appeared after two months of dead silence and called for a meeting."

Harris' voice was slightly disdainful. "And the old man gets it, just like that?"

"Not quite like that. First he had to convince Dayan that he had something. Dayan then went to the Prime Minister. It was she who gave approval for the meeting."

"You would think after being so insistent, he would at least be on time," Harris said.

"He's an old man," Eshnev said apologetically. "And he insists on using his own car, an old Volkswagen that keeps breaking down. He won't take one of ours.

If I didn't leave special word outside I'm sure they wouldn't even let him into the parking lot." The telephone in front of him buzzed. He picked it up, nodded and put it down. "The general is on his way, gentlemen."

The electronic doors opened silently and every head turned. The man who stood there was tall, over six feet, and clothed in dusty sand-encrusted Bedouin robes. The white hair and beard covering his lined, sun-blackened face made him look more Arab than Jew. Only the startling dark-blue eyes denied Arab heritage. His walk was firm and proud, as he moved toward General Eshnev. His voice was raspy as if eroded by time and the desert sand. "Lev," he said, holding out his hand.

"General," Lev Eshnev replied, rising. They shook hands. "Gentlemen, allow me to introduce General Ben Ezra." He then introduced each man, beginning counterclockwise from the old man's right.

Ben Ezra looked directly into each man's eyes and repeated his name. When the introductions were completed, they sat down.

Eshnev turned to the old man. "It's your meeting, general."

"Thank you." The old man spoke in unaccented English. "I suppose you have all been made aware of the buildup along the Suez Canal by the Egyptians and by the Syrians along the Golan Heights. And I suppose you are also aware of the new military equipment that is arriving in greater quantities than ever before from Russia and China. I suppose you realize that if this rate of supply continues they will soon achieve a military parity and perhaps a strike potential in excess of our own within a very short time."

"That's true," Eshnev said. "We know all that."

"I'm sure you also know of the heavy influx of North Korean fighter and bomber pilots."

"Yes," Eshnev said. "But we also know that Sadat is under heavy criticism from the moderates about the Russian influence."

Ben Ezra nodded. "But we can't allow that to lull us into a false sense of security. For the first time they are building a capable war machine. And that's something you don't do unless you intend to use it."

"Granted," Eshnev said. "But, it could be another year and a half before they are ready."

"No," Ben Ezra said. "They are ready now. They can strike anytime."

"Then what are they waiting for?" Eshnev's voice was polite but there was a faint note of impatience. "So far you've told us nothing we do not know."

Ben Ezra was unruffled. "This time, we cannot evaluate their decisions simply on a military basis. Other factors play a part in their plan. They have been infiltrating the Western world through financial investments. In addition, they are lining up the oil-producing countries to create an economic force that can be used to reduce the support we've been getting from the technological countries. They will strike when they have those plans worked out and not before."

"Do you have specific information on that?" Eshnev asked.

"No. All I know is what I have picked up in my wanderings. There are rumors in the Sinai that the Fedayeen are exerting pressure on the moderates. They are selecting targets among the Arabs themselves in order to coerce cooperation from the rich oil producers."

"Any specifics on that?"

The old man shook his head. "That's why I asked for this meeting." He looked across the table at the Americans. "I thought our busy friends might have some knowledge of that pressure."

Harris looked at his companions. "I wish we did," he said. "But there is very little we do know."

Ben Ezra's face was inscrutable. "You're State Department?"

Harris nodded.

"That's understandable," Ben Ezra said. He looked directly at the CIA man. "How about you?"

Smith was uncomfortable. "We're aware of their economic plans."

"Yes?"

"But we haven't been able to tie them together," Smith said. "The economic thrust seems to be under the direction of one man, Prince Feiyad's personal representative, Baydr Al Fay. But he appears to be completely independent, a known conservative and an advocate of rapprochement with Israel. Not because he likes you but because he thinks it would bring about an economic solution that would benefit the entire Middle East. But we have no way of knowing for sure. We haven't been able to infiltrate his organization so far."

Eshnev looked at him. "You haven't?"

The American shook his head. "No."

Eshnev smiled with faint triumph. "Then maybe we can be of help. We have a man in there."

There was a moment's silence around the table. It was Ben Ezra who broke it. "So?" he asked.

Eshnev's voice was calm. "Al Fay's principal interest at the moment seems to be his desire to make a film based on the life of Muhammad, to be called *The Messenger*. We also know that he has rejected a proposal by Al-Ikhwah to handle certain purchases for them."

Ben Ezra looked at him. "Was Ali Yasfir involved in that proposal?"

It was Eshnev's turn to be surprised. "How did you know that?"

"I didn't," the old man said. "But Yasfir just turned up in one of the Al-Ikhwah training camps in Lebanon with what they call the most important recruit they ever made. The daughter of the richest man in the Arab world. Does this man have a daughter?"

"He has two," Eshnev said. "One is married and lives in Beirut near her mother, Al Fay's former wife. The youngest is in a school in Switzerland."

"You're sure of that?" Ben Ezra asked.

"We've had no word to the contrary," Eshnev said. "But we can check on that easily enough."

"He has other children?"

"Yes. Two sons with his present wife, an American. The eldest son, now ten, is to be appointed by Prince Feiyad as heir to the throne."

"Then if they have the girl, they may have the key to Al Fay," Ben Ezra said.

"Possibly."

"I'll see what can be found out in the Sinai," Ben Ezra said. "You people pursue your sources."

"We'll do that," Eshnev said.

"Agreed," Smith added.

"That still leaves us with the important question," Eshnev said. "When do you think they will attack?"

Ben Ezra looked at him. "Right after the feast of Ramadan," he said flatly.

Eshnev could not keep the shock from his voice. "But that's around the High Holy Days. They wouldn't do that. Respect for the laws of Moses is still an important part of their religion."

Ben Ezra got to his feet. "Not as much as it is of ours."

Eshnev looked up at him. "If they come we'll be ready for them."

"I hope so," the old man said. "But there are better ways."

"Preemptive strike?" Eshnev asked, but didn't wait for an answer. "You know we can't do that. Our allies won't permit it."

Ben Ezra looked at him, then at the Americans. "Maybe they will if they realize that without us they lose their power in the Middle East. The Sixth Fleet can't cross the desert and occupy the oil fields."

"It is the belief of the State Department that there will be no attack by the Arabs in the foreseeable future," Harris said stiffly.

Ben Ezra smiled. He looked at the CIA man. "Is that also your opinion?"

Smith didn't answer. It was not his place to make official statements.

Ben Ezra turned to the American soldier. "Installation of the latest Russian ground-to-air missiles have been completed in the Suez and on the Golan Heights. I've seen them with my own eyes. Don't you agree that the time to attack has come when your own defenses are set?"

Weygrin nodded. "I would think so."

Ben Ezra looked around the table. "Then they're ready." He paused for a moment. "All they're waiting for now is to get their house in order."

"How will we know when that is?" Eshnev asked.

"We won't," the old man shrugged. "Until they attack. Unless—"

"Unless what?"

A thoughtful expression came into the old man's eyes. He seemed lost for a moment in memory, then his eyes cleared. "It may sound strange to you but in an old man's bones there is a feeling that we may find the answer in Al Fay. The winds that blow across the desert no longer originate in the East—they come from the West. The Arab sheiks have awakened to the power of their wealth. That will be the real end of Russian influence. Communism has no answer for them. And control of the Middle East is only the beginning. If they invest their wealth wisely they may be able to soon control the world without ever firing a shot."

He looked around the silent table. "I hate to disillusion you, gentlemen, but the fact is that we are no longer important to Islam except to their pride. They must achieve some victory no matter how minor just to regain face. The big thrust will come after the battle is over."

He turned to the Americans. "We will need your help. For now. Later, you will need ours."

Harris was polite but disdainful. "What makes you think that?"

"Because we, more than anyone in the world, understand them," the old man said, his face settling into grim hawklike lines. "And because you, not we, are the real target."

Again there was silence. Finally Eshnev spoke. "You will continue to keep us informed of what you learn?"

The old man nodded. "Of course. I would also appreciate a favor."

"If I can do it, it will be done," Eshnev answered.

"I would like a complete dossier on Al Fay. His whole life. Everything—personal and business. I want to know all about him."

Eshnev looked around the table. There were no objections. He nodded. "It will be done immediately."

"You will relay my opinions to the Prime Minister?" Ben Ezra asked.

"Yes, I will."

"Also give her a kiss for me," Ben Ezra said, smiling. "I think she could use it."

There was a polite murmur of laughter around the table. The telephone rang and Eshnev picked it up. He listened for a moment then put it down. "There's been another hijacking," he said. "A Lufthansa plane out of Düsseldorf. It's on its way to Beirut."

Ben Ezra shook his head sadly. "How sad. How stupid." He looked at the Americans. "The net effect is nothing but headlines. And while we are distracted by the news, quietly, under our very noses, without anyone really being aware of it, they are hijacking the world."

BOOK TWO

The End of Summer

1973

CHAPTER 1.

YOUSSEF entered the restaurant at Tahiti Plage through the roadside door. He looked out of place in his dark suit, white shirt and tie as he threaded his way through the half-naked men and women to the beach. He blinked his eyes as he came out into the bright sunlight once again. Squinting, he looked around at the tables. After a moment he saw him, seated near the frond-covered beach bar. He was talking earnestly to a good-looking young black man.

Jacques looked up as Youssef's shadow fell across him. "Youssef," he said in French, rising. "What a pleasant surprise. We weren't expecting you."

Youssef didn't return his smile. "I can see that," he said coldly. "Tell your petit ami to get lost."

A sullen look crossed Jacques' face. "What right have you—"

Youssef didn't let him finish. "I own you, you cunt!" he snarled. "Now, tell him to get lost, or I'll throw you back into the gutters of Paris where I found you! Hustling tourists for ten-franc blow jobs!"

The black man got to his feet, the muscles tensing in his arms as he tightened his fists. "Do you want me to get rid of him for you, Jacques?"

Youssef stared at Jacques. Jacques' eyes fell after a moment. "I think you better go, Gerard." He didn't look at the black.

Gerard's lips curled contemptuously. "Poule!" he snapped at Jacques, then turned his back on them. He dropped to the sand a few feet away and covered his eyes with his arm, seeming to pay no attention to them.

The waiter came up as Youssef sat down in the chair the black had just vacated. "Monsieur?"

"Coca. Beaucoup de glace." He turned to Jacques, who was sinking back in his chair. "Where is she?"

Jacques didn't look at him. "How the hell should I know?" he retorted sullenly. "I've been waiting here on the beach for her almost two hours."

"You're supposed to know!" Youssef snapped. "What the hell do you think I am paying you all this money for? To fuck around with petits nègres on the beach?"

The waiter put the Coca-Cola on the table and went away. Youssef picked it up and drank thirstily. "Were you with her last night?" he asked.

"Yes."

"The pictures? Did you get them?"

"How could I?" Jacques asked in return. "She never came to the apartment. She left me in the disco at three o'clock and told me to meet her on the beach today at noon."

"Were you with that black all night?"

"What was I supposed to do?" Jacques answered defensively. "Save myself for her?"

Youssef reached into his inside coat pocket and took out his new gold cigarette case. He opened it slowly and carefully took out a cigarette. He tapped the cigarette on the cover of the case. "You're not very smart," he said, placing the cigarette between his lips and lighting it. "Not smart at all."

Jacques stared at him. "How can I get the pictures when she does not come to the apartment? Never. Always we do it where she chooses." He looked over Youssef's shoulder at the sea. "Ah, she is coming now."

Youssef turned to look. The big San Marco was heading toward the shore from the open sea. He reached into his jacket and threw a key on the table in front of Jacques. "I have an apartment reserved for you at the Byblos. All the equipment is there. The room is bugged and a photographer will be waiting in the next room for you to let him in. You get her

there. I don't care how you do it but you get her
there. You have only this night left."

Jacques stared at him. "What is the sudden rush?"

"I have a telegram in my pocket from her husband.
Tomorrow afternoon she will be on a plane to California."

"What if she does not want to stay? What am I
supposed to do, hit her on the head? If it is like last
night she will leave at three o'clock in the morning,
return to the San Marco and go back to Cannes."

Youssef got to his feet and looked down at Jacques.
"I will see to it that the San Marco will have engine
trouble. The rest is up to you." He glanced over his
shoulder at the sea. The San Marco was trolling slowly
into the shallow waters near the beach. "Go down to
the water, lover boy," he said sarcastically, "and help
the lady ashore."

Silently, Jacques got out of his chair and started
toward the beach. Youssef watched him for a moment,
then turned and made his way back through the restaurant to the road where he had parked his car.

He got into the car and sat there for a moment before turning the key in the ignition. If only Jordana
didn't hate him. Then none of this would be necessary.
But he knew how many times she had tried to turn
Baydr against him because she resented their relationship. And after all, he was only an employee while she
was the boss's wife. If it came to a showdown there
was no doubt in his mind who would be the victor.
She would win hands down. But if Jacques came
through tonight that would never happen. The threat
of presenting Baydr with proof of her indiscretion
would be enough to keep her in line. Youssef knew
that the best ally was a conquered enemy.

JORDANA opened her eyes the moment the heavy roar
of the engines died down to idling speed. She glanced
at her watch. It was forty minutes since she had left
Cannes. By road, with all the traffic, it could have
taken an hour and a half. This was not only faster

but the sea had been smooth and she had slept all the way.

She sat up, reaching for her bikini top and shirt. She looked down at herself as she fastened the brassiere. Her breasts were as tan as the rest of her body, a golden nut brown, and her nipples were a purple plum color instead of their normal red rose. She was pleased with herself. Her breasts were still firm. She hadn't yet begun to sag like so many women her age.

Instinctively she glanced over her shoulder to see if the two sailors at the helm of the speedboat had been looking at her. Their eyes were studiously turned away but she knew that they had been watching in the rear-view mirror mounted on the windscreen in front of them. She smiled to herself. To tease them, she cupped her breasts with her hands suggestively so that her nipples hardened. Then she fastened the bra.

A paddle boat came by with two topless girls. They looked at the seventy-thousand-dollar San Marco with undisguised hope and curiosity. Again she smiled to herself as the look of disappointment crossed their faces when they saw that she was the only passenger. They were so obvious. The pedalo turned away slowly.

" 'Allo!" The call came from the other side of the boat.

She turned. Jacques had come out in a small dinghy with an outboard motor. His blond hair had completely whitened in the summer sun, making his tan even darker by contrast. She waved without speaking.

"I've come to take you ashore," he shouted. "I know how you hate to get your feet wet."

"I'll be right with you," she called. She turned to the sailors. "Wait out here," she told them in French. "I'll call you when I'm ready to leave."

"Oui, madame," the sailor at the helm replied. The other sailor started back to help her over the side. She gave him the large beach bag she always took with her. Inside were her shoes, a change of wardrobe for the evening, the walkie-talkie for communication with the speedboat, as well as cosmetics, cigarettes, money and credit cards.

The sailor reached over the side and pulled the dinghy closer to the speedboat. He dropped the bag into Jacques' hands, then held Jordana's arm as she stepped over. He cast the dinghy free as soon as she sat down.

She sat facing the rear of the dinghy. Jacques sat at the tiller of the outboard motor. "Sorry to be late," she said.

"That's all right," he smiled. "You sleep well?"

"Very well. And you?"

He made a moue. "Not too well. I was too—how you say?—frustrated."

She looked at him. She couldn't quite figure him out. Mara had said he was a gigolo but the several times she had given him money he had returned it with a hurt look. This was not business, he had said. He was in love with her. But it still didn't make sense. He had an expensive apartment in the Miramar, right on the Croisette in Cannes, and a brand-new Citroën SM and never seemed to be short of money. He never let her pick up a check as so many of the others did, gigolos or no. Several times she had seen him eying some boys but he had never made any overt moves while she was around. At one point, she was fairly sure that he was bi and that perhaps his real lover was a man who had sent him down to the Côte d'Azur for the summer, but that didn't disturb her. She had long ago come to the conclusion that bisexual men made the best lovers.

"With all the talent available in that discotheque?" she laughed. "I wouldn't have thought you would have any problems."

"I didn't," he said to himself, thinking of his night with Gerard. He felt himself growing hard as he thought of the black towering over him, and peeling the fore-skin back on his giant black shaft to expose the red-dish purple swollen head. He remembered going down on his back like a woman and raising his legs, and the exquisite agony of the big penis forcing its way roughly into his anus. He had whimpered like a woman and then yelled as his orgasm overtook him and his semen squirted up on their bellies that were pressed tightly together.

"Look," he said aloud, releasing his erect penis from his bikini. "See what you do to me? The moment I see you. Three times last night I had to relieve myself."

She laughed. "Didn't anyone ever tell you that was bad for you? You could stunt your growth doing it so much."

He didn't laugh. "When are you going to spend a whole night with me? Just one time so that we could make love without my feeling that you always have one eye on the clock, so that we can fully take our pleasures of each other."

She laughed again. "You're too greedy. You forget that I am a married woman with responsibilities. I must be home every night so that I see my children when I wake up in the morning."

"What would be so terrible if you did not?" He pouted.

"Then I would be remiss in the one duty that my husband demands of me," she said. "And that I would not do."

"Your husband does not care. Otherwise he would have come to see you and the children at least once during these past three months," he said.

Her voice went cold. "What my husband does or does not do is none of your business."

He sensed instantly he had gone too far. "But I love you. I am going crazy for wanting you."

She nodded slowly, relaxing. "Then keep things in their proper perspective," she said. "And if you're going to keep playing with your cock, you'd better take the boat back out to sea before we crash on the beach."

"If I do, will you suck me?"

"No," she said sharply. "I'm more in the mood for a cold glass of white wine."

SHE was high. Papagayo was packed. The strobe lights were like a stop-motion camera on her eyes, the heavy pounding of the rock group tortured the ears. She took another sip of the white wine and looked down the table. There were fourteen people, all shouting at one another to be heard over the din in the discotheque.

Jacques was talking to the English woman on his right. She was an actress who had just finished a picture with Peter Sellers, and had been with a group of people who had come down from Paris for the weekend. Jordana had begun collecting them on the beach that afternoon. She'd completed the group at L'Escale, where they'd had cocktails and dinner. About midnight they had gone to the discotheque.

The reason for gathering the people was that she had been annoyed with Jacques. He seemed to take too much for granted. In some ways he was like a woman, only in his case he seemed to think that the world revolved around his cock. She was beginning to be bored with him, but apart from an occasional visiting male there was nothing really dependable around. It was the boredom that had led her to smoke a joint. Usually she never smoked in public. But when the Englishwoman had offered her a toke in the ladies' room, she had stayed until they finished the cigarette between them.

After that, she didn't mind the evening at all. It seemed that she had never laughed so much in her life. Everyone was excruciatingly bright and witty. Now she wanted to dance but everyone was too busy talking.

She got out of her chair and went to the dance floor alone. Pushing her way into the crowd she began to dance. She gave herself to the music, happy that she was in the south of France where no one thought it

strange that a woman or a man wanted to dance alone.
She closed her eyes.

When she opened them, the tall good-looking black
man was dancing in front of her. He caught her eye
but they didn't speak. She had noticed him earlier that
day on the beach; later at cocktail time he had been at
the bar in L'Escale; now he was here. She had seen
him sitting at a table not far from her own.

He moved fantastically well, his body fluid under
the shirt, which was open to his waist and tied in a
tight knot just over the seemingly glued-on black jeans.
She began to move with him.

After a moment, she spoke. "You're American,
aren't you?"

His voice was Southern. "How did you know?"

"You don't dance like a Frenchman—they jerk up
and down—the English hop and dip."

He laughed. "I never thought of that."

"Where are you from?"

"Cracker country," he said. "Georgia."

"I've never been there," she said.

"You're not missing anything," he replied. "I like
it better here. We could never do this back there."

"Still?" she asked.

"Still," he said. "They never change."

She was silent.

"Je m'appelle Gerard," he said.

She was surprised. His French was Parisian without
a trace of accent. "Your French is good."

"It should be," he said. "My folks sent me over
here to school when I was eight. I went back when
my father was killed—I was sixteen then but I couldn't
take it. I headed right back to Paris the minute I got
enough bread together."

She knew what French schools cost and they weren't
cheap. His family had to have money. "What did your
father do?"

His voice was even. "He was a pimp. But he had a
finger in every pie. But he was black and the honkies
didn't like that, so they cut him up in an alley an'

blamed it on a passing nigger. Then they hung the nigger an' everything was cool."

"I'm sorry."

He shrugged. "My father said that was the way they would do it someday. He had no complaints. He had a good life."

The music crashed to a stop and the group came down from the stage as the record player came on with a slow number. "Nice talking with you," she said, starting back to the table.

His hand on her arm stopped her. "You don't have to go back there."

She didn't speak.

"You look like a fast-track lady and there's nothin' but mudders back there," he said.

"What've you got in mind?" she asked.

"Action. That's something I got from my father. I'm a fast-track man. Why don't you meet me outside?"

Again she didn't speak.

"I saw the way you looked," he said. "You gotta be turned off on that crowd over there." He smiled suddenly. "You ever make it with a black man before?"

"No," she answered. She never had.

"I'm better than they say we are," he said.

She glanced at the table. Jacques was still talking to the Englishwoman. He probably had not even noticed that she had left the table. She turned back to Gerard. "Okay." she said. "But we'll only have about an hour. I have to leave then."

"An hour's enough," he laughed. "In one hour I'll have you on a trip to the moon and back."

CHAPTER 2.

WHEN she came out he was on the quai opposite the discotheque, watching the last of the sidewalk artists pack up their wares for the night. He turned when he heard the sound of her high-stacked shoes on the sidewalk. "Any trouble getting out?" he asked.

"No," she answered. "I told them I was going to the ladies'."

He grinned. "Mind walking? My place is just up the street past Le Gorille."

"It's the only way to fly," she said, falling into step beside him.

Despite the hour there were still crowds walking back and forth. They were engaged in their principal form of amusement, looking at each other and the beautiful yachts tied up right alongside the street. For many, it was the only thing they could afford to do, after paying the exorbitant seasonal prices for their rooms and food. The French had no mercy for tourists of any nationality, even their own.

They turned up the street past Le Gorille with its smell of fried eggs and pommes frites and began to climb the narrow sidewalk. Halfway up the block he stopped in front of the door of one of the old houses which had a boutique on the ground floor. He opened it with a heavy old-fashioned iron key and pressed the button just inside to turn on the hall lights. "We're two flights up."

She nodded and followed him up the old wooden staircase. His apartment was at the head of the second flight. This door had a more modern lock. He opened and held it for her.

She stepped inside. The room was dark. The door closed behind her and at the same time she heard the click of the light switch. The room filled with soft red light from two lamps, one on either side of the bed against the far wall. She looked at the room curiously.

The furniture was cheap and worn, the kind with which the French supply the summer vacationer. In the corner of the room was a sink and under it was a bidet on a swivel. The WC was behind a narrow door that looked like a closet. There was no tub, shower or kitchen, only a hot plate on the top of a bureau next to an armoire.

He caught her look. "It's not much," he said, "but it's home."

She laughed. "I've seen worse. You're lucky the toilet's not in the hall."

He went over to the bureau and opened a drawer. He took out a joint and lit it. The sweet acrid smell of the marijuana reached her nostrils as he held it toward her. "I don't have anything to drink."

"That's okay," she said, taking a toke from the reefer. "This is good grass."

He smiled. "A friend of mine just in from Istanbul dropped it off. He also laid some righteous good coke on me. Ever use it?"

"Sometimes," she said, passing the joint back to him. She looked at him as he dragged on it. She put down her beach bag and moved toward him. She felt the buzzing in her head and the wetness between her legs. It was really good grass if one toke could do that. She pulled at the knot of his shirt. "Are we going to talk or fuck?" she asked. "I only have an hour."

Deliberately, he placed the joint in an ashtray and then pushed the see-through blouse down from her shoulders exposing her naked breasts. He cupped one in each hand, squeezing the nipples between a thumb and forefinger until the pain suddenly flashed through her. "White bitch," he said, smiling.

Her smile was as taunting as his own. "Nigger!"

His hands pressed her to her knees in front of him.

"You better learn to beg a little if you want some black cock in your hot little pussy."

She had the shirt untied, now she pulled at the zipper on his jeans. He wore nothing underneath and his phallus leapt free as she pulled the pants down around his knees. She put a hand on his shaft and pulled it toward her mouth.

His hand held her face away from him. "Beg!" he said sharply.

She looked up at him. "Please," she whispered.

He smiled and relaxed his hands, letting her take him in her mouth while he reached into the open bureau drawer and took out a small vial filled with coke. The tiny gold spoon was attached to the cap with a small bead chain. Expertly, he took a spoonful and snorted it up each nostril. Then he looked down at her. "Your turn," he said.

"I'm happy," she said, kissing him and licking at his testicles. "I don't need any."

He pulled at her hair, snapping her head back. "White bitch!" He lifted her to her feet and filled a spoon and held it under a nostril. "You do as I say. Snort!"

She sniffed and the powder lifted from the spoon into her nose. Almost in the same second he had the filled spoon under the other nostril. This time she snorted without his saying a word. She felt the faint numbness in her nose almost immediately, then the powder exploded in her brain and she felt the strength pouring right into her genitals. "God!" she exclaimed. "That's wild. I came just sniffing it."

He laughed. "You ain't seen nothin' yet, baby. I'm goin' to show you some tricks my pappy taught me with that stuff."

A moment later they were naked on the bed and she was laughing. She had never felt so good. He took another spoonful and rubbed it on his gums, making her do the same. Then he licked her nipples until they were wet from his tongue and sprinkled a little of the

white powder on them and began to work them over
with his mouth and fingers.

She had never felt them grow so large and hard.
After a few moments, she thought they were going to
burst with the agonizing pleasure. She began to moan
and writhe. "Fuck me," she said. "Fuck me!"

"Not yet," he laughed. "We only beginning." He
jackknifed her legs back and sprinkled the coke over
her clitoris, then put his head between her legs.

After a moment she was screaming as she never had
screamed before. Each orgasm seemed to take her
higher than she had ever been. She reached down for
his phallus and finding it, pulled herself around so
that she was able to take him into her mouth. Greedily
she sucked at him. She wanted to swallow him alive,
to choke herself to death on that giant beautiful tool.

Suddenly he held her away. She stared up at him,
almost unable to breathe. He was on his knees between
her legs, his phallus reaching out over her. He took
the vial and sprinkled the powder until the glistening
wet head looked as if it were coated with sugar. Then
he held her legs wide apart as he eased into her slowly.

She felt her lungs congest. He felt so large. She was
afraid for a moment she could not take him. Then
he was all the way inside her and for a long moment
was still. She felt the tingling reach up into her belly.
Slowly he began to move, gently at first, with long
smooth strokes, then picking up the tempo until he
was slamming into her like a triphammer.

Somewhere in the distance she could hear herself
screaming as orgasm after orgasm ripped her apart.
She had never come like this before. Never. She, who
had always thought that this kind of sexual excitement
was only something that people talked or read about.
A kind of game they played on themselves to hide
their feelings. And if it were true, she felt that it was
something beyond her capacity to feel. For her, sex
was her triumph over the male; any satisfaction in it
for her was purely accidental. But this was different.

Now she was being used, she was being pleasured, she was giving, she was taking, she was being completed.

Finally she could take it no more. "Stop," she cried. "Please, stop!"

His body came to a rest against her; he was still hard inside her. She looked up at him. In the dim red light the fine patina of sweat covering his face and chest glowed copper. His teeth shone white as he smiled. "You all right, white lady?"

She nodded her head slowly. "Did you come?"

"No," he said. "That's the on'y thing my pappy didn't tell me. Use enough to make a lady happy an' that's just enough to keep you from makin' it."

She stared at him for a long moment, then, suddenly and unaccountably, she began to cry.

He watched her for a moment, then without speaking, got out of the bed and walked over to the sink. Bending over he swung the bidet out into the room and turned on the water. He straightened up and looked at her. "You have to let it run for a few minutes if you want to get hot water," he explained.

He opened the small cabinet over the sink and took out a towel and a washcloth which he hung over the connecting pipes. With a finger he tested the water. "It's all ready for you," he said.

She looked at him without speaking.

"You did say you only had an hour, didn't you?" he asked.

She nodded, sitting up. "I don't know if I can walk."

He smiled. "You'll be okay, once you get movin'."

She got out of bed. He was right. After the first step, the strength came back into her limbs. She squatted over the bidet and took the soap and washcloth from his outstretched hand. She washed herself quickly. The lukewarm water was refreshing. She picked up the towel and dried herself, then began to dress while he washed himself. "I'm sorry you didn't make it," she said.

"That's okay," he said. "I promised you a trip to the moon and I wanted you to have it."

"I had it all right," she said. "I'll never forget it."

He was hesitant. "Maybe we could do it again sometime?"

"Maybe," she said. Dressed, she reached for her beach bag and took out some money. She ripped off a few large bills and held them out toward him. "I hope you don't mind."

He took the money. "I could use it. But you don't have to."

"I didn't give you much else," she said.

"You gave me a lot, lady," he said. "You left all your friends to come with me. That's something."

Something in his tone of voice caught her. "Do you know me?"

He shook his head. "No."

"Then why did you ask me?"

"I saw you on the beach," he said. "After that man sent Jacques out to meet you."

"You know Jacques?" she asked.

"Yes," he said. "I spent last night with him."

She was silent for a moment. "Is Jacques—"

He nodded. "He'd rather be a girl."

"And you?"

"I like to fuck," he said, "I don't give a damn as long as there's a hole to stick it in."

"Do you know the man who spoke to Jacques?"

"I never saw him before. He had dark hair and spoke French with an Arabic accent. I heard him say that Jacques had to get something by tonight because you were leaving for California tomorrow and that Jacques shouldn't worry because he had fixed it so that the San Marco wouldn't be able to take you back to Cannes."

Suddenly it all came together in her head. Youssef was the only one who knew that she was leaving tomorrow. He had come down from Paris to handle the flight arrangements for her on Baydr's instructions.

A long time ago she had heard there had once been a connection between Youssef and Princess Mara. And Mara had pushed Jacques on to her. What she didn't understand was what possible benefit Youssef could get from it. Unless—unless he meant to use it against her with Baydr.

An unfamiliar feeling of fear came over her. Youssef had never really liked her but that didn't seem to be enough of an explanation for something like this. She just didn't know. All she did know was that she had better get back to the villa tonight.

But that was a problem. There were no taxis in St. Tropez after midnight. And she had given Guy, her chauffeur, the night off so she could not call him.

She looked at Gerard. "Do you have a car?"

"No."

"Damn!" A worried look crossed her face.

"I have a bike," he said. "I'll take you back if you'll ride behind me."

"You're lovely," she said, smiling suddenly. She threw her arms around him in a sudden burst of relief and kissed his cheek. "It should be great fun."

He put her arms down, suddenly embarrassed. "Don't be too sure, lady. Just see if you think so after I get you there."

CHAPTER 3.

IT was about two hours after they had taken off from Paris. The cabin attendants were busy preparing to serve lunch. Jordana looked back at Youssef. "I think I'd like to get some sleep now."

Youssef unfastened his seat belt and rose to his feet. "I'll have them prepare your seats right away." He glanced at Diana, Jordana's secretary. She was dozing in the window seat next to his, her unfinished drink resting on the tray in front of her.

He made his way to the chief steward, who was standing near the galley. "Madame Al Fay would like to rest."

"But we are about to serve déjeuner," the steward protested.

"She is not hungry."

"Oui, monsieur," the steward said quickly. He left the galley and went back through the curtains that separated first class from economy.

Youssef turned and looked at Jordana. Her eyes were completely hidden by the large dark glasses but there wasn't a line on her face to indicate that she had not slept the night before. She was looking at the Air France magazine on her lap, and sipping from a glass of white wine.

He suppressed a yawn. He was exhausted. He had been awake since four that morning when Jacques had called him from St. Tropez to tell him that she had disappeared.

The San Marco was still in the port and there was no trace of her anywhere in the village. Jacques had been to every restaurant and discotheque that was still open. Youssef had put down the telephone still fuming.

There was nothing he could do but wait until he went to the villa in the morning to take her to the airport. He could not get back to sleep. All the money he had given Jacques, all the plans he had made, were for naught. Even telling the mechanic at the Citroën garage to take the SM away from Jacques that morning had given him no satisfaction.

Jordana had been at breakfast when he arrived at the villa about nine o'clock. She said nothing about the evening, nor did she mention anything about how she had returned home. Casually, he had found out from one of the security guards at the villa that she had arrived by taxi from Cannes at about five that morning.

In the limousine on the way to the airport he had

explained the arrangements for the flight. They had the last four seats in the first-class section. Two were for her. He and her secretary would occupy the seats directly behind. He had also reserved the first three seats in the economy section so that when she wanted to rest she could lie down there. Special handling had also been arranged for her luggage. It would be placed in the cabin so that she would not have to wait for it in Los Angeles. There would be a special U.S. Customs agent waiting for them on arrival so that they could transfer quickly to the helicopter which would take them to Rancho del Sol. ETA for AF 003 was 4 P.M. Los Angeles time; dinner at Rancho del Sol was set for 8 P.M. If everything went according to schedule, she would have ample time to dress.

The steward came back to him. "It is ready for madame."

"Thank you," Youssef said. He walked back to the seat. "It's okay," he told her.

She nodded and rose to her feet. She opened her purse and took out a small vial and shook two pills into her hand. She swallowed them quickly with a sip of wine. "That's to make sure that I sleep."

"Of course."

"Please see that I'm awakened at least an hour and a half before we land."

"I'll take care of that," he answered. "Have a good rest."

She stared at him for a moment. "Thank you."

He watched her disappear through the curtains and sank back into his seat. Beside him, Diana stirred but did not open her eyes. He looked at his watch and glanced out the window. There were still eleven hours left. This time he did not suppress his yawn. He closed his eyes, hoping that he could get some rest.

Air France had done a good job. Temporary curtains, like those used for the second flight crew or these extralong nonstop flights, had been rigged around her seats. The window blinds were drawn and it was dark as she stretched out and pulled the blanket over her.

She lay quietly waiting for the sleeping pills to take effect. She began to feel the aching protest of her body as the exhaustion seeped through her. She could still feel the pounding of the motorcycle against the road as they raced through the early dawn toward Cannes. She had made Gerard drop her at the railroad station in the center of the town. There were always taxis there.

She had offered him more money but he had refused. "You've given me enough," he said.

"Thank you," she said.

He put the bike into gear. "Look me up when you come back to St. Tro."

"I will. And thank you again."

He took the crash helmet he had loaned her and strapped it onto the back seat. "Goodbye."

"Goodbye." He gunned the engine and took off. She watched him turn the corner toward the sea, then walked over to the first taxi on line and got in.

It had been daylight and a few minutes after five o'clock when she entered her bedroom at the villa. Her suitcases, neatly packed, were against the wall and still open in case there was anything she wanted to put in at the last minute. A note from her secretary was propped against the lamp on the night table. She picked it up. It was terse, in Diana's usual style:

Departure Villa—9 A.M.
Departure Nice–Paris—10 A.M.
Departure Paris–LA—12 N.
ETA Los Angeles–4 P.M. Pacific Coast Time

She looked at the clock again. If she wanted to have breakfast with the boys at seven o'clock, there was no point in her going to bed now. She would be better off trying to sleep on the plane.

She went into the bathroom, opened the medicine cabinet and took out a vial of tablets. She popped a

Dexamyl into her mouth and swallowed it with a drink of water. It would keep her going at least until the plane took off from Paris.

Slowly she began to undress. When she was naked, she looked at herself in the full-length mirror that was built into the wall of her dressing room. There were faint bruises on her breasts where Gerard had squeezed them, but they could not be seen in dim light, and in the daytime a little body makeup would cover them. Her belly was just flat enough and there was no extra flesh on her hips or thighs. She placed her hand on her pubis and gently parting the soft blond hair, examined herself critically. Her vagina felt heavy and swollen and seemed slightly red and irritated. A faint tingling went through her as she thought about the way the black had taken her. She never dreamed that she could come as many times as she had. She turned back to the medicine cabinet and took out a packet of Massengill. A douche wouldn't hurt and at least it would be soothing. As she mixed the solution another thought flashed through her mind.

What if the black had venereal disease? There was always a possibility especially since she knew he was bi. Somewhere she had read that homosexuals had the highest rate of venereal infections. Again she opened the medicine cabinet. This time she swallowed two penicillin tablets. She put the vial in her handbag so that she would not forget to keep taking them for the next few days.

The Dexamyl was beginning to take effect and when she finished her douche she went right into the shower. Hot and cold, hot and cold, hot and cold. three times as she had learned to do it from Baydr. When she stepped out of the shower, she felt as refreshed as if she had slept all night.

She sat down at her dressing table and slowly began to put on her makeup. Afterward she dressed and went downstairs to the breakfast room to join the boys.

They were surprised to see her. Usually she did not have breakfast with them. Instead they would come to her room after she had awakened, which was generally just before their lunch.

"Where are you going, Mommy?" Muhammad asked.

"I'm going to meet Daddy in California."

His face brightened. "Are we going too?"

"No, darling. It's just a quick trip. I will be back in a few days."

He was visibly disappointed. "Will Daddy be coming back with you?"

"I don't know," she said. It was the truth. She didn't know. Baydr had only asked her to join him. He had said nothing about his future plans.

"I hope he does come," Samir said.

"I hope so too," she said.

"I want him to hear how well we speak Arabic," the little one said.

"Will you tell him, Mommy?" Muhammad asked.

"I will tell him. Daddy will be very proud of you."

Both children smiled. "Also tell him that we miss him," Muhammad said.

"I will."

Samir looked up at her. "Why doesn't Daddy come home like other daddies? My friends' daddies come home every night. Doesn't he like us?"

"Daddy loves you both, but Daddy is very busy and has to work very hard. He wants to come home to see you but he can't."

"I wish he could come home like other daddies," Samir said.

"What are you doing today?" Jordana asked to change the subject.

Muhammad's face brightened. "Nanny's taking us on a picnic."

"That should be fun."

"It's all right," he said. "But it's more fun when Daddy takes us water-skiing."

She looked at her sons. There was something about their serious faces and large dark eyes that reached into her heart. In many ways they were miniatures of their father, and sometimes she felt that there was very little that she could do for them. Boys needed to model themselves after their father. She wondered if Baydr knew that. Sometimes she wondered if Baydr cared about anything but his business.

The nanny came into the room. "Time for your riding lesson, boys," she said in her dry Scottish voice. "The teacher is here."

They jumped from their chairs and ran, whooping, to the door. "Just a moment, boys." the nanny said. "Haven't you forgotten something?"

The two boys looked at each other, then, shame-facedly, trooped back to their mother. They held their cheeks up to be kissed.

"I have an idea," Samir said, looking up at her.

She looked at the little one, a smile coming to her face. She knew what was coming. "Yes?"

"When you come back, you surprise us with a present," he said seriously. "Don't you think that's a good idea?"

"It's a good idea. What kind of a present do you have in mind?"

He leaned over and whispered into his brother's ear. Muhammad nodded. "You know those baseball caps that Daddy wears when he's on the boat?" he asked.

She nodded.

"Can you get some like those?" he asked.

"I'll try."

"Thank you, Mommy," they chorused. She kissed them again and they ran off without a backward glance. She sat at the table for a moment, then rose and went back to her room. At nine o'clock, when Youssef arrived with the limousine, she was waiting for him.

THE drone of the jets and the sleeping pills began to take effect. She closed her eyes and thought about Youssef. What had he been trying to do? Was he act-ing on his own or at Baydr's instructions? It was odd that Baydr had been away for almost three months. That was longer than they had ever been separated before. And it wasn't just another woman. She understood him better than that. She had known about Baydr and his women long before they had gotten married. Just as he had known about her passing affairs.

No, this was something else. Deeper and more important. But she would never know what it was unless he told her.

Though he had been Westernized in many ways and she had become a Muslim, they were still separated by a thousand years of different philosophies. Because although the Prophet had granted women more rights than they had ever had until that time, he still had not granted them full equality. In truth all their rights were subject to man's pleasure.

That was one thing that was clear in their relationship. She knew it and he knew it. There was nothing she had that he could not take away from her if he so desired, even her children.

A chill ran through her. Then she dismissed the thought. No, he would never do that. He still needed her in many ways. Like now, when he wanted her to appear beside him in the Western world so that they would not think him so much a stranger.

This was Jordana's last thought before she fell asleep.

CHAPTER 4.

THE noon sun filtered through the trees into the loggia outside the Polo Lounge of the Beverly Hills Hotel, tracing delicate lines on the pink tablecloths. Baydr sat in the shadows of one of the booths, sheltered from the sun. Carriage and the two Japanese were opposite him. He watched them as they finished their lunch.

Meticulously, their knives and forks were placed

lengthwise across their plates in the European manner, to signify that they were finished with the course.

"Coffee?" he asked.

They nodded. He signaled the waiter and ordered four coffees. He offered them cigarettes, which they refused. Baydr lit one and sat there looking at them.

The elder Japanese said something in his own language to his associate. The younger man leaned across the table. "Mr. Hokkaido asks if you have had time to consider our proposition."

Baydr addressed himself to the young man even though he knew that Hokkaido understood every word. "I have thought about it."

"And?" The young man could not restrain his eagerness.

Baydr saw the flash of disapproval cross the older man's face and quickly disappear. "It won't work," he said. "The arrangements are entirely too one-sided."

"I don't understand," the young man said. "We are prepared to build the ten tankers at the price you offered. All we ask is that you use our banks to finance."

"I don't think you understood," Baydr said quietly. "You are talking about making a sale and I am interested in forming a total consortium. I can see no point in our competing with one another to purchase certain properties. All we succeed in doing is driving up the price we ultimately pay. Take the Rancho del Sol deal, for example. One of your groups just bought it."

"It was another group, not ours," the young man said quickly. "But I didn't know you were interested in it."

"I was not," Baydr said. "But there is another big development in that area that we are interested in and so is your group. The end result is that the asking price has almost doubled and whichever one of us gets it has lost before we begin."

"You are negotiating through your bank in La Jolla?" the young man asked.

Baydr nodded.

The young man turned to Hokkaido and spoke quickly in Japanese. Hokkaido listened attentively, nodding, then replied. The young man turned back to Baydr. "Mr. Hokkaido expresses his regrets that we find ourselves in competition for that property but says that negotiations began before we were in contact with each other."

"I regret it also. That was why I came to you. To find a rapprochement. Neither of us needs the other's money. Each of us has more than enough of his own. But if we work together perhaps we can be helpful to one another on other matters. That is why I spoke to you about building tankers for us."

"But even that you make difficult," the young man said. "We will build the ten tankers you want but where will we find ten tankers to deliver to you immediately? There are none on the market."

"I know that, but your shipping line has over one hundred. It would be a simple matter for you to transfer them to our company, one in which we would each own fifty percent. In that manner, you are really not losing the benefit of them."

"We're losing fifty percent of the income they produce," the young man said. "And we see nothing to replace that."

"Fifty percent of the income from the additional tankers you are building will more than take care of that," Baydr said. "And fifty percent of your foreign investment supplied by me will certainly be looked on with favor by your government."

"We have been having no trouble getting our foreign investments approved," the young man said.

"World conditions change," Baydr said smoothly. "A recession in the Western world could alter your favorable balance of payments."

"There is nothing like that on the horizon at this time," the young man said.

"One never knows. A change in the world's supply of energy could bring its technocracy to a screeching halt. Then you would be faced with two problems. One, a shortage of customers: two, an inability to maintain your own rate of productivity."

Again the young man addressed himself to Hokkaido. The older man nodded slowly as he listened. Then he turned to Baydr and spoke in English. "If we agree to your proposition, would you use the tankers to bring oil to Japan?"

Baydr nodded.

"Exclusively?"

Again Baydr nodded.

"How much oil would you be able to guarantee?" Hokkaido asked.

"That would depend entirely on what my government would allow. I think under the right circumstances a satisfactory agreement could be reached."

"Would you be able to secure a most-favored-nation clause?"

"I could do that."

Hokkaido was silent for a moment. His next words were very clear and precise. "To recap, Mr. Al Fay, in effect you are saying that if we give you five ships now at half price and build five more ships for you with our own money, you will then be good enough to use those ships to bring to our country the oil we buy from you."

Baydr did not answer. His face was impassive.

The Japanese smiled suddenly. "Now I know why you are called the Pirate. You are indeed samurai. But I will still have to discuss the entire matter with my associates in Japan."

"Of course."

"Would you be able to come to Tokyo if we should desire to go ahead?"

"Yes."

The Japanese got to their feet. Baydr rose also. Mr. Hokkaido bowed and held out his hand. "Thank you for a most enjoyable and informative lunch, Mr. Al Fay."

Baydr shook his hand. "Thank you for your time and patience."

Carriage signaled for the check as the Japanese walked away. "I don't know what they're complaining about," he said with a laugh. "We're paying for the lunch." He signed the check and added, "Michael Vincent is waiting in the bungalow for us."

"Okay," Baydr asked. "What time is Jordana's plane arriving?"

"ETA is four o'clock," Dick answered. "I checked just before lunch. It's running about fifteen minutes late. We should leave the hotel no later than three-thirty."

They walked through the dark Polo Lounge and out again into the sunlight to take the path which led to their bungalows. Their footsteps echoed on the pink cement walk.

"Did you check with Rancho del Sol?" Baydr asked.

Carriage nodded. "Everything's ready. We've taken a private house for you near the main building, overlooking the golf course. The bank people have all been booked into the club itself. Dinner will be in a private room with cocktails first. That will give all of us a chance to get to know each other."

"Any cancellations?"

"No. They'll all be there. They're as curious about you as you are about them."

Baydr laughed. "I wonder what they would think if I showed up in a traditional costume?"

Carriage laughed with him. "They'd probably shit. I've already heard talk that they suspect you of being a simple savage. That's a very snobbish group down there. All WASP. No Jews, no Catholics, no foreigners."

"They should love Jordana then," Baydr said. It was true. She was a born and bred California girl and they didn't come any WASPier.

"They will," Carriage answered.

"Still, it's not going to be easy. I have noticed a lack of enthusiasm in their pursuit of new business, and we have dropped some important accounts since we've taken over the bank."

"According to their reports, they blame it on the Jewish-controlled Los Angeles banks."

"That's too easy an excuse to satisfy me. I always get suspicious when they tell me something they think I will accept. They bungled the Star Ranch offer and let the Japanese maneuver us into a bid situation."

"They said the Japanese were working through the LA banks."

"Not good enough. They were there on the ground floor. We should have had it all wrapped up before LA even heard about it. Now it's had time to get all the way to Tokyo and back."

They were at the bungalow. Carriage opened the door and they went into the cottage. The cool, dark air-conditioned room felt good after the white heat of the sun.

Vincent got to his feet, the inevitable glass of whiskey on the cocktail table before him. "Baydr, it's good to see you again."

"It's always good to see you again, my friend." They shook hands and Baydr walked around the small table to the couch and sat down. "How is the script coming?"

"That's what I wanted to see you about. At first, I thought it would be easy. You know. Like my films about Moses and Jesus, there would always be some miracles to fall back on for visual excitement. The parting of the Red Sea for the Israelites, the Resurrection. But it's not like that at all. Your Prophet has no miracles going for him. He was just a man."

Baydr laughed. "That's true. Just a man. Like all of us. No more and no less. Does that disappoint you?"

"Cinematically, yes," Vincent answered.

"It would seem to me that should make the message of the Prophet even more convincing and dramatic. That a man, just like any of us, should bring the revelations of Allah to his fellow men. What about his persecution by the pagan Arabs and the taunts of the Jews and Christians, and his banishment and flight from Medina? And what about his battle to return to Mecca? Surely, there should be enough drama in that for several films."

"For the Muslim world perhaps, but I doubt very much that the Western world would take to the idea of their being the villains of the piece. And you did say that you wanted this film to be shown all over the world, didn't you?"

"Yes."

"There's our problem," Vincent answered. He picked up the whiskey and drained his glass. "We're going to have to solve that before we begin on the script."

Baydr was silent. The truth in the Koran was self-evident—why, then, was there always this problem? The unbelievers didn't even want to listen. If, only once, they would open their minds and hearts to the Prophet's message the light would come to them. He looked thoughtfully at the director. "If I remember your version, the film on Christ had him crucified by the Romans, not the Jews, is that right?"

Vincent nodded.

"Was that not contrary to fact?" Baydr asked. "In reality did the Jews themselves not condemn Christ to the cross?"

"There are different opinions," Vincent said. "Because Christ Himself was a Jew and betrayed by one of His own apostles, Judas, who was also a Jew, and because He was hated by the rabbis of the Orthodox temples for threatening their power and authority, many believe that the Jews pushed the Romans into crucifying Him."

"But the pagan Romans were made the villains of the film, were they not?"

"Yes."

"Then we have the answer," Baydr said. "We will build our film around the Prophet's conflict with the Quraish, which led to his flight to Medina. The Prophet's wars in reality were not with the Jews, who already had accepted the principle of one God, but with the three great Arab tribes who worshiped many gods. It was they who drove him away from Mecca, not the Jews."

Vincent stared at him. "I remember reading it but I never thought of it in that light. Somehow I felt that the Arabs had always been with him."

"Not in the beginning," Baydr said. "The Quraish tribe consisted of pagan Arabs who worshiped many gods and it was to them rather than the Jews and Christians that Muhammad first directed his teachings of the true Allah. It was they whom he first called 'Unbelievers.' "

"I'll try that approach," Vincent said. He refilled his glass and looked across the table at Baydr. "Are you sure you would not be interested in writing the script with me?"

Baydr laughed. "I'm a businessman, not a writer. I'll leave that to you."

"But you know the story better than anyone I have met."

"Read the Koran again. Maybe then you will see what I see." He got to his feet. "Youssef will be arriving later this afternoon and we'll all get together after the weekend. Now if you'll excuse me, I'm going out to the airport to meet my wife."

Vincent got to his feet. "I think you've set me on the right track. I'll get right to work on the new approach."

They shook hands and Vincent left the bungalow. Baydr turned to Carriage. "What do you think?" he asked.

"If I may say so, chief, I think you ought to pay him off and forget the whole thing. The only thing you can guarantee yourself in a film like that is losses."

"The Koran teaches that man can benefit in many ways by his actions, to seek not only the profit but the good."

"I hope you're right, but I would still be very cautious before you go ahead with the film."

"You're a strange young man. Don't you ever think of anything but dollars and cents?"

Carriage met his gaze. "Not when I'm working. I don't imagine you hired me for my social graces."

"I guess not," he said. "But there are some things more important than money."

"That's not my decision to make," Dick said. "Not when it's your money." He began to put some papers into his attaché case. "My job is to be sure that you are aware of all the risks. The rest is up to you."

"And you think the film is risky?"

"Very."

Baydr thought for a moment. "I'll keep that in mind before we proceed. We'll go into it again when the script is completed and budgeted."

"Yes, sir."

Baydr walked to his bedroom door. "Thank you, Dick," he said quietly. "I don't want you ever to feel that I don't appreciate what you're trying to do for me."

Dick flushed. It wasn't often that Baydr complimented him. "You don't have to thank me, chief."

Baydr smiled. "I'll grab a quick shower and I'll be ready to go in a few minutes. Have the car brought around in front of the bungalow."

"Will do, chief." Carriage was on the telephone before Baydr closed the bedroom door.

CHAPTER 5.

AS usual, the plane from Paris was an hour late. Silently Baydr cursed the airlines. They were all alike. They never gave accurate arrival information until it was too late to do anything but sit at the airport and wait for the plane to come down.

The telephone rang in the small VIP room and the hostess picked it up. She listened for a moment, then turned to them. "Double-O-three is touching down right now. It should be at the gate in a few minutes."

Baydr got to his feet. She rose from her desk and walked toward them. "Mr. Hansen will meet you at the gate and expedite Mrs. Al Fay through the formalities."

"Thank you," Baydr said.

There was a crowd around the arrival area. Mr. Hansen, a heavy-set man in an Air France uniform, came to meet them. Quickly, he ushered them downstairs through the restricted customs area. A uniformed immigration officer joined them and they went into the entrance room, just as Jordana came from the plane.

He nodded to himself in approval. Jordana had great instincts. The casual tie-dyed jeans and see-through clothing she affected in the south of France were nowhere in evidence. Instead, she was the fashionably dressed young California wife. The Dior suit with its modestly cut skirt, the slouch hat and lightly applied makeup were exactly right in the society they were about to enter. He moved forward to greet her.

She held her cheek for his kiss. "You look lovely," he said.

"Thank you." She smiled.

156

"The flight comfortable?"

"I slept all the way. They fixed up a special bunk for me."

"Good. We have a kind of difficult schedule in front of us."

Youssef, slightly rumpled in his dark suit, appeared behind her with her secretary. Baydr shook hands with them, as the Air France representative collected their passports for clearance. He led Jordana away from the crowd of people so they could talk privately.

"I'm sorry I could not get back this summer," he said.

"We were too. The boys especially. They gave me a message for you."

"Yes?"

"They wanted to tell you that they are doing very well in their Arabic. That you would not have to be ashamed of them."

"Are they?" he asked.

"I think so. They insist on speaking nothing but Arabic to all the help whether they are understood or not."

He smiled, pleased. "I'm glad." His eyes met her own. "And you? What have you been doing with yourself?"

"Nothing much, the usual thing."

"You look very well."

She did not answer.

"Were there many parties this year?"

"There are always parties."

"Anything exciting?"

"Not particularly." She looked at him. "You've lost weight. You look thin."

"I'll have to eat more," he said. "It would never do if I were to go back to the Middle East looking like this. They might think I was falling upon hard times."

She smiled. She knew what he was talking about. The Arabs still judged a man's success by his girth. A portly man was always more highly regarded than a thin one. "Eat bread and potatoes," she said. "And more lamb."

He laughed aloud. She knew how Western his taste was. He disliked starchy and fatty foods, preferring to eat beefsteaks. "I'll remember that."

Hansen came over to them. "Everything's okay," he said. "We have a car waiting on the field to take you over to the helipad."

"We can go then," Baydr said. He gestured to Youssef, who came toward them. "Vincent's at the Beverly Hills Hotel," Baydr told him. "You spend the weekend with him and try to find out exactly where we're at. I'll be in touch with you on Monday."

Youssef tried to conceal his disappointment. He hated to be left out of anything that might be important. "Do you think there's a problem with Vincent?"

"I don't know, but it would seem to me that in three months he should have at least made a start."

"Leave it to me, chief," Youssef said confidently. "I'll build a fire under him."

"IT will take about a half-hour to get down there," the helicopter pilot said as they lifted off.

"What's the dress for tonight?" Jordana asked. "How much time will we have?"

Baydr looked at his watch. "Cocktails are at eight, dinner at nine. Black tie."

Jordana looked at him. She knew how he hated evening dress. "You're going all out."

"That's right," he said. "I want to make a good impression. I have a feeling they resent me for taking over the bank."

"I'm sure they'll get over it once they meet you."

"I hope so," Baydr said seriously. "But I don't know. They're very clannish down there."

"They will. I know that crowd very well. Expatriate Pasadena. But they're no different than anyone else. They go with the money."

The giant bouquet of red roses presented to Jordana by the president of the bank, Joseph E. Hutchinson

III, and his wife, Dolly, when they arrived proved that she was at least partly right.

THERE was a soft knock at the door, and the muffled sound of Jabir's voice announcing, "It is fifteen minutes past seven, master."

"Thank you," Baydr called back. He rose from the small table at which he had been reading the latest bank reports. He would have time for another shower before he changed into his dinner jacket. Quickly, he took off his shirt and trousers and, naked, he started for the bathroom which separated his bedroom from Jordana's.

He opened the door, just as she rose, glistening, from the scented bath. He stood for a moment, staring. "I'm sorry"—the apology sprang to his lips without thought —"I didn't know you were still in here."

She returned his look. "It's all right," she said, a faint tinge of irony in her voice. "There's no need to apologize."

He was silent.

She reached for a bath towel and began to wrap it around her. He put out a hand to stop her. She looked at him questioningly.

"I'd almost forgotten how beautiful you are," he said.

Slowly, he took the towel from her hand. He let it fall to the floor. His fingers traced a line from her cheek, across the flushed, rising nipple, past the tiny indentation of her navel to the soft swelling of her mound. "Just beautiful," he whispered.

She didn't move.

"Look at me!" he said, a sudden insistence in his voice.

She looked up into his face. There was a gentle sorrow in his eyes. "Jordana."

"Yes?"

"Jordana, what has happened to us that we have become strangers?"

Unexpectedly her eyes began to fill with tears. "I don't know," she whispered.

He took her into his arms and pressed her head against his shoulder. "There are so many things that are wrong," he said. "I would not know where to begin to correct them."

She wanted to talk to him but she could not find the words. They came from different worlds. In his world the woman was nothing, the man everything. If she said to him that she had the same needs he did, the same sexual and social drives, he would regard it as a threat to his male supremacy. And he would think that she was not being a proper wife. Still, these needs were what had brought them together in the beginning.

She pressed her face against his chest, weeping silently.

He stroked her hair gently. "I've missed you," he said. He put a hand under her chin and raised her eyes. "There is no one else like you for me."

Then why do you stay away? Why the others? she thought to herself.

He answered as if he were reading her mind. "They mean nothing," he said. "They are only to pass the time."

She still did not speak.

"Is it like that with you?" he asked.

She stared up into his eyes. He knew. He had always known. And yet he had never once spoken about it. She nodded.

His lips tightened for a moment. Then he sighed. "A man begins his own heaven or hell right here on this earth. As I have begun my own."

"You're not angry with me?" she whispered.

"Have I the right?" he asked. "Judgment is for the time we stand before Allah and our book is read. My own sins are enough for me to bear. And you are not one of us, so even the rules that might be applied could not hold true. There is but one request that I make of you."

"What is that?" she asked.

"Let it not be with a Jew," he said. "To all others I will be as blind as you."

Her eyes fell. "Must there be others?"

"I cannot answer that for you," he said. "I am a man."

There was nothing she could say.

He raised her head again and kissed her. "I love you, Jordana," he said.

She felt his warmth flowing into her, as she clung to him. His strength hardened against her belly. Her hand dropped to encircle him. He was hard and moist in her fingers. "Baydr," she cried. "Baydr!"

He stared into her eyes for a long moment, then lifting her under the arms, he raised her into the air before him. Automatically, her legs widened to encircle his waist, then slowly he lowered her onto him. She gasped as she felt him penetrate her. It seemed as if he were thrusting a burning rod into her heart. Still standing, still holding her, he began to move slowly inside her.

The heat began to run through her and she could not contain herself. Clinging to him like a monkey she began to move spastically on him as orgasm after orgasm began to shake her. The thoughts were racing crazily through her head. It was not right. This was not right. This was not what she should have. This was not the punishment she sought.

She opened her eyes and stared wildly into his face. "Hurt me," she said.

"What?"

"Hurt me. Please. Like you did the last time. I deserve no better."

He stood very still for a moment, then slowly, he lowered her to the ground and took her arms from around him. His voice was suddenly cold. "You'd better dress," he said, "or we'll be late for the party."

He turned abruptly and went back into his room. After a moment, she began to shiver. She reached for the towel, cursing to herself. She could do nothing right.

CHAPTER 6.

THE heat from the white glaring sun seemed to bounce off the jagged rocks and the sands of the desert that stretched in front of them. An occasional wild scrub leaned brown and weary in the warm wind. The chatter of the machine gun somewhere ahead of them fell silent.

Leila lay motionless in the small foxhole. She felt the sweat gathering in her armpits, between her breasts and between her legs. Carefully, she rolled over on her back. She heaved a sigh of relief. The ache in her breasts from pressing so hard into the ground began to ease. She squinted up into the sky and wondered how long she should lie here. The Syrian mercenary in charge of their training had told her not to move until the rest of the platoon caught up to her. She glanced at her heavy man's chronograph. They should have been here at least ten minutes ago.

Stoically she forced herself to wait. Maybe it was only a training exercise but those were real bullets they were using and already one woman had been killed and three others wounded. After the last exercise, the grim joke at the camp had been the question, who would get the most credit for wiping out the Fedayeen —themselves or the Israelis?

She wanted a cigarette but did not move. A shadow of smoke in the clear air would be an invitation to draw fire. A rustling sound came from behind the fox-hole.

Silently, she rolled over on her belly and turned to face it, pulling the rifle toward her at the same time.

She inched toward the top of the foxhole and began to raise her head over the edge.

A heavy hand came down on her, jamming the steel helmet and liner over her ears. Through the pain, she heard the mercenary's gruff voice. "Stupid cunt! You were told to keep your head down. I could have picked you off from a hundred yards away."

He tumbled into the foxhole beside her, breathing heavily. He was a squat, heavy-set man, short of breath and patience. "What's going on up there?" he asked.

"How the hell should I know?" she retorted angrily. "You told me to keep my head down."

"But you were supposed to be the advance scout."

"You tell me how I'm supposed to do both," she said sarcastically, "find out what's happening without raising my head out of the foxhole."

He was silent. Without a word, he took out a package of cigarettes and held one out to her. She took it and he lit the cigarettes for both of them.

"I thought we weren't supposed to smoke," she said.

"Their mother's cunt," he said. "I'm getting tired of playing these stupid games."

"When is the platoon coming up?"

"Not until dark. We decided it wouldn't be safe for them to move until then."

"Then why did you come up here?"

He looked at her, his dark eyes moody. "Somebody had to let you know of the change in plan."

She stared back at him. He could have sent one of the others; he didn't have to come up himself. But she knew why he did. By now she must be the only one of the women in the platoon he had not had.

She wasn't too concerned. She could handle him if she had to. Or wanted to. In many ways everything had been made too easy. All the traditional taboos of the Muslim had disappeared. In the fight for freedom, the women were told that it was their duty to give solace and comfort to their men. In the new, free society, there would be no one to point a finger against them. It was just another way the woman could help win the battle.

He pulled the canteen from his belt and unscrewed the cap. He tilted his head back and let the water trickle slowly into his throat, then handed it to her. She poured a drop onto her fingers and delicately wiped her face. "By Allah, it is hot," he said.

She nodded, giving him back the canteen. "You're lucky," she said. "I've been out here two hours already. You have less than that until dark."

She rolled over on her back once again and pulled the helmet visor down so that her eyes were shaded from the sun. She could at least try to make herself comfortable while she waited. After a few moments she became aware of his gaze. Through narrowed eyelids, she could see him staring at her. She became very conscious of the dark blotches of sweat on her cotton uniform, under her arms, across her waist and in the crotch of her trousers. It was almost as if she'd marked off her private areas.

"I'm going to try to rest," she said. "This heat's worn me out."

He didn't answer. She looked up at the sky. It was that peculiar shade of blue that always seemed to come toward the end of summer. Strange that it should be like that. Until now she had always associated it with the end of summer vacation and the return to school. A memory flashed through her mind. It had been a day like this, under the same blue sky, that her mother had told her that her father was going to get a divorce. Because of that American bitch. And because a miscarriage had left her barren, so that she could not give him a son.

Leila had been playing on the beach with her older sister that afternoon when suddenly Farida, their housekeeper, appeared. She seemed oddly agitated. "Come back to the house immediately," she said. "Your father has to leave and wants to say goodbye to you."

"All right," she had said. "We'll change out of our wet bathing suits."

"No," Farida said sharply. "There's no time for that. Your father is in a hurry."

She turned and began to waddle quickly back to the house. They fell into step behind her.

"I thought Daddy was planning to stay for a while," Amal said. "Why is he going?"

"I don't know, I am only a servant. It is not my place to ask."

The two girls exchanged glances. Farida made it her business to know everything. If she said she didn't know it was because she didn't want them to know.

She stopped in front of the side entrance to the house. "Wipe the sand from your feet," she commanded. "Your father is waiting in the front salon."

They wiped their feet quickly and ran through the house. Their father was waiting near the front door. Jabir was already taking his suitcases out to the car.

Baydr turned to them and smiled suddenly. But there was a curious dark sadness in his eyes. He dropped to one knee to embrace them as they came running up to him. "I'm so glad you came in time," he said. "I was afraid I would have to leave without saying goodbye to you."

"Where are you going, Daddy?" Leila asked.

"I have to go back to America on important business."

"I thought you were going to stay," Amal said.

"I can't."

"But you promised to take us water-skiing," Leila said.

"I'm sorry." His voice seemed to choke and suddenly his eyes were moist. He held them close to him. "You both be good girls now and listen to your mother."

There was something wrong. They could feel it but they did not know what it was. "When you come back, will you take us water-skiing?" Leila asked.

Her father didn't answer. Instead he held them very tightly. Abruptly he let them go and got to his feet.

Leila looked up at him, thinking how handsome he was. None of the other fathers looked like him.

Jabir appeared in the doorway behind him. "It is getting late, master. We must hurry if we are to make the plane."

Baydr bent down and kissed them, first Amal, then Leila. "I'm depending on both you girls to take care of your mother and obey her."

Silently they nodded. He started for the door and they followed him. He was halfway down the steps toward the car when Leila called after him. "Will you be gone long, Daddy?"

He seemed to hesitate for a moment but he was in the car and the door closed without his giving an answer. They watched the car roll down the driveway and then went back into the house.

Farida was waiting for them. "Is Mother in her room?" Amal asked.

"Yes," Farida said. "But she's resting. She's not feeling well and asked that she not be disturbed."

"Will she come down for dinner?" Leila asked.

"I don't think so. Now you girls take your baths and wash all that sand off of you. Whether your mother comes to dinner or not, I want you both to be clean and fresh at the table."

It was not until later that night that they learned what was happening. Their mother's parents came over after dinner and when their grandmother saw them she burst into tears.

Anxiously she pulled them close to her heavy bosom. "My poor little orphans," she cried. "What will you do now?"

Grandfather Riad immediately grew angry. "Silence, woman!" he roared. "What are you trying to do? Frighten the children to death?"

Amal immediately began to cry. "My daddy's plane crashed!" she wailed.

"See?" Grandfather's voice was triumphant. "What did I tell you?" He pushed his wife aside and swept the oldest girl up into his arms. "Nothing happened to your daddy. He's fine."

"But, Nana said we were orphans."

"You're not orphans," he said. "You still have your mother and your father. And us."

Leila stared up at her grandmother. The heavy eye makeup the old lady wore streaked her cheek. "Then why is Nana crying?"

The old man was uncomfortable. "She's upset because your daddy went away. That's why."

Leila shrugged. "That's nothing. Daddy is always going away. But it's all right. He comes back."

Grandfather Riad looked at her. He did not speak. Farida came into the salon. "Where is your mistress?" he asked.

"She is in her room," Farida replied. She looked at the children. "It is time to go to bed."

"That's right," Grandfather Riad said quickly. "Go to bed. We will see you in the morning."

"Will you take us to the beach?" Leila asked.

"Yes," her grandfather replied. "Now do as Farida said. Go to bed."

As they started upstairs Leila heard her grandfather say, "Tell your mistress that we await her in the salon."

Farida's voice was disapproving. "The mistress is very upset. She will not come down."

Her grandfather's voice grew firm. "She will come down. You tell her that I said it was important."

Later, when they were in bed, they heard the loud sound of voices coming from downstairs. They crept out of their beds and opened the door. Her mother's voice was very shrill and angry.

"I have given him my life!" she wailed. "And this is the thanks I get for it. To be left for an American bitch with blond hair who has given him a bastard son!"

Their grandfather's voice was lower and calmer but they could still hear him. "He had no choice. It was the Prince's command."

"You defend him!" their mother said accusingly. "Against your own flesh and blood you defend the injustice. All you are concerned about is your bank and your money. As long as you have their deposits you do not care what happens to me!"

"And what is happening to you, woman?" Grandfather roared. "Is there anything you lack? You are left a millionaire. He did not take your children away from you as he could have done under the law. He gave you the property and the homes, here and in Beirut, and a special allowance for the girls. What more can you ask?"

"Is it my fault I could not give him a son?" Maryam cried. "Why is it always the woman who is to blame? Did I not bear him children, was I not a faithful wife, despite the fact that I knew he was carrying on with infidel whores all over the world? In the sight of Allah, which of us has lived a good life? Certainly it was I, not he."

"It is the will of Allah that a man must have a son," her father said. "And since you did not, it was not only his right but his duty to provide himself with an heir."

Maryam's voice was quieter now but it held a note of deadly intent. "It may be the will of Allah but he will pay for it someday. His daughters will know of his betrayal and he will be as nothing in their eyes. He will not see them again."

Then the voices dropped and they could hear no more from downstairs. Silently, the children closed the door and went back to their beds. It was all very strange and they did not really understand.

The next day when they were on the beach Leila suddenly looked up at her grandfather, who was sitting in a chair under an umbrella reading his newspaper. "If Daddy really wanted a son," she said, "why didn't he ask me? I would have been glad to be a boy."

Grandfather Riad put down the paper. "It's not as easy as that, child."

"Is it true what Mother said?" she asked. "Will we never see him again?"

He was silent for a moment before he answered. "Your mother was angry. She'll get over it in time."

But she never did. And with the passing of the years, the girls gradually began to accept their mother's attitude toward their father. And since their father made no attempt to bridge the gap between them, they finally were convinced that she was right.

THE air was growing cool as the sun began to drop and the summer blue faded into darkness. Leila rolled to her side and looked at the Syrian. "How much more time?"

"About another half-hour," he said, smiling. "There's enough time for us." He reached for her.

She moved away from him quickly. "Don't."

He stared at her. "What is the matter with you? Are you a Lesbian?"

"No," she said quietly.

"Then don't be so old-fashioned. Why do you think they're giving you girls those pills?"

She stared at him. Contempt crept into her voice. Men were all alike. "For my protection, not your convenience," she said.

He gave her what he thought was a winning smile. "Come on then," he said, reaching for her again. "Maybe I can teach you to enjoy it."

She moved quickly; her rifle prodded his belly. "I doubt it," she said quietly. "You may have taught me how to use this gun but I already know how to fuck."

He looked down at the rifle then up into her face. A genuine laugh bubbled up in his throat. "I didn't doubt that for a minute," he said quickly. "I was only worried that you might get out of practice."

CHAPTER 7.

TORTUOUSLY, Leila squirmed across the hard, sandy surface of the rock until she reached the rows of barbed wire. She stopped, gasping for breath. After a moment, she turned and peered through the pale moonlight. Soad, the big Egyptian woman, and Ayida, the Lebanese, were inching up behind her. "Where's Hamid?" she asked.

"How the hell do I know?" swore the Egyptian. "I thought he was up here in front of us."

"Jamila scraped her knee when she came across the rocks," Ayida said. "I saw him putting a bandage on it."

"That was an hour ago," Soad said sarcastically. "By now he's probably got her cunt in a sling."

"What are we going to do?" Leila asked. "We need wire cutters to get through this."

"I think Farida has a pair," Ayida said.

"Pass the word back," Leila said.

Quickly the message traveled down the line of women strung out behind her. A moment later, the wire cutters passed forward from hand to hand until they reached Leila.

Soad gave them to her. "Did you ever use these before?"

"No," Leila said. "Did you?"

Soad shook her head.

"It shouldn't be too difficult. I saw the way Hamid did it the last time."

She took the heavy wire cutters and inched up to the barbed wire fence, then rolled over on her back. She raised the cutters slowly over her head. The polished metal blades reflected the moonlight. It could only have lasted a fraction of a second but immediately the machine gun up forward began to chatter, and the bullets whined over their heads.

"Damn," Leila exclaimed in disgust, trying to press her body into the ground. She didn't dare move her head to look back at the others. "Where are you?" she called.

"We're here," Soad said. "We're not moving."

"We have to move," Leila said. "They've got us spotted."

"You move. I'm not goin' anywhere until that gun stops."

"If we crawl we're safe—they're firing three feet over our heads."

"They're Arabs," Soad said sarcastically. "And I've never known one that can shoot straight. I'm staying right here."

"I'm going. You can stay here all night if you want to."

Cautiously she rolled over on her stomach and began to crawl crabwise along the wire fence. After a few moments, she heard scratching noises behind her. She looked back. The other women were following.

Almost a half-hour later, she stopped. The machine gun was still firing but the bullets were no longer whistling over their heads. They had passed out of its range.

This time she took no chances. She smeared dirt over the blades of the cutters so that no light would be reflected. Again she rolled over on her back and reached up for the wire. It was harder than she thought it would be and the noise resounded in the stillness of the night, but no one seemed to hear. A few minutes later she had cut her way through the first row. She crawled through the opening and toward the next row. Two more and they would be in the clear.

Despite the chill, she was beginning to sweat. Anxiously she went to work on the second row. It was constructed of double strands and took almost twenty minutes to cut through. The last row was made up of triple strands, and it was forty minutes more before she was finished.

She lay on her back, gasping for breath, her arms and shoulders aching with pain. After a moment, she looked back at Soad. "We stay down until we reach the white markers. That should be about two hundred meters farther on. After that we're in the clear."

"Okay," Soad answered.

"Remember to keep your heads down," Leila said.

She rolled back on her belly and began to crawl forward. Two hundred meters seemed like a thousand miles on your belly.

Finally she could see the white markers sticking out of the ground a few meters in front of them. At the same time, she heard the voices—men's voices.

Leila held out a hand, palm backward so the women would be silent. It would be a shame if they were spotted now. They all hugged themselves into the ground.

The voices came from her left. In the moonlight, she could see three soldiers. One of them was lighting a cigarette; the others were seated behind a machine gun. The match spun away from the soldier in a flaming arc, landing near Leila's face.

"Those whores are still out there," the soldier with the cigarette said.

One of the others stood up, swinging his arms to warm himself. "Hamid's going to find himself with a lot of frozen pussy on his hands."

The soldier with the cigarette laughed. "He can give some to me. I'll show him how to thaw them out."

"Hamid gives away nothing," the seated one said. "He acts like a pasha with his harem."

A faint buzzer sounded. The soldier with the cigarette picked up a walkie-talkie. Leila could not hear what he said as he spoke into it but she could hear him addressing his companions after he put it down. "That was Post One. They had them spotted but they lost them. They think they might be coming in this direction."

"They're full of crap," one of the others said. "I can see a half a mile in this moonlight. Nothing's out there."

"Just the same keep your eyes peeled. It wouldn't look good if a couple of girls made donkey's asses out of us."

Leila smiled grimly to herself. That was exactly what they were going to do. She reached back and tapped Soad on the shoulder. She mouthed the words silently. "Did you hear?"

Soad nodded, as did the women behind her. They had all heard.

Leila moved her hand in a wide sweeping gesture. They understood. They would crawl in a wide circle that would bring them back to the machine gun emplacement from behind. Slowly, holding their breaths they began to move.

It took almost an hour and they were well behind the white markers and directly behind the machine gun when Leila gave the signal.

With a yell, the women sprang to their feet and charged. Cursing, the soldiers turned toward them, and found themselves staring into barrels of the women's rifles.

"You're our prisoners," Leila said.

The corporal smiled suddenly. "I guess so," he admitted.

Leila recognized him as the one with the cigarette. She couldn't keep the note of triumph out of her voice. "Maybe you'll think differently about women soldiers now."

The corporal nodded. "Maybe."

"Now what do we do?" Soad asked.

"I don't know," Leila said. "I think we should call in and report their capture." She turned to the corporal. "Give me your walkie-talkie."

He held it out to her. He was still smiling. "May I make a suggestion?"

"If you like." Leila's voice was businesslike.

"We are your prisoners, aren't we?"

Leila nodded.

"Why don't you rape us before you report in? We promise not to complain."

The women began to snicker. Leila was angry. Arab men were the worst kind of male chauvinist pigs. She jammed down the call button on the walkie-talkie. But before she could get a reply, Hamid and Jamila came strolling up to them, as casually as if they had spent an afternoon in the park.

"Where the hell were you?" she yelled at Hamid.

"Right behind you."

"Why didn't you help us?"

He shrugged. "What for? You were doing all right."

She looked at Jamila. The pudgy Palestinian had a relaxed look on her face and Leila knew why. She turned back to Hamid. "How did you get through the barbed wire?"

"Easily," he said, a broad smile coming to his lips. "We dug ourselves a little trench and fucked our way through it."

Leila held a straight face as long as she could, then started to laugh. The Syrian mercenary had a strange sense of humor but he was funny. She handed the walkie-talkie to him. "Here, call us in," she said. "Maybe you can get them to send a truck out for us. I think we could all use a hot bath."

THE steam rose over the tops of the barracks shower stalls. Above the splashing of the running water came the chatter of the women.

The stalls each had four jets and were designed for communal use, four women to a shower. Since there were only two stalls, there was always a line of women waiting for a shower to open up. Leila liked to wait until most of the others had finished their baths, so that she did not have to hurry to make way for the next one. She leaned against the window smoking a cigarette, listening to the chatter.

Almost three months had passed since she had come to the camp, and all during that time she had been drilled from morning until night. Whatever fat there had been on her body had long since disappeared. Now she was lean, her belly and flank muscles firm, her breasts like two apples. Her lustrous black hair, cut short for convenience when she arrived, now fell to her shoulders.

Every morning there had been two hours of calisthenics and drill before breakfast. After breakfast there had been manual training in which the women learned about guns—how to use them and how to take care of them. They also learned about grenades and the use of plastique, the techniques of preparing and concealing letter bombs and the practicality of transistorized timer-detonator devices. Afternoons were spent practicing the techniques of manual combat, hand to hand and weapon to weapon. Later in the day, they were given political lectures. The ideological indoctrination was important because each of them was considered a missionary for a new order in the Arab world.

Later the political lectures gave way to lessons in military tactics, paramilitary infiltration and sabotage, guerrilla warfare and subversive diversion.

For the last month, they had all been training in the field. Everything they had learned had been put to use. Gradually Leila could feel herself toughening. She thought of herself as a woman less and less. The purpose for which she trained possessed her and became a way of life. It was through her and others like her that a new world would come. For a moment she thought of her mother and her sister. They were in Beirut, still living in that old world—her sister with her petty family and social problems; her mother, still bitter and resentful over the way she had been tossed aside by her father but doing nothing constructive with her life. She closed her eyes for a moment, remembering that day in the south of France before she had come here. She thought of her father and his sons water-skiing on the bay in front of the Carlton. Her father hadn't changed since she had last seen him almost nine years before. He was still tall and handsome, filled with strength and vitality. If only he could understand, if only he knew how much he could do to help free the Arab from the imperialism of Israel and America. If he only knew the need, the suffering, the oppression of his brothers, he would not stand idly by and permit this to happen. But she was only wishfully dreaming. Of course he knew. He had to know.

It was just that he didn't care. Wealth was his by birth and his only concern was to increase it. He loved the luxury and the power that sprang to his beckoning finger. And the terrible truth was that he was not alone. The sheiks, the princes and kings, the bankers and men of wealth were all the same, Arab or not. They cared only for themselves. Whatever benefits filtered down from their efforts were only incidental to their own. There were still millions of peasants in every Arab land who lived on the fringes of starvation while their rulers drove in air-conditioned Cadillacs, flew in private jets, maintained palaces and homes all over the world and then talked pompously about freedom for their people.

Eventually it had to come. The war was not only against the foreigners—that was only the first step. The second step and probably the more difficult would be the war against their own oppressors—men like her father, men who took everything and shared nothing.

A shower stall was now vacant, and Leila threw her coarse large towel over the wall panel and stepped under the streaming shower. The heat of the water spread over her like a soothing balm. She could feel the tension in her muscles loosen. Slowly, languidly, she began to soap herself, the touch of her fingers on her skin giving her a sensual pleasure.

In that she was like her father. Again she saw him on the water skis, the muscles straining against the lead, his entire being enjoying the physical effort of skill and balance.

She lathered the soft pubic hair until the dark curls were covered with the white fluff. Then she thrust her hips forward and let the shower beat directly down on her. The tingling and the warmth ran through her. Softly, almost automatically, she stroked herself. Her orgasm and the vision of her father on skis with hips thrust forward came together, taking her by surprise. Before she could stop another orgasm shook her body. She felt shock, then anger, then disgust at herself. She was sick to even allow such thoughts. Violently she turned off the hot water and held herself rigid under the icy stream until her flesh was blue with the cold. Then she stepped from the stall, wrapping the towel around her.

It was crazy. She had never had thoughts like that before. But it was in her blood. Her mother had said so many times. She was like her father. His body ruled him; his lusts and appetites were never to be satisfied. Her mother had told them stories about him and his women. He was not a man who could ever be satisfied with one good woman. Bad blood, her mother had said in warning.

She rubbed herself dry and then, tying the towel around her, went into the barracks.

Soad, whose bed was next to her, was almost dressed. "What are you doing tonight?"

Leila reached for a robe. "Nothing. I thought I would just stay in bed and read."

Soad began to apply her lipstick. "I've got a date with Abdullah and a friend of his. Why don't you come along?"

"I don't really feel like it."

Soad looked at her. "Come on. It would do you good to get out."

Leila didn't answer. She remembered Soad on her first day here. She had come to be near her boyfriend and had told everyone how she couldn't wait to be with him. But when he didn't appear she hadn't been upset. She took her female liberation seriously. Women had equal rights in this army and by now she had

fucked her way through the entire camp and made no
bones about it. "Cairo was never like this," she'd say
with a burst of raucous laughter.

"Tell you what," Soad said seriously. "If you come
along I'll let you have Abdullah. He's the best cocks-
man in the camp. I'll settle for his friend."

Leila looked at her. "I don't think so."

"What are you saving it for?" Soad asked. "Even if
you don't want it for yourself, it's part of your duty.
Didn't the CO tell us that it was our responsibility
to give solace and comfort to our men? I can't imagine a better way to combine duty and pleasure all at
the same time."

Leila began to laugh. Soad had a one-track mind.
"You're fantastic," she said. "But none of those men
appeal to me."

"You'll never know until you try them," Soad said.
"Men can surprise you. The greatest lovers look like
nothing sometimes."

Leila shook her head.

A puzzled look came over Soad's face. "Are you a
virgin?"

Leila smiled. "No."

"Then you're in love." It was a statement.

"No."

Soad gave up. "I don't understand you."

That was the truest thing Soad had ever said. But
how could she make the woman understand that there
were things more important to her than sex?

CHAPTER 8.

IT was just ten minutes after reveille when the barracks door opened unexpectedly and Hamid shouted from the doorway. "Attention!"

There was a flurry of motion as the women fell into place, in front of their beds, in various stages of dress.

Hamid stepped back from the doorway and the CO entered. Her sharp dark eyes took in the entire barracks in one sweeping glance, then she walked into the center of the room followed by Hamid. The fact that some of the women were half-naked seemed to make no difference to her.

She was silent for a long moment before she spoke. Her voice was clear and emotionless. "Today will be your last day. Your training has been completed. Our work has been done. This camp will be closed and each of us assigned to duties elsewhere."

She paused for a moment. The women did not stir, nor did they take their eyes from her face. "I am proud of you," she said. "All of you. There have been those who have looked upon us with disdain and skepticism. They have said that women, especially Arab women, could not make good soldiers, that they were only fit for cooking, cleaning and taking care of the children. We have proved them wrong. You are members of Al-Ikhwah. You are the equal of any man in our armies. You have completed the same training as the men have and you have done as well as any of them."

The women were still silent. The CO began again. "You will have exactly one hour to pack your personal belongings and be ready to leave. I will see each of you individually to give you your next assignment. This assignment is not, I repeat, is not to be discussed among you. It is your own, and highly secret. Any discussion of your individual assignment will be regarded as treason and will be punishable by death— for one poorly chosen confidence can cause the death of many of our comrades."

She walked back to the door, then turned to face them. "An-nasr, I salute you. May Allah protect you." Her hand snapped up in a salute.

"An-nasr!" they shouted, returning her salute. "Id-bah al-adu."

The room filled with their voices as the door closed behind her.

"Something big must be in the wind."

"This is a month earlier than we had been told."

"Something is wrong."

Leila didn't speak at all. She opened her locker and began to take out the clothing she had worn on her arrival. Silently she laid her uniforms and fatigues in a neat pile on the bed. Even the brassieres and panties, shoes, boots and stockings were placed into a neat stack.

She opened the small suitcase that she had brought with her. She took out the blue jeans she had bought in France just before she came and put them on. It was then that she realized how much her body had changed. The jeans, which had once hugged her, were now big around the waist and in the seat. Even the shirt was loose, and she rolled the sleeves because they seemed to have grown longer. She tied the shirt across her waist and slipped into the soft sandals. She packed her comb, brush and cosmetics, then carefully checked the locker. It was empty. She snapped the suitcase shut.

She sat down on the bed and lit a cigarette. The other women were still debating what to take and what to leave. Soad looked across at her. "You're wearing your own clothes?"

Leila nodded. "The CO said personal belongings. These are the only things that are mine."

"What about the uniforms?" one of the others called.

"If they wanted us to take them they would have said so."

"I think Leila is right," Soad said. She turned toward her locker. "I think I won't mind getting into my own clothes for a change." A moment later she gasped in dismay. "Nothing fits. Everything's too big!"

Leila laughed. "It's not too bad." She put out her cigarette. "Think of all the fun you'll have getting new things."

As she walked out of the building, the sun was coming up over the mountain. The morning air was fresh and clean. She breathed deeply.

"Ready?" Hamid's voice came from behind her.

She turned. He was leaning against the building, the ever-present cigarette dangling from his lips. "Ready as I'll ever be," she said.

He looked at her steadily. "You're not like the others, you know that."

She didn't answer.

"You didn't have to do this. You're rich. You could have everything you want." The mercenary's eyes were appraising.

"Could I? How do you know what I want?"

"You don't believe all this empty talk, do you?" He laughed. "I've been through three wars. Each time it has been the same thing. The slogans, the shouting, the threats, the promises of vengeance. Then when the bullets begin to fly it's all over. They turn and run. Only the politicians go on forever."

"Maybe someday it will be different," she said.

He fished another cigarette from his pocket and lit it from the butt of the other. "What do you think will happen if we take Palestine back?"

"The people will be free," she said.

"Free of what? Free to starve like the rest of us? With all the money coming into the Arab countries now, the people are still starving."

"That will have to be changed too."

"Hussein, the oil sheiks, even your father and his

prince, do you think they would willingly share what they have with the masses? At least now they have to do something. But if we win and there is no pressure on them, what then? Who is there to make them share? No, they will only grow richer."

"It will be up to the people to change them."

Hamid laughed bitterly. "I'm almost sorry to see this job finished. It was a good one. Now I'll have to find another."

"What do you mean?" she asked. "Don't they have another assignment for you?"

"Assignment?" he laughed. "I'm a professional. I got paid. One thousand Lebanese pounds a month for this job. I don't know any place where I can make that kind of money."

"Surely there must be a place for you in the army?"

"For one-fifty a month I can get my ass worked off," he said. "I prefer the Brotherhood. It pays better. They always seem to have lots of money to throw around."

"Don't you believe in what we're doing?" she asked.

"Sure I do," he said. "I just don't believe in our leaders. There are too many of them, each busy lining his own pockets while trying to become the top dog."

"They can't all be like that."

He smiled at her. "You're young yet. You'll learn."

"What happened?" she asked. "Why the sudden change in plans?"

He shrugged his shoulders. "I don't know. The orders came last night and the CO seemed to be as surprised as any of us. She was up all night getting things ready."

"She's an extraordinary woman, isn't she?"

Hamid nodded. "Maybe if she were a man, I would have more faith in our leaders." He looked at her quizzically. "You know you owe me something."

"I do?" she asked, puzzled. "What?"

He gestured at the barracks behind him. "There are fourteen girls in that platoon. You're the only one I haven't fucked."

She laughed. "I'm sorry."

"You should be," he said half-seriously. "Thirteen is an unlucky number. Something bad is going to happen."

"I don't think so." She smiled. "Look at it this way: You have something to look forward to."

He grinned. "I'll strike a bargain. If we ever meet again—no matter where—we'll do it."

She held out her hand. "Agreed."

They shook hands. He looked into her eyes. "You know, you're not a bad soldier for a girl."

"Thank you," she said.

He glanced at his watch. "Do you think they're ready?"

"They should be," she said. None of them had very much to take.

He threw his cigarette down and turned and opened the barracks door. "Okay, girls," he shouted in his field voice. "On the double!"

IT was almost two hours before they were ushered into the CO's headquarters. While they waited, the camp was being dismantled before their eyes. Men and trucks were moving everything—beds, clothing, weapons—out of the building. Already the camp was beginning to look like a ghost town. And with doors and windows open, the desert sand was swirling in, anxious to reclaim its own.

The women stood outside headquarters watching truck after loaded truck pull away. The headquarters building itself was the last to be dismantled. Furniture was being moved out as they were ushered in.

Following alphabetical order, Leila was the first to be called. She closed the door behind her, stepped to the CO's desk and saluted smartly. "Al Fay reporting." Somehow it didn't seem as proper in blue jeans as it had in uniform.

The CO returned her salute wearily. "At ease. Annasr," she said. She looked down at the sheet of paper before her. "Al Fay, is that your name?"

"Yes, ma'am." For the first time Leila thought of her as a woman. The CO was tired.

"You are to return to your mother's home in Beirut," she said. "You will be contacted there and directed to your next assignment."

"Is that all, ma'am? Nothing else?"

"That is all at this time. But don't worry, you'll hear from us."

"But how will I know? Isn't there a code name or some way that I will be sure of—"

The CO interrupted. "When the call comes, you will know," she said. "For now, your assignment is to go home and wait. You will not involve yourself or go near any political groups no matter how sympathetic they are to our cause. You will keep your own counsel and remain in the normal social confines of your family. Do you understand that?"

"Yes, ma'am."

The CO looked at her for a moment. She seemed about to say more but then she stopped. "Good luck," she said. "Dismissed."

Leila saluted, executed a smart about-face and left the room. She walked through the outer office. The other women looked at her with curiosity, but she didn't speak.

There was a truck parked outside. Hamid gestured toward it. "Your limousine awaits."

Leila nodded, silently climbed in the back and sat down on one of the rows of benches. It took less than a half-hour before the truck was filled.

They were peculiarly silent. Suddenly they were all strangers, bound by their orders, afraid that they might unwittingly reveal something.

It was Soad who broke the tension. "You know," she said in her coarse Egyptian voice, "I'm really going to miss this place. It wasn't so bad and I got some of the best fucking I ever had."

With that, they all laughed and began to talk at once. There were so many things they had to remember and joke about—the accidents, the mistakes, even the hardships. A half-hour passed and still the truck hadn't moved.

"What are we waiting for?" one of the women called to Hamid.

"The CO," he replied. "She'll be out in a minute."

He was right. A moment later she appeared in the doorway behind him. The women fell silent as they stared at her.

It was the first time any of them had ever seen her out of uniform. She was wearing an ill-fitting French tailored wool suit. The jacket was too short, the skirt too long. The seams of her stockings were crooked and she walked uncomfortably on the high-heeled shoes she wore to give her height. Somehow the commanding presence she had in uniform had disappeared. Even her face looked pudgy and uncertain.

If she were a little heavier, Leila thought, she would look no different than my mother. Or any of the women in my family.

Hamid opened the door and she got into the truck beside the driver. He ran around to the back and climbed in with the women. "Okay," he called to the driver.

The last of the furniture was being removed as they drove onto the road and fell into line behind the other trucks. A moment later the last truck came up behind them and blew its horn as a signal. Up front the first truck began to move and soon they were all rolling down the road toward the coast.

They had their last glimpse of the camp as they turned the curve around the mountain on the southern end. It was as empty and deserted as yesterday. Again the women were silent. There were no more jokes. They were all preoccupied with their own thoughts.

They had been on the road for less than an hour when they heard the sounds of explosions coming from behind them in the area of the camp. A moment later they heard the whine of the aircraft and just as suddenly the planes were upon them. Up ahead a truck burst into flame.

Hamid stood up in the back of the truck. "Israeli fighters!" he shouted to the driver. "Get off the road!"

But in the roar and the noise the driver didn't hear him. Instead he put on a burst of speed and crashed into the truck ahead. At the same time another jet made a pass low over the convoy.

More bullets whistled through the air. Another truck was struck and blew up. The women were screaming and trying to get off the back of the truck.

"Over the sides!" Hamid yelled. "Take cover in the ditches!"

Leila moved automatically. She hit the ground, rolled over and scrambled toward the side of the road, diving head-first into a drainage ditch.

Another jet roared down on them. This time she could see the flaming trails left by its rockets. More trucks seemed to explode in clouds of smoke.

"Why aren't we shooting back at them?" she heard someone shouting.

"With what?" someone else shouted back. "All the guns have been stowed on the trucks!"

Another woman jumped into the ditch beside her. Leila heard her sobbing. She didn't raise her head to look. Another plane was making a pass.

This time a missile hit the truck she had been on. It exploded in a thousand fragments and anguished screams filled the air. The debris that fell around her contained scraps of metal and parts of human bodies.

She burrowed further into the ditch, trying to bury herself in the fetid earth. Somehow she had to escape death at the hands of the flying monsters.

Again the planes roared by, the shrieking whistles of their jets trailing behind them as the missiles tore once more into the convoy. Then they were gone as suddenly as they had come, climbing high into the sky and turning to the west, the sunlight glancing off the blue painted stars on their sides.

For a moment there was silence, then the sound of

pain began to rise in the air. Moans and screams and cries for help. Slowly Leila raised her head from the ditch.

On the road a few people began to move. She turned to look at the woman who had jumped into the ditch beside her. It was Soad.

"Soad," she whispered. "Are you all right?"

Slowly the Egyptian turned toward her. "I think I'm hurt," she said, in an oddly soft voice.

"Let me help you," Leila said, moving toward her.

"Thanks," Soad whispered. She tried to raise her head then slipped gently back to the ground. A rush of blood bubbled up through her mouth and nose, staining the ground beneath her and then her eyes went wide and staring.

Leila looked at her. It was the first time she had ever seen anyone die, but she did not have to be told that Soad was dead. Leila felt a cold chill. She forced herself to look away and got to her feet.

She stumbled out of the ditch. The ground was covered with debris. In front of her was a severed hand. The diamond ring on one of the fingers sparkled in the light of the sun. She kicked it away and walked toward the truck.

There was nothing left but twisted wood and iron and around it were strewn broken and mangled bodies. She stared at it dully, then walked around to the front. The CO's body lay half over the driver, half out of the open door. Her skirt was twisted obscenely over her pudgy thighs.

Out of the corner of her eye, Leila saw a movement. A soldier had found the hand and was pulling the diamond ring from its finger. When he had the ring, he threw the hand away, carefully examined the diamond, then put it in his pocket. He looked up as he became aware of her stare.

She didn't speak.

He smiled sheepishly. "The dead need nothing," he said. Then he walked behind the truck.

The nausea rose in her throat and she bent double

with pain as she retched and spewed her vomit onto the road. She felt herself growing faint and was beginning to fall when a strong arm came around her shoulders.

"Easy," Hamid said. "Easy."

She was empty now but weak and trembling. She turned toward him and buried her face against his shoulder. "Why?" she cried. "Why did they have to do this to us? We never did anything to them."

"It's war," Hamid said.

She looked up into his face. There was blood across his cheek. "They knew the raid was coming, that's why they were moving us out."

Hamid didn't answer.

"It was stupid then," she said angrily. "Keeping all those trucks together on the road. Giving them a target like that."

Hamid looked at her without expression.

"Is this what we trained for? To be slaughtered like sheep?"

"It won't be like that when we listen to the radio tonight," he said. "My guess is that we heroically shot down at least six Israeli jets."

"What are you talking about?" She asked, bewildered. "Are you crazy? We never fired a shot."

He spoke in a quiet voice. "That's right. But there are one hundred million Arabs who were not here to see that."

"The Jews. They are animals. We were defenseless and still they came."

"Yesterday we won a great victory, according to the radio," he said. "In Tel Aviv a school bus was blown up, killing thirty children. I guess this was their way of showing they didn't like it."

"The Brotherhood is right," she said. "The only way to stop them is to exterminate them."

He looked at her silently for a moment, then he reached into his pocket and took out a cigarette and lit it. He exhaled the smoke through his nose. "Come, little one, let's leave this. There is nothing here for us to do and we have a long walk ahead of us."

"We could stay and help bury them."

He pointed behind them. She turned and saw men searching through the debris. "Right now, they are busy looking for whatever they can find. Later they will fight among themselves to keep what they find. After that there will be only you to fight about. You are the only woman left."

She stared at him speechlessly.

"I don't think your desire to give solace and comfort to our comrades extends to twenty or thirty men at the same time."

"How do you know they won't come after us?"

He bent swiftly and picked something up from the ground at his feet. For the first time she saw that he had an automatic rifle, then she saw the gun stuck into his belt.

"You expected this?"

He shrugged. "I told you I was a professional. I had these under my bench and grabbed them before I jumped from the truck. Besides, I had a feeling. Didn't I also tell you that thirteen was an unlucky number?"

CHAPTER 9.

BAYDR watched Jordana across the room. He felt satisfied. He had made the right decision. Jordana was just the balance he had needed. Now she was bidding good night to the Hutchinsons. She had made an impression on the wives and there was no doubt that it had made a difference in his relationships with the bank's officers. Now they were a team.

Of course his new profit-sharing proposal had been a great help. Fifteen percent of the profits to be distributed among the employees on a stock dividend basis had not hurt at all. There was one thing all people had in common—greed.

Joe Hutchinson came over to him. "I'm glad we were able to get together," he said in his hearty California voice. "It's sure good to know that the man you're working with has the same ideas that you have."

"I feel good too, my friend," Baydr said.

"The girls hit it off pretty good too," Hutchinson said, looking back at his wife. "Your little lady invited Dolly to visit her in the south of France next summer."

"Good," Baydr smiled. "You come too. We can have some fun."

The Californian winked his eye and grinned. "I heard about them French babes," he said. "Is it true they all go around topless on the beaches?"

"On some of them."

"I'll be there, you can bet on that. I never got as far as Europe during the war. I caught some flak in North Africa and the only girls I ever saw were gook whores. And no self-respecting man would touch them. Either they were full of clap or else they had a nigger up an alley to run a knife into you."

Apparently, Hutchinson didn't realize he was talking about Arab countries. In his mind there could be no association between the natives of North Africa and the man who stood before him. "The war was a bad time," Baydr said.

"Was your family in it?"

"Not really. Our country is small and I guess no one thought it important enough to fight over." He didn't mention that Prince Feiyad had entered into an agreement stipulating that if Germany won they would have been placed in charge of all the oil development in the Middle East.

"What do you think?" Hutchinson asked. "Will there be another war in the Middle East?"

Baydr looked him in the eye. "Your guess is as good as mine."

"Well, if anything does happen," Hutchinson said, "I hope you give 'em hell. It's about time somebody put those Jews in their place."

"We don't have many Jewish customers, do we?" Baydr asked.

"No, sir," the banker said enthusiastically. "We just don't encourage them, that's why."

"Do you think that's why we blew the Rancho del Sol development?" Baydr asked. "Because some of the developers were Jewish?"

"That has to be the reason," Hutchinson said quickly. "They wanted to do business with the Jewish banks in Los Angeles."

"I was curious. Somebody told me that we were underbid. LA gave them the money at prime and we wanted a point and a half over."

"The Jews did that deliberately to undercut us," Hutchinson said.

"Next time you cut right back. I want our bank to be competitive. It's the only way to attract the big deals."

"Even if they're Jews?"

Baydr's voice went flat. "Don't get confused. What we're talking about is dollars. United States dollars. That deal could have made us two million in three years at prime. If we undercut it by a half point, it would still be a million and a half. That's the kind of money I don't like to pass up."

"But the Jews would have underbid us anyway."

"Maybe," Baydr said. "But we just might remember that from now on we'll be an equal-opportunity lender."

"Okay," Hutchinson said. "You're the boss."

"By the way," Baydr said. "Is that last figure you quoted me on Leisure City still firm?"

"Twelve million dollars, yes. The Japs have forced it up."

"Put a hold on it at that figure."

"But wait a minute. We haven't that kind of money available," Hutchinson protested.

"I said put a hold on it, not buy it. I think we may have a partner by the end of the week."

"The hold will cost us ten percent, a million, two hundred thousand. If the partner doesn't show up we lose it. And there go our profits for the year. The examiners won't like that."

"I'll take the chance. If worse comes to worst, I'll put up the money myself." If everything worked out right, neither he nor the bank would have to put up a penny. The Japanese would put up six million, and the other six would come from his Middle Eastern group which the bank in New York could finance and he would have it three ways. The bank would collect interest on the money and an equity, he would collect an equity for his share in the Japanese consortium, and he also had an equity in the Middle Eastern group. Money, it seemed, had a strange power to feed on itself and grow.

Finally the Hutchinsons were gone. Jordana came back into the room. She sank into a chair exhausted. "Jesus," she said. "I don't believe it."

He smiled. "What don't you believe?"

"That there are still people in the world like that. I thought they were all gone by now. I remember them from when I was a child."

"You'll find people don't really change."

"I think they do. You've changed. I've changed."

He met her eyes. "That's not necessarily for the good, is it?"

"It depends on how you feel. I don't think I could ever go back to that kind of life. No more than you can go back home and stay there."

He was silent. In a way she was right. There was no way he could ever go back and live as his father lived. There was too much going on in the world.

"I could use a smoke," she said, looking up at him. "Does Jabir have any of that private hash of his?"

"I'm sure he has," Baydr said, clapping his hands.

Jabir appeared from the adjacent room. "Yes, master?"

Baydr spoke rapidly in Arabic. A moment later Jabir was back with a silver cigarette case. He opened it and held it out to Jordana. The cigarettes were beautifully rolled, complete with cork tips. Carefully she took one. He then turned and extended it toward Baydr, who also took one. Jabir placed the cigarette case on the coffee table in front of Jordana and struck a match. He held the flame at the right distance so that only the top touched the cigarette and none of the heat came through. He lit Baydr's cigarette in exactly the same manner.

"Thank you," Jordana said.

Jabir salaamed, in the gesture of obeisance. "I am honored, mistress." He left the room quietly.

Jordana sucked the smoke deep into her lungs. She felt its tranquil effects. "This is beautiful," she said. "No one seems to get it the way Jabir does."

"It is grown by his own family on their own farm, not far from where my father was born. The Arabs call it the stuff of which dreams are made."

"They're right." She laughed suddenly. "You know, I think I'm high already. I'm not tired anymore."

"Neither am I." Baydr sat down in the chair opposite her, put his cigarette into an ashtray and leaning forward took her hand. "What would you like to do?"

She looked into his face. Suddenly her eyes filled with tears. "I would like to go back," she said, "back to the time we first met and begin all over again."

He was silent for a moment, then he spoke. "So would I," he said gently. "But we can't."

She stared at him, the tears running down her cheeks. Then she hid her face in her hands. "Baydr, Baydr," she cried. "What has happened to us? What went wrong? We were so in love then."

He drew her head to his chest and stared somberly into space. His voice was a low rumble in her ears.

"I don't know," he said quietly, thinking how beautiful she had been the first time he saw her.

HE remembered the cold and the white blinding light reflected from the snow and the white buildings surrounding the inaugural stands. It was January 1961. The greatest country in the world was inaugurating its new President, a young man by the name of John F. Kennedy.

Six months ago no one in the Middle East had even known the young man's name. Then, suddenly, he was the candidate of the Democratic party and there was a telegram from the Prince on his desk. "What is Kennedy's policy on the Middle East?"

His reply had been terse. "Pro Israel. Not much else known."

The telephone call he had received the next day was equally terse. The Prince himself had called. "Find a way to contribute one million dollars to the Nixon campaign," the Prince had said.

"It will not be easy," he had replied. "The United States has peculiar rules about campaign contributions."

The Prince chuckled slyly. "Politicians are the same everywhere. I am sure you will find a way. Mr. Nixon and Mr. Eisenhower were very good to us when the British and French tried to take over the Suez in fifty-six. We should at least show we are grateful."

"I'll work it out," Baydr replied. "But I would like to suggest that we also make a token contribution to the Kennedy campaign, just in case."

"Why?" the Prince asked. "Do you think he has a chance?"

"Not according to the polls, but this is America. One never knows."

"I will leave it in your hands," the Prince said. "I'm beginning to think you're more American than Arab."

Baydr laughed. "The Americans don't think so."

"How are your wife and daughters?" the Prince asked.

"They're fine," he answered. "I spoke to them last night. They're in Beirut."

"You had better make a visit home," the Prince said. "I am still waiting for that heir you promised me. I would like to see him before too long. I am not growing any younger."

"Allah will preserve you," Baydr said. "You will live forever."

"In paradise I hope." The Prince's whispery laugh echoed in the telephone. "But not on this earth."

Baydr had put down the telephone thoughtfully. The Prince never said anything casually. He wondered if he had heard that Maryam could not bear any more children after the birth of the last girl. But if he had heard he would not have asked about an heir.

He would have insisted that Baydr get a divorce and marry another. Barrenness was a valid reason for divorce under Muslim law. But Baydr was reluctant. It was not that he was in love with Maryam. There never had been that between them and the longer they were married the less they seemed to have in common. She was too provincial; she really disliked Europe and America. She was only truly happy when she was in her own environment, in a world she understood. That was the real problem, Baydr thought. She was too much an Arab. And the thought of having to marry another Arab woman just didn't appeal to him.

Maybe the Prince had been right. Maybe he was too American. For he definitely preferred Western women to his own. There was a life about them, a style, a look, a freedom that Arab women didn't have.

Baydr found a way to make the contributions. Both of them. They had many friends among the businessmen in both parties. The token contribution had paid off and the Prince had received a special invitation from the inaugural committee. The Prince declined on the grounds of poor health and appointed Baydr to be his special representative at the inauguration.

Baydr was in the section reserved for the representatives of foreign countries, fairly close to the inaugural platform itself. He was uncomfortable in the freezing cold, despite the thermal underwear under his formal swallow-tail suit, pearl gray vest and trousers. The top hat, pressed down on his head to prevent it from being blown off by the gusts of wind didn't help very much in keeping his head warm.

He looked around. Some of the other diplomats and their wives were better prepared than he was. They were older and probably had been through this before. He could see them nipping from small silver flasks and there were more than a few thermos bottles in evidence.

He glanced at his watch. It was almost a quarter past twelve. They were running late. The ceremony was due to start at noon. He reached into his pocket for the dark glasses. His eyes were weary with squinting against the sun and snow, but he changed his mind. None of the others were wearing them. There was a flurry on the stands. He looked up as the applause began. The President-elect was coming onto the platform.

There was something young and very vulnerable about him as he walked forward with firm strides, the wind ruffling his hair. The cold seemed not to bother him. He alone of all on the platform wore no hat or coat.

A moment later a priest came forward and delivered the invocation. His voice was singsong and monotonous like all priests' voices no matter what their faith, but the young President stood quietly, hands clasped, his head respectfully inclined. Allah would not have insisted on so long a prayer in such cold weather, Baydr thought.

When the priest had finished, another man was led forward. He was old and white-haired and his face seemed carved out of the same granite as the building behind him. Baydr heard the whispers around him. The man was Robert Frost, one of America's great poets.

The old man began to speak, his breath smoky in the winter air. Baydr could not distinguish the words.

A moment later he stopped. There seemed to be a problem.

Another man stepped forward and held a hat over the lectern. Apparently the sun had blinded the old man so that he could not read what was on the sheet in front of him. Another whisper ran through the stand. The man who held his hat was Lyndon Johnson, the future Vice-President. The old man said something, the Vice-President elect stepped back and the old man began to recite a poem from memory. His voice rang through the public address system but Baydr had stopped listening. He had noticed a girl on the platform about three rows behind the President.

She seemed tall but he could not really tell. The platform was tiered so that all could see and be seen. She was bareheaded with long, straight blond hair, framing a golden tanned face. Her bright blue eyes were set above high cheekbones that fell into planed lines to an almost square chin. Her lips, as she listened intently to the poet, parted, revealing white even teeth. When the poet finished, she smiled and laughed and clapped her hands enthusiastically. For some reason Baydr thought, She's a California girl.

Then the President was being sworn in. The ceremony itself only seemed to take a moment, after which he turned to the lectern to begin his speech. Baydr listened carefully.

There was one line that made him wonder if the President had read the Koran. It could have been taken from the Holy Book. "Civility is not a sign of weakness, and sincerity is always subject to proof."

When the President had finished speaking, Baydr looked for the girl but she had already gone. He tried to find her in the crowds that were moving away from the platform but she was nowhere to be seen.

Still her face kept appearing before his eyes all through the afternoon as he rested in his suite in the hotel. He watched several replays of the inauguration ceremony on television, hoping to catch another glimpse of her, but the angle of the camera was always wrong.

There was only one other chance. Spread across Baydr's desk were invitations to four inaugural balls, each of which promised an appearance by the President. She would have to be at one of them, he thought. But which one? That was the question.

The answer was simple. He would go to all of them. If the President could do it, so could he.

CHAPTER 10.

BAYDR allowed himself no more than an hour at each ball. One was very much like another, crowded and noisy, the floor covered with people, drunk and sober, dancing, talking or just walking about aimlessly. The one thing they had in common was that they were all Democrats, glad to be back in the sun after eight years in the dark. After a while, Baydr began to wonder if there were any Republicans left in the country.

He arrived at the first ball just after the President had left for the second. Carefully, his eyes swept the room. He never realized before just how many blondes there were in Washington, but none of them was the one he sought. He went to the bar and ordered a glass of champagne.

A man came up to him and grabbed him by the arm. "Did you see him?" he asked excitedly.

"Who?" Baydr asked.

"The President, that's who," the man answered in an aggrieved voice. "Who else would I be asking about?"

Baydr smiled. "I saw him."

"Great, wasn't he?" The man smiled and walked off without waiting for an answer.

Baydr put his drink down and decided to go on to the next ball. It was a good thing it wasn't far because the streets were still icy. Again, the President had come and gone by the time he arrived. Baydr screened the room and when he saw that the girl wasn't there, he didn't even stay for a drink.

He got to the third ball in the middle of a dance. People were crowded around the periphery of the floor, trying to peer through the crowds.

Baydr pushed his way through. He tapped a man on the shoulder. "What's happening?"

"The President's dancing with some girl out there," the man said without turning around.

On the far side of the floor the flashbulbs were popping. Baydr made his way toward them. As he passed, he heard a woman ask in disapproving tones, "Why doesn't he dance with Jackie?"

He heard her husband's disgusted reply: "He has to do those things, Mary. It's politics."

"Then why does it always have to be a pretty girl?" the wife retorted. "I don't see him dancing with any of us who worked so hard on his campaign."

Baydr was at the edge of the floor. The photographers and cameramen were climbing over each other to get pictures of the President. For a moment, he was pinned against a post, then he managed to slip past them.

There was a small clear space around the President and his partner. The other dancers didn't really move; they just shuffled in a semicircle, staring at the President. Baydr stared too. The President was dancing with his girl.

He had a sick feeling of disappointment. From the way they were laughing and talking, they seemed to know each other fairly well. His hopes of finding someone they both knew to introduce them were dashed. One couldn't very well ask the President of the United States to introduce one to a girl. Besides, he too had heard some of the stories about the President. It seemed he was quite a man with the ladies.

As he watched, the music ended and they started from the floor. Immediately, they were surrounded by throngs of people. Photographers were taking more pictures. Then the President turned to the girl. Smiling, he said something to her. She nodded and the President turned and started away. The crowd followed him and a moment later the girl was standing almost alone.

He took a deep breath and went up to her. "Miss?"

She was even more beautiful up close than she had been from a distance. "Yes?" she asked politely. Her voice was low and slightly Western in intonation.

"How did it feel to dance with the President of the United States?"

"That's a strange question."

"What's your name?"

"Are you a reporter?"

"No," he answered. "Do you know the President well?"

"You ask a lot of questions for a man who says he's not a reporter."

He smiled. "I guess I do. But I can't think of any other way to keep you from walking away."

For the first time she looked directly at him. "I can," she said. "Why don't you ask me to dance?"

CHAPTER 11.

HER name was Jordana Mason and she had been born and raised in San Francisco. So he'd been right about one thing. She was a California girl. Her father and mother had been divorced when she was a child. Both parents had since remarried but relations were good between them, and Jordana was in close touch with her father even though she lived with her mother. She was nineteen years old, a junior at Berkeley and one of the organizers of the Students for Kennedy Movement, which was the reason she'd been invited to the inaugural.

She had caught the candidate's eye at a rally in San Francisco. His press people had made a big thing of getting photographs of him with the students and he had promised her that if he won she would receive an invitation.

She was not naïve enough to believe that he would remember the promise. She was sure that there were more important things on his mind. So she was surprised when the invitation arrived in the mail one morning.

Excitedly, she called her mother. "Isn't it wonderful?"

Her mother was cool. The whole family was solidly Republican.

"I hope they have provided a chaperon," her mother said.

"Mother," Jordana said. "This is 1960, not 1900. I'm a grown girl. I can take care of myself."

"I'm sure you can, dear," her mother said smoothly. "But have they arranged for a good place for you to stay? And who is paying for your air fare?"

"I'm supposed to take care of all that myself. The invitation is only for the inauguration. And it says I'm to have a place on the same stand with the President."

"I still don't like it," her mother sniffed. "I think you'd better discuss this with your father."

She called her father at his office in the Civic Center. He was no more enthusiastic, but he did understand how much it meant to her. He cautioned her about Kennedy's reputation, even though he knew that she could take care of herself. Besides, now that the man was President, he was sure that he would change his ways. He agreed to buy her ticket but he wanted her to check again with her mother to see if she knew some friends with whom she could stay. The hotels in Washington were notorious dens of iniquity, filled with all kinds of Southern and black politicians and foreigners who were trying to promote something. In the end they found out that all their friends were Republicans and that Jordana would be better off staying in a hotel than letting one of them know that one of their own family had gone over to the other side.

All this Baydr learned during the first dance. After the number was over, he led her in search of an empty table where they could sit and talk. They found one in a small room off the main ballroom. The waiters were scurrying about frantically trying to fill the orders that came at them from all directions.

Baydr solved the problem simply. He caught the eye of the maître d' by waving a hand in which he had concealed a ten-dollar bill. A moment later a bottle of Dom Pérignon appeared at their table.

"That's expensive," Jordana said. "Are you sure you can afford it?"

"I think so," Baydr said noncommittally. He raised his glass. "To the most beautiful girl in Washington."

She laughed. "How would you know? You haven't seen all of them."

"I've seen enough."

She sipped the wine. "This is delicious. They say California champagnes are as good as the French but they're not like this."

"California champagnes aren't bad."

"I'll bet you never drank any," she accused.

He laughed. "I went to Harvard, then spent a few years at Stanford."

"What do you do?"

"I'm a businessman."

She looked at him doubtfully. "You seem kind of young for that."

"Age doesn't matter much in these times," he said. "Kennedy is only forty-three and he's President."

"You're not forty-three," she said. "How old are you?"

"Old enough," he said, refilling their glasses. "When do you plan to go back?"

"Tomorrow morning."

"Don't go. Now that I've gone to so much trouble to find you, you can't vanish so quickly."

She laughed. "I have to be in school on Monday." A puzzled look crossed her face. "What do you mean you went to so much trouble to find me?"

"I saw you this afternoon at the inauguration ceremony. I couldn't get you out of my mind so I decided to attend every one of the balls until I found you. I was sure you would be at one of them."

"Honestly?"

He nodded without speaking.

She looked down at her glass. "I have to go back."

"But not tomorrow," he said. "There's the whole weekend before you have to be back."

"It's freezing here. I've never been so cold in my life. I haven't got clothes for this weather."

"We can take care of that. We can leave for Acapulco tonight. It's warm there."

"Is there a plane leaving this late?" she asked.

"There are always planes."

"That's crazy," she said, smiling. "Besides, how can I be sure that I'll make a connection to San Francisco. You know those Mexican airlines."

"I'll guarantee it," he said confidently. "What do you say?"

She looked at him skeptically. "I don't know. I'm not sure."

"Of what?"

"Why you are doing this. You don't even know me."

"It's one way of getting to know you better."

She met his eyes. "What are you getting out of it?"

He returned her gaze evenly. "The pleasure of your company."

"That's all? Nothing else?"

"Isn't that enough?" He laughed. "I'm not a sex maniac if that's what you're thinking. You have absolutely nothing to worry about."

"But I don't even know your name."

"We can fix that." He took his card from his wallet and gave it to her.

She looked down at it. "Baydr Al Fay. MEDIA Inc., 70 Wall Street, New York," she read aloud. "MEDIA—what does that stand for?"

"That's the name of my company," he said. "Middle Eastern Development and Investment Associates."

"You're not American?"

"No. Did you think I was?"

"I thought you were Jewish," she said.

"Why?"

"I don't know. The way you look I guess."

"Many people make the same mistake," he said easily. "I'm an Arab."

She fell silent. Again she looked at the card.

"Is there anything wrong?" he asked quickly.

"No. I was just thinking, that's all." She looked up at him. "I've never done anything like this before."

"There's always a first time for everything."

"Can I think about it and let you know in the morning?"

"Of course you can, but it would really be a shame to miss a whole day in the sunshine."

She hesitated again. "Do you really mean it? There are no strings attached?"

"Absolutely no strings."

She raised the glass of champagne to her lips and emptied it. "My room's upstairs in this hotel. I'll go upstairs and pack. I can be ready in fifteen minutes."

"Good," he said, signaling for a check. "That will give me time to make a few phone calls and arrange for the flight. We can pick up my things on the way to the airport."

It had begun to snow again as the limousine slowly made its way to the airport. Jabir sat silently on the seat next to the chauffeur, smoking a cigarette.

"I hope we won't be late for the flight," she said.

"We won't," Baydr said.

"Do you think the weather might keep us from taking off?"

"I've taken off in much worse."

The airport was practically deserted as they walked through. Jabir and the chauffeur were behind them with the luggage. "I don't see any passengers," she said as they walked toward the departure gate. "Are you sure there's a plane?"

"There's a plane." He smiled.

It wasn't until they were on the ramp, climbing up the steps into the Lear Jet, that she realized they were boarding a private plane. She paused on the top step and looked at him.

He nodded reassuringly.

The steward was waiting just inside the door. "Good evening, madame. Good evening, Mr. Al Fay." He turned to Jordana. "Let me show you to your seat, if I may."

He led Jordana to a comfortable reclining chair and took her coat. He then leaned across and fastened her seat belt. "Are you comfortable, madame?"

"Very, thank you."

"Thank you, madame," he said and walked away.

Baydr sat down next to her and fastened his seat belt. A moment later the steward was back with a bottle of Dom Pérignon and two glasses. At a nod from Baydr, he filled the two glasses and went forward again.

Baydr raised his glass. "Welcome aboard *The Star of the East*."

"You didn't tell me it would be your own plane," she said.

"You didn't ask me. You only asked if I were sure there would be a flight."

She sipped at the champagne. "This is good. You know a girl could get hooked on stuff like this."

"I can think of worse." Baydr smiled.

The plane began to move out toward the strip. She reached for his hand automatically. "I always get nervous at takeoff."

He smiled, holding her hand gently. "There's nothing to worry about. I have two very good pilots aboard."

She glanced out the window into the falling snow. "But they can't see very much."

"They don't have to," he said. "It's all worked by radar and instruments."

There was a surge of the jets; a moment later they were airborne. When they were above the snow and clouds high in the star-filled night, she turned and saw that her hand was still in his. She looked at him. "You're a strange man," she said softly. "Do you do things like this often?"

"No," he said. "This is a first time for me too."

She was silent for a moment while she took another sip of her champagne. "Why me?" she asked.

His eyes were as blue as the night sky. "I think I fell in love with you the moment I first saw you."

The steward came back, refilled their glasses and disappeared. She sipped at the wine, then suddenly laughed. She saw the puzzled look on his face. "I just had the funniest thought," she said.

"Tell me."

"In all the movies I've seen, the sheik comes riding in from the desert, sweeps the girl up on his white charger and gallops off into the night. In a way isn't that what you're doing?"

"I should hope so," he smiled. "You see, I intend to marry you."

CHAPTER 12.

THEY were to be together for three years before they were married. And that was only after the birth of their first son, Muhammad.

During those three years they were inseparable.

Wherever he went in the world, she went with him. Except when he returned to the Middle East. There she would not go.

"Not until we are married," she said. "I will not be treated as a concubine."

"We can be married," he said. "Under Muslim law I am allowed four wives."

"Fine," she said sarcastically. "Marry three other Arab girls."

"That's not the point, Jordana," he said. "I don't want to marry anyone else. I want to marry you."

"Then get a divorce."

"No."

"Why not?" she asked. "You don't love her. You never see her. And divorce is simple for a Muslim, isn't it? You said so yourself."

"We were married by the Prince's command. I would need his permission to divorce and he would not give it so that I could marry an unbeliever."

"Baydr, I love you," she said. "And I want to be your wife. But your only wife. Do you understand that? That's the way I was brought up. One wife at a time."

He smiled. "It's not that important really. It's just the way you look at it."

"Okay, then," she said with finality. "That's the way I look at it. I won't change."

He didn't answer. Actually he was not that anxious to get married again. Not that there were other women. There had been very few since he had been with her. And then only on those rare occasions when they happened to be apart. When they were together, he never felt the need for another woman.

At first, her parents had been aghast at her actions. It was not until Baydr placed substantial brokerage accounts with her stepfather that they began to come around. After that, they would sometimes have dinner with her parents when they were in San Francisco. But the dinners were always private family affairs. No one wanted to explain that Jordana was living in sin, especially with an Arab.

Baydr bought a villa in the south of France and they spent as much time there during the summers as they could. Jordana studied and became proficient in French. She loved the Riviera. It was gay and bubbly and everyone was there for a good time. People cared nothing about your private life. Only that you had the money to enjoy it.

During the winter, they lived in New York and vacationed in Acapulco, where he bought the house in which they had spent their first weekend together. Occasionally they would go skiing but since he disliked the cold, she couldn't persuade him to go very often. Every three months Baydr returned home for two weeks. While he was away, Jordana would visit her family in San Francisco. But always when the two weeks were up, she would be there to meet him in New York or London or Paris or Geneva or wherever he had to be on business.

Only one time when he came into the apartment in New York she was not waiting to greet him. "Have you heard from the madame?" he asked the butler, who took his hat and coat at the door.

"No, sir," the butler answered. "As far as I know, madame is still in San Francisco."

He waited all day for her to arrive and finally, after dinner that night he called her mother's house in San Francisco. Jordana answered the telephone.

"Darling, I was beginning to worry," he said. "When are you coming home?"

Her voice was tired. "I'm not."

"What do you mean, you're not?" The shock crept into his voice.

"Just what I said. I'm twenty-one and I have to do something with my life. I'm not coming back."

"But I love you."

"It's not enough," she said. "I'm tired of living in limbo. I think two years of that is enough for any girl. It's time I grew up."

"Is there someone else?"

"No. You know better than that. There has been no one else since you."

"Then what is it?"

"Would you believe that I'm just tired of the way we're living? Tired of playing at being Mrs. Al Fay when I'm not." She began to cry.

"Jordana."

"Don't try to talk me out of it, Baydr. I'm not like the Arab women you know. I just can't accept it. I have a mind of my own."

"I won't try to talk you out of it. I just want you to think it over."

"I have thought it over, Baydr. I'm not coming back."

He felt the anger rising within him. "Then don't expect me to come running after you," he said. "I did that once."

"Goodbye, Baydr."

The telephone went dead in his hand. He looked at it, then slammed it down angrily. For a few minutes he stared into space, then he picked up the telephone and called again.

This time it was her mother who answered. "May I speak with Jordana, please?" he asked.

"She ran up to her room," her mother said. "I'll call her."

Baydr held on until her mother came back on the telephone. "She said she doesn't want to speak to you."

"Mrs. Mason, I don't understand what's happening. What's the matter with her?"

"It's quite normal, Baydr," she said calmly. "Pregnant girls are usually quite excitable."

"Pregnant?" he shouted. "She's pregnant?"

"Of course," Mrs. Mason said. "Didn't she tell you?"

SEVEN months later, he stood at the side of her hospital bed. His son lay in her arms.

"He looks exactly like you," she said shyly. "The same blue eyes."

He remembered what his father had once told him.

"All newborn children have blue eyes," he said. "We'll name him Muhammad."

"John," she said. "After my grandfather."

"Muhammad," he repeated. "After the Prophet." He looked down at her. "Now will you marry me?"

She met his gaze. "Will you get a divorce first?"

"I cannot have an unbeliever as my only wife," he said. "Will you take the faith?"

"Yes," she said.

He picked up the child and held it close to him. The baby began to cry. He looked down at Jordana with a proud father's smile. "Our son will be a prince," he said.

THE old Prince looked up as Baydr came into his room. He gestured with his hand and the young boy who had been sitting at his feet rose and left the room. "How are you, my son?" the old man asked.

"I bring you news of an heir to the throne, your highness," he said. "I have a son. With your permission I shall name him Muhammad."

The old man looked at him shrewdly. "The child of an infidel concubine cannot pretend to a throne of the Prophet."

"I will marry this woman," Baydr said.

"Will she accept the faith?"

"She already has," Baydr replied. "And already she knows the Holy Koran better than I."

"You have my permission then to marry this woman."

"I request a further boon of your highness."

"What is that?"

"It is not seemly that the heir to the throne is issue from a second wife in the house. I ask your permission to divorce first."

"There must be grounds," the Prince said. "It is forbidden by the Koran to divorce because of vanity or whim."

"There are grounds," Baydr replied. "My first wife has been barren since the birth of her last child."

"I had heard such talk. Is it true?"

"Yes, your highness."

The Prince sighed. "Permission is then granted. But the settlement must be just and conform to the Holy Writings."

"It will be more than just."

"When you have married this woman, I would like you to bring her and your son to see me."

"It shall be as you wish, your highness."

"All is the will of Allah," the old man said. "When your son reaches the age of ten years he will be named my heir." He leaned and Baydr kissed his hand and nose. "Go then in peace, my son."

AT their marriage, Jordana pleased and surprised him and his parents by speaking to them in Arabic. Unknown to him, she had hired tutors and taken a crash course so that she now spoke the language well but with a delightful, soft American accent that made it sound almost musical. Baydr remembered how fascinated his mother and sisters had been by her hair, how they touched it, almost caressingly, remarking upon its softness and its spun-gold color. He remembered too how proud his father had been when he held his first grandson in his arms. "My little prince," Samir said softly.

After the marriage ceremony, they made the pilgrimage to Mecca, not by camel across the desert as his father and mother had done, but by Lear Jet, which made the trip in hours instead of days. Together, they stood in the calm quiet of the square, dressed as were the other pilgrims in white flowing robes, and when the call to prayer came, they prostrated themselves on the ground before the Kaaba, the Holy House of Allah.

Afterward in the plane on their way to visit the Prince, he turned to her, speaking in Arabic. "Now you are truly Muslim."

"I have been from the moment we first met," she said. "I just didn't know it."

He had taken her hand. "I love you, my wife."

In the Arab tradition she raised his hand to her lips and kissed it. "And I love you, my master."

"If your son is to be my heir," the old Prince had said, "you will make your home near mine, so that I may see him grow and prosper."

Baydr had seen the startled look in Jordana's eyes above the traditional veil she wore for public meetings. He shook his head so that she would not speak.

"You will live in a house," the Prince continued, "within the palace walls so that you may be guarded from evil."

"But my work, your highness," Baydr protested. "It keeps me away most of the time."

The Prince smiled. "In that case you will arrange to come home more often. It is not good for a man to be separated from his family for too long."

That night in their own chambers, Jordana spoke to him. "He can't mean it," she said. "There is nothing for me to do here. I'll go crazy."

"It won't be for long. We have to humor him for a little while, then I will tell him I need you to help me in my work and he will understand."

"I won't do it!" she exclaimed. "I'm not an Arab woman who can be ordered about like a slave!"

His voice grew cold. It was a side of Baydr she had never seen before. "You are a Muslim wife," he said, "and you will do as you are told!"

Perhaps it was then that things began to change between them. Baydr was true to his word. But it was six months before he could convince the Prince that they would have to make their home elsewhere. By that time the damage had been done. For both of them.

An invisible barrier had grown between them and their love and no matter how they tried, they could not break it down.

CHAPTER 13.

JORDANA could not sleep. Her eyes wide, she stared into the darkness, listening to his soft deep breathing on the far side of the king-size bed. Nothing had changed. Not even Jabir's stuff of dreams could bring them together now.

Before they were married, their sex had been warm and filled with lovely tender moments, despite the fact that there were certain acts of love he would not permit. He would kiss her breasts and belly but he would not engage in oral sex with her. Many times she had tried to lead him to it and although he delighted when she took him in her mouth, he would never allow her to assume the superior position so that she could control their movements. Without putting it in words, he had let her know that the things she wanted him to do were beneath his dignity as a man. A man should never be subservient to a woman in any way.

Still none of this had mattered. He had been a good lover. But she noticed a change soon after they were married. Sex became almost perfunctory. He entered her without preparation and was quickly finished. At first, she blamed it on the pressure of his work. The Prince was making greater and greater demands upon him. His business was expanding into all the countries of the Western world and his organization was increasingly complex. Gradually Baydr gathered a staff of young men who, like himself, were of Middle Eastern extraction and versed in the ways of the West. These staff members were stationed in the countries with which they were most familiar, and it was their job to keep a day-to-day watch on his investments. But Baydr himself traveled from one to the other to make the final decisions and coordinate the various endeavors into a profitable whole.

To meet the pressures on his time, the Lear Jet had given way to a Mystère Twenty, then to a Super Caravelle and finally to a Boeing 707 InterContinental. Now he could cover long distances without having to make a stop, but even so, his travel kept them more and more apart. There was always some other place he had to be, some other emergency that only he could resolve. Their summers in France fell by the wayside, and more often than not the giant yacht they had bought for their mutual enjoyment lay idle in the harbor.

Soon after the birth of Samir, their second son, their lovemaking seemed to disappear altogether. And one night, when in her despair she reached for him, he took her hand and placed it on the cover between them. His voice was cold. "It is unseemly for a wife to make advances."

Stung by the rejection, she started to cry, then became angry. She turned on the light, sat up in bed and reached for a cigarette. Carefully she lit it and took a deep puff, trying to compose herself. "What is it, Baydr? Don't I do anything for you anymore?"

He didn't answer.

"Is there someone else?"

He opened his eyes and looked at her steadily. "No."

"Then what is it?"

He was silent for a moment, then got out of the bed. "I am tired," he said. "I wish to sleep."

She looked up into his face. "And I want to fuck," she said bluntly. "Is there anything wrong with that?"

"It is enough that you are acting like a whore," he said. "You do not have to speak like one."

"You should know," she said bitingly. "You spend enough time with them."

His face darkened with anger. "What I do is none of your concern."

"I am your wife, and you have not been with me in months. What do you mean that it is not my concern?"

"It is a wife's duty to bow to her husband's will."

"Marrying you did not make me a second-class citizen," she snapped. "I have rights and feelings too."

"You have forgotten what is written," he said. "You are my wife, my possession, and you are only entitled to those rights and feelings which I allow you."

She stared at him. "Then I ask you for a divorce. I won't live like this."

"I reject your request," he said. "You will live as I order you to."

"This isn't the Middle Ages," she said. "Neither are we in the Middle East, where you can lock me in a harem. Tomorrow I will leave for home and file for divorce."

His eyes were ice cold. "If you do," he said quietly, "you will never see your children again. You know I have power."

The hurt and shock leaped into her voice. "You couldn't do a thing like that!"

"I can and I will," he said flatly.

The tears flooded her eyes and she could not speak.

He stared down at her for a moment, and when he spoke it was without any sympathy. "There will be no divorce. There is too much at stake. I will not have my son's accession to the throne despoiled by scandal. Not after I made so great a sacrifice to obtain it for him."

She looked at him incredulously. "What sacrifices have you made?"

"I swallowed my pride and asked permission to marry an infidel despite all the counsel I received against such an act. But I wanted the throne for my son. It had been promised."

"But I took the faith, didn't I?" she cried.

"With your lips but not with your heart. If you accepted it truly you would know your position and not question my acts."

She covered her face with her hands in despair. "Oh, God!" she cried.

"What God do you call on?" he asked in a cruel voice. "Yours or mine?"

She lowered her hands and looked at him. "There is no God but Allah."

"Say the rest of it."

She was silent for a moment, then her eyes fell. "And Muhammad is His prophet," she whispered.

He took a deep breath and started for the door. "Remember that."

"Baydr." Her voice held him. "What do you want me to do?"

He looked at her steadily. "I grant you freedom to do whatever you wish as long as we remain married, but there are two restrictions. The first is discretion. You will do nothing to bring disgrace upon our house. To the world our marriage must appear as it always has been."

"And the second?"

"You will avoid Jews. That I will not tolerate."

She was silent for a moment, then she nodded. "It will be as you wish."

He went into the other room, leaving the door open behind him. A moment later he was back, a yellow metal box in his fingers. He shut the door behind him and walked to the edge of the bed and looked down at her. He opened the box and placed it on the night table beside the bed. She saw the ampules in their yellow netting. "You know I don't like amyl nitrite."

"I don't care what you like or what you do not," he said harshly. "You act and speak like a whore—you will be treated as one."

He unbuttoned his pajama top and took it off, then pulled the cord on the pants. They fell to the floor and he stepped free of them. "Take off your night dress," he commanded.

She did not move.

Quickly he reached down and, grasping the front of it, tore it from her. Her breasts leaped free and he cupped one in his hand. "Is this what you want?" he asked.

She did not answer.

He increased the pressure. The pain made her gasp involuntarily. She looked into his eyes for a moment, then her gaze fell to his hand. He was holding his rapidly hardening phallus toward her. "Is that what you want?"

"Baydr!" she cried.

He thrust himself into her mouth. She choked and coughed. His voice was derisive. "That is not what you want, infidel whore?" He held her face away from him and looked into her eyes. "Perhaps you will like this better."

Quickly he pushed her flat on the bed and thrust three fingers deep into her. It was swift and unexpected and the tearing brought a moan of pain to her lips. Rapidly he began to move his fingers in and out while with his free hand he took an ampule from the box.

She felt the explosion in her brain as he broke the capsule under her nose. Her heart felt as if it would burst in her chest and in spite of herself she began to feel the throes of orgasm begin to rack her body.

Abruptly he withdrew his fingers and turned her belly down on the bed. "On your hands and knees like the infidel bitch that you are!" he commanded.

She could not move.

His open palm slashed across her buttocks. She screamed. Again and again his hand cracked across her flesh. She began to writhe and moan. It was crazy. I am crazy, she thought. I can't like this. But she was beginning to enjoy the heat spreading through her loins.

"Like a dog, woman!" he commanded.

"Yes, yes," she moaned, pushing herself back on her knees, holding her buttocks high in the air. Her

breasts hung toward the bed as she leaned on her el-
bows. She felt him positioning himself behind her and
turned to look at him.

"Don't look at me, infidel bitch!" he shouted, roughly pulling her hair so that her face turned away from
him.

The trembling she felt inside rapidly spread throughout her body, even her knees were shaking. Once she
had seen a mare trembling, waiting to be mounted by
a stallion. She knew now exactly how the animal had
felt. Then she remembered the stallion with its giant
red shaft springing from him and ripping into the
mare and how the mare had gone to her knees with
the fierceness of the onslaught.

He pulled her head back by her hair so that her
neck was stretched taut and exploded another capsule
under her nose. Again the orgasm began.

She heard him break another capsule but this time
it was not for her but for him. Then she felt the
hardness of him tear into her and the fierce slamming
thrust of his body against her buttocks.

She screamed once with the pain and the violence
of her orgasm as he began to thrust into her. Then,
like the mare, she went down under the impact.

Afterward she lay very still on her side of the bed,
the pain and trembling slowly leaving her body. He,
too, was silent. He made no gesture. There was no
communication between them.

After a moment, he spoke. "Now, woman, do you
understand your position?"

She felt the tears come to her eyes. "Yes," she
whispered in a low voice.

AND that was how it had been ever since. It was no
longer an act of love, not even an act of cruelty. Purely and simply, it was an assertion of his power over
her.

It was later that summer that she took her first
lover. After that it was easy. But with very few of

them did she achieve satisfaction. Still there was something she did get. Whether it was true or not, whether they felt it or not, whether she paid them or not, they all made love to her.

And that was something Baydr never did.

CHAPTER 14.

THE buzzing of the electric razor woke her. Jordana rolled over in the bed. Through the open door leading to the bathroom she could see him standing in front of the mirror, a towel wrapped around his flat waist. The look of concentration on his face was familiar. Shaving seemed to absorb him completely.

She sat up in the bed and reached for a cigarette. It had been a strange weekend. Strange, because there had been moments when they had seemed to be approaching the closeness they once had. But each time it happened, one or the other would draw away or do something to destroy the feeling.

Twice that weekend they had made love. The first time she had ruined it by her request for pain. "Hurt me," she had said and, as she said it, felt him turn off.

The second time had been the night before, after they had smoked Jabir's cigarette. This time she was ready. The hashish had relaxed her and she felt slow and easy. She wanted only to make love beautifully and simply. She wanted him to be as he had been when they first met.

But it wasn't like that at all. He had taken her roughly, thrusting himself into her. Three times, he went in and out of her; the fourth time he emptied himself. Taken by surprise at his quickness, she had stared up into his face. It was impassive, as if nothing were happening to him. She could see neither joy nor pleasure.

A moment later he left her and was on his side of the bed, asleep. She had lain for a long time without sleeping and had thought about that first time when he had taken her without love and made her feel as if she were nothing but a receptacle for his own use and convenience. He had made it clear then that it was the way it would be and it had been like that— until this weekend.

After the first failure, she had hoped that there would be another, better time together. But it was not to be. Whatever he had sought from her at the beginning of that weekend was over. And she wondered if she would ever get another chance.

He came out of the bathroom, wet from the shower, and looked down at her. "We're leaving for Los Angeles this morning," he said in a casual voice. "What are your plans after that?"

He was acting as if they were strangers. "So nice to see you," she said. "Look forward to seeing you again."

A puzzled look crossed his face. "What did you say?"

"Nothing. I haven't made any plans."

"Are you going back to France?"

"What about you?" she asked. "It wouldn't be a bad idea if you saw the children. You've been gone all summer and they miss you."

"I can't," he said flatly. "There's just too much to do right now. Besides, I plan to spend some time with them in Beirut this fall. I will be there at least six weeks."

"A few days would mean a lot to them."

His voice grew edgy. "I said I can't spare the time." He crossed to the dresser and took out a shirt. "I may have to leave for Japan immediately."

"I've never been to Japan. I hear it's fascinating."

He was buttoning his shirt. "Tokyo's a madhouse,"

he said noncommittally. "Traffic is awful and everything is so crowded that you can't breathe."

She gave up. He didn't want her with him. He had no use for her there. "I think I may stay in LA a few days. I'll see some friends and then maybe go up to San Francisco to visit my family."

He slipped into his trousers. "That's not a bad idea. But arrange to be back in France by the beginning of next week. I don't want the boys to be left alone too long."

"I'll arrange that," she said. With four servants, two bodyguards and the nanny, the children weren't exactly alone.

The telephone rang and he picked it up. He listened for a moment, then nodded, pleased. "Good, Dick," he said. "Call the plane and tell them we'll leave as soon as I get to the LA airport."

He put down the telephone. "I'm leaving for Tokyo right away," he said. "You can use my bungalow at the hotel if you like."

"That would be nice."

"Youssef is there in the hotel meeting with Vincent. If there's anything you need, you can call on him."

"Thank you."

He slipped into his shoes and walked to the door. "How long do you think it will take you to get ready to leave here?"

"Not long."

He nodded and left the room. For a moment, she sat without moving. Then she ground out the cigarette and got out of bed. She stood in front of the mirror, let her gown drop to the floor and looked at her naked body.

Physically, she was still the same. Perhaps her breasts had become slightly fuller since the birth of the children but they were firm and her body had the muscle tone of her youth. She should have been pleased. But she wasn't. The abundance of wealth and the comforts it brought were just not enough. There had to be more to life than standing by and waiting to be used.

The telephone in Youssef's bedroom began to ring. He didn't move, hoping it would stop. He was exhausted. The young American man he had met in After Dark last night had worn him out. He had been insatiable. Finally, when he could scarcely move, Youssef had given him fifty dollars and sent him away.

The man had looked at the fifty-dollar bill, then back at him. "Do you want me to call you?"

"I won't be here. I'm leaving in the morning."

"I'd like to see you again."

Youssef knew exactly what he wanted to see. Another fifty-dollar bill. "I'll let you know when I get back to town."

"I don't have a telephone, but you can leave a message for me with the bartender."

"Okay," Youssef said.

The man left and Youssef sank into the sleep of the dead. Now the damned telephone would not stop ringing. If Baydr were still in town, he would have leapt for the phone, but Baydr had left for Japan last night.

The phone in the bedroom stopped ringing, but started up in the living room. Youssef pulled one of the pillows over his head and tried to get back to sleep, but a moment later the bedroom phone began again.

Cursing, Youssef reached for it. "Hello," he growled hoarsely.

The words were spoken in French but with a heavy Arabic accent. "Monsieur Ziad?"

Automatically Youssef answered in Arabic. "Yes."

The voice switched to their native language. "We have not met in person but we have spoken over the telephone. And we were at the same party aboard the Al Fay yacht, the night of Madame Al Fay's birthday. My name is Ali Yasfir."

"Ahlan wa Sahlan," Youssef said, now wide awake. He knew of Ali Yasfir.

"Ahlan fik," Yasfir replied formally.

"How may I serve you?" Youssef asked politely.

"If you can arrange the time, I would like to meet with you on matters of important mutual interest."

"Where are you?"

"Here in Los Angeles. Perhaps we might take lunch together?"

"It can be arranged. Where would you like to meet?"

"Anywhere. At your convenience."

"One o'clock. In the Polo Lounge, here in the hotel."

He put down the telephone. He knew the results of Baydr's last meeting with Yasfir. He was also sure that Yasfir knew that he knew. Still, something big had to be under way for Yasfir to contact him. Yasfir usually went right to the top.

He reached for the telephone again. "Good morning, Mr. Ziad," the operator said cheerfully.

"Would you ring Mr. Vincent's room for me." There was no way he could have two lunches at the same time. Vincent would have to be put off.

IN accordance with Arab custom, Ali Yasfir did not come to the point of the meeting until their coffee had been placed before them. "I understand your importing company is beginning to bring many things from abroad into the United States."

Youssef nodded. "That is true. It is amazing to discover how many things we can have manufactured in the Middle East that Americans will buy."

"I also understand that it is your responsibility to discover the small factories in the Middle East whose products you think can be marketed in America."

Youssef nodded.

"I, too, represent certain manufacturers who are desirous of expediting shipment of their products to the United States. At the moment we deal with the European exporters and we are having many problems with them."

Youssef was silent. He knew of the problems. Too many shipments had been intercepted by the Federal Bureau of Narcotics. There were rumors in the Middle East that certain inportant people were very disappointed in Yasfir's performance. "I had understood that you were moving a great portion of your operation to South America," he said.

"That is true"—Yasfir nodded—"but that is part of our expansion program. The demand for our other products is as great as ever."

"I wish I could be of service to you," Youssef said smoothly. "But Mr. Al Fay has already formed our policy and I doubt whether he would change his mind on my advice."

"I'm sure that Mr. Al Fay does not concern himself with the details of each item that you import. I'm sure that is left in your more than capable hands."

That was true. Baydr did not have to know. Thousands of dollars' worth of small items were shipped, and without his knowing what they were.

"A most lucrative arrangement would be made for you if we find a way to work together." Ali Yasfir smiled. "You know the prices our merchandise brings. Sometimes as much as a million dollars for a shipment that takes no more space than a crate of dolls from Egypt. You could enjoy a bonus of ten percent merely for your good offices. There would be no risk involved."

Youssef looked at him. It was a lot of money. Reluctantly, he shook his head. He hated to let it pass. But despite what Yasfir said, it was too risky. Sooner or later, there would be a leak. And then, it would all be over. "I'm sorry," he said. "At this time we do not have the facilities. Our operation is just beginning. Perhaps, later, when we are bigger and better equipped."

Ali Yasfir nodded. He was satisfied. Sooner or later, Youssef would agree. It was simply a question of raising the stakes until it reached the point where he couldn't resist. "You think about it. We will talk again when you return to Paris."

"Yes," Youssef said. "Perhaps by then the situation will change."

Ali Yasfir raised his coffee cup. "Mr. Al Fay is on his way to Japan?"

Youssef nodded. He had never realized that they kept such a close watch on Baydr's movements.

"His negotiation with the Japanese is very enterprising," Ali Yasfir said.

"I know very little about it," Youssef said quickly.

Yasfir smiled. "Even more important than the little business we discussed would be an association with him. He is very highly regarded by us."

"By everyone," Youssef added.

"Still, we feel that he could be more influential in our cause," Yasfir said. "If he were to become more assertive, perhaps it would have a greater influence on those who, like him, hold more conservative views."

Youssef didn't speak. Yasfir was right. This was a great deal more important than the transshipment of narcotics.

"If you could find a way to influence him to support our cause," Yasfir said, "you would spend the rest of your days in luxury and Allah would shower His blessings on you for the help given to His oppressed people."

"Mr. Al Fay is not a man who is easily influenced."

"He is human," Yasfir answered. "A way will be found. Sooner or later."

Youssef signaled for the check and signed it. On their way out of the Polo Lounge, they ran into Jordana.

"I thought Mr. Vincent was joining you for lunch," she said, "and I just was going to stop by and tell him that I would be happy to attend the party tonight."

"I will tell him," Youssef said. "Perhaps we can go together."

She noticed Ali Yasfir standing nearby. He bowed.

"Madame Al Fay," he said. "So nice to see you again."

Youssef saw the puzzled look on her face. "You remember Mr. Yasfir," he said quickly. "He was at your birthday party on the boat."

"Of course," she said. "How are you, Mr. Yasfir?"

He bowed again. "I am fine, and you are even more beautiful than I remembered. But I must apologize. I am already late for an appointment."

She watched him hurry down the lobby then turned back to Youssef. "I hope Baydr does not have any business with that man," she said.

Youssef was surprised. It was the first time he had ever heard her say anything about Baydr's business associates. "I don't think so," he answered. Then his curiosity overcame him. "What makes you say that?"

A veil seemed to drop over her eyes. "I don't know," she answered. "Maybe it's woman's intuition. But I sense something dangerous in him."

CHAPTER 15.

JORDANA glanced around the large darkened living room and reached for her glass of wine. The other guests sat on couches and chairs around the room, staring in absorption at the big motion picture screen at the far end. It was not the fun kind of Hollywood party she had expected. It had all been rather solemn and dull.

She looked toward the back of the room where the host sat by himself at the bar, his back to the screen. It seemed that the moment the picture had begun he had lost all interest in his guests. Maybe that was what was called the star's privilege.

Rick Sullivan had been a film star for many years in what was called the big picture, the kind of spectacle that had been made by C. B. DeMille and more recently by Michael Vincent but was no longer in vogue. Actually Sullivan had played the lead in Michael's film about Moses and that was the reason for this dinner. The word had gone out in Hollywood that Michael was about to make another big score and Sullivan thought it would not be a bad idea to remind the director that he was still around.

Not that he needed the money. Or the work. For the past five years, he had had one of the most successful series on television. But for his own ego television was not the same as motion pictures.

He did not like large parties so he had kept his guest list to about sixteen. Of course, his agent and his publicity man were there, as well as one of Hollywood's leading columnists. Other guests were mutual friends of Vincent's and his, several actors and actresses who were not important enough to threaten his status as the star of the evening.

Sullivan turned from the bar and saw the look of complete boredom on Jordana's face as she watched the screen. She had not been at all what he had expected.

For some reason, he had expected an older woman. Perhaps it was because he assumed that a man with as much money as her husband was reputed to have should be further along in years. He glanced across the room, looking for the man called Ziad who had come with them. He was sitting next to Vincent on the large couch. At first he'd thought the man might be the woman's lover but then he dismissed that idea. The man was clearly a homosexual. He had to be a watchdog.

Dinner had been pleasant, the conversation self-serving and filled with mutual flattery. Everybody loved everybody—typical Hollywood table talk. At the end of the meal, he announced that he had obtained a print of Michael Vincent's great film and was about to screen it for them. Michael was pleased and the guests seemed happy as they went into the living room to take their places in front of the screen.

Rick picked up his drink, walked over to Jordana and sat down in the chair next to hers. He looked up at the screen, then almost immediately turned away. It was one of the early scenes where the young Moses first confronted the Pharaoh. It had been almost twenty years since the film had been made and he hated to look at pictures of himself as a young man. They made him too aware of his age.

He saw her watching him, and smiled ruefully. "I don't like to watch myself. I think it's the height of vanity or something."

"I can imagine that might be a problem," she said politely.

"You don't seem too interested in the picture either."

"I've already seen it," she answered frankly. "It wasn't my thing at that time either."

He laughed. "What kind of pictures do you like?"

She thought for a moment. "Modern pictures. You know, the kind of pictures they make today."

"You don't mean the X-rated pictures?"

"I've never seen an X picture."

He looked at her for a moment. "Would you like to see one?"

She met his gaze. "I suppose so. But I can't imagine going into one of those sleazy theaters."

"You don't have to do that. I can arrange a screening for you."

"That might be interesting. When do you think you might be able to do it?"

"How about right now?" he asked. He saw the puzzled expression on her face as she glanced quickly around the room. "In another room, of course."

"But what about the others?" she asked.

"They won't miss us. This picture runs another two and a half hours. We'll be back before then."

No one even looked up as they left the room. She followed him into the hallway and then to his suite. He closed the door behind him. He gestured casually. "I hope you don't mind watching it in my bedroom?"

"Not at all," she said. "But I don't see a screen."

He laughed, pressing a button on the wall. There was a whir of machinery and a platform dropped from the ceiling over the foot of the bed. On the platform was a giant television set, angled downward. "I've had the films transferred to videotape," he said. "The only handicap is that you have to watch from the bed."

"The bed doesn't look that uncomfortable."

"I'll have to put a tape on the machine," he said. "I'll be back in a moment."

"Okay."

He started for the door, then stopped and gestured toward the night table. "The silver box has cigarettes of the finest Colombian grass; the pink glass bottle with the gold spoons around it holds the best coke in town."

"Lovely," she smiled. "Then may I ask you to bring back a bottle of cold white wine. Dope always dehydrates me."

When he came back, she was lying naked on the bed, holding a joint carefully between her fingers. The film was already in progress.

Quickly, he stripped and sat down on the bed beside her. He reached for the coke bottle and a spoon. "How about a hit?" he asked. "This stuff will blow your mind."

"Sounds good."

He took a heavy snort up each nostril, then held the spoon for her. He could see her eyes brighten as the dope hit her. "How is it?" he asked.

"Couldn't be better." She reached for him. "You are a big man."

"I used to think so, until I saw that little man up there on the screen. He's really big."

She giggled. "I don't believe it. He's got to be a freak." She stared at the screen fascinated. "Oh, no!"

she exclaimed. "That girl can't take it all in her mouth. It has to be a trick."

"It's no trick," he said. "Since this picture has come out, she's made a fortune teaching Beverly Hills ladies how to do it. It's all in the way you relax your throat, she says."

She leaned over, her tongue delicately licking at him. "I'll be happy if I can take half of yours."

He laughed aloud and she looked up at him questioningly. "You know, when I first met you, I thought you were a very straight lady."

"I am a very straight lady." She smiled demurely. "I've never watched a fuck movie before." Then she went down on him.

"Beautiful," he said, watching her as he reached down the side of the bed to press the invisible button that would start the videotape recorder. He didn't tell her that the only pictures he liked to watch of himself were those taken in this bed by a hidden camera. "Just beautiful."

AFTER a while Youssef grew tired. It seemed the movie would never come to an end. Idly he glanced around the room. Suddenly the picture was forgotten. Jordana was gone. And so was the host. He was angry with himself. He had not seen them leave.

He rose from his seat. Vincent looked at him. "I have to go to the bathroom," he explained in a whisper. He tiptoed silently from the room and stood in the corridor.

It was a large house. They could be in any one of a half-dozen rooms. He tried the study, the dining room, the breakfast room, the patio, but they were nowhere to be found.

Annoyed, he went into the bathroom and washed his face and hands with cold water. He was stupid. He should have known she would be off with him. He was a big man, attractive and, most of all, a movie star. He was nothing like the gigolos she found on the Riviera.

He came out of the bathroom and walked down the hall toward the living room. It was then that he noticed the whir of machinery coming from behind the closed door. He paused, thinking it might be the air-conditioning unit. The Americans had a way of installing that kind of equipment in closets. But then he heard the faint hum of what sounded like voices coming from a speaker. He reached for the knob. The door wouldn't open. It was locked.

He looked around quickly to make sure the corridor was empty. Youssef had learned many tricks, including the use of plastic credit cards.

A moment later the closet door was open and Youssef was staring in surprise at the small monitor of a videotape recorder. The sound volume was depressed but the picture was in color and bright as day. Jordana was naked, on her back, her face contorted in the throes of orgasm. She seemed to be staring directly up into the camera as her legs gripped tightly around the waist of the man who was bucking like a bronco rider. The faint echo of her gasp whined in the speaker as the man began to spend himself inside her. Then slowly he rolled over on his side and came out of her, damp and already softening. He turned toward Jordana and smiled, his hand dropping to the side of the bed. Youssef had just enough time to recognize the face of their host before the screen went black.

He was frozen for a moment, then moved quickly. He knew the machine. Baydr had the same system installed on the boat, but only the playback units, not the recorder. Youssef depressed the key which released the videotape cartridge and took it from the machine. Placing it under his jacket, he stepped back into the corridor. He closed the door and heard the lock click.

He walked down the hall to the foyer. A servant rose from a seat near the front door, and he opened it as Youssef approached.

"Is the gentleman leaving?" he asked.

"No. I just thought I could use a moment of fresh air."

"Very good, sir," the servant said, closing the door behind him.

Youssef walked to his car. The chauffeur came out of the front seat. "Is my attaché case still in the trunk?" Youssef asked.

"Yes, sir." The chauffeur went to the back of the car and opened the trunk. He took out the case and gave it to Youssef. Quickly, Youssef placed the video cassette inside and locked it. He gave it to the chauffeur. "Remind me to take it when we go back to the hotel tonight."

"Yes, sir."

Youssef watched the man replace it in the trunk, then went back into the house. He could feel his heart pounding. This was even more than he had planned, more than he had hoped for. Now it was simply a matter of deciding when it should be used.

He slipped back into the seat beside Vincent and looked up at the screen. Vincent turned to him and whispered, "Rick made a fantastic Moses, don't you think?"

"Yes," Youssef answered. "How did you know he'd be so good in the part?"

Vincent turned to him with a smile. "I couldn't go wrong," he said. "Sullivan changed his name from Solomon when he went into pictures. How could a Solomon be bad at playing Moses?"

Youssef stared at the closeup of Moses that filled the entire screen. Of course. He wondered why he had not seen it before. The man had the face of a Jew.

There was a sound at the back of the room. Jordana and Rick were back. From the corner of his eye he watched them cross to the bar and sit there. He saw Rick glance over his shoulder at the screen and say something to her. She laughed and picked up the fresh glass of wine the barman had placed before her.

Youssef felt a rush of hatred. "Laugh, you bitch!"

he thought savagely. "That's it. Laugh, you Jew-fuck-ing bitch!"

He knew now exactly what he was going to do with the tapes. Baydr would be eternally grateful to him for protecting his name by keeping from the world the knowledge that his wife had betrayed him with a Jew.

CHAPTER 16.

LEILA looked across the room at her mother. "I told you, Mother, many times. Hamid is just a friend, that's all. I am not serious about him. I do not intend to marry him. He's just a friend."

Maryam sighed heavily. "I don't know what's wrong with you. He's just an ordinary Syrian, not even from a good family. I can't imagine what you see in him."

Leila lit a cigarette. "I have to talk to someone."

"There are many nice boys you can talk to. My father said the industrialist Fawaz spoke to him. His son is of the marrying age and they are interested in you."

"Who?" Leila asked sarcastically. "Fawaz or his son?"

"Don't be disrespectful. Grandfather means nothing but the best for you."

"Like he did for you?" Leila asked pointedly.

"It wasn't his fault," Maryam said defensively. "None of us knew then what your father was like. We did everything correctly. No one can point a finger at us."

"I don't see anyone pointing a finger at my father

either," Leila said. "Apparently nobody cares what you do as long as you have enough money."

Maryam shook her head in exasperation. "It's just as I've always said, you take after your father more than you do me. You only see things the way you want to see them. I should never have allowed you to go away to school in Switzerland. The only thing they taught you was how to talk back to your mother. Your sister doesn't act like that."

"My sister is stupid!" Leila snapped. "All she cares about is her home and her children and her problems with servants."

"That's all a woman has to care about," Maryam said. "What else is there?"

Leila gestured toward the window. "There's a whole world out there, Mother. Can't you see it? For too many years we've been oppressed, our people have been ridiculed and enslaved. Our brothers cry under the yoke of the Jews in Palestine. And you ask what else there is."

"Those are the problems that men must solve," Maryam said. "We should attend to our own affairs."

"There's no use," Leila said in disgust. She walked to the door. "I'm going out."

"Where are you going? To meet that Hamid again?"

"No. Just out. That's all."

"What's the hurry then? It's almost dinnertime."

"I'm not hungry. Don't wait for me."

Maryam watched the door close behind her. A few minutes later she heard the car start up in front of the house. She got out of her chair and walked to the window just in time to see the small Mercedes convertible turn into the street.

Leila was like her father. There was no one who could talk to her. She thought about the day last month when she had shown up at the front door with her friend the Syrian, Hamid. They were so ragged and dirty that at first the servant, who was new to the house, would not let them in. Finally, reluctantly, she had called her mistress.

Maryam was shocked at the way her daughter looked. Her skin was dark and leathery as if she had spent days in the desert sun, and there wasn't a curve on her body. She was as thin and straight as a boy.

"What happened?" she cried.

"Nothing, Mother," Leila replied calmly.

"But, look at you, you're in rags. You look as if you hadn't had a bath in months."

"I'm all right, Mother," Leila said stubbornly.

"Where did you come from? I thought you were still in school."

"We hitched our way home," Leila answered.

"What for? All you had to do was telephone. We would have bought you a ticket."

"If I had wanted a ticket, I would have called. I wanted to do it this way."

For the first time, Maryam noticed Hamid, standing outside the threshold. She looked at him, then at her daughter.

"This is my friend Hamid," Leila said. "He's Syrian."

Hamid took a step forward. He touched his finger to his forehead. "Tasharrafna."

"Hasalli sharaf," she replied automatically. She did not add the other customary words of welcome.

"I met Hamid on the road," Leila said. "He's on his way home to Damascus."

Maryam said nothing.

"He was very nice to me," Leila said. "If it weren't for him, I might have had some trouble."

Maryam turned back to the Syrian. "Enter," she said. "And make yourself welcome in our house."

He bowed again. "Thank you, madame, but I have some friends I can stay with."

She did not demur. He seemed too coarse and common. But then so did most Syrians.

"I am glad you are home," he said to Leila. "Now I must be going."

Leila held out her hand to him. "You will get in touch with me before you leave Beirut?"

He nodded, and they shook hands. Despite their formality, Maryam sensed the familiarity between them. "I will call you," he said.

But that had been almost a month ago and still he had not left Beirut. What he was doing, she did not know. But she did know that he and Leila met almost every day at the Phoenicia Hotel. She had been told that by friends who had seen them sitting in the coffee shop drinking Coca-Colas.

SHE parked the car in the street and went into the coffee shop through the outside entrance. She did not like to walk through the ornate lobby with its crowds of packaged American and European tourists. He was sitting alone at his usual table in the corner near a window. The inevitable Coca-Cola with its slice of lemon was in front of him. He looked up as she sat down opposite him. Without a word, the waitress brought her a Coca-Cola.

He waited until the waitress had gone. "I'm leaving tomorrow," he said.

She looked at him. His face was expressionless. "Home?" she asked.

"Might as well," he said. "There's nothing going on here and I had a letter from my cousin. I can get a sergeant's job in the army with time and bonuses. They're recruiting veterans with experience."

"I don't understand it," she said. "I haven't heard a word and it's almost a month now."

He shrugged.

"Maybe they think I was killed with all the others."

"They know you're here. I told them when I went in to collect my last pay."

"Then why don't they call me? I'm going crazy waiting around here. My mother never stops nagging me."

"They have other things on their mind. There was a story going around that Al-Ikhwah wanted your father to handle their foreign investments."

"I know. He turned them down. That happened before I left France." She sipped her drink through the straw. "They're crazy. My father won't lift a finger to help anyone but himself."

"They're going back to him again. They seem to think he's important."

"I wish them luck. There's only one way they'll ever get him to help them. At the point of a gun."

"What makes you say that?"

"I know my father. He still thinks that money will cure everything."

"Anyway I'm leaving tomorrow. That army job is better than nothing."

"Maybe I should go down and talk to them. I didn't get all that training to sit here in my mother's house."

"Don't do that," he said quickly. "Your orders were to wait until you were contacted."

She looked at him. "Do you have to go?"

"I have to do something. My money's almost gone."

"I have money."

"No."

She was silent for a moment, staring down at her drink, then she looked up at him. "I was hoping we would be sent on a mission together."

"I'm not the type," he said. "They would rather have students for missions. People pay less attention to them."

"You're not that old. You could still pass for a student," she said quickly.

"Maybe," he laughed. "In the dark."

"If you go back in the Syrian army, they'll never let you get out."

"Maybe I won't want to. The way we're building up and the way Egypt is preparing, the chances are something is going to happen. And if there is a war, I can make officer."

"Is that what you want?"

"No."

"What do you want then?"

"Just to make a lot of money"—he smiled—"like your father."

"Stop talking about him!" she snapped, suddenly

angry. That's all I hear everywhere I go. My father this, my father that. Even my mother never stops talking about him."

"Did you see the paper today?" he asked.

"No."

"You should have. Maybe then you would know why they talk about your father."

"What did he do?"

"He just closed the biggest oil tanker deal ever made with Japan. He bought ten ships and they're building twenty more for him. All supertankers. It will be the largest Arab-owned shipping line in the world."

"Allah be praised," she said sarcastically. "How much richer does that make him?"

"At least he's doing something. There's no reason for the Greeks and all the others to monopolize the shipping from our ports."

"How does that help the Palestinians?" she asked.

He was silent.

"I'm sorry," she said quickly. "I didn't mean to quarrel with you. I'm just getting edgy sitting around."

"That's all right."

She looked at him. "Would you like me to go back to your room with you?"

"Okay," he said, then he smiled. "But is it all right with you if we go to a movie first? The only pictures playing in Damascus are at least ten years old."

BAYDR felt the warm sake buzzing in his head as he put down his cup. Almost as soon as it touched the table, the geisha sitting on her knees just behind him filled the tiny cup. Baydr looked at it. He wasn't used to drinking. A glass of champagne occasionally but no more. And though he had only had three of the tiny cups he felt them.

"Enough," he said, starting to get up. He felt slightly dizzy as he rose. The geisha was there to help him as soon as he put out his hand. He smiled at her. "Sleep," he said.

She looked at him blankly.

"Sleep," he repeated. He placed the palms of his hands together and held them at the side of his face, closing his eyes.

"Hai! Hai! Sleep."

He nodded.

Still holding one arm under his elbow, she reached out and slid back the screen separating the rooms. She led him into the bedroom and closed the panel behind her. The bed was very low to the floor and he almost fell backward as he sat down on it. He thought that was very funny and began to laugh. She laughed with him.

"I almost fell."

"Hai, hai," she said, reaching behind him and pulling open the sash that held his robe. Gently she slipped it from his shoulders and he rolled back onto the bed as she pulled it from him.

"Tired," he mumbled into the pillow. He rolled onto his stomach, face down. As if from a great distance, he heard the gentle rustle of her kimona. He smelled the faint perfume of the talcum powder settling on his skin like a soft cloud.

Her hands felt like gentle feathers as they softly stroked his back, her fingers tracing his spine from his neck to his coccyx. A moment later, she began kneading his flesh with slightly warmed oil. He sighed in contentment.

Her hands went down his back, cupping and stroking his buttocks. Then he felt her slowly part them, and gently place a probing finger inside him. She found his prostate and massaged it in a circular motion.

Almost asleep, he felt himself growing hard and began to move to his side. Gently but firmly, she held him so that he could not move. Her other hand, moist with the warm oil, began to stroke his throbbing phallus.

He tried to move with her but couldn't. Then he became aware that there was not one but two geishas in the room. The second woman came around the other side of the bed and knelt before him. Now there were four hands instead of two. There was no part of him that was not being touched, stroked, caressed all at the same time.

The pressure on his prostate and testicles, the increasing rapidity of the moving hand on his penis became too much. He felt himself begin to contract into a knot. The agony became almost unbearable. A groan escaped him. He opened his eyes.

The tiny Japanese woman still clad in her kimono smiled sweetly at him. Then she opened her mouth to gently encircle his glans. The explosion came and for a moment he felt close to death as the semen flooded forth like a gusher. Explosion followed explosion until he was completely drained and all that was left was a mildly pleasant emptiness.

He was still watching the tiny geisha as she rose to her feet and moved silently away. He felt other hands draw the soft sheets around him. He closed his eyes and fell into dreamless sleep.

When he awakened it seemed as if he had slept for only a few minutes. But it was broad daylight and Jabir was standing over his bed.

"I'm sorry to disturb you, master," he said, "but this cable just arrived and Mr. Carriage said it was most important."

He sat up slowly and took the yellow sheet. The message was simple and one that only he and the Prince could understand.

THE DATE HAS BEEN SET FOR THE INVESTITURE OF YOUR SON AS MY HEIR. PLEASE RETURN AT ONCE TO COMPLETE ALL ARRANGEMENTS. [signed] FEIYAD, PRINCE.

He was wide awake now. He knew that it had nothing to do with his son. A long time ago they had agreed on the meaning of this message.

War. War with Israel. The time to avenge themselves for the defeat of 1967 was close at hand. Or so they thought. A feeling of sadness came over him.

It was too soon. Much too soon. Perhaps they would win a minor victory at first, but the Israelis were too experienced for them. If the war ràn more than a week it would mean another defeat for the Arabs.

Even the Prince agreed with him about that. But there was much to be done. If the world thought they were united perhaps more than a minor victory could be won. Not on the battlefield where men died, but in the banks and boardrooms where they lived.

ANOTHER PLACE: OCTOBER 1973

THE dusty dung-colored Volkswagen, its paint pocked by years of desert sand and wind, coughed and sputtered to a stop a few yards short of the parking lot gate. The sentries watched curiously as the old man in equally dusty Bedouin robes climbed out and walked around behind the car. He raised the trunk lid, exposing the engine, and stared at it dolefully.

One of the sentries walked over. "What is the trouble, old man?"

"I wish I knew. Even a camel needs water sometimes. But this creature—I tell you there is something ungodly about a creature that never needs water. If it were a camel I would know what to do."

The young soldier laughed. "What would you do if it were a camel?"

"I would give it some water. Then, if that didn't work, I would kick it in the ass."

"Why don't you try that?" the soldier suggested.

"I already did. It doesn't work. Nothing works."

Leaving the old man staring at the engine, the soldier looked into the car. The interior was as decrepit as the exterior. The upholstery was in ribbons, and the gauges were encrusted with a layer of dust. The soldier reached in and wiped the dirt from the gas gauge, then he straightened up and turned to the old man. "You're out of gas."

"I don't understand that. It never happened before."

"It's happened now," the soldier said, with a faintly condescending air.

The old man shrugged. "Oh, well, I'm glad it was nothing serious. I was afraid the poor thing had died." He started for the gate. "Push it over to the side," he called back over his shoulder. "I'll send someone out to fill the tank."

"Wait a minute, old man!" The sentry ran in front of him. "You can't go in there without a pass. That's a top-level security area."

"I have a pass," the old man said, holding out his hand. The sun reflected from the plastic card like a mirror.

The soldier took the card, looked at it and snapped to rigid attention. "I beg your pardon, general," he said, saluting.

Ben Ezra returned his salute. "It's all right, soldier. At ease."

The young man relaxed. "Do you know the way, sir?" he asked respectfully.

"I know the way," Ben Ezra smiled. He held out his hand. "May I have the pass back?"

"Yes, sir," the sentry said quickly. "And don't worry about your car, sir. We'll take care of it."

The general smiled. "Thank you." He turned and started off, his Bedouin robes flowing gently with his stride.

"Who was that?" the other sentry asked curiously.

The first soldier's voice was hushed and respectful. "General Ben Ezra."

"The Lion of the Desert?" There was a note of surprise in the other soldier's voice. He turned to look after the old man. "I thought he was dead."

"Well, he's not," the first soldier said. "Come on. Give me a hand with the general's car."

THERE were only five men seated around the table in the conference room. The three Americans who had attended the earlier meeting, Ben Ezra and General Eshnev.

"I'm sorry for the small turnout, gentlemen," Eshnev apologized. "But all the others are at the front."

"No need to apologize," Weygrin said. "We understand." He smiled. "Incidentally, congratulations. Your boys did a good job of boxing in the Egyptian Third Army."

Eshnev nodded grimly. "You're anticipating. We're not that sure yet."

"You've got them," the American colonel said confidently.

"We still need help," Eshnev said. "Lots of help. We paid too high a price letting them get the jump on us."

"Who ever would have thought they would launch the attack on Yom Kippur?" Harris of the State Department asked, trying to be consoling.

Ben Ezra's voice was matter of fact. "I did. I thought I made that very clear at our last meeting."

"It was a wild guess," Harris said defensively.

"Everything's guesswork," Ben Ezra said quietly. "But even if it hadn't been, you people weren't going to do anything about it, were you?"

Harris didn't answer.

"Tell me," the old general's voice was confidential. "Did you report back to your chief?"

Harris nodded. "Of course."

Ben Ezra looked at him. He shook his head sadly. "All this tragedy could have been prevented."

"I don't see how," Harris said.

"We should have done what we did the last time. The war would have been over now."

"And world opinion would have been against you," Harris said.

"A lot of good world opinion is doing us now," Ben Ezra retorted. "I don't see any armies coming in to help us."

"It's all after the fact," Eshnev said quickly. "That's not the purpose of this meeting, general. We're here to listen to your evaluation of the present situation."

"So that you can ignore it as you did the last time," Ben Ezra said sarcastically. He saw the expression of hurt in Eshnev's eyes and was instantly contrite. "I'm sorry, my friend," he said in a gentler voice. "I forgot that your frustrations must be even greater than mine."

Eshnev didn't answer.

Ben Ezra looked across the table at the Americans. "It is lonely when you grow old," he said.

No one at the table spoke.

"Would you gentlemen be kind enough to answer a question for me?" he asked. "Tell me, why are you at this meeting? It must be as obvious to you as it is to me that nothing will come of it, nothing will be changed, nothing will be done."

"That's not true, General Ben Ezra," Colonel Weygrin said quickly. "We have the highest respect for your opinions and ideas."

Ben Ezra smiled. "And I for yours. If only I could understand them. I still can't make up my mind whether you love us or hate us."

Again Eshnev tried to bring the meeting back on track. "You received the Al Fay file?"

"Yes," Ben Ezra nodded.

"What conclusions do you draw from it?"

"If the Arabs were smart they would disband their armies, find three more like him and conquer the world without firing a shot."

"How could that be done?" Harris asked.

Ben Ezra permitted himself a smile. "Simply enough. They would buy the world."

No one laughed.

"The war is already lost, you know that," the old man said.

"What do you mean?" Weygrin asked. "It's not over yet. The Israelis are on the move into Egypt and Syria. Sadat is already talking peace. He knows when he's licked."

"He knows when he's won," Ben Ezra said dryly. "What he wanted to do was to restore Arab pride. He's done that. The Arab soldiers have fought bravely. Their honor has been restored. That was what he set out to do." He reached into his robe and took out a sheet of paper. "We might still win this war but it depends on how much time you will allow us."

"I don't quite understand," Harris said.

"We need two more weeks," Ben Ezra said. "Egypt is no longer important. We must bypass Cairo, occupy Libya on one side and take Syria. If we do that, we break the back of the threatened oil blockade; if we do not, then it's just a question of time and we will be isolated."

"What have we got to do with giving you time?" Harris asked. "Russia is already putting on the pressure for a cease-fire."

Ben Ezra looked at him. "You can't be that stupid." He shook his head sadly. "Where was Russia when the Arabs were winning? Trying to protect us with a cease-fire demand? No. They were silent until the tide of battle had turned. Now they want a cease-fire to protect their gains. The Arabs have come up with a better weapon than they ever dreamed of—an oil embargo. That can stop the Western world faster than an atom bomb.

"If we control the oil of Libya and the Syrian pipelines, the embargo would fall apart. We could supply the whole world if we had to. Iran is already in the Western camp, Jordan would jump in quickly and there would be no threat.

"But if we do not, the whole world economy may come tumbling down around our ears. The Arabs will split the world. France will immediately try to leap into the breach and break the European entente. Japan will be forced to go along because they get eighty percent of their oil from the Arabs. Bit by bit, the Arabs will turn the countries of the world away from us. And I would not blame them, because their own survival is as important to them as ours is to us."

"If you pushed the war into Syria and Libya, Russia might intervene," Harris said.

"I doubt it," Ben Ezra said. "They are as fearful as you are of a confrontation."

"That's your opinion," Harris said coldly.

"True," the old man said. "Still, if your Mr. Kissinger would slow down just a little, we could accomplish it."

Harris looked at Eshnev. "Fortunately this is not your government's policy."

Eshnev nodded reluctantly. "It is not."

Harris turned back to Ben Ezra. "It is Mr. Kissinger's hope to have an effective cease-fire agreement in two days."

"My congratulations to Mr. Kissinger." Ben Ezra's voice was sarcastic. "He may yet prove himself the Neville Chamberlain of the seventies."

"I think this discussion is beyond the scope of our meeting," Harris said stiffly, "and should be dealt with on a higher level. What we are most interested in now is what we can say about Al Fay."

Ben Ezra looked at him. "I don't think there is anything we can do about him except to pray that he continues to resist the pressures from the left and holds as close as he can to the middle course. He certainly isn't interested in turning his wealth and power over to the masses, any more than any of the other rich sheiks. But they are all walking a narrow line. How long they can maintain it is anyone's guess." He turned to Eshnev. "Have you had any further information about him since the war began?"

"Very little," Eshnev replied. "Communication has been difficult. Al Fay was called home just before the conflict began and has remained there ever since. We know that he is going to head up the unified investment committee for all the oil-producing countries but that the actual oil negotiations are to be conducted by a joint committee of the foreign ministers of those countries. They are being very cautious about separating the exploitation of oil as a political tool and the use of the money they receive from its sale. Internally, they are deemphasizing the profit line. The new line is 'Oil for justice.' "

"Do you think he will have any influence over the oil policies?" Harris asked.

"Very little at first," Eshnev said. "Perhaps more later when they realize that slowing down or collapsing the world economy will only result in losses of their own investments. I think Al Fay and his Prince Feiyad recognize that and that is the reason he took over that committee rather than playing a more political role. By virtue of being nonpolitical he will be in a good position to negotiate freely with both sides."

"Where is his family?" Ben Ezra asked.

"His wife and sons are still in Beirut," Eshnev answered. "Also his ex-wife and daughter."

"The one that was in the Swiss school?" the old man asked curiously.

"Yes," Eshnev answered.

"Not anymore." For the first time the CIA agent spoke. "The younger daughter, Leila, left three days ago on a flight to Rome. There was another girl and a young man with her."

Eshnev was surprised. "How did you happen to find out?"

"The young man," Smith answered. "We've had him under surveillance for a long time. He was mixed up in the drug traffic in Vietnam and lately moved over to the Middle East." He reached for a cigarette. "He used to be associated with the Mafia but recently went to work for Ali Yasfir."

"What's the connection with the Al Fay girl?" the old man asked.

"We're checking into it," Smith said. "I have some information already. She left school last spring for guerrilla training. For some reason, after she got out she spent the entire summer at home. Then this man contacted her and in less than a week they took off."

"Does our intelligence have this information?" Eshnev asked.

"Yes. I passed it on to them the same day I got it."

"Are they still in Rome?" Eshnev asked.

"I don't know," Smith answered. "They split up at the airport. The girls got in one taxi and the man in another. My man could only follow one cab. He stuck with the man."

"Is the man still in Rome?" Eshnev asked.

"Yes. In the morgue. He was killed two hours after he arrived. The police think it was a gang killing. It probably was. The Mafia doesn't like losing one of its soldiers to the competition."

"We should locate the girl," the old man said.

"I'll have our people get on it," Eshnev replied. He got to his feet. "I guess that does it, gentlemen. Unless you have anything further to discuss?"

The Americans looked at one another. The meeting was over. They rose and shook hands. Colonel Weygrin and Harris were very formal with the old man but Smith was different.

He wrinkled up his face as he stared up at Ben Ezra. "You know, general," he said in his nasal Midwestern voice, "you're absolutely right. I wish more of our people would listen to you."

"Thank you, Mr. Smith. I wish they would too."

"You have my card," the CIA man said. "Give me a call if there's anything I can do for you."

"Thank you again," Ben Ezra said.

The Americans left the room and the two Israelis looked at one another. "What do you think, Isaiah?" Eshnev asked.

The old man shrugged. "Do you speak Yiddish, Lev?"

"No," Eshnev answered. "I'm sabra. I never learned it."

"They have a saying," the old man said. "I think

it originated many years ago in Poland or Russia during one of the pogroms. 'Schver tzu zahn a Yid.' "

"What does that mean?" Eshnev asked.

The old man smiled, but there was no humor in it. "It's tough to be a Jew," he said.

BOOK THREE

The End of Autumn

1973

CHAPTER 1.

DICK Carriage knocked on the door of Baydr's bedroom. Baydr's voice came through the door, slightly muffled. "Come in."

Dick opened the door and blinked for a moment. The drapes were drawn wide and the room was flooded with the Swiss morning sun. Baydr was seated at the small desk with his back to the window. His face was shadowed by the light coming from behind him. He looked up at Carriage. "Yes?"

"The French are here, chief."

Baydr looked at his watch. "They're up early."

Carriage smiled. "They're taking no chances. They don't want anyone to get to you before they do."

Baydr laughed. "That's the nice thing about the French. You can always depend on them not to honor any allegiances except to themselves."

"What shall I tell them?"

"Tell them to wait." He held some papers out to Carriage. "What do you know about this?"

Carriage took the report and looked down at it. The block letters printed across the top read: ARABDOLLS LTD. Inside the folder was a series of shipping tickets and billing invoices. Each bill was stamped paid. He looked back at Baydr. "No more than you do, except that they pay their bills promptly."

Baydr took back the folder. "That's just it. It's out of character. Do you know any Lebanese who pays his bills promptly?"

"I don't understand. They're good customers. What have we got to complain about?"

"Another thing," Baydr said. "They're paying premium for express delivery. What the hell is so important about dolls that they should pay premium for shipment? That's out of character too. The Lebanese wouldn't be willing to pay premium for anything even if their lives depended on it."

"Christmas is coming. Maybe they want the dolls in the stores before then."

"Could be if they were shipping now. But they began in September." Baydr gave the file to Carriage. "Get me a rundown on that company."

"Will do, chief." He went to the door. "Anything else?"

Baydr shook his head. "Give the French some coffee. I'll be out in a few minutes."

When the door closed behind Carriage, Baydr rose, opened the French doors behind his desk and went out onto the terrace. The clear morning air held the first promise of the coming Swiss winter. Baydr breathed deeply, taking it into his lungs.

In the distance the mountains loomed clear and blue-green, snow already gracing the peaks. Baydr looked down at the city, which was just coming awake. There was a feeling of excitement in the streets.

Geneva. It was all here. The money, the power, the diplomacy, the trading. This was where the war would be won, not on the battlefields of the Middle East. The banks and trading halls of this strange old Swiss city gave the illusion of being above strife and struggle, but they were willing to take profit from every changing wind no matter what direction it came from.

Baydr went back into his room and looked around. The suite in the hotel was leased on an annual basis and it had served its purpose for his occasional visits. But now, he wondered. For the next year he would have to spend a great deal more time here. It would not be big enough, important enough, for the entertaining he was supposed to do.

The more he thought about it the more sense it began to make. A permanent base here would not be wasted. Besides, the winter season in Switzerland was always good. Between St. Moritz and Gstaad the whole world would be there. And he had no doubt that Jordana would love it, the parties, the social scene, the winter sports.

He made a note to call her later and tell her of his decision. Also to have Carriage let the real estate broker know he was in the market for a home in Geneva and a villa in Gstaad. He was sure he would find something quickly. Money had a way of getting things done.

He walked over to the mirror and looked at himself. In his white shirt and dark slacks, he looked more European than Arab. He went to the closet. A moment later he came out with his robes in his hand. Quickly, he slipped into the dark brown mishlah and the black-banded, white headcloth that fell to his shoulders. Again he looked into the mirror. This time he nodded in satisfaction. Now he looked like an Arab. He smiled to himself as he went to the door. There were advantages in going native. Especially when it came to dealing with the French, who thought themselves superior to everyone on the face of the earth.

"WE are a small country, Monsieur Duchamps," Baydr said in French, "completely landlocked with no access to the sea except through the kindness of our neighbors, so you can very well understand our problem. Water. We have oil but no water. I have heard my prince say many times that he would gladly exchange his surfeit of oil wells for wells pumping water. With water our country would bloom."

Duchamps glanced at his associate and nodded understandingly. "Monsieur Al Fay, France has always been among the first nations in the world to understand the difficulties of the Middle Eastern nations and their desire for self-determination and freedom. We have publicly deplored the exploitation of your resources and have indicated our support of your cause, often to the detriment of our relations with the great powers and against public sentiment. Do you not remember that during the previous conflict in sixty-seven we refused Israel shipment of fifty fighter jet Mirage aircraft?"

"I remember." He did not add that he recalled that France not only refused Israel the shipment but also refused to return to Israel the hundred million dollars they had collected for the aircraft. Still he could not resist a dig. "Ever since you so generously gave Algeria its freedom, you have been in the forefront of those recognizing the great principle of Arab self-determination."

A momentary look of discomfort flashed across the Frenchman's face, then disappeared. "France stands ready now to fill any orders of matériel to the Arab countries. Our factories are in full operation, building planes, autos, tanks, almost anything the Arab world needs to demonstrate its ability to defend itself."

Baydr smiled politely. "I am pleased. I will certainly relay this message to the proper committee. As you know, I am not in military procurement. I have absolutely nothing to do with that. I am in the industrial development area. If you have a machine that will manufacture water I should be most interested."

"There are plants that can manufacture water but unfortunately they require water to start with."

Baydr allowed himself to appear naïve. "Yes?"

"Nuclear desalination plants. They are expensive but they work. Unfortunately your country is landlocked."

"True, but we have agreements with our neighbors —Syria, Iraq, Jordan, Saudi Arabia—to develop water-manufacturing resources for our mutual benefit."

"Do you represent those countries also?" the Frenchman asked.

"For the first time the Arab world is united in this area. Together we will develop our industrial and agricultural potential. We have, for example, reached a new agreement with Fiat of Italy to manufacture a version of their car. The manufacturing plants will be spread among our various countries so that the workers of each will benefit."

"Very commendable," the Frenchman said stiffly.

"Of course, it will cost us slightly more to make these cars ourselves rather than import them. But since we are not interested in profit as much as in the idea of becoming self-sufficient, we feel it very worthwhile. We are also negotiating in other fields such as household appliances and television. It is amazing how much one can do when one is willing to work."

"How much more do you estimate it will cost to make rather than buy these things?" Duchamps asked.

Baydr shrugged. "Fifty percent, one hundred percent. What does it matter? We have the money to pay for it. We can afford it."

The Frenchman was silent for a moment. When he spoke he was not quite as sure of himself as he had been earlier. "We also are interested in aiding your industrial program. I am sure that we can find many projects that would be mutually beneficial. Our manufacturing industry stands second to none in the world."

"I am glad to hear that. What is of special interest to me is your plans for nuclear desalination of water. This is certainly an area that deserves intensive study and one in which we can most certainly work together."

"That is, perhaps, the most expensive project of all," Duchamps said quickly.

"As I said, money is not important. In my small country alone, the revenues from oil exceed one million dollars a day. When you multiply that by the rest of the Arab world the sum becomes astronomical."

"France is not poor. We have all the dollars we need. More than enough in fact."

"I am aware of that, but there are other mediums of exchange, and while I am not in charge of policy my recommendations will be looked on favorably when determinations are made."

The Frenchman looked at him steadily. They both knew what Baydr was saying. The bargaining power was oil, not for money, but for cooperation. "Monsieur Al Fay," he said, "I cannot tell you how pleased I am that we have found an area in which we can cooperate. You can be sure that I will be back to you shortly with several very concrete proposals."

Baydr got to his feet. "I shall look forward to your return with great expectations." The Frenchmen also rose. Baydr bowed formally, making the conventional Arab gesture of farewell. "Go with peace."

Carriage came back into the room the moment the Frenchmen had gone. "They're beginning to back up out there," he said. "It's a minor version of the UN—Germans, Italians, Rumanians, Norwegians."

"It didn't take long for the word to get around, did it?"

Carriage shook his head. They had just arrived the day before. "They're like dogs around a bitch in heat."

Baydr laughed. "Better call the bank and see if they can lend us a couple of secretaries. Then set up an appointment schedule. We'll have to see them all."

"Why? There are very few that will have anything for us."

"I know that, but it doesn't matter. Right now they are all in shock over the embargo. They still don't believe it. When it sinks in, they will be panicky and angry. One of our jobs is to keep as many friends as we can."

"Right, chief." Carriage started for the door.

Baydr stopped him. "Dick, get Mrs. Al Fay on the phone for me. She's in Beirut at my father's house."

"Will do." The door closed behind him and a moment later the telephone rang. The Swiss telephone service prided itself on its efficiency. Jordana was on the line.

"How are the children?" he asked.

Jordana's voice was dull. "Fine."

"Are they enjoying school?"

"I don't know whether they like it or not but they're going."

"Are you very busy?"

A moment's silence. "You've got to be kidding," she said. "I'm in Beirut. There is absolutely nothing for me to do here."

"Then maybe you won't mind coming up here and helping me out. I've decided to get a house here in Geneva and a villa in Gstaad and I'll be too busy to attend to it."

"Baydr, do you mean it?"

"Why shouldn't I mean it? It looks like we'll be spending a great deal of time here in the near future. Will you come?"

She laughed. "I'll be on the next plane."

"Good." He smiled into the telephone. "Let us know the flight and I'll have Jabir pick you up at the airport."

Dick came back into the room as soon as he had put down the telephone. There was a strange look on his face. "There's a girl outside to see you."

Suddenly Baydr was annoyed. "You ought to know better than that, Dick," he said sharply. "I have too much to do to bother with girls today. Send her away."

"I did that once already, sir," Dick said. "But she came back a few minutes later with Jabir. He said you would want to see her."

Baydr found that curious. Usually Jabir never concerned himself with the women. "Who is she?"

"I don't know, sir. Neither she nor Jabir would give me her name. They said they wanted to surprise you."

Baydr thought for a moment. It had to be something important. Jabir wasn't given to playing games. "Okay, I'll see her," he said. "But only for a moment. And tell Jabir that I'm doing this only as a favor to him and that I don't want it repeated."

"Yes, sir."

Baydr walked over to the sideboard and filled a cup with coffee. Holding it in his hand he walked back toward his desk. He heard the door open behind him and turned toward it.

A young woman stood in the doorway almost shyly. Baydr looked at her. There was something vaguely familiar about her. She was beautiful, her face almost heart-shaped, with dark blue eyes and shining black hair that fell past her shoulders. She was dressed in the shirt and blue jeans that most of the young people wore these days, but from what he could see, her figure was good. He noticed the hint of fear creep into her dark blue eyes. Suddenly it all came together.

"Leila!" he exclaimed.

A tremulous smile broke through the fear. "Hello, Father," she said softly.

He crossed the room and took her in his arms.

CHAPTER 2.

"I'M almost nineteen, Father, and it's not happening for me in school," she said. "Too many important things are going on out there and I want to be a part of it."

He smiled. There was so much about her that reminded him of himself. The same impatience, the same curiosity and desire to participate. "Exactly what is it you want to do?"

She was vague. "I don't know. All I know is what I don't want to do. I don't want to be like my sister. I don't want marriage and a family to be the only goals in my life. There must be something I can do."

"Have you talked to your mother about this?"

"You know Mother. She doesn't understand. She thinks I should do exactly what I said I don't want to do. Grandfather even has someone picked out for me to marry."

Baydr was amused. "Your grandfather hasn't changed. I suppose it's a rich man from a very good family?"

"Of course." She laughed. "Grandfather Riad has always been very good at that."

Baydr laughed. "I should know that. But seriously, there are many things you could do. Like teaching. We need all the teachers we can get."

"You mean the accepted ladylike professions." She could not keep the slight note of scorn from her voice. "I don't want that either. I just don't want to do the things that women have been permitted to do for generations. I want to be involved in something real, something that moves us forward. In my way I want to do what you've been doing, by helping to bring us into today's world, and making the world accept us on our own terms."

"It's not as easy as that. Do you know how many people in this world still have the idea that we are a primitive people?"

"I know," she said quickly. "And that's what I want to change. Now that we have won the war, we have a chance to make the world recognize that we are as good as they are."

"Do you believe we won the war?" Baydr asked curiously.

"I know we did. If we hadn't been forced into a cease-fire, we could have destroyed the Israeli armies once and for all. They were moving right into the traps set for them in both Syria and Egypt."

Baydr looked at her. There was so much she did not know. This was the standard line fed to the people by the pan-Arab propagandists. It was a source of continual amazement to him that the majority of Arabs believed it. That Israel had cut off Egypt's Third Army and in a few days more could have occupied both Cairo and Damascus never seemed to enter their minds. "I still don't know what you can do," he said.

"I have an idea."

"What?"

"I could work for you." She looked into his eyes.

She was so intent that he did not smile. "Doing what?" he asked gently.

"I could be your assistant," she said seriously.

"Mother always said that I should have been a boy. That I was exactly like you."

"I'm afraid not," he said kindly. "My assistants all have had special training for their positions. Much of the work is highly technical and specialized."

"I don't mean right away," she said quickly. "I could start as a clerk or maybe a secretary until I learned enough."

"Can you take shorthand and type?" he asked.

"I can type a little."

He was silent, then he shook his head. "I'm afraid not. Even for those jobs we need someone who has been trained."

"I could be a receptionist. I'd be willing to start anywhere."

"You're my daughter. How do you think that would look?"

"No one would have to know. We could keep it secret."

"No. It wouldn't work. There are no secrets in this business."

She was crestfallen. "I won't go back to that school," she said stubbornly. "I hate it."

"You don't have to. I have another idea."

She looked up at him hopefully.

"If you are serious about what you say, I could arrange for you to go to a university in the States where you can major in business administration. In a few years you would know enough to fit in some place in the organization."

"That would take years," she said impatiently. "What about now? By the time I finish school everything will have been done."

He laughed. "I don't think so. There's more than enough to last both our lifetimes."

"Can't I go to school right here?" she asked. "That way I can work after school and learn at the same time."

"It's not the same. All they could teach you is

stenography, typing and maybe some simple accounting."

"It would be a start, then if I found that I was good at it, I could go to school in the States."

"Let me think about it."

"There's nothing to think about," she said positively. "I heard your man calling the bank for secretaries. While you're waiting for them, I could answer telephones and act as your receptionist. I'm very good on the telephone. Really."

He began to laugh. "You're a very determined young lady."

She met his eyes. "You just don't know how much."

"I'm beginning to get the idea." He chuckled, then the smile left his face. "You know I'll have to talk to your mother about this."

"Why? You never talked to her about me before."

"Is that what she said?"

"Yes." Her eyes fell for a moment, then she looked up at him. "Why didn't you ever want to see us after you left?"

Baydr met her gaze. "Is that what your mother told you?"

She nodded.

Baydr was silent. There was no point in telling her of the many requests he made to see her or have her visit him only to have Maryam refuse by saying that she wanted nothing more to do with him. Leila knew only that he had left them and that was the way it should remain. He took a deep breath and then let the air slowly out. "Well, it's not true," he said quietly.

She didn't speak.

He sensed her doubt. "But it doesn't matter now," he said gently. "You are here and I am seeing you."

She nodded, still silent.

"Tell me," he said awkwardly. "How is your sister?"

"Fine. She's married. I don't see much of her or her husband. We don't have much in common. They're very social. And, oh yes, Amal thinks she might be pregnant."

He smiled. "You mean I'm about to become a grandfather?"

"It's possible."

He let out a slow whistle.

"That's very American," she said quickly.

"What is?"

"That whistle. What does it mean?"

He laughed. "I have a lot of adjustments to make. First I have to realize that I'm the father of a nineteen-year-old, now suddenly, I'm a grandfather."

Leila laughed. "Don't count on it. Amal thinks she's pregnant every month. This might be like all the others."

"You know, you have two brothers."

"I know. Muhammad and Samir."

"You know their names?"

"It's not exactly a secret. The newspapers always have stories about you. And pictures."

"They're good boys. You would like them."

"I want to meet them."

"You will. Soon." He got to his feet. "Where are you staying?"

"With a girl friend," she said. "Her family lives in Geneva."

"Swiss?"

"Yes."

"Would you rather stay there or would you like to move in here with me?"

"Whatever you would like," she said, her eyes falling away from him.

"Get your things together then," he said. "Can you be back here in time for dinner?"

She raised her head. Her eyes were smiling. "I think so."

"Okay, get going then. I have work to do."

She rose from the chair and threw her arms around him. "Thank you, Father."

He kissed the top of her head lightly. "Don't thank me. After all, I am your father, aren't I?"

*   *   *

SHE stood in the doorway of the coffeehouse and scanned the tables. The restaurant was almost empty, just a few office workers dallying over their morning coffee before going to work. She looked at her watch. Eleven o'clock. They should be here any minute now. She went to a table and sat down.

A waiter appeared instantly. "Oui, mademoiselle?"

"Coca avec citron."

He brought the drink and went away. She lit a cigarette, then sipped at her drink. It was sweet. Not as sweet as the Coca-Cola in Lebanon but sweeter than the French, although it was served French style. One small stingy piece of ice floated on the top, not quite enough to cool the drink unless you sipped the liquid past it.

Two young men and a young woman appeared in the doorway. They were dressed much like she was in jeans, shirt and jacket. She waved to them and they came to her table and sat down. Again the waiter appeared. A moment later he brought their coffees and went away.

They looked at her expectantly. She looked back without speaking. Finally, she put down her cigarette and held up her two fingers in a V sign.

The others broke into a smile. "It went all right?" the woman asked in hesitant English.

"Perfectly."

"He didn't ask any questions?"

"Only the usual fatherly questions," she answered. Then she broke into a grin. "You know I'll have to talk to your mother about this," she imitated.

An expression of concern crossed the woman's face. "What if he does?"

"He won't," she said confidently. "I know my mother. She hasn't spoken to him in ten years and she's not going to now."

"Are you going to work for him?" one of the young men asked.

"Part-time. He thinks I should go to business school

first to learn some skills. Then I can go to work full-time."

"Are you going to go?" the woman asked.

"Of course. If I didn't, he might get suspicious. Besides, it will only be for a little while."

"What's he like?" the woman asked.

Leila looked at her as if seeing her for the first time. "My father, you mean?"

"Who else would I be talking about?" the woman retorted. "Is he anything like those stories we've read about him? You know, a playboy the ladies can't resist and all that?"

Leila's eyes grew thoughtful. "I suppose so," she said hesitantly. "But I don't see him like that at all."

"How do you see him?"

Leila's voice grew bitter. "I look at him and I see all the things we're fighting against. The money, the power, the ego. The kind of person who is concerned only for himself. He couldn't care less about the struggle of our people. He thinks only about the profit he can make from it."

"Do you really believe that?"

"If I didn't believe it," Leila answered in a hard flat voice, "I wouldn't be here doing what I agreed to do."

CHAPTER 3.

THE first thought that flashed through Leila's mind as Jordana came into the room was how beautiful she was. Tall, honey-colored blond hair, tanned California glow, slim body and long lovely legs. She was everything an Arab woman could never be. For a moment, she understood why her father had done what he did.

Then the old bitterness and animosity bubbled up and she had all she could do to keep it from her eyes as Jordana came toward her.

"This is Leila," Baydr said proudly.

Jordana's eyes were clear and direct, her smile genuine and warm. She held out her hand. "I'm so glad to meet you at last. Your father used to speak often about you."

Leila took her hand. Jordana's grip was as warm as her greeting. "I'm pleased to meet you too," she said awkwardly.

"Baydr, your father, tells me you are planning to stay."

"If I'm not in the way."

"You won't be," Jordana assured her. "And I'm delighted. Now, maybe, I'll have someone to talk to when he's away. He travels quite a bit."

"I know," Leila said. She looked at her father. "I'm sorry. I'm a little tired. Is it all right if I skip dinner and go right to bed?"

Baydr cast a quick glance at Jordana, then back at Leila. "Of course."

"And you won't mind, will you?" she asked Jordana. "Besides, you two must have many things to talk about."

"I don't mind," Jordana answered.

"Good night then."

"Good night."

When the door had closed behind her, Baydr turned to Jordana. "What do you think?" he asked.

"I think she doesn't like me."

"How can you say that?" The surprise echoed in his voice. "She doesn't even know you."

"Your daughter is jealous."

"You're being foolish," he said, annoyance creeping into his voice. "What has she to be jealous of? I asked her to stay, didn't I?"

Jordana looked at him. There were some things

men would never understand. But she remembered how possessive she had been about her father and how she had felt when she had seen him with his new wife for the first time. "It doesn't really matter," she said. "I'm glad for you."

He didn't answer.

"She's a very pretty girl," she said.

"Yes."

"What made her decide to leave school so suddenly?"

"She said she felt life was passing her by," he answered. Then he chuckled. "At nineteen."

"That's not so funny," she said. "I can understand that."

"You can?" He was surprised. "Then maybe you can explain to me why after all these years she suddenly wanted to see me?"

"Why shouldn't she? You are her father. Girls have a very special thing for their fathers."

He was silent for a moment. "I should call her mother and tell her."

"I have a feeling you won't have to. That her mother already knows."

"What makes you think that?"

"Your father told me that she had spent almost the whole summer with her mother, and that she just left Beirut a few weeks ago. Her mother must have known where she was going."

He stared at her. That was strange. Leila had led him to believe that she had come from school. She had said nothing about being at home. He wondered why she didn't tell him, but decided to say nothing to Jordana. "I think I'll call my father," he said. "I'll let him talk to her mother."

Jordana smiled. In some ways he was very transparent. He did not want to talk to his former wife. "The boys asked if they could come to visit when we get a house. They've never had a chance to play in the snow."

Baydr laughed. "You tell them that they can come up here the very first day the snow begins to fall."

DICK Carriage leaned back in his chair and took off his reading glasses. He took a tissue from the box on his desk and, turning his chair away from the bright Tensor lamp, slowly began to wipe the lenses. Large white lazy flakes floated past the window.

They had been in Switzerland almost a month before the snow began to fall and Baydr, true to his word, had his sons flown in the same day. Now they were in Gstaad for the weekend. He had remained in Geneva to clean up the pile of paperwork. Baydr had called that morning in very good humor. The boys were really enjoying themselves.

Carriage smiled to himself. Fathers were pretty much alike no matter what their background. Baydr felt much the same as he did about his own sons. He swung back to the desk and looked at the photographs of his wife and sons. The picture, taken in his garden in California, suddenly made him feel very much alone. They were a long way from the snow in Switzerland.

He heard the click of the front door latch outside the study that he and Baydr used as an office when they were in the big house in Geneva. He looked at his watch. It was a little after two o'clock in the morning. He heard the sound of hard-soled shoes on the marble floors of the entrance foyer. They had an unmistakably feminine rhythm. It had to be Leila. She was the only member of the family who had not gone to Gstaad. She had said something about special classes at school on Saturday but then she hadn't gone. Instead she had stayed in her room until after lunch, then she had gone out and had not returned until just now.

There was something strange about her, he thought. Despite the outward pleasantness and apparent willingness to cooperate, he sensed a certain withdrawal, a restraint in her calculating eyes. Occasionally he would catch a glimpse of her resentment, especially toward

Jordana, although she obviously tried to keep it concealed.

The footsteps reached the staircase and began to ascend, then they came to a stop. A moment later the knob on the study door moved tentatively. "Come in," he called.

The door swung open and Leila stood there, dressed in her inevitable blue jeans. Sometimes he wondered if she owned any other clothes.

"I don't mean to disturb you. I saw the light coming from under the door."

"It's okay. You're not bothering me. I was just taking a break anyway."

She came into the room and he could see the flakes of snow melting in her hair and on her clothes. "You haven't stopped since my father left yesterday morning."

He smiled. "It's the only chance I have to catch up on the paperwork. When he's around I don't have much time for it."

"Don't you ever take time off?"

"Sure. When we were in California a few months ago, I had a whole week with my family."

"But since then," she persisted. "You don't even take time for yourself on weekends."

"What for?" he asked. "There's nothing I want to do."

"You could go out to dinner. Go to a movie."

"I'd rather work. I don't like doing those things alone."

"You don't have to be alone. There are lots of girls in Geneva looking for dates."

He laughed. "There are lots of girls everywhere. But, you forget. I'm a married man."

"My father is a married man and that doesn't stop him," she said.

He looked at her sharply, wondering how much she knew. "There are certain things your father has to do," he said quickly. "That's his business."

"Is it? I've heard lots of stories about him."

He was silent.

"I've heard stories about Jordana too." Her eyes were challenging. "Is that business also?"

He met her gaze coolly. "There are always people who are quick to gossip. Most of them don't know what they are talking about. I've learned that the most important contribution I can make toward your father's business is to mind my own."

She laughed. "I can see why father trusts you so much. You are loyal to him."

"He's my employer," he said stiffly. "I respect him a great deal."

"But do you like him?" she asked pointedly.

His answer was prompt and direct. "Yes."

"Even if he doesn't give you any days off?"

"That's my option," he said evenly. "If I choose not to take them, it's my own affair."

She walked around the corner of his desk and glanced down at the pile of papers. "Money buys a lot of things, doesn't it?" It was a statement not a question. "You're as much a slave to the system as anyone."

"The only better way I know to make a living," he answered in Arabic, "is to have a rich father."

He saw the quick anger flash in her eyes and knew he'd hit a nerve. "I don't have—" Then she caught herself and stopped abruptly.

"You don't have—what?" he asked softly.

The anger was quickly replaced by self-control. She smiled. "Nothing. Where did you learn to speak Arabic so well?"

"At home."

She was surprised. "I thought you were American."

"I am," he smiled. "But my parents came from Jordan. Their name was Khureiji. My father changed it to Carriage before I was born, when he opened his first restaurant. He thought it would be easier for Americans to say Carriage House than Khureiji House."

"Are they still alive?"

"No."

"Didn't they ever want to go home?"

"Yes."

"Maybe it's just as well they didn't," she said quickly. "Not as long as the Jews were on their doorstep."

He looked at her without speaking. The real tragedy was that they had gone back. Perhaps if they hadn't, they would still be alive today.

She took his silence for agreement. "It won't always be like that. Soon we will get rid of the Jews. We almost did this time, but we were betrayed."

"By whom?"

"Some of our own people. People who thought only of their own pockets, their own power. If they hadn't stopped us, we would have driven the Jews into the sea."

"I still don't know who these people are."

"You'll find out," she said, suddenly secretive. "Soon enough." She smiled and changed the subject. "Would you like me to make some coffee?"

"That's very kind of you. But I don't want to put you to any trouble."

"It's no trouble at all. Besides, I'd like a cup myself. American or Turkish?"

"Turkish," he said, though he much preferred American.

"Good," she said, starting for the door. "I'll be right back."

He stared at the door after she had gone. She was strange. If only he could discover what she was really thinking. Idly he picked up the next folder from the pile of papers. It was the report Baydr had asked him to get on Arabdolls Ltd. His vision blurred and he put it back on the desk. He was more tired than he had realized. It could wait until after he'd had coffee.

It was almost a quarter of an hour before she came back with the coffee. When he saw her, his mouth almost fell open in surprise. She did have other clothes. Instead of the perennial blue jeans, she was wearing a white caftan with gold piping which led

down the front and followed the lines of the buttons
that joined the two sides of the garment. Flashes of
her golden, tanned body, visible through the spaces in
the caftan revealed that she wore nothing beneath it.

She placed the silver coffee tray on a small table
in front of the couch. The white steam rose in curlicues
as she slowly poured the coffee into the small cups.
She looked up at him. "You can come out from behind that desk for the coffee," she said. "I promise
not to tell my father."

He smiled and got to his feet. "Something tells me
you wouldn't anyway."

"Right."

He sat down on the couch beside her. She picked
up a cup and handed it to him. "Taste it."

Obediently, he sipped at it. The sweetness almost
gagged him. He took his coffee without sugar.

"Sweet enough?"

"Perfect," he said with a straight face.

She smiled, pleased. "I love my coffee extra sweet."

"It's very good."

She sipped at her coffee. "Do you smoke?" she
asked.

"I have cigarettes on the desk," he said, beginning
to rise.

Her hand stopped him. "I don't mean that kind."

"Oh," he said, looking at her. "Sometimes. But not
when I'm working."

She opened the small silver box which was on the
tray next to the coffee pot. "Don't you think you've
worked enough for tonight?"

He looked down at the neatly rolled joints.

"Jabir gave me these," she said. "He's got the best
hashish in the world. He rolls them especially for my
father."

"I know," he said.

She took a cigarette and struck a match. The flame
glowed for a moment as the sulfur burned off, then
she held it to the cigarette. After she had taken a
few puffs, she held it out to him.

He looked at it, without moving.

"Come on," she urged. "Relax. Loosen up a little. The work will still be there in the morning."

"Oh, okay," he said. He took the cigarette from her hand and dragged on it. After a few tokes he gave it back to her. "It is good," he said.

"That's better," she said, dragging on the joint again. She smiled. "You know, for the first time you're beginning to look human."

He took the cigarette from her and puffed on it. He began to feel a buzzing in his head. "How do I usually look?"

She leaned back against the couch. "Very serious usually. Very businesslike all the time. No expression. You very rarely smile. You know what I mean."

"I didn't realize that."

"Most people aren't aware of how they look." She looked at him. "You know you'd be kind of handsome without those glasses." She reached out and took them from his face. "Go look in the mirror and see for yourself."

"I don't have to. I know what I look like. I shave myself every morning."

She began to laugh. "That's very funny."

He smiled. "Is it?"

She nodded. "You know you're not too bad for an American. I usually don't like Americans. But you seem different. Maybe it's because your parents were Arabs."

He didn't speak.

She stared at him silently for a moment, then leaned forward suddenly and kissed him on the mouth. He was caught by surprise and held very still.

She drew back and looked into his eyes. "What's the matter? Don't you like it?"

"That's not it," he said awkwardly. "After all, I'm a married man."

"I know that, but your wife is at the other end of the world."

"Is that supposed to make a difference?"

"Does it?" she asked looking at him.

He didn't answer. Instead he took another drag on the cigarette. The buzzing suddenly left his head, leaving it extraordinarily clear. He felt as if all his senses had been sharpened. He was no longer tired. "What is it exactly that you want from me?"

She met his eyes. "I want to learn everything about my father's business. And you can help teach me."

"I would do that without you having to sleep with me." He didn't tell her that Baydr had instructed him to encourage her interest in the business.

Her eyes were steady. "But I want to sleep with you."

He reached for her but she held out a hand, stopping him. "Wait just a minute."

He watched her get to her feet and cross to his desk and turn off the light. It seemed almost as if she were floating. She went around the room slowly turning off the lights except one lamp in the far corner. Then she came back to the couch and, standing in front, slowly undid the buttons down the front of her caftan and let it fall to the floor around her.

He held out his arms toward her and she came down into them. He pressed his mouth to her lips almost roughly.

"Take it easy," she whispered. "You still have your clothes on." She began to undo the buttons on his shirt. "Relax. Let me undress you."

Later, when she was moaning beneath him, when he was marveling at the firm strength in her young rounded body, when he felt the power of her clutching loins drawing him into her like a vacuum, he heard her begin to whimper almost inaudibly.

He forced his mind to clear so that he could listen to her words. They were the same word over and over as she was caught in the throes of strange physical and mental orgasm.

"Daddy! Daddy! Daddy!"

CHAPTER 4.

DESPITE the late November chill and rain that covered Paris like a gloomy gray wrapping, Youssef felt good as he walked up Avenue George V, turning past Fouquet's into his offices on the Champs-Elysées. He entered the narrow French elevator, closed the gate and pressed the button for the top floor. Slowly the iron cage climbed toward the roof.

He smiled to himself, thinking about his new little friend, a Greek boy, slim and young, with dark black ringlets around his face and enormous dark eyes. The boy was in love with him. He was sure of that. It had to be the real thing. When he had offered him money, the boy had been hurt, his eyes filled with tears. He apologized quickly and kissed away the tears. The boy had smiled radiantly when he promised to see him the following evening.

The iron cage creaked to a stop at his floor. He left the elevator, closing the gate carefully behind him, so that it could respond to another summons. In true French style the office door was wooden with the company name stenciled in black lettering on the large pane of opaque glass: MEDIA (FRANCE) SA.

His secretary, who also served as the receptionist, looked up as he came in the door and smiled. "Bonjour, Monsieur Ziad."

"Bonjour, Marguerite," he answered, walking past her into his office. He closed the door behind him, took off his raincoat and went to the window. Despite the rain the Champs-Elysées was crowded. Already tourists were buying tickets for tonight's performance at

276

the Lido on the other side of the boulevard, and the stores were filled with customers.

The door opened behind him and, without turning around, he held out his raincoat. "Anything new?" he asked, as the woman took the coat from him.

"There was a telex from Genève on the machine when I arrived this morning," she answered.

"Where is it?"

"In the folder on your desk. I put it on top of the other papers."

He opened the folder, picked up the yellow telex sheet and read it quickly.

ZIADMED. CANCEL FILM PROJECT AND SETTLE VINCENT CONTRACT IMMEDIATELY STOP. ALSO REFUSE FURTHER SHIPMENTS ON A/C ARABDOLLS UNTIL FURTHER NOTICE. WE HAVE COMPANY UNDER INVESTIGATION STOP. INFORM ME OF TERMS VINCENT SETTLEMENT SOONEST. STOP. REGARDS. ALFAYMED.

He felt a clutch of pain in his bowels. He sank into his chair, and the sweat broke out on his forehead. Thoughts raced through his brain. Something had gone wrong. Somehow he had been discovered. He felt the nausea in the back of his throat and barely made it to the bathroom.

After he had thrown up, he felt better. He took a glass of water from the carafe on his desk and sipped it slowly as he reread the telex. His stomach began to settle down. Maybe it wasn't at all what he had first thought. It had been his own guilt and fear that had choked him. Baydr could have had a thousand valid business reasons for his decisions other than the ones he feared.

He had to remain calm, so that he could think and determine the true reasons for Baydr's actions. Then he would know what to do. He lit a cigarette and turned the telex face down on the desk. Right now, he had to execute the orders he had received. He picked up the telephone. "Locate Michael Vincent for me," he said to his secretary.

"Oui, Monsieur Ziad," Marguerite answered. "Do you wish to speak with him?"

"Not just yet," he replied. "First I want to speak with Monsieur Yasfir. You will have to locate him also."

He put down the telephone and started trying to get his thoughts in order. He had received four hundred thousand dollars on Vincent's account already but he had only disbursed half of that amount to him. He wondered if he could make a deal to close at that figure. They would then be out only for what they had already paid. Baydr could not help but be impressed by that. He began to feel better. Maybe things were not as bad as they had seemed.

The telephone on his desk buzzed. It was his secretary. "I have Monsieur Yasfir on the telephone for you."

"Where is he?"

"In Genève."

He punched the button, and spoke in Arabic so that if anyone overheard they would not understand. "I have received instructions to stop shipments for Arabdolls. Do you have any idea why?"

Yasfir's voice was calm. "No. Did they give a reason?"

"Not really. All they said was that they had the company under investigation."

Yasfir was silent.

"I will have to cable our office in Beirut," Youssef said.

"No." Yasfir's voice was cold. "We have shipments scheduled twice a week until Christmas. This is the most important season of the year for us."

"I can't help it," Youssef explained. "If I do not comply it will mean my job."

"Then you have a problem, my friend. If those shipments are not made my associates could lose more than twenty million dollars. And that is something they would not care to do."

"I can't help it," Youssef repeated. "I don't like to lose my commission either. But I must keep my job."

"You are missing the point," Yasfir said. "To be unemployed and alive, or to be employed—and dead."

Abruptly the connection was broken. The French operator came on quickly. "Avez vous terminé, monsieur?"

Youssef stared at the telephone a moment. "Oui," he answered quickly. Again he felt the pain in his bowel, and the sweat came out on his forehead. He placed his head in his hands. He had to think. He had to find a way to make Baydr change his mind.

The telephone buzzed again. He picked it up. His secretary's voice was annoyingly cheerful. It was amazing how the French considered each successfully completed long-distance call a personal victory. "Monsieur Vincent has just left London for Paris," she said. "He is expected at the George V at one o'clock."

"Leave word that I must see him for lunch. It is most important."

He put down the telephone and picked it up again almost immediately. "Bring me two aspirin," he said. "And then get Monsieur Carriage in Genève."

The aspirin didn't help much and now the circuits to Geneva were busy. Youssef looked at his watch. It was after eleven o'clock. Ordinarily he was not a drinking man but this time he could make an exception.

He got to his feet and left his office. "I will return in a few moments," he said to his secretary.

Marguerite was puzzled. "Are you all right?" she asked in a concerned voice.

"I'm fine," he snapped. He went out into the hallway and got into the iron cage, which slowly took him down to the ground floor. He walked out of the doorway of his office building and turned left into Fouquet's.

He walked up to the bar. The bartender came forward immediately. "Bonjour, Monsieur Ziad. What is your pleasure?"

"What do you have to settle a nervous stomach?"

The bartender looked at him. "Alka-Seltzer. I find that very effective."

"No." Youssef was abrupt. "Something stronger than that."

"Fernet-Branca, monsieur," the bartender said quickly. "It is an old remedy but still the best."

"I will have that. And make it a double."

"A double, monsieur?" The bartender looked at him strangely.

"Yes. And be quick about it." Youssef was annoyed. Why did everything have to be so difficult?

"Oui, monsieur." The bartender turned and took down a bottle. A moment later the dark brown liquor was in an old-fashioned glass in front of Youssef. "Je pense que c'est trop, monsieur," he said. "Va doucement."

Youssef looked at him with contempt. The French always insisted that you had to do things their way. He picked up the glass and threw the drink back. For a moment, he stood paralyzed as the horrible-tasting liquor burned its way down his throat. Then clapping his hand over his mouth, he turned and ran up the stairs to the washroom.

MICHAEL Vincent was relaxed as he opened the door for Youssef. He smiled and held out his hand. "I have good news," he said warmly. "I've completed the first draft of the screenplay."

Youssef looked at him without enthusiasm. "We have problems we must discuss, my friend."

Vincent was instantly wary. He knew that "problems" in the lexicon of the film business was a word of doom. But he also knew better than to respond directly. "There are no problems that cannot be solved."

Youssef looked at the American. For the first time since he had met him, the man seemed completely sober. Why did it have to be at this time? He always felt better dealing with Vincent when he was partly drunk. "I have taken the liberty of reserving a table downstairs for lunch," he said.

Vincent smiled. "Excellent. I'm starved. I haven't had any breakfast."

"What would you like to drink?" Youssef asked after they had been seated at their table.

Vincent shook his head. "Never drink on an empty stomach."

Youssef turned to the captain. "We will see the menu then."

"We have an excellent poached salmon, Monsieur Ziad," the captain suggested.

Youssef didn't care what he ate. "That sounds fine." He looked at the American. "How about you?"

"Sounds good to me too."

Youssef cursed to himself. The man was entirely too pleasant. He had hoped he would take a drink. "A bottle of Montrachet," he said to the captain. Perhaps a good white wine would help.

The captain bowed and went away. For a moment the two men were silent. Vincent spoke first. "You mentioned problems?"

"Yes," Youssef replied seriously. He looked at Vincent and decided to use a direct approach, however foreign it was to his own nature. "I have just received instructions this morning to cancel the project."

There was no expression on Vincent's face. Then a small sigh escaped his lips. "I thought something like that might happen. It was going too well to be true."

"You're not surprised?"

The director shook his head. "No. Not since I read in the Hollywood trades a few weeks ago that another company was ready to begin filming a story of the Prophet in Morocco next spring."

Youssef felt an immediate sense of relief. So that was the reason for the telex. At least it was not because they suspected his arrangement. "Yes," he said, keeping his face impassive."

"Don't look so glum," Vincent said. "If you'd been

around the film business as long as I have, you would have seen worse."

"Even so," Youssef said, "there is still an unpleasant matter for us to deal with. I have been asked to work out a settlement of your contract."

Vincent was alert. "There is nothing to settle. My contract is firm. I receive a million dollars regardless of whether or not the film is made."

"I don't think so. As I understand it, half your fee is to be paid during the filming. If we do not begin production that would mean payment would not be made. Also the million dollars includes two hundred thousand for expenses contingent on performance. If that is halted we do not have to pay that sum either."

"I read the contract differently. I think I can enforce the payment of the whole amount."

"How?" Youssef asked flatly. "If you read the contract, you will find that the laws of Lebanon govern the agreement and any questions regarding it are to be settled in Lebanese courts. Do you think that you, a foreigner, would have a chance against Al Fay? You would get nothing. In fact you would probably not even find an attorney who would take your case against us."

Vincent was silent. That was the one clause in the contract he had not liked. It was also the one clause in the contract they had been firm about. Now he knew why.

Youssef felt more secure now. "Friends have no place in a court of law," he said. "It would be much more agreeable to work out a settlement between us. The world is small. You never can tell when we may be of help to one another in the future."

"What do you suggest?"

"You have already received two hundred thousand. Payment of another one hundred thousand completes our obligation for the screenplay. I suggest that we stop at that."

Vincent was silent.

"And I will waive my commission," Youssef said

quickly. "I think that's only fair, since the project did not go through. That way all the money would be yours."

"What about my expenses?" he asked. "One hundred thousand of that was supposed to be paid during the writing of the screenplay."

Youssef thought for a moment. What the American said was true. In addition, he already had the money with which to pay him so there would be no problem. As far as Baydr knew the money had already been dispersed. Still, he could not suppress his natural greed. "If we pay the expenses then I will insist on my commissions."

Vincent did the arithmetic in his head. Three hundred thousand dollars net or four hundred thousand less twenty percent. The difference was only twenty thousand dollars but it was better than nothing. He laughed suddenly. "Agreed," he said. "With one condition."

"What is that?" Youssef asked cautiously.

"That you use every effort to get me on the other picture."

Youssef smiled in relief. "We would do that anyway," he said.

The wine steward arrived, opened the bottle with a flourish and poured a taste for Youssef's approval. "Trés bon," Youssef said, gesturing to the steward to fill Vincent's glass.

Vincent held up his hand. "I've changed my mind," he said. "Bring me a double Scotch on the rocks."

CHAPTER 5.

ALI Yasfir walked into the cafe across the street from the President Wilson Hotel in Geneva. He looked at his watch. It was almost six o'clock and the cafe was crowded with office people having a drink before they left the city for their homes in the outskirts. He found a quiet table in the back of the restaurant against the wall, ordered a coffee and prepared to wait. She had told him she didn't think she could get away much before six o'clock. He opened his copy of the Paris *Herald Tribune*.

The newspaper was filled with stories of the panic in the United States over the oil embargo. At first the country had been in a state of shock. People could not believe that it was really happening to them. But then they had settled in and begun to maneuver to increase their supplies. He smiled to himself. There was not very much they could do. By winter they would really feel the pinch. By spring, when they realized it would take five years for them to redevelop their own sources of oil which they had allowed to lapse because of the cheapness of import, they would be on their knees begging for mercy.

That is, if the Arabs were able to maintain their unity. Already chinks were beginning to develop in the armor. There were rumors that oil tankers bound for America were still slipping through the Gulf of Oman not only from Iran but also from the United Arab Emirates, Kuwait and even Saudi Arabia. He never doubted for a moment that the rumors were true. All of those countries were tied to America not only by sentiment but by cold hard money. Their investment in the American economy was so great that they dared not tamper with it too much for fear that it would lead to chaos and the loss of all their investments. The fact that their self-interest stood in the way of complete freedom for the Arab world meant nothing to the select few who ruled those countries. They only used the crisis to enhance their own power and wealth. These were men like Al Fay—perhaps the worst of all—men who would have to be purged before the Arabs could assume their rightful place in the sun. What they gave to the movement was a mere pittance when measured against their own benefit.

The Prophet had said, "Look to the day of judgment." But they were not ready to wait that long. Already plans had been made to turn the power of these men against themselves. Soon it would begin and in time they would feel the wrath of a people betrayed.

Ali Yasfir was on his second cup of coffee when the young woman came in and stood before him. He gestured to the chair across the table without speaking.

She sat down and the waiter appeared. "Coca-Cola avec citron," she said. When the waiter had gone, she looked at him. "I'm sorry I'm late, but it was difficult for me to get away on such short notice."

"I would not disturb you if it were not important."

"I understand that." The waiter came with her drink and went away again. "What is happening?" she asked.

"Many things," he said heavily. "Perhaps the worst is that the embargo is in danger of being bypassed."

She sipped at her drink without speaking, her eyes fixed on his face.

"The United States is bringing a great deal of pressure to bear on men like your father. They threaten confiscation of their investments in the States."

"I haven't seen anything like that. And I am in the office every day. I read almost every piece of paper that comes through."

"They are not that stupid. There are some things that would never be committed to paper. But the threats are still there. And your father is responding to them."

"How? My father has nothing to do with the allocation of oil."

"But his influence in the council is great. Sooner or later they will listen to him and others like him."

She lit a cigarette and inhaled deeply. "Things are never really what they seem, are they?"

Ali Yasfir nodded. "We may have to take action sooner than we had thought."

She let the smoke drift slowly from her mouth.

"You have not changed your mind?" he asked quickly. "You are still of the same beliefs?"

"I have not changed my mind. How can I? I still remember the atrocity perpetrated on us by the Israeli planes. I can still see the dead bodies and faces of my friends. I have seen the unprovoked cruelty of the Israelis. I will not change my mind until they are all dead."

He relaxed slightly. "I was afraid your American lover might have changed your beliefs."

She met his eyes steadily. "He is not my lover," she said coldly. "I use him so that I can have access to what is going on in my father's business."

"Then you know about the order to stop the shipments from Arabdolls?"

"Yes."

"Do you know why?"

"I'm not sure but I think they suspect that Ziad has been taking money from them on the side. They are investigating now to find out if that is true."

"It is very important to us that those shipments continue. It is our main source of American dollars. Do you think you have enough influence with your American friend to get those orders rescinded?"

"I don't know," she said doubtfully. "He was instructed by my father to stop those shipments." She looked at him. "What if I spoke directly to my father?"

"No. Your father knows nothing about those shipments. If he did, he would surely halt them. He refused us before."

"I don't know what I can do then."

"Perhaps you can persuade the American to report to your father that there is no problem with the shipments, that Ziad is not getting any money from them."

"Is that true?"

"Of course not," he said testily. "Don't be so naïve. How do you think we could get a swine like him to cooperate with us except by bribery? You could tell your friend that you just learned that Arabdolls is owned by friends of yours and you would not like to see them upset."

"Do you think he would believe that?"

"Who can tell? You should know better than anyone how much power you have over him."

A faint smile came to her lips. "He might do it. We have been together at least four times a day while my father has been in Gstaad. He is like a madman. He never lets me alone."

"If that is true, then you should have no difficulty with him."

"But what if he refuses?"

"You can threaten to go to your father and tell him of your affair." He saw the shocked expression on her face and added quickly, "But that is only a last resort. For now you will do no more than ask him. We will meet again at the same time tomorrow evening and you will let me know his answer."

"Is there anything else?"

"Not now."

"How long must I remain here?" she asked. "I did not spend all that time in a training camp to be a secretary. When will I get an opportunity to do something real?"

"You are doing something very important for us right now. But perhaps the other thing will come sooner than you think."

*   *   *

CARRIAGE looked up at the clock after the special messenger from the consul's office had left. Seven o'clock. He opened his desk drawer and took out the matching key that would open the pouch. It had to be something very important to have been sent by sealed diplomatic pouch on the last plane of the day from Beirut.

Inside was a single folder with one sheet of paper. Typewritten across the folder in bold red letters were the words CONFIDENTIAL REPORT—ARABDOLLS.

He opened the folder and began to read quickly. The contents were brief and to the point. Arabdolls was a front for the drug syndicate. Among its listed owners were an American Mafioso, a French Corsican who was a known operator of heroin refineries and two Lebanese, one a man who had wide contacts among the poppy growers in both Lebanon and Turkey, the other a banker who represented various Fedayeen groups in many of their financial transactions.

Now the premium paid for the shipments began to make sense. They had found a legitimate shipper to bring the drugs into the United States for them because MEDIA not only provided the carrier, but as a licensed U.S. Customs broker they also cleared the shipments for them and delivered direct to the consignee in New York. Although the New York consignee was a well-known American wholesale toy importer, he didn't doubt that they had made adequate arrangements for the handling of the shipments in the States.

Carriage picked up a telephone and placed a call to the managing director of the MEDIA shipping office in Beirut. There was one thing more he had to find out.

The director came on the line, sputtering from the honor of a personal call from Mr. Al Fay's executive assistant. It was the first time he had spoken to anyone further up in the hierarchy than Youssef. He was most cooperative.

No, he personally knew nothing about Arabdolls, only that they were very polite and that their invoices were paid promptly. He wished that all his clients were that timely but alas, you know how they are.

Dick sympathized with him, saying that Mr. Al Fay was quite aware of his problems and very understanding. Then, he inquired how they got the account—which of their agents had solicited it.

The director was apologetic. Unfortunately, none of his men had been alert enough to get the account. He had to give full credit to Mr. Ziad, who had made all the arrangements in Paris. All they had to do was service the account. And they were taking special care to see that the client had the very best service. Good accounts such as these were hard to come by.

Dick thanked him and put down the telephone. He wondered how much Youssef knew about the contents of the shipments. It was hard for him to believe that Youssef would dare proceed against Baydr's policy. Especially after the Ali Yasfir incident in Cannes last summer, he was well aware that Baydr had refused to act as a front for the illegal activities of the Fedayeen no matter how worthy they claimed their motivations were.

Still, there was only one way that the deal could have been made. Someone had to have reached Youssef. He wondered how well Youssef knew Ali Yasfir. He tried to recall if he had seen them together in Cannes but all he could remember was that he had asked Youssef to relay to Yasfir Baydr's invitation for the party on the yacht.

He had just locked the folder in the safe when Leila returned. He looked up at her, thinking as he did so that he would call Baydr first thing in the morning.

"What's wrong?" Leila asked quickly. "You look very serious."

"Too much on my mind, I guess." He forced a smile. "How were your friends?"

She returned his smile. "Silly girls. They were okay at school but now I think I've outgrown them. All they can talk about is boys."

He laughed. "That seems normal to me."

"That's all they think about too."

"And what do you think about?" ·

She came over to his desk and bent over him so that her face was almost touching his. "Fucking you," she said.

CHAPTER 6.

BAYDR came on the telephone, sounding cheerful. "Good morning, Dick."

"Morning, chief. How is it up there?"

"Just beautiful. And the boys love it. You ought to see them on skis. They're naturals."

"Good," Dick said. "I've got some business to talk about. Is the scrambler attached?"

"No," Baydr answered. "Call me back in ten minutes on the other line. I'll have it hooked up by then."

Dick put down his telephone and checked to make sure his own scrambler was tied into the line. He flipped the switch and the red light came on. It was working. He turned it off. The scrambler had been especially made for them, so that anyone who might even accidentally come on their line would hear nothing but a series of unintelligible sounds.

He thought back to last night. The affair of Arabdolls was becoming stranger by the minute. Now there was a new ramification. Out of left field Leila had shown an unexpected interest in it.

She had led up to the subject obliquely, in true Arabic fashion. They were lying naked on his bed, smoking a joint, after making love. He felt himself drifting hazily. "I wonder if we'll be able to meet like this when my father comes back," she said.

"We'll find a way."

"You won't have time. When he's around you never have a moment to yourself."

He didn't answer.

"Sometimes I think you're even more of a slave than Jabir."

"It's not as bad as that."

"It's bad enough," she said, her eyes seeming to fill with tears.

"Hey, cut that out," he said, reaching for her.

She moved her head down to his chest. "I'm sorry," she whispered. "I'm just beginning to get used to you, just beginning to discover how wonderful you are."

"You're pretty wonderful yourself."

"I have a confession to make."

"No confessions."

But she went on. "You're the first real man I've ever been with. All the others were just boys. I never felt anything with them like I feel with you."

He didn't answer.

"Is it like that with you? Do you feel the same things with your wife that you feel with me?"

He thought of his wife and sons, who were six thousand miles away, and felt a twinge of conscience. "That's not fair," he remonstrated.

"I'm sorry, that was stupid of me. I won't ask you again." She reached up and took the joint from his fingers. "Give me a toke."

He watched her inhale the sweet fragrance. After a few drags she gave the cigarette back to him. He took it and placed it in an ashtray. Then he turned her on her back and went down on her.

She moaned softly, her hands holding his face tightly against her. "By the life of Allah, how I love it!" She raised his face so that she could look at him. "Do you know you are the first man who ever ate me?"

He shook his head.

"None of the boys I went with ever did that. But they were all Arabs," she said. "Arab boys are lousy lovers. All they think about is their own pleasure. Tell me, do all Americans do that?"

"I really don't know."

"Do you like me to eat you?"

He noaded.

"Let me then," she said, pushing him over. She took his erect phallus in her two hands and covered his glans with her lips. After a moment she raised her head and looked up at him. "You have a beautiful cock, do you know that? Thick and lovely. It's very American."

He laughed aloud.

"Don't laugh, I mean it," she said seriously. "All the Arab boys I knew had long skinny ones."

He didn't tell her that might have been because the boys were young and had not reached their growth. "Is it only Arab boys that you knew?" he asked.

"No, once I had a French boy. But it was dark and he was so quick I never really had a chance to see it." She looked down at him. "You know I'll miss it."

Then unexpectedly she laughed. "I just had a crazy idea. I saw an ad in a magazine where they sold life-size inflatable doll. Do you think I might have one made of you? That way I could keep you in my room and if you could not be there in person I would just blow it up and there you'd be."

"That is crazy." He laughed.

"I bet I could get my friend at Arabdolls to make one," she said.

The warning bell in his head rang loud and clear. "I wouldn't think they were into that sort of thing," he said.

"They might do it for me. Essam Mafrad's father owns the company and he is a close friend of my mother's father."

Mafrad was the Lebanese banker who represented Al-Ikhwah, and it was more than likely that her grandfather knew him. The Lebanese banking community was a tightly knit one. But he dismissed the possibility of mere coincidence after her next question.

Sitting up in the bed, as if the thought had just come to her, she asked, "Isn't that the company my father doesn't want to handle the shipments for?"

He nodded.

"He can't do that. They're our very good friends. They would be very upset."

"Then tell your father. I'm sure if he knew that he would reconsider."

"I can't do that. You know my father. He doesn't like anyone to tell him what to do."

He was silent.

"You could do something about it. You could okay the shipments."

"Then what about your father? If he found out he would have my ass."

"He would never have to know. Just don't show him the reports. He has so much on his mind, he would never think of it."

"I couldn't do that."

"Why not? You would really be doing him a favor. Our families have been friends for years and you would be saving him a great deal of embarrassment."

"It's not my place. I haven't the authority."

"Then do it for me. And if father finds out, you tell him that I asked you to do it. I'm only trying to avoid trouble between the families."

"I'm sorry," he said firmly.

Suddenly she was angry. She got out of the bed and stood over him. "You act as if I'm a silly girl!" she stormed. "I'm all right as something to fuck but as far as anything else goes, forget it!"

"Hey, wait a minute," he said in a conciliatory voice. "I don't think anything of the sort. I have a great deal of respect for your opinion. I don't doubt that you're right, but you're asking me to do something I haven't the authority to do. But I will do something. Tomorrow I will tell your father what you told me and I'm sure he will approve the shipments."

"I don't need your favors!" she snapped. "I don't

want you to tell him anything, do you understand that? Anything!"

"I won't then, if that's what you want."

"That's what I want. If I have anything to tell him, I will tell him myself!"

"Okay, okay," he said.

She snatched her robe from the chair and walked to the door, then turned back to face him. "You're all afraid of my father, but I'm not. And, someday, all of you will find that out!"

For a long time, he had sat in bed smoking cigarette after cigarette. It had to be more than coincidence. Even if the Riad and Mafrad families were good friends, the whole thing coming from her at this particular time was just a little too pat.

He wondered whether he should tell Baydr about it, but decided against it. It would only expose their relationship and that would be the end of his job. As liberal as Baydr might be about many things, he was still her father.

Maybe by morning she would have calmed down. In the meantime, he made up his mind to do one thing.

Despite the late hour, he reached for the private telephone on his night table, pressing down the anti-eavesdropping button, so that no one in the house could listen in on an extension. He dialed the number of a private investigator the company had used several times.

When he put down the telephone after talking with the man, he felt better. From now on, whenever Leila left the house she would be under surveillance. By the end of the week he would have a good idea of who she was seeing and every friend she had in Geneva. Maybe when all of that was put together he might be able to make some sense out of her actions.

He had gone to the office before eight o'clock, when he knew there would be no one else around and he could reach Baydr at breakfast. Now it was almost time to call Baydr back. He would have the scrambler connected. He dialed the number.

Baydr answered, "Dick?"

"Yes."

"Turn your switch on."

He heard the buzz in his line and pressed down the scrambler button. Abruptly the buzz disappeared. "Okay now?"

"Perfect," Baydr said. "What is it?"

"Arabdolls." He was succinct. "They're a front. I'm afraid we've been running dope for them." Quickly he reviewed everything he had learned.

Baydr was silent for a moment. "How did we get into this?" he asked. "Was the deal made in Beirut?"

"No, in Paris. I was informed that the contract came from Youssef himself."

"I was afraid of that. I had heard that he'd been meeting Ali Yasfir. But I didn't think that Youssef would have the nerve to do anything like that on his own. The money had to be very big to move him."

Carriage was surprised. "You knew of the contacts between them?"

"Yes, but I thought it was just Yasfir's way of keeping in touch. Apparently I was wrong. I accepted all his little side deals. Those were more or less customary. But this is something else."

"What should we do about it?"

"There's not much we can do. We can't open it up because it could turn into a Pandora's box for us. One word and we lose our U.S. Customs brokerage as well as our shipping franchises. We'll have to handle it internally. The first thing to do is to get Youssef up here. We have to find out how deeply we're actually involved."

"Will you come here to meet him?" Dick asked.

"No. Geneva is filled with inquisitive eyes. Better ask him to come to Gstaad to see me."

"Okay. Would you like me to come also?"

"I think you'd better remain there. The less people he sees around the better."

Another thought ran through Dick's mind. "I've picked up some talk that Mafrad and Riad are very close. Do you think your former father-in-law might be involved with them?"

"Impossible!" Baydr's reaction was convincing. "Riad is an old-fashioned conservative. He wouldn't go near a hustler like Mafrad if he were coated in gold."

"I just thought you should know," Dick said. Again he thought of Leila. The words were almost on his lips when he reconsidered. It would keep until the end of the week, when he would know more. After he had put down the telephone, he sat for some moments lost in thought. If there was no connection between the families, why had she made such an important point of saying that there was? None of it made any real sense, at least not yet.

The door opened and his secretary came in. She paused in surprise. "Mr. Carriage," she said in her English-sounding Swiss accent. "You're in early."

"Yes. I had some important calls to make."

"Would you like some coffee?"

"Please. And bring in your book. I want to send a telex to Ziad in Paris."

When she returned with her book, he changed his mind and decided to place a call instead. He could be more casual about Baydr's summons on the telephone than in a cold telex. He was sipping his coffee when Youssef answered his phone.

"The chief asked me to call you and ask you to come up to Gstaad to see him if you're free," he said.

A note of worry crept into Youssef's voice. "Is it anything special?"

Dick laughed. "I don't think so. Between us I think he's getting a little bored playing the family man. Maybe he's looking for an excuse to get out of there."

Dick could sense his relief. "I've got just the excuse. Vincent agreed to let us out of the contract without our paying him anything more than we have already paid him. I can say that the chief has to come down to sign the papers."

"He'd like that," Carriage said.

Feeling that confidentiality had been established, Youssef let a note of camaraderie come into his voice. "What's the chief's interest in Arabdolls all about?"

Dick kept his voice on the same level. "I really couldn't say. He didn't tell me. But you know him as well as I do. He's interested in any new business that has the smell of money about it. Maybe he wants in."

"From what I've heard, it's just a small operation. I don't think it's big enough for him."

"If it should come up while you're there," Dick said, still casual, "you could tell him."

"That's an idea." Dick could almost hear the wheels turning in the man's head. "I have a few things to clean up down here. Tell the chief I'll be up there sometime this evening."

"I'll tell him," Dick said and put down the telephone.

His secretary came into the office with another pot of coffee. "Miss Al Fay is outside," she said, as she placed the tray on his desk. "She asks if you would have a moment for her this morning?"

"Ask her to come in," Dick said. Leila must have something on her mind, he thought as he poured his coffee. Usually she never came to the office in the morning.

Somehow she looked more like a young girl this morning than he had ever remembered. She stood hesitantly in front of his desk. "I won't take too much of your time."

"That's all right. Would you like some coffee?"

"No, thanks. I came in especially to tell you that I was sorry about last night."

"Forget it. I already have."

"No, I mean it," she said insistently. "I behaved like a spoiled child. I had no right to ask you things like that. I don't want it to change anything between us."

"It won't."

"Honestly?"

"Honestly," he answered.

He saw her look of relief and the strange hint of triumph hiding in her eyes. "Can I come to your room tonight?" she asked, still in the small voice.

"I would be very unhappy if you didn't."

"I promised some friends I would have dinner with them tonight. I'll get through it as quickly as I can and come home."

"I'll be waiting."

She came around the desk, took his hand and held it to her breast. "I don't know whether I can wait until tonight," she said.

The telephone rang. He took his hand from her breast and reached for it. "I'm afraid, young lady," he said with mock severity, "we'll both have to." He picked up the telephone. "Hold on just a moment," he said. Then he covered the mouthpiece with his hand and looked up at her. "You see, I have work to do."

She kissed him swiftly on the lips and started for the door. Halfway there, she stopped as if struck by an afterthought. "By the way, you're not going to mention anything to my father, are you?"

"No," he answered, his hand still covering the mouthpiece.

"Good." She blew him a kiss. "Until tonight."

He kept the smile on his face until the door had closed behind her, but a troubled look came over his face as he took his hand from the mouthpiece.

Deep in the marrow of his bones, he knew that something was wrong. Very wrong.

CHAPTER 7.

BAYDR picked up the telephone. Youssef's voice was cheerful. "I'm down at the hotel in town and I brought something very special from Paris with me," he said. "Would you like to come and have some dinner?"

"I don't think I can."

"Chief, you know me. When I say this is something special, it's something special. She's got a body you can't believe and she's crazy, completely crazy. There isn't anything you can think of that she doesn't love to do."

"Put her on ice. It will just have to be another time. We have some people in for dinner tonight."

"Maybe in the morning then."

"That's out too. I have some meetings here in the house tomorrow morning."

"Then when will you want to see me?" Youssef asked. "Lunch tomorrow?"

"The whole day is locked up. It will have to be tonight."

"Tonight?" A note of concern crept into Youssef's voice.

"Yes. My dinner guests should be gone by midnight. Supposing you get up here around half-past."

"Sure you wouldn't want to come down here?" Youssef suggested. "The girl will be very disappointed. I told her what a great guy you were."

"Buy her a little something in the jewelry shop in the hotel and give it to her with my compliments and tell her that I am as disappointed as she is."

"Okay, chief. I'll see you tonight then. Twelve-thirty, right?"

"Right," Baydr said and put down the phone. He was still sitting in the semidarkness of the library when Jordana came into the room.

"The boys are going to bed," she said. "They asked if you would come up and say good night to them."

"Of course," he said, getting to his feet. He started past her when her hand on his arm stopped him.

"Is there anything wrong?" she asked, looking up into his face.

"What makes you ask?"

"You look troubled. Who was it on the phone?"

"Youssef. He's coming up to see me after our guests leave."

"Oh."

"He's coming alone. We have some important business to discuss."

She was silent.

"You don't like him, do you?"

"I never liked him," she answered. "You know that. He's like so many of the men I see around you. They gather like predatory vultures hoping to pounce on the leavings. Meanwhile they suck up to you as if you were some kind of a god. There's another one I met, twice, once on the boat and once in California after you had gone. Ali Yasfir. He's like that."

"I didn't know he was in California," Baydr said.

"He was. I saw him going into the Polo Lounge just as I was leaving. He was going to meet Youssef. I wouldn't dare turn my back on either of them."

He stared at her. Strange that she should group the two of them together. She was more aware than he had thought.

"You better go up," she said. "The boys are waiting and there won't be much time left to dress before our guests arrive."

"Okay."

"Baydr."

He turned back again.

"Thank you."

"For what?"

"I've never seen the boys so happy. Do you know you've spent more time with them these past two weeks than you have in the past three years? They like having a father around. I do too."

"I liked it too."

"I hope we can have more of it." She placed her hand on his arm. "It hasn't been like this for a long time."

He didn't move.

"Do you think we will?" she asked.

"We'll see. There's always so much to do."

Her hand fell from his arm. She kept her face carefully expressionless. "Better hurry," she said, turning away from him. "I have to check out some last-minute dinner arrangements."

He watched her cross the room to the other door leading to the grand salon. It was not until she had gone that he went out into the hall and up the staircase to the boys' room.

They were sitting up in their beds waiting for him. He spoke in Arabic. "Did you have fun today?"

They answered in the same language, almost in chorus. "Yes, Father."

"Mother said you wanted to see me."

The children looked at each other. "You ask him," Muhammad said.

"No," answered Samir. "You ask him. You're the oldest."

"Baydr laughed. "One of you had better ask because I have to go and get dressed."

"Ask him," Samir urged his brother.

Muhammad looked at his father. His eyes were wide and serious. "We like it here, Father."

"I'm glad."

Muhammad looked at his younger brother for support. "I like it too," Samir said, in his thin voice. He looked over at his brother in the other bed. "Now you can ask him."

Muhammad took a deep breath. "We'd like to live here, Father. With you."

"But what about Beirut?"

"We don't like it, Father," Muhammad said quickly. "There's nothing to do there. There's no snow or anything."

"But what about school?"

"Our Arabic is much better now, Father," Samir said quickly. "Couldn't you—we thought—" His voice trailed off. He looked frantically at Muhammad.

"We mean," Muhammad picked up, "couldn't you bring the school up here to us? That way we could have the snow and still go to school."

Baydr laughed. "It's not that easy."

"Why?" Samir asked.

"You just can't pick up a whole school and move it. What would the rest of the students do? They'd have no school to go to."

"We could bring them along," Muhammad said. "I bet they'd like it better here too."

"Our nanny says you can do anything you want to," Samir said.

Baydr smiled. "Well, she's wrong. There are some things even I can't do. That happens to be one of them."

He saw the looks of disappointment on their faces. "But I tell you what I will do," he added.

"What is that?" Muhammad asked.

"You have another school holiday in about two months," he said. "I'll bring you back here then."

"But the snow might be all gone," Samir said.

"It will still be here. I promise you that." He knelt over and kissed each one in turn. "Now go to sleep. I'll talk to the ski instructor. Maybe he'll let us try the north slope tomorrow."

"Where the big boys ski?" Muhammad asked excitedly.

"Yes, but you'll have to promise to be extra careful."

"We will, Father," they both said at once.

"Good night, then."

"Good night, Father," they replied.

He started for the door. "Father," Muhammad called after him.

"Yes?"

"We forgot to thank you. Thank you, Father."

He stood very still for a moment. "Allah keep you, my sons. Sleep well."

Jordana was waiting in the hall when he came out of their bedroom. "Are they asleep?"

He smiled. "I've just tucked them in. Did you know what they were going to ask me?"

"No. They wouldn't tell me, only that it was important."

He started down the corridor to their suite. She walked beside him. "They said they wanted to live here. They didn't want to go back to Beirut."

She didn't speak.

"They even wanted me to move the school up here with all the pupils." He laughed. "You never know what wild ideas children will come up with."

"It's not that wild," she said. "Not when you know what they're really asking."

"And what is that?"

Her eyes looked into his. "They love you," she said. "You're their father and nothing can take your place. They want to live with you."

"Didn't you ever explain to them that I have many things to do? Surely they can be made to understand that."

"It's not as easy as you think," she answered. "How can you explain to a child that the sun in the heavens from which all life comes is something you can't have every day?"

CHAPTER 8.

DESPITE the cold, Youssef's face was covered with a
fine mist of perspiration as he carried the heavy suitcase up the steps to the villa. Jabir opened the door.
"Ahlan," he said.

"Ahlan fik," Youssef replied as he crossed the
threshold and put down the valise. He straightened
up. "Will you hold this for me until I leave?" he asked.

"It will be my pleasure, sir," Jabir replied. "The
master awaits you in the library. If you will please
follow me."

Youssef slipped out of his coat and gave it to Jabir,
then followed him through the large entrance hall to
a pair of heavy wooden doors. Jabir knocked softly.

"Come in," Baydr called.

Jabir opened the door, held it for Youssef, then
closed it softly behind him. Youssef looked around
the library. It was a large old-fashioned room with
floor-to-ceiling bookshelves. Baydr was seated behind
a desk, his back to the large French doors that led to
the garden behind him. A beautiful shaded lamp on
Baydr's desk cast the only light in the room and left
his face in shadows. He did not get up as Youssef
walked toward him.

"The villa is beautiful," Youssef said. "But then, I
expected nothing less."

"It's comfortable."

"You should have warned me about the drive up
here." Youssef smiled. "Parts of the road were covered
with sheets of ice. Especially on the curves near the
edge of the mountain."

"I didn't think of it," Baydr said politely. "I forgot

that the road sometimes freezes at night. I should have sent one of the chauffeurs down for you."

"No matter. I made it all right." He sank into the chair opposite the desk. "Too bad you couldn't make it down to the hotel tonight. The girl was very disappointed."

"The bauble didn't help ease her pain?"

"I bought her a gold Piaget. It helped."

Baydr looked at him. He wasn't very imaginative. But then what else was there to buy for a girl in Switzerland except a watch? He saw the shine of perspiration on Youssef's face. "Would you care for coffee? Or a cold drink, champagne perhaps?"

"Is there anything else?" Youssef laughed, a little too readily.

Baydr tugged the bell cord behind him. Jabir opened the door. "A bottle of champagne for Mr. Ziad."

"Did Dick tell you of the settlement I made with Michael Vincent?" Youssef asked when Jabir had gone to get the wine.

"Yes. How did you get him to let us off so easily?"

"It wasn't that easy. But I finally made him understand that it would do him no good to take us to court. That we would tie him up for years and eventually it would cost him everything he had already received in legal fees. Then I promised him we would try to get him on the other picture and if we had anything in the future we would certainly come back to him."

"That was very well done," Baydr said.

Jabir came back into the room with a bottle of Dom Pérignon in an ice bucket and two glasses on a silver tray.

"I'm glad you're pleased," Youssef said, watching Jabir open the bottle expertly and fill the two glasses. The servant left the room again and Youssef picked up a glass. He looked at Baydr. "Aren't you having any?"

Baydr shook his head. "I have to be up early. I promised the boys I would go skiing with them in the morning."

"Cheers then," Youssef said. He emptied his glass in one thirsty swallow and refilled it. "I didn't realize I was so thirsty."

Youssef sipped the second glass of wine more slowly. He leaned back in his chair, feeling a little more at ease. Baydr's next words put an end to that.

"Tell me about Arabdolls," he said.

Youssef felt the sweat break out again on his forehead. "What is there to tell? They're good clients. Other than that I know very little about them."

Baydr looked at him steadily. "That's not like you. Usually you know everything about the people we do business with. That's always been one of our cardinal rules."

"They're not a very big client. I saw no reason to look into them. They were small shipments but they paid very well."

"Premium," Baydr said. "Wasn't that enough to make you curious?"

"No, I had other more important deals on my mind."

"Didn't you think it was unusual that they contacted you in Paris instead of our office in Beirut? Certainly that would seem more normal for a business that size."

"I thought it was just a coincidence," Youssef said quickly. "I met this American in the bar at the George V and he told me of the problems he had arranging for the import of dolls into the United States and I told him to contact our office in Beirut. That we might be able to help him."

"According to the Beirut office they acted on a shipping contract sent by you. They never contacted anyone at the company."

Youssef felt the perspiration under his arms. "That could be possible. I might have left instructions with my secretary to follow through. As I said, I didn't think it important enough for me to concern myself."

"You're lying," Baydr said quietly.

Youssef was stunned. "What? What?" he stammered, as if he hadn't understood.

"I said, 'You're lying,'" Baydr repeated. "We know

everything about that company now. You've placed us
in a position of running drugs into the United States.
Because of that we are liable to lose everything we
have worked for all these years. Now I want you to
tell me the truth."

Baydr watched him reach for a cigarette and light
it with trembling fingers. "Tell me," he said softly,
"how much did Ali Yasfir give you to make those shipments?"

Youssef fell apart before his eyes. Now his voice
was trembling as well as his fingers. "He made me do
it, master," he cried. "He forced me into it. I only did
it tó protect you!"

"Protect me?" Baydr's voice was cold.

"He had pictures, master. He threatened to expose
them to the world."

"Who would give credence to pictures of me? Especially from a source like that? Why didn't you come
to me at once?"

"I did not want to hurt you, master. They were
pictures of your wife." Youssef's eyes were filled with
real tears.

"You have them with you?"

"Yes, master." Youssef's voice was hushed. "They
are in a valise I left in the entrance hall. I was hoping
it would not come to this."

"Get it," Baydr said calmly.

Youssef almost ran from the room and came back
a moment later carrying the suitcase. Baydr watched
him silently as he opened the suitcase and removed
the portable video cassette player and a small-screen
American television set. Quickly he connected the two
machines. He looked around the room for an electrical
outlet. There was one at the side of the desk. He
plugged the wire into it, then placed the cassette in
the player.

He hesitated, looking down at Baydr. "I still feel
you should not subject yourself to this, master."

Baydr's voice was almost savage. "Turn it on!"

Youssef pressed the button and the screen filled

with bright empty light. There was a faint hum from the unwinding tape. A moment later the first blurred images appeared in color. Youssef made an adjustment and the pictures were suddenly in sharp focus.

Jordana and a man were lying on their backs in bed, apparently filmed from a camera overhead. They were both naked and passing a cigarette between them while obviously watching something happening offscreen. Abruptly the screen went blank for a moment, and resumed with the sound of their voices issuing from the speaker. Jordana was going down on the man. "Just beautiful," the man said, looking down at her.

Baydr did not say a word until the cassette had finished and the screen had gone blank. Then he reached across the desk and turned it off. His face was inscrutable. "I've seen the man before. Who is he?"

"An American actor," Youssef answered. "Rick Sullivan. His real name is Israel Solomon."

"A Jew?"

Yossef nodded. "That was another reason I did not want to have the pictures exposed."

There was still no expression on Baydr's face. "When did this take place?"

"At a party at the actor's home in California after you left for Tokyo."

"Was Yasfir at this party?"

"No."

"Were you?"

"Yes. I accompanied Michael Vincent and your wife to the party. But I left early with a headache."

"How did Yasfir get this tape?"

"I don't know. He didn't tell me."

"Are there other copies?"

Youssef took a deep breath. If Baydr believed his next statement, he might still save himself. "He said he had others which he would distribute if anything happened to stop the shipments."

"Why did he leave this with you?"

Youssef hesitated. "I don't know."

"He didn't suggest to you that if there were any problems you were to show the tape to me?"

"No, master, you must believe me," Youssef said sincerely. "Only the thought that you believed I betrayed you forced me to reveal this to you." He fell to his knees before Baydr, then seized and kissed his hand. "By my father's life, I would rather die than betray you." He began to weep.

Baydr looked down at him silently for a moment. When he spoke, his voice was harsh. "Compose yourself, man. Do not weep like a woman."

Youssef got to his feet, the tears falling on his cheeks. "I must have the words of forgiveness from your lips, oh, master," he cried.

"I forgive you," Baydr said heavily. He got to his feet, gesturing to a door. "There is a washroom. Bathe your face. It would not do to have you appear thus before the servants."

"Thank you, master!" Youssef said fervently, seizing Baydr's hand again and kissing it. "The light once more comes back into my life now that the burden has been lifted from my soul."

Baydr watched him go into the bathroom and close the door behind him. He didn't believe a word the man had said. He had condemned himself with his own words. No one but Youssef himself could have obtained that tape. There was no way Yasfir could have gotten it if he was not at that party. Silently, he moved across the room and opened the door.

Jabir was seated on a bench across the corridor. He rose to his feet when he saw Baydr. Baydr crossed the hall to meet him.

"Yes, master?"

Baydr's voice was calm. "That piece of camel dung has brought grave dishonor to our name."

Jabir's eyes turned cold, the skin tightening across his cheekbones. He did not speak.

"A mile down the road there is a curve around the mountain where the cliff drops off almost two hundred meters. It is too bad that his car must skid off the icy road."

Jabir nodded. His voice was a deep growl in his throat. "It will be a tragedy, master."

Baydr went back into the library. A moment later he heard the sounds of an automobile engine coming through the closed window. He turned and looked out between the drapes in time to see Jabir's Land Rover disappear down the driveway. He went back to his desk and sat down wearily.

A moment later, Youssef returned from the bathroom. He looked more like himself. Even the tone of his voice reflected the return of his confidence. "What shall we do about this, chief?"

"I must have time to think before I can make any decision. There is nothing more we can accomplish tonight."

"I guess not," Youssef said hesitantly.

"We might as well try to get some rest. You'd better go back to the hotel."

Youssef looked at the video cassette player. "Would you like me to guard that for you?"

"No. Leave that with me." He got to his feet. "I will let you out. The servants have all gone to bed."

It wasn't until the powerful Land Rover, its headlights blacked out, came at him from his blind side, pushing his tiny rented Opel inexorably toward the precipice, that Youssef looked back frantically to see Jabir hunched grimly over the steering wheel and remembered the one thing he never should have forgotten. The thought came to him at exactly the same moment that his car snapped the frail wires that served as a guard rail at the edge of the cliff and went hurtling into the air. He never heard the scream of fear that leaped from his throat as he plunged toward oblivion, but the thought burned in his brain.

Jabir never went to sleep when Baydr was awake.

CHAPTER 9.

BAYDR was seated alone in the breakfast alcove over-looking the garden, reading the Paris *Herald Tribune* and sipping coffee when the snobbish English butler came into the room. The man cleared his throat, and Baydr looked up.

There was a disapproving tone in the butler's precise voice. "There are some gentlemen from the police asking to see your excellency."

Baydr looked at him. No matter how many times he had explained to the butler that he did not hold a rank which entitled him to be addressed as "excellency," the man refused to address him in any other manner. His last employer had been the pretender to the throne of Spain and "excellency" was about as far down as he would descend from "highness."

"Show them into the library," Baydr said. "I will join them in a moment."

"Yes, your excellency." The butler left the room, his straight back and squared shoulders somehow carrying a hint of disapproval.

Slowly Baydr folded the newspaper and placed it neatly on the table. He took a last sip of coffee, then rose and went into the library.

There were two policemen, one in uniform, one in plainclothes. The plainclothesman bowed. He spoke in English. "Mr. Al Fay?"

Baydr nodded.

The policeman bowed again. "Permit me to introduce ourselves. I am Inspector Froelich and this is my associate, Sergeant Werner."

"What can I do for you gentlemen?"

"First I must apologize to you for intruding upon your breakfast but I am afraid I bring some rather unpleasant news. Are you acquainted with a Mr. Youssef Ziad?"

"Yes. He is the managing director of my Paris bureau. We had a meeting here last night. Why do you ask about him? Is he in some sort of trouble?"

"No, Mr. Al Fay, he is in no trouble at all. He is dead," the inspector said.

"Dead?" Baydr pretended shock. "What happened?"

"Apparently he lost control of his car and went off the road. The car fell almost two hundred meters."

Baydr stared at him for a moment, then walked around behind the desk and sat down. His face was grim. "Excuse me, gentlemen," he said. "But this is quite a shock. Mr. Ziad was an old and valued associate."

"We understand, sir," the plainclothesman said politely. "We have a few routine questions but we will try to be as brief as possible." He took a small notebook from his pocket and opened it. "You mentioned that you met with Mr. Ziad last night. At what time did he arrive here?"

"About half past twelve."

"Was there any particular reason for his arrival at that late hour?"

"There were important business matters to discuss. And unfortunately my wife and I had guests for dinner which precluded our meeting earlier."

"And approximately what time did he leave?"

"About two o'clock, I imagine."

"Did Mr. Ziad have anything to drink while he was here?"

"Nothing much."

"Could you be more specific?"

"We had a bottle of Dom Pérignon. He drank almost all of it. But that shouldn't have bothered him. Mr. Ziad drank it constantly. It was his favorite wine."

"He had good taste," the inspector said. He looked at the uniformed sergeant. A subliminal signal passed between them. The inspector closed his book and turned back to Baydr. "I guess that completes our questions, Mr. Al Fay," he said, satisfaction in his voice. "Thank you for your cooperation."

Baydr rose. "I will have to make arrangements for the funeral. His body will have to be flown home. Where is he now?"

"At the police morgue." This was the first time the sergeant had spoken. "What there is left of him."

"That bad?"

The inspector shook his head sadly. "We have gathered what remains we could find. Identification was made from his wallet and passport. The car itself is in a thousand pieces. It is too bad the people don't realize what a difference even the smallest amount of alcohol can make on an icy road at night."

Baydr sat for a moment after the policemen had left, then reached for the telephone and called Dick in Geneva.

"Call me back on the scrambler," Baydr said when Dick answered. A moment later the other telephone rang and he picked it up. "Dick?"

"Yes."

Baydr kept his voice expressionless. "The police just left. Youssef ran his car off the road last night and was killed."

"My God! What happened?"

"The road was icy and the police think he had a little too much to drink. He was quite upset when he left here and he did finish almost a whole bottle of champagne."

Dick was silent for a moment. "Did you learn anything from him about Arabdolls?"

"He claimed that he was coerced into it by Ali Yasfir."

"Then we were right. Did he admit that he was paid for it?"

"No. He swore that he received no money from them."

"I don't believe that."

"It doesn't matter now, does it? He's dead and it's over."

"Is it?" Dick replied. "We don't know what Yasfir will do now."

"There's very little he can do. He knows that he can't coerce us."

"I hope so. But you never can tell with a son of a bitch like that. You don't know what he'll come up with next."

"We'll deal with him when it comes," Baydr said calmly. "Right now, we have some unfinished business. I may send you down to the Paris office next week to take over until we can find a replacement for him."

"Right."

"Meanwhile see to it that his family and the Paris office are notified of the accident. Also make arrangements with a mortician to collect the remains from the police morgue in Gstaad and ship them to his home."

"I'll take care of it."

"Alert the crew to have the plane ready for a flight to Beirut on Friday. Jordana and the boys will be going home."

"Isn't that a week earlier than planned, chief?"

Baydr's voice grew edgy. "Just do it. I think they'll be better off at home." He slammed down the receiver and sat there staring at the videotape player.

Abruptly he crossed the room and locked the doors. Then, taking the key from his pocket, he unlocked the center drawer of the desk and took out the cassette. He inserted it into the machine and pressed the start button.

The screen went white for a moment then the picture and the sound came on. He sat almost immobilized as the tape unreeled before him. It was all there, just as it had been with him. The beauty of her body, the languorous sensuous movements, the words, the tiny animal-like cries rising to screaming orgiastic crescendos. It was all there, but this time it was not for him. It was for another man. A Jew.

The screen went blank just as the knot in his

stomach exploded into blazing pain. Angrily he slammed his fist down on the stop button, almost smashing the machine. Then he held his hands in front of him and looked at his trembling fingers.

Abruptly he closed them into fists and beat them against the desk. Over and over, he pounded them in unison to his muttered words—"Damn you! Damn you! Damn you!"—until his hands were painful and swollen.

He stared again at his hands, then at the machine. "Jordana!" he cried as if she were inside the machine. "Is it for this I have made myself into a murderer?"

The screen did not answer him. It was blank. He put his face down on the desk and wept, as he had not done since he was a boy. A prayer he had not uttered since childhood came to his lips:

In the name of Allah, the Beneficent, the Merciful.
I seek refuge in the Lord of men,
The King of men,
The God of men,
From the evil of the whisperings of the slinking devil,
Who whispers into the hearts of men.

The comfort of the prayer flowed through him. The tears dropped and he felt the hurt and pain leave him. Too easily one forgot the wisdom of Allah, the wisdom revealed by the Prophet. And much too easily, one forgot that the laws of Allah, revealed by the Prophet, were given to men to live by.

For too long had he tried to live by the laws of the unbelievers but they were not for him. Now he would live as he was intended. By the one true law. The laws of Allah.

JORDANA came into the library. The shock was still in her voice. "I just heard about Youssef," she said. "I can't believe it."

"He was dung," he said coldly. "But now he stands before the throne of judgment and must answer himself for his own sins. And even Allah, the most merciful, will not find forgiveness for him. Certainly he will see the fires of hell for all eternity."

"But he was your friend." She could not understand the change in him. "He has served you for many years."

"He served only himself. He was no man's friend but his own."

She was bewildered. "What happened between the two of you? What did he do?"

His face was an impenetrable mask, his eyes hooded. "He betrayed me, as did you."

She stared at him. "Now I really don't know what you're talking about."

He looked at her almost as if he did not see her. "You don't?"

She shook her head silently.

"Then I will show you." He went back to the desk, and pressed the button on the videotape player. "Come here."

She stood behind the desk next to him and looked down at the small screen. It was white and shining for a moment then the picture came on. She half-cried, her breath catching in her throat in shocked disbelief. "No!" she cried aloud.

"Yes," he said quietly.

"I won't watch!" she said, starting to leave.

His hand gripped her arm tightly, so tightly that she felt a pain shoot up into her shoulder. "You will stay, woman, and watch."

She closed her eyes and turned her head away. His fingers gripped her chin like claws of steel, forcing her face back to the screen. "You will watch," he said coldly. "All of it. All of your shame. As I had to."

Silently she stood there as the tape unwound. It seemed to last forever. She felt the sickness in her. It was crazy. All of it. There had been a camera on them all the time and there was only one way it could have been done. Sullivan had to have controlled it himself.

Then it all came back to her. That time he left the room, just before they began. He was starting the machine. And his insistence at always staying in the upper portion of the giant bed. The camera must have been fixed to cover that area. He had to be sick, sicker than anyone knew.

Suddenly, it was over. The screen went black and Baydr turned off the player. She turned to look at him.

His face was expressionless. "I had asked discretion of you. You were not discreet. I had specifically told you to avoid Jews. The man is a Jew."

"He is not!" she flashed. "He is an actor named Rick Sullivan."

"I know his name. His real name is Israel Solomon."

"I didn't know."

He didn't answer. It was obvious that he didn't believe her.

Suddenly she remembered. Youssef had been at that party. "Did Youssef bring you that tape?"

"Yes."

"That was more than three months ago. Why did he wait so long to give it to you?"

He didn't answer.

"He had to be guilty of something," she guessed shrewdly. "And he thought by using this he could clear himself."

"He said he was coerced by someone who brought him this tape. And that unless he did their bidding they would expose you."

"I don't believe that! He was the only one there who would have an interest in getting it. He had to be lying!"

Again he didn't answer. Everything she said only confirmed his own belief.

"Are there other copies?"

"I hope not, for my sons' sake as well as your own. I would not like them to learn that their mother committed adultery with a Jew."

For the first time the pain he felt crept into his voice. "Do you know what you've done, woman? If this were to become public, Muhammad could never be adopted

heir to the throne. When we are at war with Israel,
how can any Arab accept as his ruler and spiritual
leader one whose mother has committed adultery with
a Jew? Even his own legitimacy would become subject to question. By your action you could not only
lose for your own son the heritage to which he was
born but cause the loss of everything my father and I
have struggled for all our lives."

"I'm sorry, Baydr," she said. "But we have grown
so far apart that I thought nothing between us mattered anymore. I knew of your women. I even accepted
them. Now I see I did not even have the right to accept the options you granted me. Perhaps if I were an
Arab woman I would have known that. But I am not.
And I could never live the life of pretense that they
do, seeing but not seeing, believing the words that belied the deeds."

"It's too late for that now. I have made arrangements for you and the children to return to Beirut the
day after tomorrow. You will remain there in our home
in seclusion. You are not to leave the house, you are
not to see anyone, you are not to correspond or talk
to anyone by telephone except immediate members of
our family and servants until January, when Muhammad is officially invested as prince and heir to the
throne."

"And after that?"

"The day after the investiture you will be permitted
to return home to America to visit your parents. You
will remain there quietly until you receive the papers
of our divorce."

"What about the children?"

His eyes were as dark as blue ice. "You will never
see them again."

The pain in her heart choked off her breath. "What
if I refuse?" she managed to ask.

There was an implacability about him that she had
never seen before. "You have no choice. Under the
laws of Islam the punishment for an adulteress is death
by stoning. Would you have your children see that?"

"You wouldn't!" she exclaimed, horrified.

His eyes were unwavering. "I would."

Suddenly, she knew the truth. "Youssef! You killed him!"

His voice was contemptuous. "Youssef killed himself," he said, gesturing at the videotape player. "With this."

She was beaten. No longer able to control her tears, no longer able to look at him, she sank to her knees, covering her face with her hands. Her body was racked by sobs.

He stood there impassively, looking down at her; only a pulse beating in his temple gave sign of his own effort at self-control.

After a while the tears stopped and she looked up at him. Her eyes were swollen, her face drawn with pain. "What will I do?" she whispered in a hoarse hollow voice almost to herself. "What will my life be without them?"

He didn't answer.

Slowly she rose to her feet and began to walk toward the door. Halfway, she turned back. "Baydr," she said, the pleading clear in her eyes and in her voice.

The cold implacability was still in his voice. "Don't waste your time, woman, begging my forgiveness. Instead, go and thank Allah for His mercy."

Their eyes met for a brief moment, then her eyes fell. There was no more fight left in her. Slowly she walked from the room.

He locked the door behind her and went back to the desk. He stood looking down at the videotape player for a long time, then he reached down and pressed the start button once more. Almost at the same moment, he pressed the other button, marked ERASE.

The tape raced through the machine at ten times normal playing speed. Forty minutes of tape went through the machine in only four minutes. There was a click and he pressed the stop. A moment later he pressed the start button again. This time the tape moved at playing speed. But the screen remained blank and empty.

The tape had been wiped clean.

Baydr pressed the stop button. Machines made everything so simple.

If only there were a button that one could press to wipe the ribbon of life clean so that one could begin again.

CHAPTER 10.

WHEN she boarded the plane, Jordana was surprised to find Leila there with two young men. The young men, dressed in ill-fitting dark suits with bulging pockets customarily worn by Middle Eastern office workers abroad, got to their feet politely.

"I didn't know you were coming with us," Jordana said.

There was a strange, challenging tone in Leila's voice. She spoke in Arabic. "Do you mind?"

Jordana was puzzled. Leila had always spoken to her in English or French. But perhaps it was because her friends were not as proficient in these languages as she. She dismissed the thought and answered in Arabic. "Not at all. I am glad to have you with us. I was just surprised. Your father hadn't mentioned it."

"He might have forgotten," Leila said.

He didn't forget, Jordana thought. She hadn't seen him since the morning when he told her she would have to leave. Later in the day he had returned to Geneva and had only stopped by at the house to say goodbye to the boys. "He has many things on his mind," she said, still in Arabic. She turned pointedly to the two young men.

Leila got the hint and introduced them. "Madame Al Faÿ, my father's second wife, this is Fouad Aziz and Ramadan Sidki. They are joining me for a weekend at home."

"Ahlan," Jordana said.

"Ahlan fiki," they replied awkwardly, bowing jerkily as if it were not customary for them.

Just then the two children, their Scottish nanny, Anne, and her personal maid, Magda, came up the ramp into the plane. The boys broke into happy cries when they saw their sister. "Leila! Leila!" they exclaimed, running to her.

She was almost cool to them, though when they had first met, she had made a big fuss over them and spent the better part of two days playing with them before they left for Gstaad.

Jordana thought that she did not want to bother with them because of her friends. "Take your seats, children," she said. "And remember to fasten your seat belts. We'll be taking off in a few minutes."

"Can we sit next to Leila?" Samir asked. "Can we?"

She looked at Leila. "If your sister wouldn't mind?"

"I don't mind," Leila said. Again Jordana noticed a grudging tone in her voice.

"All right, but you must behave yourselves."

"Mother," Muhammad asked, "why are you speaking Arabic?"

Jordana smiled. "I think it's because your sister's friends may not be as conversant in English as we are. That's the polite thing to do if people don't understand what you are saying."

"We speak English, ma'am," the young man called Ramadan said in a clear British accent.

"So you do," she said. She looked at Leila, whose face was impassive. "I apologize for my misunderstanding then."

Raoul, the steward, came back into the cabin. "Captain Hyatt would like to know if you are ready to take off, madame."

"We will be as soon as everyone is in their places," she said, moving to the rear seat near the round table that Baydr usually occupied.

There was a flurry of activity as the boys were strapped in and the others took their seats. Raoul and the stewardess, a pretty American named Margaret, made a swift round of the cabin checking the seat belts. He nodded to Jordana, then went forward. A moment later the big plane moved down the runway.

Once they were in the air and the seat belt sign was off, Jordana got out of her seat. She gestured to Raoul, who came forward. "Would you please prepare the bed in Mr. Al Fay's cabin. I think I would like to lie down and rest."

"Yes, madame." He signaled swiftly, dispatching the stewardess to perform the function.

The boys were crawling all over Leila, who seemed nervous and barely able to tolerate them. "Don't bother your sister," Jordana said sharply. "Maybe she's tired."

Obediently the boys returned to their seats.

"I'm not feeling too well," Jordana explained. "I thought I might lie down for a bit."

Leila nodded without speaking. She watched Jordana make her way to the rear and enter the stateroom. She really could not understand what her father saw in her. In broad daylight, she was not as pretty as she had first thought. Without makeup, her face was drawn, there were dark circles under her eyes and her hair was stringy and not quite as blond as it had seemed. Just as well the woman had gone to sleep. It might make things easier.

She looked across the aisle at Fouad and Ramadan. Fouad glanced at his wristwatch, then back at her. "Another half-hour," he said.

She nodded and leaned back against the headrest. She closed her eyes. Another half-hour was not too long to wait after all the time she had spent preparing for it.

IT seemed to Jordana as if she had just closed her eyes when in her sleep she heard a child crying. She stirred restlessly, hoping the sound would stop. But it didn't and gradually it penetrated that it was one of her children crying. She sat up in the bed abruptly, listening.

It was Samir. But it was not his usual cry or whimper. There was a peculiar note in it. A note of fear.

Quickly she rose from the bed and straightened her dress. Then she opened the door and went out into the cabin and down the narrow corridor to the forward lounge. At the entrance, she stopped, suddenly transfixed. Her mind could not take in what she saw. It has to be a nightmare, she thought wildly. It has to be.

Huddled in the area just behind the galley in the small space that Carriage used as an office when he was on board were the children, their nanny, her maid and the cabin crew, Raoul and Margaret. Raoul had one hand on the bulkhead to support himself and blood was streaming down his face from a cut on his cheekbone. In front of them stood Leila and her two friends.

But it was a Leila she had never seen before. In her hand she held a heavy automatic, from the belt of her blue jeans hung two hand grenades. The two men were even more heavily armed. In addition to the grenades hanging from their belts, each carried an automatic rapid-fire rifle.

Samir was the first to see her. "Mommy! Mommy!" he cried, breaking loose from his nanny's grasp and running toward her.

Leila made a grab for him but he was too quick. Jordana bent forward and the child leaped into her arms. The tears were running down his cheeks. "They hit Raoul and he's bleeding!" he cried.

"It's all right, it's all right," she said soothingly, holding him tightly.

Leila gestured with her gun. "Get up there with the others." Jordana stared at her. "Have you gone mad?" she said angrily.

"You heard me," Leila said. "Get up there with the others!"

Instead Jordana turned on her heel and started back down the corridor to the cabin. Leila moved so swiftly that Jordana did not know she was behind her until the sudden thrust of the gun against her back sent her sprawling in the narrow corridor, knocking the child from her arms.

Immediately, the child began to cry again. He sprang at his sister, flailing his little fists. "Don't you hit my mommy, you bad girl, you!"

Indifferently, Leila sent him sprawling with a slap across the cheeks. The child fell in a huddle against his mother and she put her arm around him.

At the far end of the cabin, Muhammad began to cry. He pulled loose from the nanny and ran to her, kneeling on the floor beside her. Jordana put her other arm around him.

"These children are your brothers," she said, ignoring the screaming pain in the small of her back as she tried to sit up. She looked up at Leila. "You will answer to God for your sins."

"Slut!" Leila's lips drew back in a snarl. "They are not my brothers. They are the children of an American whore!"

"It is written in the Koran that brothers and sisters are united by the father," Jordana said.

"Don't quote the Holy Book to me, bitch!" Leila snapped. "True brothers and sisters are united, not those you managed to convince my father were his own. I've heard all about that from my mother."

"You are still committing a crime against your father," Jordana said.

Leila laughed. "My father has betrayed any allegiance I may have felt for him. He has betrayed his own people and become an accomplice and tool of the Jews and the imperialists."

Oddly enough, Jordana thought, she felt no fear for herself, only for the children. "It will be all right," she whispered to them. "Don't cry anymore."

"On your feet!" Leila snapped.

Wincing with pain, Jordana struggled upright. Leila gestured with her gun for them to go forward. Painfully, holding Samir in one arm and leading Muhammad by the hand, she moved through the cabin.

"Give the children to their nurse," Leila commanded.

Jordana looked at her.

"Do what I say! Quickly! Or they will be the next to be hurt!"

Silently, Jordana gave the boys over to the nanny. They looked up at her with frightened eyes. She patted them reassuringly. "Don't be frightened. It will be okay."

She almost screamed with pain as she felt the prod of a gun in the small of her back. When she turned, she saw the strange look of pleasure in Leila's eyes. She tightened her lips. She would not give her the pleasure of hearing her moan.

"You go forward to the flight deck with Ramadan," Leila said.

The young man made her walk in front of him. As she opened the door to the cockpit, he shoved her violently. She stumbled forward to her knees and he sprang into the narrow space behind her.

Captain Hyatt, the copilot, Bob, and the flight engineer, George, turned around in surprise. George reached overhead for a wrench.

Moving with unexpected speed, Ramadan hit him in the side of the face with the butt of the rifle, knocking him back into his seat. Blood began spurting from his broken nose. "Don't any of you try anything foolish," he said in his clipped British accent, "or you'll kill everyone on this plane."

Andy Hyatt looked up at him, then over at his flight engineer. "Are you okay, George?"

George nodded, holding a handkerchief to his nose. Jordana got to her feet. "Where's the first aid kit?"

"In the cabinet over George's seat," Bob answered.

She took down the metal box and opened it. Quickly she stripped the wrapping from several packages of gauze bandages and gave them to George. She looked down at the captain. "Raoul has a bad cut on his cheek." She started back into the cabin.

"Wait a minute!" Ramadan blocked her path. "You're not through here yet." He turned to the captain. "There are three of us aboard and we're all armed with automatic weapons and grenades. That puts us in charge of this plane, do you understand that?"

Hyatt's voice was puzzled. "Three of you?"

"Leila is one of them," Jordana said.

"Leila?" Hyatt let out a long slow whistle. "Well, I'll be damned. This has got to beat it all. To be hijacked by your boss's own daughter."

"Now that you understand, you will follow my orders exactly as I give them to you," Ramadan said.

Hyatt glanced at Jordana. She nodded. He looked up at the young man. "Yes," he answered.

"First, you will inform Beirut that there has been a change of flight plan; you will request clearance from Lebanon to Damascus."

Hyatt made some notes on the scratch pad beside him. "Got it."

"When we get into Syria, tell them there's been another change in plans and get clearance over Iraq to Teheran."

Hyatt looked at him. "I didn't take on enough fuel to get us to Teheran."

"Don't worry," Ramadan said confidently. "We're not going there."

"Where are we going then?" the captain asked.

Ramadan took a piece of paper from his jacket pocket. He handed it down to the pilot. "That's where we're going."

The captain glanced at it then back at him. "You're

crazy," he said. "There's no place to put a plane this size down there. It's nothing but mountains."

"There is a place," Ramadan said. "I'll show it to you when we get there."

"Is there equipment for an instrument landing?" Hyatt asked.

"No," Ramadan answered. He gave a short nervous laugh. "But you have the reputation for being one of the best pilots around. Surely, Al Fay would have nothing but the best. You shouldn't have any trouble making a visual approach and landing."

"I hope you're right," Hyatt muttered. He reached for the radio switch. "I'd better get on to Beirut."

"Just a minute!" Ramadan pulled the extra set of ear phones from the flight engineer's desk and held one of them to his ear while keeping a finger on the trigger of the rifle in the crook of his other arm. "Now you can call. And, remember, no word of a hijacking or I'll kill you right in your seat. We don't want anyone to know about this. Just yet."

Hyatt looked at him grimly and nodded.

"Now can I go back to help Raoul?" Jordana asked.

"Of course." Ramadan seemed more relaxed. "And while you're about it, you can tell them that I have everything under control up here."

CHAPTER 11.

BAYDR came into Dick's office about four o'clock in the afternoon. He had been at the bank for lunch and gone to several meetings later. He glanced around the office. "Where's Leila?"

Dick looked up at him in surprise. "She went to Beirut this morning."

"Beirut?"

Dick saw the blank expression on his face. "I thought you knew. She left with Jordana and the children. She told me it was okay with you if she and two friends made the trip. She wanted to go home for the weekend."

"I must be getting old. Strange, but I don't remember a thing about it."

He went into his office, closing the door behind him. Dick stared after him, a vague apprehension beginning to build inside him. It wasn't like Baydr to forget anything. The telephone rang; he picked it up. He listened for a moment then pressed down the hold button and went into Baydr's office.

Baydr looked up from behind his desk. "Yes?"

Dick kept his voice level. "I have our man at the Beirut airport on the line. He's been there since one o'clock and the plane hasn't arrived yet."

Baydr picked up the phone, then covered the mouthpiece with one hand. "What time was it due there?"

"About one-thirty."

Baydr's face paled slightly. He removed his hand from the mouthpiece. "This is Al Fay," he said. "Call the air controller and find out if they have any word on the plane. I'll hold on."

He looked up at Dick, covering the mouthpiece again. "I hope nothing's happened."

"Don't worry," Dick said reassuringly. "Andy's too good a pilot to let anything go wrong."

A voice came back on the line. Baydr listened for a moment then seemed to relax slightly. "Okay, thank you very much."

He put down the phone. There was a puzzled look on his face. "I don't understand it. Air control in Beirut said the pilot requested clearance for Damascus."

Dick didn't say anything.

"Get on the phone to Damascus and find out if they're on the ground there."

"Right away, chief." Dick went back into his office and picked up the telephone. It took him twenty minutes to connect with air traffic control in Damascus. He listened for a moment then nodded, placed another call and went back into Baydr's office.

"Are they down there?" Baydr asked.

Dick shook his head. "No. They told me they cleared the plane for Teheran via Baghdad."

Baydr exploded. "Hyatt's gone out of his mind! He'll hear from me about this." Then he calmed down. "Put calls in to those airports and see what you can find out."

"I've already done that," Dick said.

"Good. Let me know as soon as you get word." He leaned back in his chair and watched the door close behind Dick. There was only one possible reason for the change in flight plans. Jordana. She was trying to get the children away from him. He felt anger at his own stupidity. He never should have been so confident that she would do his bidding. Not after what had happened.

A half-hour later Carriage returned. His face was grim. "They didn't land at Teheran and Baghdad reports that there was no radar track of their crossing Iraqi territory. I checked back with Damascus and they report no signs of trouble or any word from the plane since it flew over them at about two o'clock this afternoon."

"The plane couldn't have vanished just like that without leaving a trace." Baydr was silent for a moment. "I think we'd better call for a search."

"Before we do that I have a man outside I think you should talk to," Dick said.

"Tell him to come back," Baydr snapped. "I have more important things on my mind right now than business!"

"I think what he has to say could have a bearing on where the plane might be."

Baydr stared at him. "Show him in."

Dick opened the door. "Would you please come in, Mr. Dupree?" A medium-size man in a nondescript gray suit came through the door. Dick walked with him to the desk. "Mr. Dupree, Mr. Al Fay."

Dupree bowed. "Honored, monsieur."

Baydr nodded but did not speak. He looked questioningly at Dick. "What has he got to do with the plane?"

"Maybe nothing," Dick said quickly. "But first perhaps I'd better explain."

Baydr nodded.

Dick cleared his throat. It was evident that he was uncomfortable. "Mr. Dupree is a private investigator. We have used him several times before on confidential matters and he has proved himself to be completely trustworthy. Early this week because of certain remarks that Leila made I took it on myself to have him place her under surveillance."

Baydr's voice was cold. "Why?"

Dick met his gaze. "Because the day after we stopped the Arabdoll shipments she asked me to let them continue. When I refused because it was against your orders, she said that the Riad and Mafrad families were old friends and that her grandfather would be very embarrassed by it. She also said that I could have the shipments continued and that you would never have to know about them." He took a deep breath. "When I found out from you that they were not friends I decided to learn what I could about her."

Baydr turned to the private detective. "What have you found out?"

Mr. Dupree took some papers from his inside jacket pocket and unfolded them. He placed one copy on the desk before Baydr, gave one to Dick and held the other in his own hand. "Typewritten on that sheet of paper are the names of every person your daughter came into contact with this week, together with the times and places of their meetings."

Baydr looked down at the paper. One name stood

out above all the others: Ali Yasfir. Leila had met with him five times this week, twice yesterday. Several other names were repeated but they were not familiar to him. He looked up at the private detective.

"I'm afraid your daughter has been keeping dangerous company, monsieur," the detective said. "Almost all the names on that list are known Arab terrorists or partisans and, as such, are kept under close surveillance by the Swiss police. They are young and a man called Yasfir appears to be their greatest financial supporter.

"So the Swiss police gave a sigh of relief when Fouad Aziz and Ramadan Sidki, the two who were considered the most dangerous because they were both experts in the use of bombs and weapons, boarded the plane with your daughter and left the country. You may be sure that they will never be granted a reentry visa."

Baydr studied the paper for a moment. "Is there anything else?"

"Only this, monsieur," Dupree answered. "I took the liberty of calling the school your daughter used to attend in Montreux. I hoped to get some information on several of the girls she had been seeing. But they couldn't tell me anything, except that they had not seen your daughter since early last May, when she left school in the company of a gentleman named Mr. Yasfir who represented himself as an associate of yours. The school was told that they were going to join you at the Cannes film festival. She never returned."

Baydr looked at Dick, then turned back to the private detective. "Thank you very much, Mr. Dupree. You've been most helpful."

The detective sighed. "The children nowadays." He opened his hands in a typically Gallic gesture. "I have a teen-age daughter myself. One never knows what they're up to." He bowed. "If there's anything further I can do for you, Monsieur Al Fay, please do not hesitate to call on me." He bowed to Dick and left the office.

Dick turned to Baydr. "I don't like what I'm thinking, do you?"

"No." Baydr let out a deep breath. "But at least now we know the plane is safe, even if we don't know where it is."

"It's a big plane. They can't hide one that size for long."

"Maybe." Baydr's voice was noncommittal.

"What do we do now?"

"Wait."

"Wait?" There was surprise in Dick's voice.

"Yes." Baydr looked up at him. "We were wondering what Ali Yasfir's next move would be. Now we know. Soon he will be in touch with us to tell us what he wants."

THEY stood at the edge of the small forest and looked back at the silver 707. Nine men were scrambling over the plane, putting the camouflage netting in place, so that it would be concealed from aerial view. Another plane would have to fly over it at less than twenty feet to spot it.

Jordana turned to Hyatt, who was standing near, his eyes fixed on the plane. "You put her down beautifully, captain. Thank you."

"It was a little hairy there for a moment. I thought we were going to run into those trees at the end of the runway." He turned back to the plane. "Why do you think they built a runway as big as this up here? From the looks of it, it's at least three years since it's been used."

"I wouldn't know, captain," she said.

The man called Fouad came up to them. "Okay. Move out." His English bore an American accent. He gestured with his gun toward the forest.

Jordana walked over to the children, who were standing between their nanny and her maid, Magda.

The boys were watching the camouflaging of the plane with great interest. She took their hands and waited.

In front of them stood two soldiers in rough, poorly fitted battle uniforms. There were no markings on them to indicate what army, if any, they belonged to. At a signal from Fouad, they began to lead the way. Several other soldiers came up and walked beside them; others fell in behind. All held their rifles pointing at them.

Jordana walked silently with the children. Leila and Ramadan were nowhere to be seen. They had been the first off the plane and a few minutes after landing, they had disappeared.

The forest grew thicker and the branches of the trees and the bushes caught and tore at their clothing. Jordana tried to protect the children but within ten minutes there were scratches all over their arms and faces. She called to the nanny. "Anne, if you, Magda, Margaret and I walk in front with the children close behind us, they won't get as many scratches."

The nanny nodded and the other girls came up to join them, forming a semicircle with the children in the middle.

A few minutes later they came out of the forest onto a narrow dirt road. Two jeeps were parked there, each with a driver.

"Into the cars," Fouad said. "The ladies with the children in the first car, the men in the second."

A moment later the cars started up the road. It was narrow and bumpy and filled with potholes, a winding road that seemed to lead in and out of the forest but climbed continually up the side of the mountain. After about ten minutes, the air began to feel cooler.

Jordana looked up at the sky. It was growing dark. Evening had come. She turned to the boys, wishing she had thought to bring their coats. But they had been left aboard the plane along with everything else.

Five minutes later they came out of the forest into a clearing. At the edge of the clearing was a group of dilapidated wooden buildings. The buildings were surrounded by a low wall, on the top of which were mounted heavy machine guns at intervals. Each gun was attended by two soldiers. And there were searchlights on each corner.

Jordana looked up at the soldiers as they drove into the camp, and they returned her gaze with open interest. A few called ribald comments after them but they could not be heard over the noise of the rattling jeep engines.

The jeeps pulled to a stop in front of the largest of the buildings. The driver gestured for them to get out.

Two men came out of the building and stood watching them. Ramadan, now dressed in uniform, was one. But Jordana had to look twice before she recognized the other. It was the uniform that fooled her. The second soldier was Leila.

Leila came toward her. Somehow, in the uniform she seemed larger and coarser. All the prettiness that Jordana had seen in her was erased by the hardness of her manner. "You will occupy one cabin with the children and the other women," she said. "The men another. Dinner will be brought to you in one hour. After you have eaten, the lights will be extinguished for the night. No smoking will be permitted after dark. From the sky the light from a cigarette can sometimes be seen for miles. Any infraction of our rules will be severely punished. Do you understand that?"

"You won't get away with it," Jordana said. "When your father learns about this there will be no place left on earth or in heaven for you to hide."

Leila stared at her with contempt. "My father will do as he is told—that is, if he ever wants to see any of you alive again."

CHAPTER 12.

IT was the next morning before they heard from him. His voice crackled over the wire. "We have important matters to discuss," he said. "Much too important for the telephone. I think a meeting between us would be of mutual benefit."

Baydr's voice was cool. "It might."

"Where would it be convenient for you?" Yasfir asked.

"I'm in my office."

"I don't think that would be a very good idea. With all due respect to you, there are too many opportunities to be overheard."

"We would be alone."

"Only Allah knows how many bugs lie hidden in the walls of buildings," Yasfir said.

"Where do you suggest?"

"A mutually agreeable place, perhaps a bench in the park across the street from your hotel."

"When will you be there?"

"I can be there in fifteen minutes."

"I will be there." Baydr put down the telephone. He pressed the buzzer on his desk. Dick came into the office. "He wants me to meet him in the park across the street from the hotel. Do you think our electronics man can pick up our conversation with a telescopic microphone from here?"

"I don't know. We can try."

"Get him up here then. We only have fifteen minutes."

The man was in the office in less than ten. Baydr

took him to the window and pointed to the park across the street. "Can you get us from here?"

"Maybe," the man answered. "It depends on a lot of things. Street noises. Movement. It would help if you were to remain in one place."

"I don't know," Baydr answered. "A great deal will depend on the other man."

"I'll set up. We'll see what happens."

The man worked swiftly. He was checking out his amplifiers when Dick stuck his head in the door. "It's almost time."

Reluctantly Baydr got ready to leave. He would have preferred to wait a few minutes more to find out whether the electronic eavesdropper would work but he was afraid to be late. He walked through the outer office to the door. Jabir rose to follow him.

Baydr gestured. "Wait here," he said.

Jabir returned to his seat. As soon as the door had closed behind Baydr, Dick beckoned to him. "Your master will be in the park across the street," he said. "Follow him but keep your distance and do not allow him to see you. I fear for him."

Jabir nodded and without speaking left the office. When he came out of the entrance to the hotel, Baydr was already crossing the street. Jabir stationed himself near the corner, where he could keep his eyes on him.

Baydr crossed the street and entered the small park. An old woman was sitting on the first bench, wrapped against the cold autumn winds, feeding the pigeons. Baydr sat down on the far end of the bench away from the old woman. He looked up and down the path. There was no one there—not even office workers taking a shortcut on their way to work. He reached for a cigarette.

Fifteen minutes later, he was on his fourth cigarette and beginning to wonder whether Yasfir had led him on a wild-goose chase when abruptly the old woman got up and left the bench. His eyes followed her curiously as she walked to the curb outside the park and got into a taxi. Odd that a woman dressed as shabbily as she should be able to afford a taxi. Then the thought struck him. He looked at the corner of the bench where she had been sitting. There under the bag of peanuts she had left behind was a sheet of ordinary white paper. His eyes scanned the typewritten message.

My apologies for not meeting but urgent business has taken me from the country. Besides, our meeting would serve no effective purpose for our requests are simple and can be transmitted on this sheet of paper. I am pleased to inform you that your wife and children have arrived safely at their destination and are all well. Tomorrow morning you will receive a tape of your wife's voice reassuring you of this fact. In order to guarantee our continued interest in their well-being you will comply with the following requests:

1. Deposit $100,000 U.S. each morning before 12 noon to the account No. AX1015 at the Banque d'Assurance in Geneva. This is to reimburse us for the care given your family while they are our guests.
2. Allow the shipments previously rescinded to continue as planned. The next shipment will take place four days from now to be followed by a shipment every other day until the end of the year.
3. You will have prepared and signed by yourself, in blank, an effective instrument of transfer in the amount of a 50 percent equity in your company. This together with a payment of $10,000,000 U.S. will be turned over to the account of the bank listed above not later than 5 Jan. 1974.

In the event that all of the above conditions are met promptly, your wife and sons will be returned to you before 10 Jan. in time for the investiture of your eldest son as prince. Any breach of the confidentiality of this agreement or any failure to meet with the terms exactly as specified could lead to the death of one or all members of your family. As further indication of our good will and in order to assure you of their continued well-being, you will receive each day at your office in Geneva a tape of your wife's voice in which she will read a headline from the previous day's Paris *Herald Tribune* and give you some personal words regarding their general condition. Of course, your aid in the war against our common enemies is expected. IDBAH AL-ADU!

It was signed BROTHERHOOD OF PALESTINIAN FREEDOM FIGHTERS.

Slowly Baydr got to his feet and started back to his office in the hotel. Dick was waiting for him as he came in the door.

"What happened? We didn't see anyone and we couldn't pick up anything."

"No one came," Baydr said. "Only this." He gave the paper to Dick, who followed him into his office.

He went behind the desk and sank heavily into his chair. Dick continued to read the paper while the electronics expert quickly gathered his equipment and left.

"They're crazy," Dick said when he had finished. "There's no way you can comply with this."

Baydr nodded in weary agreement. There was no way he could satisfy the third and last request. He didn't own fifty percent of the companies in his name. At best, he averaged a twenty percent equity. "I know that and you know that," he said in a tired voice. "But they don't know that. And how do you negotiate with someone who won't talk to you? Someone you can't find?"

"We'll have to find him. There must be a way."

"We'll find him all right, but what worries me is

what will happen to the children and Jordana when we do."

"Then what can we do?" Dick asked.

"First we'll make arrangements to make that deposit every day and let the shipments go through as they requested. That will buy us time."

"Those shipments can cause the death of hundreds of people in the States. I wouldn't want that on my conscience."

"Neither do I. We will have to find a way to stop the shipments on the other side."

"How do you plan to do that?"

"I have a friend in New York, Paul Gitlin. He is an attorney, a man of great moral force, and with a strong sense of justice. I am sure that he will understand my position and respect our confidence. He will find a way to stop the shipments there and protect us at the same time."

"And then?"

"We must use our time to find out where they are keeping my family and get them out." He rose from the chair and walked to the window. "Arrange the bank deposits and place the call to New York," he said, without turning around.

"Yes, sir," Dick said, starting from the office.

"And, Dick."

Dick turned back.

Baydr was facing him. There were lines on his face that Dick had never seen before. "Call Uni-Jet and charter a plane for me. I will pick up my father in Beirut and we will go together to see the Prince. Perhaps he will be able to help us."

THE old Prince finished reading the sheet of paper, then took off his glasses with palsied fingers. His wrinkled hawklike face under the ghutra looked at Baydr and his father sympathetically. "I know of this organization," he said. "They are a splinter group expelled from Al Fatah because of their nihilistic aims."

"I had heard that, your highness," Baydr said. "I thought that with your sponsorship we could gather enough support to force them into the open."

"And then what would you do?" the Prince asked.

"Destroy them!" Baydr said savagely. "They are thieves, blackmailers and murderers. They demean and bring dishonor to the cause they pretend to serve."

"Everything you say is true, my son. But there is nothing we can do."

"Why not?" Baydr demanded. He had all he could do to contain his anger. "It is your heir, the heir to your throne, whose life they endanger."

The old man's eyes were weak and rheumy, but his words were clear and distinct. "He is not yet my heir. And he will not be until I appoint him."

"Then you offer no help?" Baydr asked.

"I cannot—officially," the Prince replied. "And neither can the heads of any other states you might go to. This organization that calls itself the Brotherhood has garnered great support among certain elements. Even Al Fatah finds that it must leave them alone." He picked up the sheet of paper and held it toward Baydr.

Baydr took it silently.

"Unofficially, if you can locate where these fiends are holding your family, you can call on me for as many men and as much money as it takes to free them."

Baydr rose to his feet with a heavy heart. "I thank you for your boons, your highness," he said properly. But he knew it was of no use. Without official help they would never be found.

The old Prince sighed as he held out his hand. "If I were a younger man," he said, "I would be at your side in your search. Go with God, my son. I shall pray to Allah for the safety of your loved ones."

Outside the great palace, in the blinding sun, Dick waited in the air-conditioned limousine. He saw them walking toward the car. "What did he say?" he asked.

"There's nothing he can do," Baydr's father answered.

Baydr stared out the window as the car began to roll down the road. "It's hopeless," he said in a dull voice. "There's nothing anyone can do. There's no one willing to help me."

Dick was silent for a long moment. So much was at stake, so many years. All the work, all the effort that had gone into getting him here would go down the drain. But there were some things that were more important than work. Like the lives of innocent children. He thought of his own two and how he would feel if they were in the same position. That was what finally decided it.

He turned on the jump seat so that he could face Baydr. "I know of some that would help you," he said.

"Who?"

Dick's voice was quiet. "The Israelis."

Baydr's laugh was bitter. "Why should they want to help me? I was born their enemy."

Samir looked at his son. "Men are not born enemies. That is something they learn."

"What difference does it make?" Baydr retorted sarcastically. He turned back to Dick. "Why should they help me?" he asked again.

Dick's eyes went straight into his. "Because I'll ask them to," he said quietly.

Baydr was silent for a moment. Then a small weary sigh escaped his lips. "You work for them?"

Dick nodded. "Yes."

"You're not Israeli," Baydr said. "Why?"

"My parents went back to Jordan to live," Dick said. "One day a man named Ali Yasfir came to visit them and asked them to allow his organization to use their small village as a base. After a few months, during which three girls were raped and many were abused, the villagers demanded that they leave. What the Fedayeen gave them in answer was death. Ali Yasfir personally led his men on a systematic house-by-house extermination of the village. Only a small boy and two girls managed to escape. They told us the true story, while the Fedayeen loudly proclaimed the latest Israeli atrocity. The two girls personally saw Ali Yasfir slaughter my mother and father."

"And so now that you have betrayed me," Baydr said bitterly, "you think that you should help me."

Dick met his look honestly. "Not for that reason. But because we both believe that the Arabs and Israelis can live and work together in peace. It is men like Ali Yasfir who kill this possibility. They are our enemies. They are the ones who must be destroyed."

CHAPTER 13.

BAYDR looked at the two men in the doorway. If anything, they looked more Arab than either his father or himself. The old man was tall. His headcloth almost hid his face except for the large hawklike nose, and his dusty faded jellaba trailed to the floor. The young man was dark and swarthy with a heavy Syrian mustache over his lips. He wore faded tan khaki shirt and trousers.

Baydr and his father rose as General Eshnev led them to him. "Dr. Al Fay, Mr. Al Fay—General Ben Ezra."

The general stared at Samir for a moment, then smiled. "It has been a long time, my friend."

Samir's face suddenly went pale. He felt himself trembling inside. From the corner of his eye he looked at Baydr, hoping that his nervousness would not be noticed. Baydr was looking at the general.

"And this is your son," the general said. "Allah has been good to you. He is a fine man."

Samir's nervousness left him. "It is good to see you again, general."

Baydr looked at his father. "You know each other?"

His father nodded. "Our paths crossed one time in the desert. Many years ago."

General Eshnev spoke quickly. "I must repeat our official position, gentlemen, so that we may all understand it clearly. A very delicate cease-fire exists at the moment so we dare not condone any official action which might involve entering enemy territory. Such an action could destroy the sincere efforts that are being made to maintain the peace that Israel so profoundly desires."

He paused for a breath. "But there is nothing that we can do about the actions of private citizens as long as we are not aware of what they are doing. Have I made myself clear?"

The others nodded.

"Good," he said. "General Ben Ezra is of course a private citizen. He has been retired from the Israeli army for many years. And so is the young man with him. A former first sergeant in the Syrian army, he was taken prisoner on the Golan Heights and at the general's request was released in his custody. He goes by the name of Hamid."

The Syrian bowed respectfully. "I am honored."

"The honor is ours," Baydr and his father replied.

"And now, gentlemen, I must leave you," General Eshnev said. "Unfortunately I have duties that take me elsewhere."

When the door closed behind him, they sat down at the small round table. From beneath his jellaba, Ben Ezra produced several rolls of maps. He spread them open on the table. "One week ago, after your arrival in Tel Aviv, I was told of your problem. On my own, I undertook to examine the feasibility of a rescue plan. But first I knew we had to locate the camp in which the prisoners were held. In order to do that, I asked that Hamid be released in my custody. Many years ago, when we were both very young, Hamid's grandfather and I soldiered together in the British army and Hamid in the family tradition grew up as a professional soldier. I knew that before the war Hamid's last job was as an instructor in a particular camp where the Brotherhood was training a women's corps similar to that of Al Fatah. It failed."

He looked at Baydr, then continued in the same even tone. "Your daughter, Leila, spent three months in that camp. Hamid reports to me that she was a good soldier, much more serious than most in her application to duty and much more idealistic in her politics. After her stint at the camp, Hamid accompanied her to Beirut, where he remained until he decided to return to Syria for military duty since there were no longer any opportunities for mercenaries among the Fedayeen."

Baydr looked at Hamid. "Then you knew my daughter?"

"Yes, sir."

"Did she ever talk about me?"

"No, sir."

"What did she talk about?"

"Freeing Palestine mostly," Hamid answered. "It was her feeling that it was not only the Jews who held back the liberation but also the wealthy, elite Arabs who wanted to perpetuate their power over the land and its peoples."

"Do you think she included me in that group?"

Hamid hesitated, then nodded. "Yes, sir, I believe she did."

Baydr turned back to Ben Ezra. "I'm sorry, general, I'm still trying to understand what happened."

The general nodded. He looked down at the map and pointed to a spot. "We think we have located the one camp where they might be. You say your plane was a 707?"

"Yes."

"Then I'm sure we have it," he said, a faint note of triumph entering his voice. "There is an old camp, built by the Syrians and abandoned more than ten years ago. It is located just north of the Jordanian border, west of your own country. At the time it was built, they had planned to use it as a base for giant bombers but since they could not purchase the planes, the entire project was given up. But the airstrip is still there and there have been rumors in the countryside that the camp has been occupied by the Brotherhood. There is one major difficulty however: the airstrip is in the mountains on a plateau seven hundred meters up and the camp itself is one hundred and fifty meters higher. There are only two ways to penetrate. We could go in by air, but the sound of planes would give them too much warning and they would have the captives executed before we could get to them. The other way is to go on foot. To avoid detection we would have to set down at least fifty miles from the camp, concealing ourselves by day and traveling by night through terrible terrain. We would have two nights of forced march and attack on the third night. My estimate based on the size of the camp is that they may have as many as one hundred men there. So even if we are successful in freeing the captives, we will still have the problem of getting them to safety before we are pursued."

He looked up at them. "That's my speech. Any questions?"

"How do we know that we're going to the right camp? Or that they will be there when we get there?" Baydr asked.

The general's voice was flat. "We don't. But that's the chance we take. Right now it's the only possibility we have. Unless you know of another place where a 707 can land."

"I don't know of any other."

"Then it is you who must make the decision to go or not to go."

Baydr looked at his father for a moment, then he turned back to the general. "I say we go."

The general smiled. "Well said. Since this is an unofficial action we will need to recruit volunteers. I say fifteen, not more than twenty men. Any more than that would be unwieldy and make us too visible. They will be paid very high wages, of course, for such dangerous work."

"I will pay whatever they ask."

"Good. I know of ten men I can be sure of."

"I would like to volunteer," Hamid said. "I have been at that camp once. I know the layout."

"Accepted," the general said grimly. "Even though you have already been drafted."

"My prince promised me as many men as I needed," Baydr said.

"Are they good?"

"His personal guards are all mountain warriors from the Yemen."

"They'll do," the general said. The Yemeni mountain men were considered the most savage fighters in all Islam. "We will need equipment, guns, grenades, portable rocket launchers, food, water and other supplies as well as planes to get us to our starting point. It will be expensive."

"You will have them."

"And one more thing. We will need a helicopter to get us out. We will time its arrival at the airstrip with our attack."

"That too," Baydr said.

The general nodded.

"How long will it take to get ready?" Baydr asked.

"Three days if you can get your men here by then."

"They'll be here," Baydr answered. He turned to his father. "Would you be kind enough to see the Prince and ask him for the assistance he promised? I would like to remain here with the general and see that everything is in readiness."

Samir nodded. "I will do that."

"Thank you, Father."

Samir looked at him. "They are my grandchildren also." He turned to Ben Ezra. "My heartfelt gratitude, my friend," he said. "Once again, it seems, Allah sent you to me in my time of need."

"Do not thank me, my friend," Ben Ezra said in Arabic. "It would seem to me that we are both blessed."

CHAPTER 14.

"MOMMY, when will Father come for us?"

Jordana looked down at Samir's little face peering at her over the edge of the blanket that was tucked under his chin. She glanced at Muhammad in the other cot. He was already asleep, his eyes tightly shut, his face pressed against the hard pillow. She turned back to Samir. "Soon, my darling, soon," she whispered reassuringly.

"I wish he would come tomorrow," Samir said. "I don't like it here. The people are not nice."

"Daddy will come soon. Close your eyes and go to sleep."

"Good night, Mommy."

She bent and kissed his forehead. "Good night, darling." She straightened up and walked back into the other room of the small two-room cabin in which they were living. A small oil lamp glowed in the center of the little table where they took their meals. The three other women were sitting around the table, staring into the lamp. There was nothing for them to do, nothing to read. Even conversation had run dry. After two weeks there was nothing left to talk about, and they hadn't had much in common to begin with.

"The children are asleep," she said, just to hear the sound of a voice.

"Bless the little darlings," Anne, the nanny, answered. The others did not even raise their heads.

"My God!" Jordana exclaimed. "Look at us. We're as tatty a bunch of females as ever existed."

This time they did look up. "We have to make up our minds," she said forcefully. "Tomorrow we'll have to do something about ourselves. Surely there has to be a needle and thread somewhere in this damned camp."

"If there is," Margaret, the stewardess, replied, "they probably won't let us have it. We have all the clothes we need down on the plane but they won't send anyone to get them for us."

"We'll have to insist."

"It wouldn't do any good," Margaret said. She looked up at Jordana. "I don't understand why Mr. Al Fay won't pay the ransom and get us out of here."

Jordana looked at her. "How do we know that he hasn't? And that they are holding out for even more?"

"It doesn't make sense to me," Margaret said. She covered her face with her hands and began to cry. "It's terrible here. They won't let us out except to go to the toilet, and then the guard stands in front of the open door watching. They won't let us talk to the men. We don't even know how they are. They may be dead for all we know."

"They're okay," Jordana said. "I saw a man bringing them their food trays the other day."

Abruptly the stewardess stopped crying. "I'm sorry, Mrs. Al Fay. I didn't mean to let it out on you. I guess it's just gotten to be too much for me, that's all."

Jordana nodded sympathetically. "I think it's too much for all of us. The real hell is not knowing what is going on. They know that and that is why they keep us the way they do."

She walked over to the boarded window and peeked through a tiny crack between the boards. She could see nothing except the darkness of the night. She went back to the table and sat down in the vacant chair.

A moment later, she, too, was staring into the glowing lamp.

She lost all track of time. She didn't know whether it was a half-hour, an hour or two hours later when the cabin door was abruptly thrown open. She, like the others, stared at the two soldiers in the doorway in surprise.

One of the soldiers pointed to her. "You," he said harshly in Arabic. "You come with us."

"Me?" she asked, stunned. It was the first time this had happened. Even the daily tape recordings were made in the cabin. She would be handed a small clipping from the *Herald Tribune* carrying the date and a headline and nothing else. She would read it into the microphone and then add a few words about herself and the children. Then the microphone and recorder would be taken away. She could only guess that the tapes were being used to assure Baydr that they were alive and well.

"Yes, you!" he repeated.

The others looked at her fearfully. "Don't worry," she said quickly. "Maybe the information we have been waiting for has come. I'll be back soon and tell you all about it."

She rose from the chair and went out the door. The soldiers fell in beside her and silently walked her to the command cabin. They opened the door for her and, after closing it behind her, remained outside.

She stood, her eyes blinking at the unaccustomed brightness of the light. There were no little oil lamps here. Somewhere behind the building a generator hummed. Electricity. In the background a radio was playing Arab music.

Leila and Ramadan were sitting at a table with a third man she did not recognize until he rose and turned to greet her. "Madame Al Fay." He bowed.

She stared at him. "Mr. Yasfir!"

He smiled. "I see you remember my name. I am honored."

She didn't answer.

"I trust that you are comfortable," he said smoothly. "I regret that we cannot reciprocate the lavishness of your hospitality, but we do the best we can."

"Mr. Yasfir," she said coldly. "Why don't you just skip the bullshit and get to the point!"

Yasfir's eyes hardened. "I had almost forgotten you were American." He reached behind him and picked up a sheet of paper from the desk. "You will read that statement into a tape recorder."

"And if I refuse?"

"It would be most unfortunate. You see, the message you are to read into the tape recorder is our last effort to save your life and the lives of your children."

She looked from him to Leila. Leila's face was devoid of expression. A Coca-Cola bottle stood half-empty on the table before her. She turned back to Yasfir. "I'll do it."

"Over here." He led her to the far corner of the room, where the tape recorder had been set up on a table between two chairs. He picked up the mike and gave it to her. "Speak slowly and distinctly," he said. "It is important that every word on this tape be understood." He pressed the start button. "Now."

She looked down at the paper and began to read it aloud.

"Baydr, this message is being read by me because it is a final warning and they want me as well as you to know it. It has just been learned that every shipment made under their agreement with you has been confiscated in the United States. It is believed that you are responsible for those losses and you are hereby assessed $10,000,000 additional to be paid into the account agreed upon not later than the Monday following the receipt of this tape. Your failure to do so and any further confiscation of shipments will constitute a breach of the agreement and will result in an immediate application of the extreme penalty. Only you can now prevent the execution of your family." She paused and stared at him in horror.

He gestured her to read on.

"It has also been learned that you have applied to your prince and various other Arab sources for assistance. We trust that you are convinced by now that the Arab world is with us. And we advise you to cease wasting your time searching for help you will not get."

He snatched the microphone from her hand and spoke into it. "This is our final message. There will be no further warnings. Only action." He pressed the stop button.

"You can't mean that," she said.

He smiled at her. "Of course not," he replied. "But your husband is a very difficult man as you must know. He must be convinced of our threat." He got to his feet. "You must be exhausted," he said. "May I offer you a drink?"

She sat numbly without answering. Suddenly it had all become too much for her to understand. It was more than just a kidnapping; there were political implications that had not occurred to her before. It seemed to her that there was no way in God's creation that Baydr could live up to all the demands being made upon him.

She was going to die. She knew that now. And in a strange way it no longer mattered. Even if she lived there would be nothing in life. She herself had destroyed any chance she might have had for Baydr's love.

Then a chill ran through her. The children. They had done nothing to bring this upon themselves. They should not be made to pay for the sins of their parents.

She got to her feet. "I think I will have that drink now," she said. "Do you have any wine by chance?"

"Yes." He turned. "Leila, bring the bottle of wine."

Leila stared at him, then slowly got to her feet. Reluctantly she went into the next room and came back with the wine. She placed it on the table and began to return to her seat.

"Two glasses, Leila," he said.

She walked to a cupboard and came back with two ordinary tumblers. She placed them beside the wine and sat down. "We have no opener," she said.

"It doesn't matter," Yasfir said. He picked up the bottle and crossed to a washbasin in the corner of the room. Sharply he rapped the corked neck of the bottle against the porcelain. The neck broke cleanly away. He had been so expert that only a few drops of the wine had been lost. He came back, smiling, and filled the two glasses. Picking them up, he turned to Jordana and held one toward her.

She stared in fascination at the redness of the wine in the glass. She didn't move. The color reminded her of blood. Her blood. Her children's blood.

"Take it," he said harshly.

His voice broke through the paralysis that had gripped her. "No!" she suddenly screamed, striking the glass from his hand. "No!"

The glass flew against his chest, staining his suit and shirt with the red wine. He looked down at himself, then back at her, a violent anger leaping into his eyes. "Bitch!" he cried, hitting her in the face.

She fell to the floor. Strange that she felt no pain, only a dull shock. The room seemed to be reeling about her. Then she saw his face bending over her and his hand. She closed her eyes as the pain began to explode in her face, first on one cheek, then the other. In the distance she thought she heard the sound of Leila's laughter.

Then the explosions ended and she felt hands tearing at her clothing. She heard the ripping of the cloth as he pulled at the front of her dress. She opened her eyes. Suddenly the room had filled with soldiers.

Yasfir stood over her, his face flushed with exertion; next to him was Leila, a strange kind of joy in her eyes. Slowly she turned her head. The two soldiers who had brought her here were looking down at her, and next to them were the two guards who had been outside the cabin, behind them there were other soldiers she had never seen before. But all the faces seemed the same, all were wearing the same fiercely sensuous expression. Only Ramadan had not moved. He remained in his chair, an expression of disdain on his face.

Suddenly she became aware of her nakedness. She moved her hands, trying to cover herself from their searching eyes.

Leila laughed again. "The slut hides what she once was so proud to display." She dropped to one knee and grabbed Jordana's wrists, forcing them away from her body, spread-eagling her on the floor. She looked up at the soldiers. "Who will be the first man to avail himself of my father's whore?"

"Your father's wife!" Jordana screamed, struggling against Leila's grip. "We were married according to the Koran in the eyes of Allah!"

There was a sudden silence in the room, a subtle change had come over the soldiers. Awkwardly, uncomfortably, they looked at each other, then slowly, they began to shuffle to the door.

"Are you cowards?" Leila screamed after them. "Afraid to match your manhood against this whore?"

The soldiers did not look back. One by one, they filed from the cabin. Only Yasfir remained, looking down at them. Then he, too, turned away and went back to the table and sat down. He lifted the glass of wine to his lips with trembling fingers and drained it in a single swallow.

Abruptly, Leila let go of her wrists and rose to her feet. She glanced at the two men seated at the table, then went to the far corner of the room. She sank into the chair next to the tape recorder and sat silently, not looking at them.

For the first time Ramadan moved. He knelt beside Jordana and slipped a supporting arm under her shoulders. Gently, he raised her to her feet.

Vainly, she tried to cover herself with her torn dress. He guided her toward the door and took a soldier's coat that was hanging on the wall and wrapped it around her. He opened the door and called to the soldiers outside. "Escort Madame Al Fay back to her cabin."

"Thank you," she whispered.

He didn't answer.

"There is no hope for us?" she asked.

Though he did not speak, a subtle change in the expression of his eyes gave her the answer.

She looked up into his face. "I don't care what you do with me. But my children. Please don't let them die."

"I am nothing but a soldier who must obey the orders he is given," he said, not without sympathy. "But I will do what I can."

She looked into his eyes, then nodded and turned away. She felt weak and stumbled slightly. One of the soldiers put an arm under her elbow to support her. Oddly enough, she felt her strength returning as she walked toward their cabin.

There was some hope. Maybe not much. But some.

CHAPTER 15.

HAMID lowered his night glasses. From his position in the trees just outside the camp he had been able to determine which cabin held the women. The men had to be in the cabin next to them. Carefully, soundlessly, he slipped down the trunk of the tree.

Ben Ezra looked at him. "Well?"

"I have located the cabins which contain the prisoners. They are in the center of the camp. We must pass all the other cabins to reach them. The first cabin holds the men; the second, the women. Each cabin has two guards stationed in front and two behind. The command cabin is the large one just beyond the entrance. At the moment, there are three jeeps parked in front of it."

"How many men do you estimate they have?"

Hamid calculated swiftly. Twelve machine guns mounted on the walls, two men to a gun always on duty. If each man covered for twelve hours that alone would account for forty-eight men. Eight guards for the prisoners' cabin. Plus the others he had seen. "Ninety, one hundred maybe."

Ben Ezra nodded thoughtfully. He had at the most eighteen men he could use in the assault. He had to leave two men behind to secure the airstrip which they had taken less than one hour ago. There had been seven Brotherhood soldiers there. Now they were all dead. The Yemenis had requested permission to take the airstrip and he had given it. Too late he had remembered that the Yemenis might take no prisoners.

He had wanted Baydr and Carriage to remain at the airstrip but Baydr insisted on coming with him so he'd had to assign two of his volunteers, men that he could sorely spare. He looked at his watch. It was ten o'clock. At four o'clock in the morning, the larger helicopter that Baydr had secured would be waiting for them at the airstrip. Dr. Al Fay with a complete medical team would be on it. Everything had to be timed to the split second so that they would reach the airstrip before a pursuit force could be mounted.

The attack had to begin at two o'clock. They had to be on their way down to the airstrip not later than three. One hour was barely enough time to allow for the journey on foot, especially when they didn't know the condition of the eight captives. He hoped they would be strong enough to make it without help. If any of them had to be carried, he might not have the men to spare.

He checked his watch again. Four hours to zero. He looked at Hamid. "Do you think you can get inside and plant the plastiques?"

"I can try."

"The first things I want knocked out are those four giant searchlights. Then the jeeps."

Hamid nodded.

"I want all the timers set for two hundred hours."

"It will be done," Hamid answered.

"Will you need help?"

"I could use one man," Hamid said politely.

Ben Ezra turned and looked back at the soldiers. They were professionals, all of them highly trained. There was really none that he could spare; he had work for each of them. His eyes fell on Jabir. The man was not young but he had an air of quiet competence. He caught his eye and gestured to him.

"Hamid needs one man to help with the plastiques," Ben Ezra said. "Will you volunteer?"

Jabir glanced back at Baydr. "I will be honored, if you will guard my master in my absence."

Ben Ezra nodded. "I will guard him as my own." Later the thought of what he had said would come back to him. He was his own.

He called the Israeli corporal in charge of that group. "Set the rocket launchers and aim them at the walls below the machine guns. After that the target will be the command cabin."

The Israeli saluted and went away.

He motioned to the Yemeni captain. "I have selected your soldiers to lead the assault. At the first detonation of the plastiques, you will pick off as many of the men on the machine guns as you can. Then, without waiting for results, you will follow me through the gate and deploy your men around the soldiers' cabins while we seek out the captives."

The captain saluted. "We are grateful for the honor you have given us. We shall fulfill our duty unto death."

Ben Ezra returned the salute. "I thank you, captain."

He turned and looked back at the walls of the camp. They gleamed ghostly white in the faint moonlight. He turned back. Already the men were scattering, taking up their positions, preparing for the attack. He walked slowly back to Baydr and Carriage and sank down on his haunches beside them.

"How is it going?" Baydr asked.

Ben Ezra looked at his son. How strange, he thought. There is so much we might have been to one another. And yet, the ways of the Lord were beyond human understanding. After so many years to be brought together in an alien world, to reach across the borders of hatred, to answer in each other a common need.

The old man seemed lost in thought. "How is it going?" Baydr repeated.

Ben Ezra's eyes cleared. He nodded his head slowly. "It goes," he said. "From this moment on we are in the hands of God."

"What time do we attack?"

"At two hundred hours." His voice grew stern. "And I don't want you to get in our way. You are not a soldier and I don't want you getting yourself killed. You wait out here until I send for you."

"It's my family in there," Baydr said.

"You will do them no good if you are dead."

Baydr leaned back against the tree trunk. The general was a remarkable old man. In two nights of long and arduous march over the worst terrain Baydr had ever seen, the general had moved as agilely and rapidly as any of them. Not once had Baydr seen him weary. What was it the Israelis called him? The Lion of the Desert? It was a name truly given.

BEN EZRA turned to the Israeli corporal. "Fifteen minutes to zero hour. Pass the word."

The soldier immediately ran off. The general looked worried. "Hamid and Jabir have not yet returned."

Baydr got to his feet. He looked toward the camp. All was quiet.

There was a rustle from the trees to one side. A moment later, Hamid and Jabir appeared.

"What took you so long?" the general asked angrily.

"We had to work around the guards," Hamid said. "They're crawling around the place like flies. I think my estimate may have been low. There are maybe a hundred and fifty men in there."

"It changes nothing," Ben Ezra said. "You stay close to me when we go in. As soon as the rockets are gone, the Israelis are coming in to help us with the captives."

"Yes, sir." Hamid looked around. Baydr was out of earshot. "I saw his daughter. She was in the command cabin. There were two men with her. I recognized one of them as Ali Yasfir. I didn't know the other."

Ben Ezra made a face. Like it or not she was his grandchild. "Pass the word not to harm the girl if possible," he said.

"Yes, sir." Hamid ran off and disappeared among the trees.

Ten minutes to zero. Ben Ezra reached under his jellaba and unfastened his sword belt. Swiftly he buckled it outside his flowing robe. Reaching across his waist, he drew the scimitar from its scabbard. The gracefully curved steel glinted in the light from the moon. Ben Ezra felt himself grow young once more. The sword without which he had never gone into battle was at his side. All was right with the world.

LEILA took a fresh bottle of Coca-Cola and brought it back to the table. "When are you going back?" she asked Ali Yasfir.

"In the morning."

"I wish I were going with you. I'm going crazy up here. There's nothing to do."

"The only girl with one hundred and forty men and you're bored?"

"You know what I mean," Leila said angrily.

"Soon it will be over. Then you can come back to Beirut."

"What happens to them when it's over?"

He shrugged his shoulders.

"Do we have to? Even if my father gives us everything we've asked for?"

"There are too many of them. They can always identify us."

"But the children, do they have to die also?"

"What's come over you? I thought you hated them. They stole your heritage."

"Not the children. Jordana and my father, yes. But not the children."

"Children can identify us also."

She sat silently for a moment, then got to her feet. "I think I'll go outside for some air," she said.

After the door had closed behind her, Yasfir turned to Ramadan. "If I don't get back in time you have your orders."

"Yes," Ramadan replied.

"She must go first," Yasfir said. "She, more than any of them, can get us hanged. She knows too much about us."

The night air was cool and it felt good against her face. Leila walked slowly in the direction of her own cabin. So much had happened that she hadn't anticipated. There was none of the glamour and excitement that she had envisioned. Mostly it was just boredom. Boredom and empty days and nights.

And there was none of the feeling of participating in the cause of freedom. She had long given up trying to connect what was taking place here with the struggle to free the Palestinians. All the soldiers were mercenaries. And very well paid too. Not one of them seemed to care about the cause. Only about their monthly pay. It was not at all what the boys and girls in school had talked about. Here, freedom was just another word.

She remembered that Hamid had once tried to explain that to her. But she refused to understand it then. It seemed so long ago, but it had been only six months. Why was it that she had felt so young then and so old now?

She paused at the entrance to her cabin and looked out at the camp. It was quiet. Something disturbed her but she didn't know what it was. Her eyes caught a glimpse of motion on the wall. One of the machine gunners had straightened up to stretch. Against the pale moonlight, she could see his hands reach toward the sky. Then, suddenly, he pitched forward head-first into the camp. A moment later there was the crack of a rifle shot. Even as she froze in surprise, the skies seemed to open up and the fires of hell to pour down on them.

The thought flashed crazily through her mind even as she began to run. Now she knew what had disturbed her. The quiet. It had been much too quiet.

CHAPTER 16.

THE children came awake screaming with terror. The tiny cabin reverberated with the concussions coming from the explosions that seemed to be taking place all around them. Jordana leaped from her cot, ran to them and held them close to her.

She heard one of the women in the other room screaming but she could not tell who it was. Through the cracks in the boarded-up windows, she could see flashes of red and orange light. The whole cabin seemed to shudder convulsively as another explosion tore the night.

Oddly enough she wasn't frightened. For the first time since the hijacking, she felt secure.

"What's happening, Mommy?" Muhammad asked, between tears.

"Daddy's come for us, darling. Don't be frightened."

"Where is he?" Samir asked. "I want to see him."

"You will," she said soothingly. "In just a few minutes now."

Anne, the nanny, appeared in the doorway. "Are you all right, madame?" she called.

"We're fine," Jordana shouted back over the noise. "And you?"

"Magda's got a splinter of wood in her arm but otherwise we're all right." She paused as another violent concussion rocked the cabin. "Do you need any help with the children?"

"No, we're fine," Jordana said. She remembered something from a war movie she had once seen. "Tell the girls to lie down on the floor with their hands over their heads. They'll be safer that way."

"Yes, madame," Anne answered, her Scottish imperturbability unruffled. She disappeared from the doorway.

"On the floor, boys," Jordana said, pulling them down with her. They stretched out, one on either side, and she placed her arms over them, sheltering their heads under her shoulders.

The noise from the explosions was diminishing. Now more and more she heard the sounds of rifle fire mixed with the noises of men running about and shouting. She held the children tightly and waited.

LEILA ran through the camp, which was filled with men running back and forth in confusion. The attack seemed to be coming from all sides.

Only one man seemed to have a purpose. She saw Ramadan, his rifle in his hand, running toward the women's cabin.

Suddenly she remembered the automatic in her belt and pulled it out. The cold steel weight was comforting in her hand. Now she did not feel as alone and unprotected. "Ramadan!" she yelled after him.

He didn't hear her and kept going, disappearing from sight around the corner of the women's cabin. Without knowing why, she ran after him.

The door of the cabin was open when she got there. She ran inside and suddenly stopped in shock. Huddled against the wall of the back room, the women had gathered in a group around Jordana and the boys. Ramadan, standing in the narrow doorway between the rooms, his back to her, was bringing his automatic rifle up to firing position.

"Leila!" Jordana screamed, "they're your brothers!"

Ramadan wheeled, the rifle turning toward Leila.

It wasn't until Leila saw the cold absence of expression on Ramadan's face that she realized the truth. She meant no more to Al-Ikhwah than her brothers. They recognized the ties of blood even if she hadn't. To them, she was only a tool to be used and discarded when their need of her no longer existed.

She held the heavy automatic in front of her with both hands. By reflex, her fingers tightened on the trigger. It wasn't until the clip had emptied itself and Ramadan had pitched violently onto the floor that she realized she had pulled the trigger.

Looking across his body, she saw Jordana quickly turn the faces of the boys away from the sight of the blood welling from Ramadan's body.

Suddenly she felt a strong pair of arms seize her from behind, pinning her own arms against her body. Violently she struggled to free herself.

"Leila! Stop it!" a familiar voice snapped in her ear.

She twisted her head to see who it was. "Hamid!" she exclaimed in surprise. "Where did you come from?"

"Time for that later." He pulled her backward through the doorway. Loosening his grip but holding on to one arm, he dragged her after him through an opening that had been blasted in the camp wall.

When they got to the edge of the forest, he pushed her down flat against the earth. She raised her head to look at him. "What are you doing here?"

He pushed her head down again. "Don't you remember the first thing I taught you?" he said harshly. "Keep your head down!"

"You didn't answer my question," she said, her voice muffled.

"I came to get you."

"Why, Hamid, why?"

"Because I didn't want you to get yourself killed, that's why," he said huskily. "You always were a lousy soldier."

"Hamid, you love me," she said, a note of wonder coming into her voice.

He didn't answer.

"Why didn't you ever say anything?"

He turned to look at her. "What right have I to love a girl like you?"

BEN EZRA strode about, directing his soldiers, his scimitar flashing over his head.

He glanced around fiercely. The resistance seemed to be slowing down. He looked around for Hamid, but he was nowhere to be seen. Aloud he cursed him. He hated soldiers who became too involved in the battle to remember their orders. He had told him to stay near him.

He signaled the Israeli corporal. "Gather your men!" A moment later he caught Jabir's eye "Fetch your master," he shouted. "We're bringing out the captives!"

There was a burst of gunfire on the other side of the camp. He saw several of the Yemenis run toward it. He nodded to himself grimly. He had made the right choice. They were magnificent fighting men.

BAYDR was the first to enter the cabin. He felt his heart leap as he saw his sons. He dropped to one knee to bring them in his arms as they ran to him, screaming, "Daddy! Daddy!"

He kissed one then the other, and felt the salt of his own tears on his lips.

"We weren't frightened, honest, Father," Muhammad said. "We knew you would come for us."

"Yes," Samir piped up. "Mommy told us that every day."

He looked up at her. His vision was blurred with tears. Slowly he rose to his feet.

Jordana didn't move; her eyes were fixed upon him.

Silently, he held out his hand to her.

Slowly, almost tentatively, she took it.

He looked into her eyes for a long moment. His voice was husky. "We almost didn't make it."

She smiled tremulously. "I never for a moment doubted."

"Can you forgive me?" he asked.

"That's easy. I love you," she said. "But can you forgive me?"

He grinned. Suddenly he was the Baydr she had first known and loved. "Easy," he said. "I love you too."

"Move out," the Israeli corporal yelled from the door behind them. "We haven't got all night!"

BEN EZRA was standing near the camp entrance. "Anyone else?" the general asked.

"That's all of us," the corporal answered.

He turned to the Yemeni captain. "Rear guard posted?"

"Yes, sir," the captain replied. "Four men with automatic rifles ought to keep them occupied for a while. We're not to wait for them. They'll backtrack and we'll pick them up in our original landing place in a few days."

Ben Ezra nodded. That was good soldiering. "How many casualties?"

"One dead, a few superficial wounds—that's all."

Ben Ezra turned to the Israeli.

"Two dead."

"We were lucky," the general said grimly. "We caught them with their pants down!" He looked out on the road. The captives were in the midst of a joyous reunion. The men of the flight crew were in good shape and so were the women. They huddled together in a tight group, all trying to talk at once. "Better get them started," Ben Ezra said. "It won't take our friends very long to figure out how few of us there are and then they'll be coming after us."

The Israeli started off. Ben Ezra called him back. "Did you see the Syrian?"

The soldier shook his head. "I haven't seen him since we first went in after the rockets were fired. He was in front of me and then he just disappeared."

Ben Ezra was puzzled. It didn't make sense. Unless the man had been killed and was lying undiscovered somewhere. But, no, that wasn't possible. The Syrian was just too good a soldier. He would turn up sooner or later. Ben Ezra turned and started down the road after them. He looked at his watch. Three o'clock. Right on schedule.

Now, if the helicopter made it on time, they would be having breakfast at the Prince's palace in the morning.

CHAPTER 17.

DICK Carriage moved slowly through the camp. Through the open gate, he could see the others going down the road on their way to the airstrip. But he wasn't ready to leave yet. There was still some unfinished business for him to attend to.

The sporadic sound of rifle fire came from the various corners of the camp. The Yemenis were doing their job. Slowly, carefully, he opened one cabin door after another and still there was no sign of him.

Yet the man had to be there. He could not have gotten out before the attack. No one could have left the camp without being seen. Besides, he had heard Hamid report to the general that he had seen him fifteen minutes before the attack had begun.

He turned to look back at the command cabin. In front of it were three burned-out jeeps. Thoughtfully he turned and walked back to it. He had already gone through the cabin once but maybe there was something he had overlooked.

Cautiously he approached the door again. His automatic in his hand, he stood to one side and pushed it wide. He waited for a moment. There was no sound from inside.

He went through the doorway. The first room was a shambles. The rockets had torn gaping holes in the sides of the cabin. Papers and furniture were scattered around the room as if a tornado had struck.

He went through into the other room. Slowly he looked around. It was impossible. There was just no place for the man to hide. He started back outside then stopped.

He felt the hairs on the back of his neck begin to rise. The man was here. His instinct told him. It didn't matter that he couldn't find him. The man was here.

He turned and slowly looked around the cabin again. Nothing. He stood very still for a moment and then went over to the bench beside the washbasin where he had noticed several oil lamps.

Breaking them open, he quickly scattered the oil around the room. Then he took a chair and put it in the outer doorway and sat down on it, facing the room. He took a book of matches from his pocket, struck one, held it until the book erupted in flames then threw it into the room.

The fire raced rapidly across the floor, reaching, then climbing the walls. Smoke began to fill the room and still he sat. The heat grew intense, but he did not move.

Suddenly there was a faint sound from inside. He tried to peer through the smoke but saw nothing. Again the sound came, a creaking sound, as if a door were opening on rusted hinges. But he could see through to the other room and there were no other doors.

Then something on the floor moved. He got to his feet. Part of the wooden floor seemed to be shifting. He moved toward it on catlike feet.

He stopped at the side of the floorboard. Now he

took out a handkerchief and held it over his nose and mouth to protect himself against the smoke. Suddenly the floorboard was flung to one side and a man sat up, coughing.

The Israeli agent nodded to himself in satisfaction. This was the man he had come to get. It was never the idealist who had to be feared, only the man who corrupted the ideal. This man was the corrupter. Slowly, deliberately, before the man even realized he was there, Dick emptied the clip of his automatic into him.

Then he turned and without even a backward look walked out of the cabin toward the road, leaving the dead Ali Yasfir lying in his fiery coffin.

He was a quarter of a mile down the road when he came upon them. He had just walked around a curve as they emerged from the forest. They stopped, staring at one another.

"Leila!" he said.

Hamid turned to her. He saw the strange look on her face. He remained silent.

"Dick," she said in a strained voice. "I—"

The sound of a rifle shot interrupted her. A look of intense surprise suddenly appeared on Dick's face. Then a strange bubble of blood appeared in the corner of his mouth and he slipped slowly to the road.

Hamid reacted immediately. Throwing Leila to the ground, he flung himself on his belly, facing the direction from which the shot had come. A moment later, he saw the man between the trees. Carefully, he lined the sights of his automatic rifle between the two trees where the man would pass. He waited until the man was dead center, then he squeezed the trigger. The automatic rifle almost cut the man in half.

He turned back to Leila. "Come on," he said hoarsely. "Let's get out of here!"

Dick moaned.

"We can't leave him here," Leila said. "He'll die!"

"He'll die anyway," Hamid said callously. "Let's go."

"No. You'll have to help me get him to the others."

"Are you crazy? Do you know what will happen to you if you go back? If they don't hang you, you'll spend the rest of your life in jail!"

"I don't care," she said stubbornly. "Are you going to help me or not?"

Hamid looked at her and shook his head. He gave her the rifle. "Here, carry this." He bent over, picked Dick up and slung him over his shoulders. "Let's go. There'll be others behind that one in just a few minutes!"

BEN EZRA checked his watch. It was almost four o'clock. "Where's that damn helicopter?"

No sooner were the words out of his mouth than the sound of the plane came from the distance. He peered into the sky, but now that the moon was gone, he could see nothing but the blackness of the night.

Ten minutes later, the sound came from overhead. A moment afterward it passed the crest of the mountain and disappeared.

A crackling of rifle fire came from the direction of the road through the forest. The Israeli corporal came running up. "They're coming down the road after us!"

"Keep them busy. The helicopter should be down any minute."

But the gunfire grew more intense and still the helicopter did not come down. Occasionally the sound of the engines could be heard, but then it would vanish.

The Israeli corporal returned. "We better make it quick, general," he said. "They're coming down with some real heavy stuff now."

"Get back there!" Ben Ezra snapped. He peered up at the sky. "You know what I think? I think the damn fool up there is lost and can't find us in the dark."

"Maybe if we light a fire," Baydr suggested. "It would serve as a beacon for him."

"Good idea," the general said. "But we've got nothing to make a big enough fire. It would take us an hour to gather enough branches and they wouldn't burn anyway. Everything's too damp from the night moisture."

"I've got something that will burn."

"What?"

Baydr gestured to the 707 under the camouflage. "That would make a hell of a fire."

"You wouldn't?" Ben Ezra's voice was questioning.

The sounds of the fighting grew closer. "I came to get my family out of this and that's what I'm going to do."

He turned to Captain Hyatt. "Andy, how would you go about setting it on fire?"

The pilot looked at him.

"I'm not joking, Andy," Baydr snapped. "Our lives depend on it!"

"Open the wing tanks and fire some incendiaries into it," Hyatt said.

"Open them," Baydr ordered.

Andy and his copilot ran to the plane. They climbed up into the cabin. One ran to either side of the plane. In less than two minutes they were back.

"We're ready now," Andy said. "But you better move everybody down to the far end of the strip just in case she blows up."

Ben Ezra bellowed his orders. It took almost five minutes to get them all down at the other end of the field. "Get down, everybody," he said, giving the signal to the riflemen.

The automatic rifles set up a screaming chatter. A moment afterward there was a strange hiss, then a groan as the giant plane blew. A geyser of flame climbed a hundred feet into the air.

"If they don't see that, they're blind," Hyatt said sadly.

Baydr saw the look on his face. "Don't feel bad. It's only money," he said. "If we get out of here, I'll get you another one."

Hyatt smiled half-heartedly. "I'll keep my fingers crossed, chief."

Baydr's eyes were grim as he scanned the sky. Behind them the sound of gunfire came closer. He moved toward Jordana. "You all right?"

She nodded, the boys clinging to her. They all searched the sky.

"I think I hear it!" Muhammad yelled.

They listened. The faint sound of the rotors came toward them, growing louder with each passing moment. Two minutes later it was overhead, reflected in the glare of the burning plane. Slowly it began to descend.

The flashes of gunfire were almost at the side of the airstrip now as the soldiers fell back according to plan.

The helicopter touched down. The first man off the plane was Baydr's father. The two boys ran to him. "Grandfather!"

He scooped them up in his arms as Baydr and Jordana came toward him. Everybody began to converge on the helicopter. The boarding was swift, just a few men still in the field holding off the guerrillas.

Baydr stood at the foot of the ramp, next to Ben Ezra. "Everybody on board?" the general asked.

"Yes," Baydr answered.

Ben Ezra cupped his hand around his mouth. "Bring them in, corporal!" he yelled in a stentorian voice that could be heard all over the field.

Another fuel tank blew on the 707, bathing the entire field in a daylight glow. Baydr could see the soldiers backing in from the edge of the field, their guns firing into the forest.

A moment later they were almost at the foot of the ramp. The first of them turned and started up the stairs. Ben Ezra swatted him on the behind with his sword in an approving gesture.

The yellow light from the burning plane reached the edge of the forest. Baydr, watching, thought he heard someone calling him. Then suddenly he saw her, running from the forest. Behind her was a man carrying a body across his shoulders.

Automatically a soldier swung his rifle toward her.

Baydr struck at the gun so that the barrel pointed at the sky. "Hold it!" he yelled.

"Daddy! Daddy!" Leila cried.

Baydr ran toward her. "Leila! This way!" he shouted.

She turned, making a straight line for him, and ran into his arms. A soldier came dashing up to him. "We've got to get out of here, sir!"

Baydr gestured toward Hamid. "Help him," he said to the soldier.

He turned and with one arm around his daughter went up the steps into the plane. Hamid and the soldier, carrying Dick between them, were right behind them. Ben Ezra came up the ramp and stood in the open door.

Already Hamid and the soldier had placed Dick on a cot, and Dr. Al Fay and the medical team hooked up the plasma and glucose. "Take it up!" Ben Ezra yelled.

As the big rotors began to turn sluggishly overhead Hamid went back to the general. Behind him, Hamid could see the guerrillas running onto the field. "I wouldn't stand there if I were you, general," he said respectfully.

"Where the hell were you all night?" Ben Ezra shouted angrily as the helicopter began to lift heavily.

"I was merely obeying your orders, sir," the Syrian said with a straight face. He gestured toward Leila, who was kneeling beside Dick. "I was making sure that no harm would come to her."

"You were ordered to stay at my si—!" The anger faded from the old man's voice and was replaced with a note of surprise. "Oh, my God!" he exclaimed. The scimitar fell from his suddenly nerveless hand. He took a tentative step toward the Syrian, then began to fall.

Hamid caught him in outstretched arms. He felt the old man's blood gushing through the soft Bedouin robes. Hamid lurched and almost fell as the helicopter seemed to leap into the air. "The general's been shot!" he yelled.

Baydr and his father were at his side almost before

the words had left his mouth. Gently, they moved Ben
Ezra to a cot. Dr. Al Fay rolled him on his side,
quickly cutting away his robe.

"Do not bother, my friend," the general whispered.
"Save your time for the young man there."

"The young man will be all right!" Samir said almost angrily.

"So will I," Ben Ezra said softly. "Now that I have
seen my son, I am not afraid to die. You have done
well, my friend. You have raised a man."

Samir felt the tears blur his eyes. He knelt down
and placed his lips close to the old man's ear. "For too
long I have allowed him to live a lie. It is time for him
to learn the truth."

A faint smile came to the dying soldier's lips. "What
is the truth? You are his father. That is all he needs
to know."

"You are his father, not I!" Samir whispered vehe-
mently. "He must learn that it was your God who
brought him into this world!"

Ben Ezra looked up with rapidly glazing eyes. His
gaze turned to Baydr, then back to the doctor. His
voice was faint as he summoned all his strength into
this last breath. He was dead the moment the words
had left his lips.

"There is but one God . . ."